MARILYN

MARILYN

SHADES OF BLONDE

EDITED BY

CAROLE NELSON DOUGLAS

A TOM DOHERTY ASSOCIATES BOOK

NEW YORK

MARILYN: SHADES OF BLONDE

This book is printed on acid-free paper.

Designed by Michael Mendelsohn of MM Design 2000, Inc.

A Forge Book
Published by Tom Doherty Associates, Inc.
175 Fifth Avenue
New York, NY 10010

Forge® is a registered trademark of Tom Doherty Associates, Inc.

Library of Congress Cataloging-in-Publication Data

Marilyn : shades of blonde / Carole Nelson Douglas, editor. — 1st ed.
        p.   cm.
    ISBN 0-312-85737-3 (acid-free paper)
      1. Monroe, Marilyn, 1926-1962—Fiction.   2. Motion Picture actors
and actresses—United States—Fiction.   3. American fiction—20th
century.   4. Short stories, American.   I. Douglas, Carole Nelson.
PS648.M53M37   1997
813'.0108351—dc21   97-1160
                                                                          CIP

First Edition: August 1997

Printed in the United States of America

0   9   8   7   6   5   4   3   2   1

For Bob Gleason,
with thanks for steering me
toward the enigma of Norma Jeane

CONTENTS

INTRODUCTION

BY CAROLE NELSON DOUGLAS

*er death was the best thing
that could have happened to her.*
—film director Joseph Mankiewicz

 MORE THAN ANYTHING ELSE, Mankiewicz's brutal epitaph at the time of Marilyn Monroe's death debunks any lurid murder theories about her passing. Why use assassins when attitudes can be so much more lethal?

Mankiewicz's assessment that screendom's "zany, wonderful dizzy blonde" would have been "a pitiful, dreadful mess" as an aging woman, that early death was a blessing in disguise, reflects the built-in obsolescence Hollywood expects of its onscreen women.

But by the time she died, barely thirty-six, Marilyn Monroe had spent half her life confounding the expectations and exploitations of the men who made the movies.

She had made herself, perhaps in their image at first. Later, she set about looking for substance. Time has proved she found it, despite a tragic family background, despite her need to be loved by proxy on the screen.

"I want to say that the people—if I am a star—the people made me a star. No studio, no person—but the people did."

She astutely remarked later that the studio bosses never forgave her for saying that. Old Hollywood expected starlets to twinkle on casting couches, then vanish once the moviemakers had used them up. Many actresses who became stars in the movies' first three decades were sexually active, or even married, by sixteen. Marilyn Monroe was no exception. Her fear of aging beyond her image was no neurotic self-indulgence, but hard-headed realism.

In fact, Mankiewicz's cruel summation was a lie.

In the last months of Marilyn Monroe's life, one fact is inarguable: This was not a woman preparing to be pitied. She had lost twenty-seven pounds in recent months and gave upbeat, impressive interviews only days before her death. Long-lost reels of her aborted final film, *Something's Got to Give,* reveal a radiant beauty with miles to go, who adds an uncanny emotional depth to the light material. The famous nude swimming scene outakes Marilyn herself engineered put the plastic surgeons at bay.

Today's female film stars have managed to maintain careers for an extra decade beyond thirty. Yet fortyish-plus actresses, even those always taken seriously, still find new roles slim, or slight.

The Hollywood studio system may have died with Marilyn, but today's young female "stars" seem designed for the same preprogrammed obsolescence: all nearer twenty than thirty, all giving way to a new generation every four years or so. All stripping for the screen or the cover of *Vanity Fair* between "serious" assignments with weary *déjà vu.*

Oh, yes, we survivors of a certain age say now, we the people would have respected Marilyn's ambitions and her talent, we would have seen beyond the tinsel and the sleeping pills. We wouldn't have killed her softly with our sexism and stereotyping. We know better. Now.

Do we?

This collection invited writers known for a variety of fiction to re-examine Marilyn. Most who accepted came from the crime fiction field, and many looked beyond the fascinating mystery manqué of her death—the whodunit, howdunit, and whydunit—to the greater enigma of her life, work, and legacy. As many men were invited as women; more women accepted. Most of the writers were children, or very young adults, when Marilyn Monroe died in 1962. No limits were set, only that the writers look at Marilyn. Look at Norma Jeane. Really look and speculate on the past and future Marilyn, as we do with any too-soon-gone mythical figure who instills people with hopes of a return, like King Arthur, like Elvis. Like JFK.

This collection will succeed if it stimulates readers to mirror the journey many of these writers made to find their own "real" Norma Jeane/Marilyn Monroe.

So, go ahead: Read the books, this one of fiction, the many of nonfiction. Look at the pictures that she made for us, still and moving. Still and moving, she is there yet.

You will find her best between the lines, the voluminous, often scurrilous lines of the Marilyn Monroe Memoir Industry. Rent the movies. Pore over the coffee table books, stare past the camera's mechanical eye.

Maybe you'll find my favorite Marilyn: sincere Norma Jeane, the brown-haired girl who had a corner on radiance long before they straightened her hair and her smile and bleached her to the white luminosity of old bones.

You will surely find Elton John's "Candle in the Wind" in the elusive magic of her unretouched smile. You will trace tragedy in the sexpot wound of her meticulously painted lips.

But you will find your own Marilyn or Norma Jeane somewhere, beyond the contradictions and the obvious misrepresentations and the fan worship, behind the microscopic pixels of photographs and film stills; the Marilyn Monroe she secretly collaborated with all of us to compose: part siren, part child; part performer, part victim; part strumpet, part saint, or half-canonized martyr, anyway.

As her former husband Arthur Miller wrote about another moribund American archetype, the salesman Willy Loman, "Attention must be paid."

Attention must be paid not because she was that supreme saleswoman, Marilyn Monroe: self-made star, mistress of modeling herself to the camera's needs and her times, actress-in-training and mother-in-waiting, but because she was an all-too-human being.

The writers in this anthology—who kindly rooted through their own pasts to find photos of themselves from 1962 for use in this collection—have sorted through the trunk of Marilyn Monroe's life and death, hunting unexamined mementos. Two-thirds of them chose to examine the postmortem Marilyn, so their visions focus on what may be this woman's most enduring role on the moving screen of our times: not as sexpot, not as star, not as victim, but as eternal spirit.

Call her Marilyn or Norma Jeane, like a lost child . . . a half-forgotten friend remembered . . . a memory of a bad time that could have been better . . . she haunts.

"I'm trying to prove to myself that I'm a real person. Then maybe I'll convince myself that I'm an actress."

She haunts.

BLONDE NOIRE

BY MARTIN MEYERS AND ANNETTE MEYERS

THE SKY IS different in California.

The highway outside my window was a straight line away from the horizon.

I live and work in a squat two-story, fake pink hacienda on Ventura Boulevard in Van Nuys. Apartment upstairs, office down. The sign on the pebbly glass door of my office says JOHN MARLEY, PRIVATE INVESTIGATIONS.

Don't go by the movie crap. I'm no Dick Powell, or Bogart. The one gun I own is a small .22 Colt automatic, and it only comes out of my desk drawer on exceptional occasions. Like if the Japs invaded.

I'm five-ten, a hundred and sixty pounds. And the only fights I win are the ones where I'm sneaky. Though, I must admit, I am pretty good at that.

That morning, light blue sky had mingled with white clouds, which, to the east, grew into a giant mass of ever-darkening cotton balls. It all looked like a perfect backdrop curtain that didn't quite reach the desert floor. Between the space created by the bottom of the cloud curtain and the horizon was the emerging orange glow of the sun coming up from behind the foothills.

At the end of the road a stumpy, geometric block of a building stood between me and the hills.

All of a sudden the blinding sun appeared beneath the cotton ball curtain and above the geometric block.

It was beautiful. And not quite real.

Like the blonde sitting across from me a couple of hours later.

She wasn't one of those Jean Harlow types that get it from a bottle. More natural. What they called dirty blonde: loose ringlets of light brown with glints of sunshine in them.

She had—the only way to say it is—pneumatic breasts. Even so, she looked like somebody's kid sister, twenty at the most, come right off a farm, busting out with good farm girl health. Her skin was pink-white. I wanted to touch it. Anywhere. Everywhere.

The girl had a small birthmark on her left cheek, just above the laugh line, which I wasn't seeing now because she was nervous as a wild cat in a pen. She smelled of Chanel No. 5 with an Ivory soap chaser. She took off her sunglasses and abstractedly chewed one of the temple bars. Her dark eyes were bright, the whites were clear. This girl had a kind of innocent beauty. She was a humdinger.

On my desk the front page of the *L.A. Times* lifted and fell to the steady breeze from the fan overhead. In the center of the page, above the fold, was a four-column-wide picture of Franklin Delano Roosevelt and the dates: 1882–1945. The headline was: FDR IS DEAD; TRUMAN SWORN IN; OUR OKINAWA GUNS DOWN 118 PLANES.

On the large Philco console standing next to my desk, I'd found the only station that wasn't talking about the dead president or the new one: Harry Truman. What they had was the Andrews Sisters singing "I'll Walk Alone."

"Isn't it sad?" she said, her mouth pouting up.

"What? The song?"

"No. The president dying." She put on her sunglasses. "He's the president, for God's sake. Don't you have any respect?" When I declined to comment, she said, "Maybe I should go?" Her chair creaked but she didn't get up.

I reached over, turned off the radio, and waited her out.

She wasn't wearing a milkmaid costume. To the contrary, she was poured into a white sharkskin dress pressed and buffed to a bright sheen. Her white gloved hands held a large white handbag in her lap and a thin green book. In spite of the desert sun she wasn't wearing a hat. She sighed and shifted in the chair, squaring her shoulders, giving me another angle of those magnificent breasts.

Her face was average—longish nose, sulky mouth. Her head was a little too big for her spectacular body.

"Stop that." She stood up. The book fell to the floor. She didn't stamp her foot, but it felt as if she had.

"Stop what?" I asked innocently.

"Stop staring at my breasts." Her voice was like a child's whisper.

"Sorry, can't blame a guy."

"Yes, I can. It's rude," she squealed. She was about five foot five or six—add two inches for heels—and all of it choice. She hadn't finished scolding me yet. "And I don't like it. I won't put up with it." Her upper lip trembled with the smile she flashed at me when she was done chewing me out.

Overhead the Hunter fan made a click-click noise. It didn't bother me. But it was annoying the hell out of the blonde, who kept looking up at it. I keep a pint bottle of Seagram's Seven in my lower right desk drawer. I brought it out. "Care for some?"

"I don't indulge." She plumped down hard on the chair. It creaked again in protest. Her face held onto a vacuous expression. Her lips were wet, pouty, over slightly protruding teeth, her mouth partially open. That delicious mouth put ideas in my mind. After a moment she methodically put on the sunglasses, not saying a word. This was going to be a barrel of laughs.

I shrugged. "Cigarette?"

The blonde had walked in off the street nursing a broken heel and a problem she was evidently reluctant to talk about.

She whipped off her glasses and frowned. The whole thing seemed rehearsed. She'd put on the damned glasses just so she'd be able to take them off like that. "I don't like cigarettes," she said.

I came from around my desk. We both leaned forward and reached for her book on the floor at the same time. I got there first. Our fingers touched. I tried not to look at her breasts. Oh, yes I did. Oh, my God. I wondered how it would be to have her on the floor right then and there.

I did nothing about my fantasy. Instead I placed the book on my desk. *Letters to a Young Poet* by Rainer Maria Rilke. I never heard of her. Him? I nodded at the book. "Good stuff?"

"I don't know." Each breathy word was rationed out as if in short supply. And each was given the same value as the others. "I haven't read it yet."

Since that was a dead end I said, "I can just make out the ridge of wedding band under those sweet white gloves."

She laughed. A queer kind of throaty sound. "It's a friendship ring."

"Makes no diff to me." I lit a Camel.

She wrinkled her nose, lifted her shoulders, then let them settle. I enjoyed watching.

"You're right. I'm saving my modeling money in order to go to Las Vegas for a divorce. I want to be free, so I can become a starlet."

"A nice enough ambition. With money tight like that maybe you can't afford to hire me. What about that? You do want to hire me, don't you?"

She tilted her head up at me and pursed those wet lips.

I was sweating. I went back to my seat, feeling as if she'd won that round. "I charge ten bucks a day, and expenses. What can I do for you, Mrs. . . . Miss?"

"My name is Norma Jeane . . . Mortensen." She laid the glasses on my ash-dusty desk and sat up straight to give me the whole effect. Don't get me wrong, she wasn't throwing herself at me, but still, I got the feeling she wanted to please me. Make me like her.

I nodded at my door. "John Marley. At your service."

"Pleased to meet you." She was sitting in the chair like the good little girl in school, but her eyes were impish, as if her coming here was all a big joke. "I'm a model. Doing some stuff for the army."

"I'm 4F myself. Punctured eardrum."

"I didn't ask." Her sentences were short, breathless, and her voice was timid. "I'm staying across the road." She threw her arm out vaguely, "At the La Fonda Motor Lodge. I'd been working all morning with my photographer, David Conover. About an hour ago, there was a knock on my door."

I was fascinated by the way she chewed the red from her lips. She caught me watching her and widened her eyes. "Go on." My voice was hoarse, my throat gummy. "So, what happened?"

"I was just back from lunch." She snuggled into the chair with a shy smile. "Alone. I wanted to take a shower. After a shower I love walking around in the nude." This delightful little girl next door was absolutely luminous. And, obviously, a tease. "Don't you find that stimulating?"

I cleared my throat. "Walking around nude? Or hearing you talk about it?"

She blew some of the ash dust off my desk, wrinkled her nose at the inadequate results, set her elbows on the desk, and rested her chin in her cupped hands. "Take your pick."

I had to keep myself from getting lost in her. "Go on," I said.

"The young man told me he just wanted to show me his stuff. He was selling."

"I'll bet."

"Don't be fresh." She shook her finger at me like a schoolteacher to the class brat. "He was selling sterling silver carving sets on the installment plan."

"In a motor lodge? Sounds like a line to me."

"To me, too," she said in her breathy voice. "But he was cute, so I listened to what he had to say."

"And?" I snagged my handkerchief from my hip pocket and wiped the sweat from my lip and the back of my neck. My shirt was sticking to my chair.

"The phone rang. The room is a small hall and a bedroom. I went maybe ten steps into the bedroom to answer it."

"Without closing him out in the hall?"

The blonde shook her head. She looked so sad.

"Not smart."

She took a deep breath, her nostrils quivered. So did those breasts. Oh, Lord, she was something else. I glanced down at Mr. Roosevelt. The sight of the dead president cleared my head. The doll was playing me. Every move, every gesture, every quiver was all deliberate. She knew what she was doing; yes, she did. Of all the dames I've ever met, Norma Jeane, if that was really her name, was the world champion first-class tease.

This time she waited me out. Since I saw she wasn't going to talk, I figured I'd better, although I hadn't seen the color of her money yet. "I bet he's 4F, too."

"Bet he's not."

"Let's ask him."

"Can't. He's dead."

We were holding the drinks I'd poured neat into the two chipped coffee cups.

"Who was on the phone?"

She tossed back half the drink, about a shot's worth, and began coughing.

"Easy does it. You said you didn't drink."

"Did you think I was lying?" Those lovely dark eyes glistened with the suggestion of tears.

"Maybe yes, maybe no."

Surprisingly she nodded.

"Who called?"

"No one. The operator told me he hung up."

"That figures. He?"

"What?"

"The operator said 'he'?"

"I think so."

"The body?"

"Lying in the hall of my room in the La Fonda Lodge." Her nostrils quivered. "With a knife in his back."

"Don't tell me. A sterling silver carving knife." She didn't tell me. "Why me? Why not call the cops?"

"I can't." A surprise. She practically screamed that. After all that controlled and sensuous banter, this dame suddenly seemed borderline hysterical. An hysteric. Hysteria made more sense than her earlier act. That's how most people would behave after having someone killed practically in front of them. If her story was true.

"Why can't you call the cops?"

Her lips twitched undecided, hesitant, searching for the smile. But she didn't answer my question.

I returned to a previous tack. "How'd you come to me?"

"I was so scared I ran out and jumped into my car. I was barely on the road when I crashed."

"Into what?"

"One of the palm trees."

"Oh."

"Some fellows in a truck stopped and pushed my car to your side of the road for me. I didn't know what to do, but God provided . . ."

"Yeah. You looked up and there I was."

Her lips trembled. Her hands. Her hands crushed the white purse. "It was gruesome," she said, "being there with a dead body." Her lips twitched. She found the smile, but couldn't hold onto it.

"While you were on the phone could you see . . . the salesman?"

"I c-c-c-could have if I l-l-l-looked. I didn't look. My b-b-b-back was to him." Now she was stuttering. This kid was a packet full of troubles.

"You're very trusting."

"I c-c-c-concentrate on one thing at a time. Besides, I was brought up to trust p-p-p-people. I'm a Christian Scientist."

"Oh."

As if to prove the force and efficacy of her faith, she said, "Peter Piper picked a peck of pickle peppers," without a flaw. The stutter was gone as quick as it had come. "I'm an actress."

"Don't I know it?"

"You're being mean. Some day I'm going to be a big star."

"I have no doubt of that."

"If I bleached my hair, do you think I could be the new Harlow?"

"Why not?" Norma Jeane's case, if it was a case, didn't look like it was going anywhere. It sure wasn't putting any money in my pocket. But what the hell, the phone wasn't ringing off the hook, and sitting opposite this dame sure beat reading about Mr. Roosevelt or the war, winding down though it was, or listening to a bunch of kids from Van Nuys High School reciting "Oh, Captain! My Captain!", Walt Whitman's farewell to Lincoln, on the radio.

"I'm going to be a star." Now she gave me the full force of her baby-face stare.

"I believe you."

"What about Beverly Hills?"

"What about it?"

"To live in, silly. No. Too snooty. But I do want to be rich. Maybe live in Brentwood. A small house will do me, Spanish, sort of. With a pool. Kidney shaped. Like the stars have. A special place where I can be protected from everything out here."

"That sounds nice." I drained my cup and poured a refill. I wondered what had really happened to the salesman. If he was a salesman.

"But I want my life to mean something. I want kids. Lots. And a poodle. Or maybe a collie, like Lassie."

"That sounds like a fair ambition."

"I had a collie once. Muggsy. She died."

"That's too bad."

The fan chugged overhead, putting out its muffled worthless breeze. I watched my seersucker jacket hanging on the peg on the wall moving to the fan's rhythms.

Somewhere outside somebody was yelling at a kid. Or a dog. My Camel smoldered in the thick glass ashtray. I lit a new one from the butt and stubbed the butt out. I got up, cranked open the blinds, and gave us both a limited view of the La Fonda Motor Lodge across Ventura. There was a beat-up old yellow Pontiac convertible at the curb. Hers.

The sunlight through the blinds cast bright stripes on her. I pictured her walking around in her birthday suit after her shower. In my fantasy her flesh was warm and alive. God, she was gorgeous.

The blonde looked from the window, to the fan, to me. All three were irritating her. "You have a soul, don't you?"

"Doesn't everyone?"

"I think you could be my best friend. And I do need a friend."

Wow. She was good. She was real good. Underneath the dumb blonde act was there a sparkling sensitive intelligence? I couldn't be sure. I studied her for a long time. My contemplation was a bit intense, I guess, because she flinched.

She was almost childlike in her desire to please. She was trying hard to be my friend. She stared at my shirt. "That's a beautiful shirt. A really wonderful shirt."

"Thank you." It was only a shirt. And one that had seen better days. "When are you going to tell me the real story?" I was losing patience and beginning to be annoyed by her little girl tricks.

She looked startled. "What do you mean?"

"I believe you about the dead body. But that's all I believe. Do you want my help? Just put twenty dollars on the desk and we can keep talking."

She fumbled with her purse. A tear rolled down her pink-white cheek.

"Come on, cut it out." I pulled my handkerchief from my back pocket. It was clean; I shoved it at her.

"No, thank you," she whispered. She produced a wad of bills from the purse and counted out four tens on the desk. Then she dried her eyes with a little square of lacy pink cloth. "Take your money. Forty ought to get me twice as much."

I picked up the crumpled bills and slipped them into my shirt pocket.

"Do you believe me now?" She narrowed those beautiful dark eyes. "Is that the way it works? If I give you money you believe me?"

"Keep talking." My receipt pad was in the top drawer of my desk next to the little .22 Colt automatic. I wrote out a receipt and handed it to her. "Where'd you get all that money, Norma Jeane?"

"I . . . I . . ." She broke off with a startled hand to her mouth. "I don't know," she said in that soft child's voice. The words were so blurred that for a moment I couldn't make them out.

"Let's go across the road and have a look see," I said.

"I'm going to be a great movie star someday," she whispered, not moving. "I'm going to be a movie star. Whatever I do is an investment in myself. Do you like my dress? I've got to have nice things when I go out on a job. If you're dressed well, they pay higher fees."

"Let's go, Norma Jeane," I said. I held out my hand.

The blush bled through her pink white skin. She made a pleading gesture with her hands.

All of a sudden she thrust her right hand out. I took it. She shook my hand firmly once. Like something she'd seen in a movie. "Thank you."

"Lead the way," I said.

She winked at me and squealed her deep-seated laugh. "Walk this way," she said. But I couldn't. Not ever. I don't think there were even women who could emulate that rolling walk of hers. I don't know if it was the broken heel or what. Whatever made the walk work, she was as lovely aft as fore. And didn't she know it.

She was out the door singing snatches of "I'll Walk Alone."

After only a second's thought I grabbed my gun and rig from the desk and my jacket from the hook. This was an exceptional occasion. Not the Jap invasion, but it would do. I take dead bodies seriously. If there was a dead body. Hot as it was, I put the rig on and hid it by wearing the jacket.

My Ford coupe was in the little lot beside the office. I opened the passenger side and she hopped in.

"Ooh," she cried, "hot seat." Then she laughed in an altogether natural way. I was taken by the innocent awe in her face. "What a yummy car. I love red."

I closed her door. A lot she knew. I'd been nursing the coupe since '41. If the war lasted much longer I'd be getting around on a Schwinn. When I got in on my side I saw she'd put her sunglasses back on. I gunned the Ford and squealed it across the highway to the La Fonda. I was in that kind of mood. "Which is yours?"

"That one." She pointed to the last yellow cabin. I pulled in right next to a black Caddie.

I got out and opened her door. She didn't get out, she didn't even move. I couldn't see her eyes, but I knew she was looking at the Cadillac. "So how about it?" I offered my hand.

She removed the sunglasses and stared at me as if she'd never seen me before.

"I'm an orphan," she said in a tiny voice.

She was a real nut job. Too bad, I thought. "Norma Jeane, do you want to show me the dead guy?"

"Oh," she said. "I forgot." She got out of the car, then reached in for the white purse on the seat. Her dress rode up to her crotch. Jesus, she wasn't wearing anything underneath.

I must have made a sound because she straightened her dress and shot me a hurt look. I was sweating like a goniff under the lights in the back room of a police station.

"You go first," she said. "I'm scared."

"If he's dead, he can't hurt you," I said, walking in front of her, imagining how she looked when I was behind her. The path was spread with little white stones. A phallic cactus leaned against her cabin.

The door was wide open. I drew my Colt, just in case. Just in case what, I thought. I had no idea.

"Oh, my God," she said. She was breathing down my neck, pushing up against me. I won't tell you what I was thinking. "Do you see him?" she whispered.

The little hall was empty. Measuring my steps, I walked into the bedroom. Not a soul. Dead or alive. There was a sharp morbid smell in the air. The bed looked as if she'd just crawled out of it after an active few hours. The night table was full of bottles of makeup, some containers of pills, and a dusting of spilled powder.

A pair of blue jeans lay on the floor, a man's white shirt drooped from the doorknob of the bathroom door. The place was a mess. On the bureau was half a hamburger with raw onion and an empty Coke bottle. The smell was coming from the hamburger, which was going green. But no dead man.

"Oh," she said, taking it all in, then giving me that tremulous smile of hers.

I holstered my Colt, reached into my shirt pocket, and handed her her forty bucks.

She gave me two tens back. "Because you were kind," she said.

The phone rang. She stared at me as if waiting my permission. I nodded. By the time she said hello, I was gone. Before I closed the door I heard her say, "What should I wear?"

It was one of those things, you know. I knew she wasn't all there, but I couldn't get her out of my mind. I just drove for a while. That was extravagant, what with gas rationing, but I needed to think. Or not to think. Still at a loss, I went to see a movie at a second-run house in LA. One I hadn't seen the first time around in '44. Edward G. Robinson and Joan Bennett in *The Woman in the Window*.

Here was a real bright guy, his life and career ruined because of a dame. So he tries to cover everything up and comes unglued. All because of a dame. There was a trick ending to the movie. When all was said and done, it turned out it was just a dream. But the point was made.

Ordinarily I would have wondered how Robinson's character could let a woman do that to him, but having met Norma Jeane and listened to her dead body story, I wasn't so sure it couldn't happen to me. I was happy to be rid of her. After the movie I had a couple of beers and went home. But she haunted my sleep.

"I'm an orphan," she said. "There's something missing in orphans. We want everybody to love us." Her juicy red lips pursed and came close to me. Like an extreme close-up in a movie. "Do you love me?" The lips came even closer, all distorted like that Spanish fellow Dali paints them, begging me to kiss them. "He's dead," she whispered. "Why don't you believe me?"

The blonde was getting into the black Caddy bare ass naked when I woke up in a pool of sweat. I took a cold shower and put on yesterday's shirt because I forgot to get my other three out of the Chinese.

When I went down to my office, I saw that her Pontiac convertible was gone. I walked on out to the parking lot, got into my coupe, gunned the motor, and made a U and pulled up in front of her cabin. Her Pontiac wasn't there either. Neither was the Cadillac.

What I should have done then was pulled the car across the road, parked it, and got on with my life. But no, I had to know more.

I could see the maid running the vacuum in the next cabin. I got out of my car and walked to Norma Jeane's cabin. Again, the door was wide open.

"Norma Jeane," I called. "You there?"

No answer. I stepped inside. The makeup and pills were gone. The clothes lying around, gone. All that remained was the rumpled bedclothes, the dusting of powder on the night table, and a crumpled paper bag on top of the bureau. That and the sharp morbid onion smell mixed with just a hint of Chanel No. 5 and an Ivory soap chaser.

I sat on the bed. The temperature had already hit ninety and the heat was getting to me. Maybe, just like Edward G. Robinson, I dreamed the whole damn thing. I stood up and something shiny caught my eye from under the bureau. A piece of jewelry or something.

I knelt down. The case of the mixed-up blonde didn't exist. And the case that didn't exist was over with. Finished. Still, there I was, John Marley, real-life private eye, crawling around a dead-smelling cabin in the La Fonda Motor Lodge, waving his hand around under a dusty old bureau. Searching for whatever it was. I touched it, and quick pulled my hand away. I'd cut myself. Sitting on the bed again, I inspected the slice in my finger as the blood beaded up from it. "God damn."

I wrapped my handkerchief around the finger and got to my feet. This time I was smarter. I lifted the end of the bureau and set it down a few inches away, uncovering the shiny thing.

It was a silver carving knife. My blood was on it. From what I could see there were no stains to show that somebody else's blood had been on it, too. But that didn't prove anything.

I reached down and picked it up.

"Hello," someone called.

"Yeah," I answered. Quickly I uncrumpled the bag and put the carving knife in it.

The Spanish girl came into the room. "I thought you checked out."

"I did," I said. "I just came back to see if I forgot something."

The phone rang.

The maid looked at me. "Maybe it's for you," she said. She had no accent at all.

"Maybe?" I said. I picked up the phone, extremely conscious of the knife in the bag. "Yeah?"

But there was no one there.

AFTERWORD

In 1962 the Supreme Court said no to school prayer. Johnny Carson on late-night TV was a new phenomenon. So was Bob Dylan's recording career. The New York Mets lost 120 games their first year. Adolf Eichmann was captured, tried, and executed by the Israelis.

Barbra Streisand debuted on Broadway in *I Can Get It for You Wholesale.* She stole the show. She was nineteen. In the fall James Meredith would be the first black admitted to the University of Mississippi and President John F. Kennedy would face down Khrushchev over missiles in Cuba.

Marty was acting periodically on the TV shows *Naked City, The Defenders,* and *Car 54, Where Are You?* Annette was assistant to Harold Prince on *A Funny Thing Happened on the Way to the Forum,* which opened on Broadway May 8 and was a huge hit.

August 5, 1962, Marilyn Monroe, supposedly a suicide, died in her bedroom, from an overdose of sleeping pills. She ended up as fantasy for the world and grist for everyone's mill.

To Marty, Marilyn was the obvious: SEX.

To Annette, she was a stunning entertainer-comedienne until she did *The Misfits* in 1961 and proved to be a brilliant actress. What a performance.

Looking back, Marilyn is still the sex symbol. But the price Norma Jeane paid to be Marilyn was horrendous.

—**Martin Meyers and
Annette Meyers**

HUSH MONEY

LYNNE BARRETT

 MY NAME IS Annie O'Malley. You may have seen my work behind the famous as they relax in their gardens in *People* or *In Style*—that's what I do, I'm gardener to the stars.

My profession requires me to live with secrets. This isn't so easy—a secret can be poison, burning in your mouth till you have to spit it out. I sometimes think that's really what motivates those who tattle to the tabloids, more than money or attention. My solution has been to write things down. I tell myself that I want the truth to be known someday, that I'm interested in justice, but mostly I just need to spill the beans.

I'd only been in Hollywood for a year or so. I'd finished the all-green garden of the producer Paul Ferris (another story) and moved on to landscaping the place of Jill Santiago, an ex-girlfriend of his. His ex-girlfriends were all fond of him, they formed a regular club, and in a way I was a member of it, too, so they were each in turn hiring me. Jill had begun as a starlet in adventure films, had failed in a couple of more serious flicks, and now, having decided to get rich, was a sensational bitch on a nighttime soap. She had honed her figure into an instrument with which she tortured men, something it turns out women enjoy watching.

In person, Jill was a combination of pragmatic and crazy that is quite common out here. She was happy with me because I had succeeded in moving into her yard an espaliered wisteria complete with its very nice old wall that went back to the Spanish settlement of California and cost a fortune, but the point was that Jill needed the wisteria to look as if it had been there behind her house (built in 1986) for generations and to bloom in just the shade she wanted behind her when Barbara Walters interviewed her. This had gone off perfectly. She looked gorgeous as they talked, her hair baby blond against the lavender blue wisteria, and Barbara had been so mellowed out by the breeze and blossoms that she didn't press Jill on the rumors that her body was surgically contrived. Somehow the old Spanish wall vouched for Jill's genuineness.

Jill cheerfully paid the bill for the crew and equipment I'd used, said I was a genius, and gave me the assignment of going up to this property in Northern California she'd bought. Her accountant said she needed to use the place, and it was up to me to decide how. "Not grapes," she said, "grapes take too long. I heard from Paul that that vineyard of his won't produce anything worth drinking for seven years. Coolidge (the acountant) says it would be good if I took some losses as write-offs—but I'd rather see a profit. I want a business hobby. It should be intelligent, feminine, unusual—but do-able."

"A lot of people are raising exotic animals," I told her. "Ostriches or giraffes."

"Animals steal scenes. Think of a good plant," she said, "in my color range, of course."

You may think this was an idiotic assignment, but I found it amusing. That's what it takes, I guess, to be gardener to the stars.

The property was not far from Geyserville, in Lake County. Late in the afternoon I came up a twisting road in the car I had rented in San Francisco, admiring old estates and picturesque shacks, roadsides bright with poppies and fields planted in tight rows of grapevines, just sprouting in early April. The road wound nauseatingly along a ridge, and after I passed a funny encampment of pink cottages at the peak, it plunged down and died out. You could see the trail beyond it where the road had once continued, but it was overgrown and flinty, so I decided I'd need a four-wheel drive to take it on. I went back uphill to the pink cottages and parked under a vast hedge of rosemary, thinking I'd ask if there was another way in. The cottages, four of them, formed a rough quad around a fragrant garden. I knocked on the blue front door of the biggest house and waited, admiring the generous patches of lavender and thrift. I was squatting before columbines in blossom, when a gruff and rusty voice behind me said, "Get the hell out of here."

I turned and saw an old lady, tall and tanned to leather, wearing many silver bracelets and a purple bath towel. Her white hair was pulled up in a big purple clip and her legs were wet. Behind her water dripped from what I realized was an outdoor shower closed in by lattice overgrown with wild pink roses.

"I'm terribly sorry," I said. "I'm trying to get over to the next property, over there. The owner sent me to—"

"It got sold again?"

I nodded. My heart, I realized, was still beating hard in shock. "The owner is Jill Santiago and she sent me up to look it over, see what it needs." I handed her my card.

She looked it over. "L.A." Her laugh was a caw. "People in L.A. have been selling that property to each other for forty years," she said.

"What happened to the road?"

"Flooded out. That road extended right across a streambed, joins up with the creek down there. Floods every ten years or so. Last couple of times nobody came in to rebuild it—nobody complained. I sure didn't."

Though her voice was rough and her stance unfriendly, I admired her. How magnificent to be an old lady living out here, I thought, showering among the roses. She was a vision of the kind of old woman I'd like to be someday.

"I'm sorry to have intruded," I said. "You'll be seeing me go through here, but I'll try not to disturb you again."

"I'm sure," she sighed, "this is only the beginning of disturbances."

"I'm sorry," I said again, and turned to go back to my car.

But she said, "Come on in," and led me into the cottage with the blue door. The main room was a kitchen. She said to me, "Hang on," and went into another room for a moment. I waited, mildly confused at the shift into friendliness—if it was friendliness. She came back in a long yellow Mexican dress. "You must forgive me," she said. "I'm out of practice seeing people. Mostly it's just the men who come to work on the grapes. I lease the vines to a winery down the valley—Mea Vinca, you ever have that wine? That's got some of my grapes in it. I get cases of it, free. Want some?"

"Huh?"

"Want some wine?"

I nodded, and she went to a green painted sideboard and brought out a bottle and green chunky glasses and poured us each a good slug. I drank, standing, not really certain of my welcome. She stood too.

"So you work in L.A.," she said. "I used to live there. During the war and right after."

"Long time ago," I said.

"Oh, I'm sure it's the same," she said. "Underneath the surface, not much really changes. L.A. is a place full of cannibals. Well, all of California, really. You know about the Donner party? Cannibalism founded California and cannibals we remain," she said.

"That's harsh," I said.

"Where are you from?"

"Massachusetts."

"You'll learn," she said. "Maybe you're already learning." She laughed—that caw again. "I learned, but it took me a few years. I knew Marilyn Monroe," she said.

"Really? Well—I guess she got eaten up all right. I see what you mean."

"Hah," she barked. "I doubt you do."

"How did you know her?"

"See," she said, "you're hungry too. You want to taste that stardust."

I must have looked confused—I wasn't sure if I should be amused or offended. I swallowed my wine—a fiercely tannic cabernet—and started moving to the door. "Well, I thank you very much for the drink. You'll see me going by."

She reached out and shook my hand. "I'm Mrs. Donofrio," she said. "Forgive me if I startled you. Like I said, I don't see so many people. When my husband was alive we had more company."

I left and when I got in my car said *Whew*. On the way back down the ridge I saw that quite a bit of what must be her land was

planted with grapevines, their rows of T-shaped trellises oddly geometric in contrast to the hodgepodge of her cottages and garden.

I drove back into Geyserville, where I'd arranged to stay in a
bed-and-breakfast. I asked about Mrs. Donofrio, but the owners
didn't know much—they'd bought the B & B only a few months
before, moving up to flee L.A. My host told me tales of the people
living in the inaccessible spots here, old hippies who'd stayed on,
pot farmers, people who liked to be beyond easy reach of the law.
He told me I was lucky nobody'd taken a shot at me. But somehow
none of these stories fit my old woman. She had seemed awkwardly
friendly, lonely. I studied a county map they had and saw a stream
bed that marked the line between the properties. I had to call over
to Calistoga to make arrangements to swap my rental car for a Jeep
next day.

This time I was able to get down the hill and across and I walked all
over the property. There was a tumble-down house—turn of the
century, it looked, the ghost of a white villa. The land was hillside
meadow, full of lupine and campanula and other wildflowers I
didn't recognize. Old unpruned lilacs were in bloom and there was
a dark blue hedge I knew Jill would like—some kind of heather. At
lunchtime I had a picnic with some sandwiches and Calistoga
water I'd brought and realized that I could spy on the old lady of
the pink cottages. She kept busy. She repainted some blue window-
boxes and then dug out what I imagined would be a vegetable
patch. The woman had a smooth, easy motion with a shovel.
Watching her work made me feel lazy and I leaned back and went
into a kind of doze, wondering what I was going to tell Jill to do
with this place. The house could be beautiful if someone put in a
lot of time and money, but I couldn't imagine Jill coming to live
here—too far from everyone who mattered to her. And the logical
thing to plant was grapes, but she had already nixed that. I felt reluctant to plant the place up with something she didn't really care
about, something that would only get neglected again after her
need for a hobby to display had been satisfied. I thought about
Mrs. Donofrio's cannibals and I'm afraid got into a very unpleasant

dream about several famous people threatening me with knives.

When I woke up I felt headachy—I'm a bad napper—and decided to pack it in for the day. But as I jounced across the stream bed, I saw Mrs. Donofrio up ahead, waiting for me. Who's going to disturb who here, I thought, but I pulled up beside her.

I declined her offer of wine—said my head hurt—and she said she had an herbal tea that would help. I was curious about her life up here, so I said sure and let her lead me into the east cottage, which was a reading room, with redwood shelves floor to ceiling and a comfortable-looking couch covered by an old quilt. She went over to a side table, where she had an electric kettle, and while she made my tea I walked around exclaiming over the hundreds of books.

"Erle Stanley Gardner camped over there on your boss's land at one time. You know he used to go around California in his camper. Traveled with his girl secretaries—a couple of 'em. Dictated three books at once, they said. We liked him, my husband and I. My husband collected all his books. I guess that's what got us started." She showed me the shelves of Erle Stanley Gardner—paperbacks with lurid covers. The ones from the forties might have been valuable, but they were just stacked up, not displayed. I moved along, noticing sets of Stevenson and Twain, encyclopedias, some dinged-up science texts. Then I reached a shelf of old gardening books that made my mouth water. She had volumes of Jepson's *A Flora of California* and a gilt-edged Gertrude Jekyll from 1904, *Old West Surrey,* that goes for $250 if you can ever find it. I started talking about them—babbling—and saw she was listening to me amusedly. "Maybe you'd like to borrow one or two of these," she said.

I took the Gertrude Jekyll—determined to photocopy every page of it—and a book on California wildflowers. While her rosemary tea cleared my head, she told me how she'd never had much education, but once she lived up here she'd started reading. As I listened I noticed that though her voice was gruff and low there was a music to it I liked.

In the days that passed I got in the habit of stopping by at the end of the day. I'd identified monkshood and shooting star and seven shades of nemophilas. I made a map and sat on Jill's land reading books and making plans—she could raise roses, I thought one day—maybe she should make a country garden, I thought the next. I made sketch after sketch, but nothing satisfied me. After this I would stop at Mrs. Donofrio's and we would have a glass of wine. I showed her some of the wildflowers I'd sketched and she told me how the Indians had used blue curls for medicine and once went to war to drive settlers off their fields of camas, the wild hyacinth whose bulbs they ate in ceremonies. I told her a few tales of Hollywood—she liked the one about the old man I'd met who was one of the gardeners that planted and tended a thousand Scottish heather plants for Samuel Goldwyn's *Wuthering Heights*. But she didn't again mention Marilyn Monroe.

Then the winery men came one day. They appeared to be doing some careful pruning. I saw them taking turns going into her bathroom and spreading their lunch at a table outside. Mrs. Donofrio didn't come out. I was doing soil tests—using my pH kit, sampling and labeling. It was precise work and I nearly jumped when someone cleared her throat and I saw Mrs. Donofrio sitting above me on a jag of rock.

I looked over at the men. "Did they drive you away?"

She shrugged. "You get used to the quiet."

"What are they doing?"

"Oh, it's all a science now—they have systems for arranging every leaf to get the most sun and air. Not the way it was when I first came up here, when the old men from Italy tended the vines."

"Well, I'm sure they were trying to wring as much as they could out of nature, too."

"You're a nice girl," she said. "I think you should leave Los Angeles."

"Actually I can't," I said. And I told her some personal things, how I came out to look after my sister (another story) in the first place but then lucked into this work. Back East, without the graduate degree or connections to get hired at one of the big botanical gardens, I had just labored for landscapers. Now I felt I'd pulled something off getting these Hollywood people to pay for my garden dreams.

Maybe I even told her who I was carrying the torch for. The point is, I offered her some secrets of mine.

"I see," Mrs. D said. She sat with her arms clasped around her knees, like a young girl, looking across at her own home. "My first name is Wanita," she said. Her voice hit a rusty patch just then, so I got the idea she hadn't spoken her own name in quite a while.

"Juanita's a beautiful name."

"W-a-n," she said. "My mother heard it in a song but she didn't know how to spell it. They were Okies, my people, trekked out here, didn't know a Spanish soul then. Wanita. Maybe the exotic name is what put it in my head to go to L.A."

"Where were you living?"

"I grew up near Sacramento. I was a big girl always, tall, with large hands and feet. Not beautiful—no, I had no illusions about that. Still, I had something going for me. Men paid attention to me. But this was during the war, there weren't so many men around. I thought I could do better in L.A." She gave her harsh laugh. "And maybe I thought someone would discover me, doll me up and put me in the movies. Sure.

"I was eighteen when I got there, in 1944. I fell in love right away with a sailor who was about to ship out. Jimmy Blue Eyes, I called him—I guess he reminded me of Frank Sinatra. Before the war he'd been a salesman—sewing machines, mainly—and he'd traveled all over the state. He talked about coming up here someday, to run some tourist cabins, maybe to farm. He wanted to marry me, but he said it wasn't fair to do that to me and then ship out and get killed. So he left me in L.A. and he didn't expect me to be a good girl, and I wasn't.

"I dated a lot of men—soldiers, sailors, four-flushers. Hollywood was loaded with four-flushers. What? Oh, a four-flusher was 4F, bad lungs, flat feet, some bit of him disabled him for war. Not that you could tell—big strapping handsome men there were who couldn't go to war, while my Jimmy Blue Eyes was a skinny guy, but he was in the Pacific on a destroyer.

"Early in the summer of '45 I met Norma Jeane. I was in a gambling club in Santa Monica—a night on the town with some fella— Hal? Harry? No, I don't remember his name. Anyway, she was a pretty girl, no question about it. Not as beautiful as she was later. That was something I noticed about her—she got more beautiful all the time—I could see that even in a matter of weeks. Later, people said she had surgery on her nose, but there are things you can't get by cutting. She had a lovely smile. And she had wonderful feet— I must have noticed that because my own were big and boney. You didn't often see a girl with pretty feet—back then we all squeezed into too-small shoes and ruined them. Vanity. Hers stayed nice— you can see her feet in those late pictures where she's naked in a swimming pool. I've often wondered about her feet, how they stayed beautiful—silly I guess.

"Her date knew mine and so we gambled—or they did and we clung to their arms—and we went off to the powder room together. You probably don't know what powder rooms were like back then. The clubs had attendants in uniforms and an array of anything you might need for repairs to your dress or your face. We carried just these little clutch bags because we knew we could get help anywhere along the way—at dinner, night club, gambling house. I see you young women dragging those shoulder bags and I laugh.

"Norma Jeane seemed real insecure. I remember she chattered even while she tinkled in the stall next to mine—" At my expression Wanita roared with laughter. "I pissed with Marilyn Monroe. I can see you don't really believe in the humanness of these people. But in your line of work you ought to know. You'll get to know. Anyway, 'Do you think he really likes me?' she said, and I noticed she stuttered a little. Real insecure. I tried to reassure her and when we came out and let the attendant brush us up a bit, she said, 'I can tell your guy is crazy about you. You know just how to talk to him.'

"Don't look surprised. It was true. I spoke to men with respectful sweetness. I had doted on my dad, I guess that's why. But on top of that I'd been having elocution lessons, trying to get the Okie out of my voice, so I was flattered by her. I figured I must sound real proper." She laughed and shook her head.

"When we got back to the table my date was winning big and after he ran up a good sum we quit and went dancing with Norma Jeane and her date. Her date was a good-looking boy. Mine was kind of an ordinary guy, maybe a little dull, but winning brightened him up and he bought us all a late dinner and next day he sent over this bracelet here—" She showed me a silver piece with green stones carved into Aztec faces, one of the heaviest of the many she wore. "I started collecting these then. I liked Mexican jewelry— thought it went with my name. Norma Jeane was at my place when it arrived. She'd called me and come over early, when I was still in bed, and we sat around and had some toast and talked. I had a swell little apartment. In Hollywood then they had buildings that were really swank. Downstairs there'd be a lobby like a hotel's and no one came up without asking at the desk. Your phone was on a switchboard. It was a nice place, hard to come by in the war, but a gentleman I knew owned the building."

Here Wanita went off into space for a minute, thinking, I sup- posed, about the man who owned the building, so I asked her what she and Norma Jeane had talked about that day.

"This and that. I learned she was married but planning to di- vorce the fellow, who was overseas. She was doing some modeling and trying to study acting, living a life much like mine, working a bit and mooching off men to get by.

"Anyway, Norma Jeane was a fun girl and she gave me a rush— invited me to the beach, I recall, and set up several double dates. When we were on our own she was *so* interested in me—made me tell long stories about growing up in the Sacramento Valley and how I came to L.A. and all my adventures while I waited for Jimmy Blue Eyes. Even I thought they weren't that fascinating, but she would listen, all attention. By then I thought she was my best friend. I remember her curled up on the day bed I had filled with pillows in pretty textiles. She had light brown curly hair then and wore a little sundress with red bobbles on it that I liked—oh, she was a picture. I had told her about Jimmy Blue Eyes and our dream of coming up here after the war, if he would only live that long, and I must have expressed some confusion about loving him and going out with all these fellows, because she said, 'You can't help it, can you?'

"And I was touched that she understood. 'No, honey, I really can't,' I said. 'I see these men and they're just so appreciative, you know, and—' We didn't have such good words for sexy things then.

Later, I'd have said they turned me on, but in the forties I said, 'They get to me,' and Norma nodded.

"She had told me herself that she wasn't so interested in sex as in ambition. She wanted to be an actress. She talked about her mother, the woman she didn't want to be—deserted, pathetic, nuts. And she told me about the actresses she'd seen when she was a girl, when her mother worked at a film lab. There was one actress whose walk she said she'd practiced—not somebody famous—she was not that pretty maybe or maybe she got in trouble with a man, I forget, but Norma Jeane said she had a sensational walk. Norma Jeane described how she'd practiced it, when she was still just nine or ten. I wish I could recall her name now. Nobody you'd have heard of.

"Hey," Wanita said. "Let's have some dinner."

I was surprised to realize the sun had dropped. I'd been off in the forties with Wanita and Norma Jeane. The men who'd been working on the vines were gone. I gathered my things and drove her back over to her place. She sent me into her garden to pick arugula and sorrel for a salad. She blendered a gazpacho and grilled some salmon. "Fish and raw stuff," Wanita said, "that's the secret to long life. And wine."

We talked for a while about Jill's land and what might be done with it. I was anxious to assure her that whatever it would be wouldn't interfere with her too much, but Wanita just shook her head.

"I'll be watching reporters chase her, before you're through. I can tell she's a cannibal princess."

"Well, it won't last long," I said.

Wanita smiled. "Their fancy moves on."

"What about Norma Jeane?" I asked. "Was that the whole story?"

"No, not quite. If I tell you," she said, "you'd have to keep the secret."

"I'm good at keeping secrets," I said. Well, I thought I was.

"Maybe it might help you out, in your work, help you to understand."

I tried to look receptive, ready to learn. We went out on the lawn and sat in old metal lawnchairs, eating fresh figs and goat cheese, drinking more wine. As darkness fell I could hardly see Wanita, just hear her. Her voice had warmed up—I was beginning to picture the charming girl from Hollywood, who appealed to men.

"After a bit more time—I don't recall exactly—she dropped me. No tiff happened or anything, she just moved on. I knew she was around and I saw her across the dance floor in nightclubs a couple of times—she had lost weight and was even prettier. The war ended but it still took eight months for Jimmy to be discharged. When he got out he took me out to Chasen's to celebrate and there she was. With some real swell. She didn't notice us but we were in the next booth and I was waiting to catch her eye, when I heard her speak and my mouth just fell open—"

Wanita stared off to her left, her mouth agape.

"What?" I asked.

"Well, she was talking like me. It wasn't just my pronunciation either, it was my voice itself. And, I mean, I knew my voice was what men liked. I'd seen men's glance go right by me and then they heard me talk and they were on me like bees on a honeysuckle. And when she did it, I could see why. I asked Jimmy to listen and he heard it too—he said, 'She sounds just like you. Who is she?' And even he was drawn in, cause I mean, you put my voice into a person who looked like Norma Jeane and it was devastating. You bet I got him out of there fast."

She must have felt that I was sitting up straighter in my seat and peering over, trying to see if she was making all this up. "Don't look at me like that," she said. "I know I don't sound that way anymore. Isn't that just what I'm telling you about?

"I called Norma Jeane up and asked to meet her and I could tell she knew what it was about. She came to see me, looking much more swank than before, wearing a white suit with light blue satin trim. She greeted me with a kiss, she exclaimed at how well I looked, she fussed over my bracelets and teased me about Jimmy—said she'd seen us leave—but I wasn't pleased because she did it all in *my* voice. Her own, you know, was a little shrill, and she sometimes stuttered.

"She saw it wouldn't wash. She sat down.

" 'Don't be mad at me,' she said.

" 'Talk like yourself,' I said.

" 'I can't anymore, honey,' she said. 'I didn't just learn your way of speaking. I had to—I had to give mine up.'

"I goggled at that. 'What do you mean?'

"She said, 'You know, Wanita, the first time I heard your voice I felt that really it *was* mine. The way I was supposed to be, I mean. So I listened, I practiced, and then one day it was just the only way for me to speak. I can't even remember how I talked before.'

" 'But honey,' I said, 'it isn't yours, it's mine.'

" 'Wanita,' she said, 'I need it more than you do. You're going to marry that sweet Jimmy Blue Eyes and be happy talking just to him. You can leave Hollywood and go have that place you dreamed of.'

" 'Actually, honey, we're going to be here for a while.' Did I mean to threaten her? I guess I did. 'Jimmy and I can both get work here and we'll have to save a long time before we can afford to buy land up north.'

"And Norma Jeane said she could help us. And so, by God, I sold my voice to her."

I said, "What?" I had been mesmerized, for as Wanita talked, I had been trying to catch the breathy speech of Marilyn Monroe somewhere behind her own deep tones.

"I sold her the right to my voice, the voice of Wanita Gregg, for a chunk of hillside in Lake County and twenty-seven years with Jimmy Donofrio."

"And you had to stop speaking that way yourself?"

"No, that happened later. This land belonged to the same man who owned the other piece, a producer. Norma Jeane didn't really have any money then, but she got him to give us a mortgage on it— I guess she used herself as the downpayment. We didn't ask. We got married and drove up here in a '36 Ford and lived in a tent till Jimmy built the first cottage. We were in love, we were delighted. My dad came to live with us and Jimmy built another cabin for him, so he was with us but we had our privacy. Things were just getting going up here with the wine business. We didn't have the capital for that, but we leased our land and Jimmy also took sales jobs from time to time and we eked along. Later we had two kids, a son and a daughter, and Jimmy enlarged the big cottage and built the other two to rent out, but that never did work out, really—we just used the space ourselves. Jimmy had more ideas than sense, if you know what I mean.

"I think the first inkling I got of my problem was in 1952, when I was in the hospital in Sonoma having my son. I heard two nurses outside the room, laughing at me. They thought I was imitating her. Marilyn Monroe.

"When the baby was three months old I left him with my dad one day and went in to the movies—over in St. Helena—and listened for myself. You know, I hadn't felt so bad when I talked to her face to face, but movies magnify everything. And maybe I'd already gotten some distance from who I'd been.

"The first thing that upset me was the elocution. When I heard Marilyn Monroe I realized that when I was trying to sound so smart I just sounded dumber—she had gotten it exactly, you see, so you heard the correct pronunciation but also that shade of tentativeness of someone who had to work so very hard not to make a mistake and a kind of proud glee that she was pulling it off. So it was comical. Well, I dropped that instantly. I went back to my Okie from Lodi voice just fine—in fact, I probably already had, with my dad around. But that still didn't do it. I remember we went to a party— the launching of a winery in Napa, a friend of Jimmy's threw it— and Gentlemen Prefer Blondes was out, and when I spoke, there were giggles. I pretended I had a cold, then, made myself hoarse. And after that—I tried to talk firmer and lower, but on many occasions, with strangers, I shut up altogether. And all this time she was getting more and more famous and inescapable."

Wanita leaned back in her chair and looked up at the stars, which were thick over the dark hillsides. "My dad, I'll say this for him, he never fell for her. As long as he lived—he died in 1956—he called her a poor imitation of me."

"And Jimmy?"

"Well, he said the same, but I didn't believe him. I got to thinking when he held me in the dark he thought he was holding Marilyn Monroe. That shut me up too. And I was changing. Two kids, you know, you have to control them—I'd find myself yelling out across the hills, trying to get them home for dinner. You don't stay the same. . . .

"But I kept sneaking out to see her movies, too, and each time, I'd learn something about myself. She sounded—I'd sounded— like somebody who'd just had sex. Not somebody all keyed up for sex—I always felt Ava Gardiner had that sound, Lauren Bacall— deep and teasing. Marilyn Monroe sounded like someone who just had sex and was grateful, flattered even. It made men feel bolder be- cause she—I—sounded like we'd already done it and we'd be sure to do it again. I noticed how they were casting opposite her. She didn't get the handsome young guys—it was all older men or wimps or someone totally naive like the cowboy in *Bus Stop*—and I decided it was because of her voice, because it had the effect of en- couraging *unconfident* men. The bolder sorts like to go up against more of a challenge. So I realized something about Jimmy."

"That he wasn't confident?"

"You know, I grew up thinking men were a big deal," Wanita said, with a sigh. "I don't know where I got that idea—books, movies. It was literally years before I realized that Jimmy couldn't really do much of anything for long—that he'd been just a strug- gling salesman when the war came along. Which was no disgrace, but after a while it did start to get me that he was content to live for the rest of his life mostly off this land that came from a woman."

"Well, but he was paying it off."

"Oh no. Did I leave that out? She'd sent us money more than once—we really needed it then, too. Checks made out to the Wanita Gregg Donofrio Elocution School. Her joke. And then she paid off the whole mortgage, in the mid-fifties. It was a year before my dad died, cause I remember we told him. You see, I wanted to turn it down. Stupid, really. I thought that would somehow give me the right to my voice back—the right to be unself-conscious again. Well, anyway. There was no going back. But I noticed that neither my dad nor Jimmy had any problem taking the money my voice had earned us, and I guess that bothered me. Certainly it was after that Jimmy started telling me I'd become grumpy and a nag about money. And I was always harping at the kids to study and work to make something of themselves. They have, too. Jim studied wine-making, even went over to France, and now he's working for a winery in Australia. Wendy's an oceanographer, knows everything about seaweed—you remind me of her, a little. Listen, let's open another bottle and drink to Marilyn Monroe."

She went inside and I noticed that I was feeling pretty crocked already, but somehow I didn't want to move and miss the end of the story. When Wanita came back out she had a merlot—"I actually bought this one," she said. She poured and smelled it deeply before she drank. She seemed to have forgotten the toast.

I asked what happened after that.

"You know as much as me. After the mortgage was paid off, we didn't hear from her. I guess she felt she'd discharged the debt. But of course we heard about her. Successes. Divorces. Seems to me I was aware she had health problems—she lost her pregnancies, was into hospitals for rest. But it was only later all this other stuff came out."

I breathed the pungent breeze from her garden and thought of all the sad stories I'd heard about Marilyn Monroe.

"You ever see her when she sang Happy Birthday to JFK? If you believe even half of it her life was a mess. She should have been screeching, angry, scared, but there she was singing like the happiest piece of fluff on earth, like she was just taking a little break between fucks, pardon my language. See—her problem was she couldn't knock it off. No matter what, she sounded like grateful, dim, sexed-up Wanita Gregg, age twenty. Poor kid."

I was going to ask which kid she meant, young Wanita or MM, but as I went to speak I yawned and realized I was way drunk. I felt dizzy, like I was going to roll right down the hill and tumble in the creek.

"Cut both ways," she said. "On the one hand, she couldn't get anybody to take her seriously. She went East to study acting and it was like this big delicious joke—Marilyn studies Stanislavsky. People laughed when she even *said* Stanislavsky. On the other hand, she used to make those studio jackals kiss her ass if they wanted her to work, and it was always poor sweet child. Still is."

"So you resented her?"

"Sure I did. Now I don't. Or maybe I do. You always kind of want to have your silly young self back, don't you? I think because of her I toughened up too soon. I mean, you do as you age, anyway, but I . . . Sometimes I wonder whether, if I'd kept my voice, I'd have done something foolish, had affairs, run off. As it was, I kind of went into myself more. Especially after Jimmy got cancer—from cigarettes— he died too young, only fifty-six. And the kids went off, into the world, and I looked around and realized I'd become a recluse. Happens easily up here. It's beautiful and you forget you're alone."

I had slid off my chair and was sitting beside a bed of lavender, letting it tickle my face. I remember Wanita saying, musingly, "I always wished I had beautiful feet."

I think I laughed and hiccupped then and Wanita helped me up and put me to bed in the book cottage and I slept it off.

In the morning, while she gave me some toast and juice, I asked her if all that story was true, and she just cackled. "I jabbered more last night than I have in years. Don't know what I said."

And I told myself it couldn't be true. I took a shower out among the roses—something I'd been wanting to do—and standing naked and wet with their pure pink faces around me, I had a clear sense of what to tell Jill about her land.

I called her from my B & B (where they carefully didn't ask me why I'd been away all night). I stressed how inaccessible the land was, how much money and time would have to be put in just to get the road fixed, let alone electricity and water, then suggested she could leave it as it was and call it a wildflower preserve. I described some of the varieties I'd found there, including rare gentians that shouldn't be picked.

"That's it," said Jill, and she called me a genius some more as she told me she'd been approached about lending her name to a cosmetics line.

So I went home and waited while she got the deal lined up. I made a trip up in the fall to cultivate and seed some of the barer spots (flax, penstemons, blue-eyed grass—Jill wanted blues—but I put in Pink Maids and Kisses and Venus' Looking Glass, just for the names). And the following April there we were, back up in Geyserville, shooting some ads with Jill knee-deep in purple lupine, Jill in a white dress under the lilacs, Jill in old jeans, artlessly natural out in a fresh blue field. The art director loved the ruined house, romantic and worn. I borrowed some hanging fuschias and rustic chairs for the porch from Wanita, who stayed inside as the crews from interview shows passed on their way to get Jill Santiago's eloquent defense of the healing powers of native plants.

The actual ingredients for the shampoo and skin cream, of course, came from elsewhere, and the factory was in Long Beach. Jill agreed with me that the property was unworkable for her; in fact, she had some choice things to say about the guy who sold it to her. When I told her I'd someday like to retire to such a place myself, she consulted Coolidge (the accountant) and sold it to me at a (tax deductible) loss. I'm pretty sure she was such a doll because she liked my work. Though it's true I dropped the fact that I knew, from her ex-boyfriend Paul (yes, he blabbed), that she got the surreal extravagance of her curves by taking out her bottom pair of ribs.

I go up when I can to work on the house (I'm letting the meadow evolve). Wanita treats me with amused tolerance, though since we've become neighbors it's awkward to confide. I keep remembering the afternoon we were having a good-bye drink, after Jill had finished and gone home. We sat outside, in the garden, watching the men from the winery work, and I asked her again if that story had been true.

She took a swig of cabernet, gargled with it and swallowed, dimpling a bit and touching her piled white hair. Then she looked over at the viner who was driving in some stakes and said, "Honey, you oughtn't to work so hard in the hot sun. You could get"—a little breath—"sunstroke."

"Hey, pretty good," he said. "Marilyn Monroe, right?"

She looked at me, triumphant. I was stunned. Her voice had been a powder puff, a cobweb of sex. "Do it again," I said.

She shook her head. "I should keep my big mouth shut. Go on back to the land of the cannibals," she said. "But watch out."

"They won't get me," I said.

"No?" she asked. I can still hear the softness of her voice.

Lynne Barrett, left

AFTERWORD

I'm interested in identity and mirrors, privacy and fame. I deliberately avoided doing Marilyn Monroe research until I'd fully drafted my story, to let myself explore my own impressions. Then I looked at the books and found it was easy to tuck my incident into the proper moment in her pursuit of stardom. I was glad I hadn't read any of the biographies or memoirs beforehand, because some of them did sway my sympathies, simply by being so scummy.

Marilyn Monroe's death is the first thing I remember knowing about her. I was a kid on the beach in New Jersey, lying on a towel, feigning sleep, while around me the women gossiped, doing their best with the bits of information they had (if they'd only known!). I doubt I'd seen any of her movies then, so that as I saw them over the years they were always edged by my knowledge of her death. Many years later I watched a documentary on her life which I realize influenced my thinking about her a lot. I was especially struck by the way she presented herself in moments of public distress—announcing her divorce to a baying crowd of reporters, for instance—humble, careful, destroyed but polite. It made me suspicious.

—Lynne Barrett

LOVE ME FOR MY YELLOW HAIR ALONE

(32 SHORT FILMS ABOUT MARILYN MONROE)

BY CAROLYN WHEAT

*O*nly god, my dear
could love you for yourself alone
and not your yellow hair
— W. B. Yeats

1. the watcher

 THE HOTEL DEL CORONADO squats on the silver strand of beach like a fat, aging duchess. Huge, sprawling, its rust-red roof like a giant mushroom cap, it dominates the Coronado oceanfront.

The woman sits on a beach chair, her face upturned to catch the rays of the sun she professes to hate. She is blonde and pale; sun will dry and wrinkle her skin, she says often. Yet she inhales the sun's heat, she revels in the languorous feeling it spreads through her body. She undulates in her beach chair, shifting her perfect anatomy to expose more skin to the blinding light. She disdains the hat her companion proffers, waving it away with an impatient hand whose fingernails are meticulously manicured but unpainted. Not Hollywood hands, but the hands of a secretary or a bookkeeper.

The companion is a middle-aged woman with a soft, lived-in look. She wears a shapeless black dress; her feet are encased in support hose and orthopedic sandals. A Jewish housewife, thinks the man with the binoculars. He knows her husband is the high priest of Method acting, but he does not know that the Jewish housewife is herself an accomplished actress, a woman who is not permitted to work because of the blacklist. He thinks the high priest has sent his wife to baby-sit the temperamental star.

2. the extra

And, boy, was she ever temperamental! She never, but absolutely never, got to the set on time. Once she showed up at noon for a nine o'clock call, and the minute she got there, Mr. Wilder picked up his megaphone and called "Lunch."

I was an extra on that movie, one of twenty Coronado kids who got to sit around on the beach and get our pitchers took, as my Okie grandfather said with a cackle when I told him about my summer job.

We were military brats, my pals and me. We grew up surfing before anybody in the rest of the country knew what a surfboard was. We bummed around on the beach and took jobs at the Del for pocket money, clearing tables or carrying suitcases and waiting for the day when we'd take the ferry to San Diego and start college and never come back to boring old Coronado where there was nothing to do.

Johnny Benson told me about the movie coming. You remember Johnny—his dad was Navy all the way and Johnny was supposed to go to Annapolis, only he didn't want to. His idea of heaven was MIT; kid was great at math and science. Only his dad thought scientists were pointy-headed weirdos who were either Jewish or faggots or both, and he was god-damned if any son of his was going to—

Well, you get the picture. So that was Johnny, and you wouldn't think a kid like that would care much about the movies or even about Marilyn Monroe, but you would be wrong because Johnny was seriously in love with Marilyn and the minute he heard that movie was coming, he decided he had to meet Marilyn. Really meet her, not just sit on the same beach as her, watching her through binoculars like all the other goofballs on Coronado.

3. the private eye

I was a Rita Hayworth man myself. That long, red hair, those full lips. Plus, she could dance. I'm not much of a dancer myself, but I love a woman who can dance. Marilyn, you could see she'd had to take a lot of lessons before she danced on screen, but Rita was a natural.

But a job is a job is a job, to quote that dyke writer in Paris. And besides, I always had a soft spot for Joltin' Joe. So he was divorced from her, that doesn't mean he can't take an interest? He can't hire a guy or two to keep an eye on her, he knows she's in some kind of trouble?

I wouldn't of taken the job if I hadn't believed I was working for DiMaggio. Honest. I would have turned that money down cold, even though making a living as a P.I. in San Diego was no picnic in those days. America's Finest City was fine, all right—too fine to need a lot of guys wearing gumshoes.

But I wouldn't have taken the money if I'd of known.

Honest.

4. the director's assistant

Mr. Wilder was so patient with her. Like a father with a fractious child, he told her over and over again just what he wanted. He'd say the same thing twenty different ways, trying for the one phrase that would connect and bring out a performance. The other actors, Curtis and Lemmon and Raft, all they needed were one or two takes and they'd have it right. But Marilyn would shake her head and her lip would tremble and a tear would fall down the perfect face and then Makeup would have to come over and do her up again.

I'd stand there in the hot sun, holding an umbrella over Mr. Wilder's head so he wouldn't get heatstroke, and I'd watch her stumble over a line and stop, demanding another take.

Even when she got the lines right, she wasn't satisfied. "I need to do it again," she'd say in that baby voice. "It wasn't right."

Mr. Wilder would lean forward and whisper in her ear. I'd have to lean forward too, so the umbrella would shield him. She'd shake her head and wave him away. "I need to think," she'd say. "Don't talk to me, please. I'll forget how I want to play it."

As if she could know how to play the scene any better than Mr. Wilder did! As if she were some kind of genius and Mr. Wilder was nothing more than a ham-handed amateur who might screw her up.

The nerve of that little bitch, I thought, gripping the umbrella with white-knuckled hands.

Until I saw the rushes. Until I saw the tiny, subtle differences between the scene as Billy had instructed her to do it and the scene the way she felt it from within.

She was magic on the screen. Even Mr. Wilder said so. Later.

Much later.

5. the hotel maid

He was always in the room. Whenever I came to clean, there he'd be, sitting on one of the wicker chairs on the balcony or writing at the desk by the window. He'd nod politely and tell me to go ahead even though I always told him I could come back when it was more convenient. That was what the management wanted us girls to say, so I said it. Some rooms the maids didn't get to clean until 5:00 in the P.M. on account of the movie people kept pretty strange hours.

"My wife's on the set," he'd say. I'd nod as if to say, where else would the star of the movie be?

But she wasn't on the set. Everybody knew Mr. Wilder and the other actors were going nuts because Marilyn didn't show until afternoon. Everybody knew except Mr. Miller. Except the husband.

The husband is always the last to know.

6. on the beach

"She's just a *pretend* lady," the chubby little boy with the potbelly confided.

"I know," the little girl replied. She was an inch shorter than the boy and her hair was the exact same baby blonde as the real lady's hair.

"She's a man dressed up like a lady," the boy went on. "For the movie."

"I know," the little girl said again. She walked toward the approaching waves; she stood on the hard sand and waited for the cool water to lick her toes. When the wave washed over her feet, she jumped and squealed, then ran back to the soft sand.

The lady who wasn't a lady walked funny. She wobbled and her heels buckled under her and the people crowding around laughed.

The little girl wasn't sure why the people laughed when the pretend lady walked. The real lady wobbled when she walked, too, only the people didn't laugh.

Once she wobbled so much she fell down on the stairs. If the pretend lady had done that, everyone would have laughed. But nobody laughed when the real lady did it.

7. the New York journalist

"Hollywood," quips Bob Hope, "where every Tom, Dick, and Harry is Tab, Rock, and Rory." And where a white-trash California girl named Norma Jeane Baker transformed herself into the most glamorous sex symbol of her time.

California is the edge of America. It's where you go to reinvent yourself, where you can leave behind the person you were and become someone new, shedding the past like a worn-out snakeskin. You expect the freeways to be littered with crackling, near-transparent carapaces of dead selves.

I gotta cut that last bit. Too goddamn literary for this rag. Maybe I can pull it out and reshape it for a piece in the *Times*. Yeah, the *Times*'ll eat that crap with a spoon. But for the *Mirror,* I need a little dirt.

She's late on the set. She's always late, they tell me, but this time it's different. This time she's not in Hollyweird; she's at this godforsaken hole near San Diego. So what the hell's she doing every morning instead of showing up for work?

She's not doing the horizontal mambo with her hubby, that's for sure. She leaves the room, but she doesn't go down to the set.

Miller thinks she's with Wilder; Wilder thinks she's with

Miller—and the whole thing smells to me like a nice big fishy story. A story I can clean up a little for the *Mirror* and spice up a little for *Hollywood Confidential.* In this business, there's nothing better than getting paid for the same story twice.

Three times, if I can toss in enough bullshit for the *Times.*

8. the watcher

He trains his binoculars on the silver strand of beach. The prop men from the movie have strategically placed several wicker beach chairs that wrap around the sitter like a cocoon. In the movie, Tony Curtis, dressed like a twenties playboy, will sit in one of the chairs and Marilyn will mince past him and strike up an acquaintance.

He thinks it would be interesting if someone walked past the wicker cocoon and discovered that the person sitting inside, facing the ocean, had been dead for some time.

9. the private eye

This thing is a security nightmare. I can't believe Wilder lets everyone and his twin brother watch the shooting on the beach. They put up ropes to hold back the crowds, but any nut could pull out a gun and shoot Marilyn where she stands. Hell, someone with a good aim could pot her from a passing boat—and a lot of boats go by, people training binocs on the shore to get a glimpse of the stars.

Wilder's there in his white cloth cap, a cigarette dangling from yellowed fingers. He looks like a cabbie, not a famous director.

Lemmon's wearing a girl's bathing suit from the twenties. He's standing next to Marilyn, and they're both laughing. I can't hear what they're saying, but I have a good idea why Lemmon, at least, is enjoying himself.

He doesn't have to wear high heels on the beach.

10. the drama student

I saw him on Orange Avenue this afternoon. I don't know why, but I thought he was taller. And I definitely visualized him wearing a suit and tie. But he had on a pair of slacks and a striped T-shirt and a baseball cap. He looked like a father on his way to his son's Little League game.

The most famous American playwright of our time, and he was walking along Orange Avenue just like anybody else.

He walked faster than everyone else; he kept moving around other people. I guess they walk a lot in New York City.

He's here because of Her, of course. I don't imagine a man like him would even step foot in California if it weren't for being married to Her.

How can he write with all the distractions She brings into his life? How can a man of his genius be content to play second fiddle to a silly movie star? Why doesn't he realize that she can bring him nothing but pain, that he needs a woman of high intellectual attainment, a woman who will devote herself to nurturing his art, not pursue her own meaningless career?

11. the actor

You do the work. Forget this self-indulgent bullshit about being ready or not ready. Forget this Method crap about getting in touch with your inner feelings. You show up, you hit the marks, you say the lines—hell, first you *know* the lines; you don't show up three hours late and ask for cue cards.

She was just off a movie with Larry Olivier. Can you feature that? I've been in the business since I was younger than Marilyn and nobody ever let me get close to a movie with Olivier, and that no-talent blonde gets a movie with him and screws it up.

I'm a character actor; you could see this movie nine times and still not really notice my performance. Which is another way of saying it's a good performance, since I'm not supposed to be noticed.

Her husband, now, he understood what professional was. He was a writer, he knew how to produce. He knew that you have to put your keister in the chair and pound away on the typewriter every day whether or not you feel like it. He wanted Marilyn to act like a pro, to give a damn about the other people on the set. Every time she threw one of her tantrums or burst into tears, he died a little.

You could see it; he'd grimace like a father whose kid is acting bratty at the officers' club.

12. the acting coach

I know what they call me on the set: the wicked witch of the East. They hate Easterners out here, which is amusing, really, because so many of them are from the East themselves. But they've gone Hollywood and I haven't.

The sun gives me terrible headaches, which is why I dress like a Bedouin, and yet I sit with Marilyn on the Ocean Terrace, going over lines and working on the scenes. I pass on bits of wisdom from my own acting days, spiced with little sayings from Lee, from the Studio.

"A scene is like a bottle," I tell her. "If you can't open it one way, try another."

She mumbles something I have to ask her to repeat.

"Maybe I should just throw the bottle away," she says in her wispy voice, which almost but not quite gets swept out to sea by the strong breeze.

13. the cameraman

You know how they say in Hollywood that the camera loves somebody. It sounds kind of stupid when you say it; I mean, how can a camera love anyone? But it's true. You take Marilyn, now. All I do is point the camera at her and she lights up. Her face plays to the camera, tilting ever so slightly to catch an angle of light. Or she widens her eyes and the camera zooms right in on her baby blues. She tosses her head and the camera records the swirl and fall of fine, golden hair.

We're shooting black-and-white, remember. And yet the camera catches, somehow, the precise shade of her blonde hair, the wide blue eyes. She is going to look wonderful on screen, lit from within like a Japanese lantern.

We're shooting black-and-white because of the boys. Wilder says if we were doing the movie in color, the drag bits wouldn't work; the makeup would be too garish.

He's right. The studio bitched at first, said nobody would ever pay good money to see a black-and-white picture again, color was here to stay. But for this movie, they'll pay. Curtis is great, Lemmon is greater, and then there's Marilyn.

The camera loves her, and I think I do too.

14. the local reporter

I can't believe this quote! Little old me from sleepy little San Diego with a quote that's going to make headlines around the world.

TONY CURTIS ON MARILYN: "KISSING HER LIKE KISSING HITLER."

Can you believe my luck in being actually in the room when Tony Curtis tells the world his glamorous costar is really more like the hated dictator?

Of course, I go on to explain in the article that what he really means is that in her relentless drive for perfection in every little thing she does, Marilyn sometimes drives her costars to distraction. But rest assured, I intend to tell the movie-going public, the results on screen will be worth it! They always are with La Monroe, aren't they?

15. the studio doc

You don't get rich in Hollywood by saying no to big stars. And Marilyn was one of the biggest. When she was in a picture, everyone on the set lived on Marilyn time. The stars, the extras, the director all sat around waiting for Her Highness to show up. On a good day, she made it before the lunch break. On a bad day, she didn't make it at all.

She lived on champagne, caviar, and Nembutal. Once, I tried to tell her she needed to taper off, not use the pills every night, especially if she was serious about wanting a baby. She looked at me with her beautiful, bleary eyes and said, "What night? My life is one long, goddamned horrible day that never ends."

I shut up and wrote another prescription.

16. the continuity girl

That last picture she made with Wilder, she didn't even have a name. Her character was called The Girl. That's all, just The Girl, as if any bubble-headed blonde in the world could have walked in and played the part.

That's what Wilder really wants from her. That she play The Girl, not a real person.

I'm forty-two years old. I've been in the picture business since I was nineteen. When I started, I *was* a girl, I guess. But now, it sounds pretty silly when people introduce me as "the continuity girl." Not bothering to find out my name, just calling me "the girl."

Just like Marilyn in *Seven Year Itch.*

I know where she goes in the mornings. I've seen her. I know I should tell Mr. Wilder. And I will—the first time he calls me by my name.

17. the drama student

He's writing a movie for Her. The greatest playwright of the twentieth century, and he's wasting his time writing a stupid movie.

I can't believe it. I can't believe he's that besotted.

If only I could talk to him. If only I could make him understand that he has a duty to his art. He needs to know there are people like me, who love him for what he's done. He needs to know he doesn't have to prostitute himself.

I have to talk to him.

18. the psychiatrist

It was a classic case of Electra complex. Marrying an older man, a father figure. And of course, there was already a father figure in Lee Strasberg, not to mention her way of playing bad little daughter with her directors. She craved their approval, and she refused to earn it by behaving properly.

Classic.

Classic, and tragic. By the time she was making that movie, any competent therapist could have told her the marriage was coming apart at the seams. Anyone could have told her nothing would save it; certainly not a baby.

19. the hairdresser

Sweetie, this movie is going to be a *hoot*. You haven't *lived* until you've seen macho Tony Curtis mincing around in high heels! The poor boy looks *so* uncomfortable. I'd just *die* if one of his butch friends like Kirk or Burt came on the set and saw his Cupid's bow lips. Honey, he's the *spitting image* of Clara Bow!

Oh, all right, I'll lay off the camp. Just for you, sweetcheeks.

Oh, don't be such a closet queen. I won't tell your Navy buddies who you like to kiss on weekends, so just relax, will you?

What's she like?

The truth? She's like a poisoned bonbon, beautiful to look at, but, oh, Mary, don't—

All *right*.

She's like a child. A mean little child who'll do anything to get her own way.

God, what hets go through for a little taste of sex on the silver screen!

20. on the beach

"Here comes the lady," the boy said. He squatted on the sand next to the sand castle he'd made with his pail and shovel. It was a simple castle; all he'd done was turn over a pailful of hard, wet sand and dig a little moat around it for the water to run in.

The little girl kicked at the shell and drew her foot back with a cry. "It hurts," she said. "It's too sharp." She picked up the offending object and threw it as hard as she could into the water. It landed with a plop about three feet away.

The lady came every morning. She walked along the beach in her bare feet, but she wore pants instead of a bathing suit. And she wore a scarf over her blonde curls. It was a funny way to dress for the beach, the little girl thought. Her mother wore a bathing suit and a white cap with a rubber flower on the side.

Maria turned the pages of her book. It was a book with pictures, and it was written in Spanish. She watched the approaching woman with an expression of indifference. She knew the blonde lady was in the movie they were making at the big hotel, but it would never have occurred to her that the pasty gringa with the capri pants and the head scarf was *La Magnifica* herself.

The blonde scuffed her feet in the water, sending salt spray up in little fountains.

"Hi," she said as she got closer. "Catch any fish today?"

"How could we?" the boy replied with a crowing laugh. "We don't have any fishing poles."

"Oh, you don't need poles," the lady said with a shake of her head. "All you have to do is want the fish, and they'll swim right over and ask you to catch them."

"That's silly," the boy retorted.

"Would the fish die if we caught them?" the little girl wanted to know. "I wouldn't like it if they died."

"Oh, no," the lady answered. "That wouldn't be nice at all. The fish wouldn't die. They'd swim into your little moat here and you could scoop them up and take them home and put them in a glass bowl and watch them swim around."

"You still need poles," the little boy pronounced. He walked over to his sand castle and began to kick it with his tanned bare feet. "I saw the men fishing on the pier, and they all had poles."

"The fish I'm talking about are called grunions," the blonde lady explained. Her forehead creased as she talked, like someone who really wanted them to understand. "They swim very close to shore, and you can really catch them in a bowl if you want to."

"Do you have any little girls?"

The lady stood very still. She looked toward the place where the sun would be if the fog weren't so thick. One hand touched her tummy very lightly and she said, "I hope I'm going to. Very soon."

She smiled, and the smile was like the sun breaking through the Southern California morning fog. "Very, very soon," she repeated.

21. the extra

If Johnny had just kept his mouth shut, he might have gotten away with it. But then, if he had, nobody would have believed him, so what would have been the point?

The whole point was that he had to kiss Marilyn and all the guys on Coronado had to know he kissed her. That way, his father couldn't get away with calling him a faggot on account of he wanted to go to MIT instead of Annapolis.

He started out just wanting to meet her, but all the guys razzed him when he talked about it, so he bet Carl Rasmussen that he wouldn't just meet Marilyn, he'd kiss her.

He'd kiss her right in front of the Del.

And Carl could watch, and then Carl could pay up, 'cause he, Johnny, was going to do it, and when he said he was going to do a thing, that thing was as good as done.

Which I could have told Carl was the truth because I was there that time in seventh grade, which Carl wasn't, being as his father was stationed in Hawaii that year. And I knew that if Johnny Benson said he was going to kiss Marilyn Monroe, then she was going to get kissed, come hell or high water.

What I didn't know was exactly how much hell there was going to be.

22. the director's assistant

"When Marilyn Monroe walks into a room, nobody's going to be watching Tony Curtis playing Joan Crawford."

That's an exact quote, I can assure you. I was in the room when she said it, right to Mr. Wilder's face. She made him reshoot the opening, said she wouldn't finish the picture unless he—

Yes, she said Joan Crawford—and isn't Miss Crawford just going to die when she sees that in print? I mean, I can't look at Tony in his costume any more without thinking of Joan.

Did I hear what Mr. Wilder said about doing another movie with Marilyn?

Well, yes, but I don't think I really ought to—

Well, since you already know, I guess it won't hurt to—

He said, "I've discussed the matter with my doctor and my accountant, and they tell me I am too old and too rich to go through this again."

Yes, that's what he said. But please don't quote me.

23. the studio doc

You've had two tube pregnancies, I reminded her. And then I had to explain for probably the fifteenth time exactly what that meant. You have two Fallopian tubes, Miss Monroe, I said. And what they're supposed to do is carry your eggs down to your womb so that if you get pregnant, the baby can grow in your womb like it's supposed to. Understand?

I was using words I'd use to explain menstruation to a slow thirteen-year-old, and the look I'd get from her was as if I was trying to explain Einstein's theory. No comprehension.

Your trouble is that your eggs don't travel all the way to the womb. They stay in the tubes, so that when the sperm fertilizes the egg, it starts growing in the tube. This is called an ectopic pregnancy, and it won't work. The baby can't grow that way.

Your chances of having a normal pregnancy, Miss Monroe?

Slim to none, I'd answer. With your history, slim to none.

24. the private eye

This job is pointless. I've got a film of Unguentine on my face so thick it traps gnats, that's how long I've been out in the sun watching Monroe. And so far, nobody's come close to her except a couple of toddlers, only it was her got close to them instead of the other way around.

If something doesn't happen by the end of the day, I'm off this job. Money or no money, DiMaggio or no DiMaggio.

25. the drama student

He wouldn't listen. He wrote me an autograph and said I should keep studying. He said he'd write me a recommendation to the Yale Drama School if I wanted him to, but he wouldn't listen.

I looked up into his face, all white and drawn with suffering, and I knew what I had to do.

I was wrong trying to talk to him. He's too noble and good to betray the woman he loves. The woman he thinks he loves.

Next time I'll talk to Her.

Only I won't just talk.

26. the extra

Johnny had it all planned. He needed a diversion, he said. Just like in the war. He needed somebody to help distract the people around Marilyn so he could step in and make his move.

He didn't mean any harm.

Honest.

He was just a kid who wanted to impress his buddies.

So we started by tossing a flying saucer back and forth on the beach. You know, those round disks you throw and somebody catches them? Anyway, Tug Murphy had one and we tossed it around, getting pretty close to where the grips were setting up the next shot. One of the grips yelled at us to move away, but we hollered and pretended not to hear. So the grip steps over to Tug and says something and Tug said something back, and pretty soon a lot of grips were walking over to straighten things out.

Marilyn was just standing there, in this funny bathing suit that didn't show nearly enough of her attributes, if you know what I mean. She was shivering on account of it was breezy out there by the shore. Nobody from the movie was standing near her. It was weird, like none of them wanted to be close to her. The funny old lady with the big black hat was sitting in one of the canvas chairs, watching like a hawk, but she was too far away to do anything.

Which was why Johnny made his move. He ran out of the crowd and made straight for Marilyn.

27. the drama student

I was watching in the crowd, waiting for my opportunity. I'd been there the day before, and the day before that, and there hadn't been an opportunity, but I was certain that today was the day my luck would change. And it did.

It was a boy, a stupid boy. He ran out of the crowd toward Her as if he was going to catch her in a flying tackle.

She screamed and her hand flew to her mouth and she jumped back. She jumped back toward me. Toward where I stood in the crowd with my knife at my side, waiting for my opportunity.

Waiting to liberate the greatest playwright in the English language from his stupid mistake.

28. the private eye

Like everybody else, I saw the kid. Like everybody else, I reacted— only, being a professional, I reacted a little faster. The trouble was, I was reacting to the wrong threat. I didn't see the girl until it was too late.

Until the little bitch raised the knife and screamed like a banshee in heat and lunged at Marilyn.

I had the kid in a wrestling hold I learned in high school, but I let him go and went after the girl.

But the kid was young and strong and I was getting beerbellied and slow. He got there first—and so did the knife.

By the time the cops came, I had her under control and the knife in my hand.

But the kid had been cut. Cut bad, too, judging from the amount of blood seeping into the white sand.

28. the extra

Johnny saved her life. At least that was what she said.

All around her, people were yelling and screaming. Some of the women ran backwards, screeching as if they'd seen a hundred mice. The big guy grabbed the girl around her waist and took the knife away from her, but she wouldn't stop crying that she was going to kill Marilyn and nobody was going to stop her. Johnny and the big guy already had stopped her, but she didn't recognize that.

With all the yelling and running, you'd have thought Marilyn would take off for safety, run over to the old lady in the black hat or something. But she didn't. She just stood there while everyone else went crazy and then she knelt down in the sand and picked up Johnny's head and put it in her lap.

And when the guys with the stretcher came pushing through the crowd, she bent down and kissed him on the lips.

Which is when I turned to Carl Rasmussen and told him he'd better pay up or else. I didn't spell out what the or else was going to be because my voice was shaking so bad I thought I was going to cry.

Which was pretty weird on account of all that happened was that Johnny did what he said he was going to do.

29. the cop

Sure, the movie people hushed it up. Can you blame them? The kid was okay—well, okay if you think thirty-eight stitches in the shoulder is okay, but you get my point. Nobody died or anything. They took the girl over to the state hospital, but this kind of publicity the movie didn't need, so they asked us all to keep it as quiet as possible.

And no, this isn't Hollywood, it's Coronado, but have you ever been anyplace where money doesn't talk?

Well, I haven't. So when the Chief said the whole thing never happened, I saluted smartly and said, What never happened, sir?

You'll go far, boy, the old man replied. And he was right.

30. the actor

Three words of dialogue; sixty-five takes. Sixty-fucking-five. That's the story of this picture in a nutshell. Wilder's going nuts, the actors are going nuts, the crew's loving the overtime, and this picture may sink into the ocean like a chunk of cliff in an earthquake.

31. the letter

She sits at the little round table in her room. There's a piece of Hotel Del stationery in front of her, and a powder-blue typewriter in a plastic case.

She smiles at the paper, picks up a pencil, and draws on the hotel's logo at the top of the page. It shows the sprawling building, with its distinctive mushroom rooftop, beside the beach. She makes a quick stick-figure drawing of herself in the billowing waves and writes the word "help" next to it, as if the figure were drowning.

Then she slips the paper into the carriage return, smartly maneuvers it to a space below the logo, and types in the date: September 11, 1958.

The letter is to a friend in New York. She tells him that the boat she is on is sinking and refers to the Straits of Dire. She adds that she has nothing to worry about as she has no phallic symbol to lose.

She smiles wryly, then hits the carriage bar several times to leave room for the oversized signature she intends to write. Another thought strikes her, and she adds:

PS "Love me for my yellow hair alone"

32. the local doctor

"I asked for a doctor, not a nurse," the tall man with the dark-rimmed glasses said when he answered my knock.

I've heard this before; female doctors are not usual, even in the field of gynecology. "I am a doctor," I said, keeping my tone even. "May I see your wife, please?"

He stepped aside and let me in.

"She's in the bathroom," he said. There was an edge of disgust in his tone; he turned abruptly and made for the door. "Tell my wife I'm going down to the set to tell the director that she's too sick to film today." He was speaking loudly enough for the woman in the bathroom to hear, and he pronounced the word "sick" with quotation marks around it. I had the distinct feeling I had been summoned as a witness to the fact that Miss Monroe was feigning her illness.

I'd heard the rumors; I'd even read a movie magazine or two. I knew Marilyn's reputation as a difficult actress, and as a woman who ingested pills the way other people chewed gum.

So I stepped into the bathroom with a brisk, businesslike air, expecting to see a spoiled star with a barbiturate hangover.

She squatted on the toilet seat, her head between her knees. She groaned weakly and sobbed as I approached. Her arms hugged her stomach; on the floor next to the commode lay a silk slip soaked in blood.

POSTSCRIPT

Marilyn Monroe, who had all but completed shooting the new Billy Wilder comedy Some Like It Hot, *was hospitalized today in Southern California. Doctors announced she had suffered a miscarriage; Miss Monroe is married to Pulitzer prize–winning playwright Arthur Miller. Mr. Miller, emerging from his wife's bedside at an undisclosed hospital, declined to be interviewed.*

—New York *Mirror*

AFTERWORD

I chose to write about the filming of *Some Like It Hot* because one week of shooting took place at the Hotel Del in Coronado, and I've been living in San Diego for six months. I drove to Coronado and walked through the Victorian monstrosity, strolled the beach, and thought about how it must have appeared to Marilyn at the time. (During the writing of this story in 1995, the Post Office issued its Marilyn Monroe stamp. There was a ceremony at the Del, with Tony Curtis saying nice things about his dead costar. Nicer things than he said at the time, as this story reveals.) As I read about that period in Marilyn's life, I couldn't help but be struck by the contrast between the frothy fun of the movie and the real-life sadness of the disintegration of her marriage to Arthur Miller and her loss of yet another baby.

—Carolyn Wheat

DA SVIDANIYA, KHRUSHCHEV

BARBARA COLLINS

THE MUSHROOM CLOUD, rising grotesquely upward toward an awaiting heaven, life-choking smoke and debris shooting outward in all directions with insidious speed, accompanied by a deafening roar, then a low rumble, filled the little silver screen.

"Remember," said an ominous male voice from the rattle and hum of the projector, "in the event of nuclear attack, *duck and cover.* This action can save your life."

Light, ebullient music swelled absurdly in contrast to the words THE END which forebodingly filled the screen, then faded.

The only sound in the classroom was the snap, snap, snap of the celluloid film whirling around as the reel ran out.

Mrs. Hahn, a seventh-grade teacher at Emerson Junior High in West Los Angeles, looking matronly beyond her years in a drab cotton dress and brown oxford shoes, shut off the machine, then turned on the lights.

She crossed the gleaming wooden floor to the front of the room and turned to face her students. Four dozen frightened eyes stared at her.

"Are there any questions?" she asked. "Comments?"

"Yeah," came a sullen voice from the back. Harold Johnson, a dark-haired boy with piercing brown eyes, sat slouched at his wooden desk. "That duck and cover malarkey is a bunch of hooey. If the Ruskies send one over, there ain't gonna be nothin' *left* to duck and cover *under.*"

"That's not so, Harold," Mrs. Hahn said tersely. Why must the boy always be difficult?

"I oughta know," he shot back. "My old man was at Nagasaki after the war." He paused and looked smirkily at his classmates around him. "The *lucky* ones got killed. The not so lucky ones got to see their hair fall out, an' their skin peal off—just like a snake— then they started pukin' up their guts. . . ."

Seated next to the boy, a frail-looking girl with red hair and badly cut bangs began to cry.

"Harold! That's enough!" snapped the teacher. "There aren't going to be any Russian bombs."

"Oh, yeah?" the boy sneered. "Last week they shot that rocket an' hit the moon. We're *next*. They'll bury us, that's what they said."

"I said that's enough!" shouted Mrs. Hahn, upset more than she wanted to admit by the boy's outburst. "Report to the Principal's office at once."

Harold shrugged and got up from his desk and sauntered out of the room.

Mrs. Hahn turned her attention back to the rest of her students. "Class," she said calmly, firmly, "don't pay any attention to Harold. He's . . . he's just trying to scare us." She squared her shoulders, hands clasped under her bosom, and pronounced, "President Eisenhower would *never* allow a nuclear war."

She moved to her desk. "Now, get out your Social Studies book and turn to chapter four."

As the students rustled in their desks, she gazed out the window onto Selby Avenue, where cars and pedestrians bustled along in pursuit of the American dream on this beautiful September morning.

President Eisenhower would never allow a nuclear war. Wasn't that why he'd invited Nikita Khrushchev over? To straighten all this silliness out?

A nuclear war could *never, ever* happen again!

Could it?

Across town, in a bungalow behind the Beverly Hills Hotel, more bustling was going on.

It was 9:00 A.M., and Marilyn Monroe's personal masseuse, Ralph Roberts, was just leaving. Agnes Flanagan, her colorist who years ago dyed Jean Harlow's hair, was waiting in the wings.

"I want it white, Agnes," Marilyn instructed. "White as the driven snow." She giggled. "*Siberian* snow."

The older woman, short and stout with white hair herself, nodded, and set about her work.

Around 10:30 A.M. Whitey Snyder arrived to do Marilyn's makeup. He had been with Marilyn since her first screen test at Fox, and together they had invented her "look," defining and refining, and redefining it over the years.

Marilyn, in a tattered old robe, was quiet, withdrawn. It was nothing personal, he knew. She was saving her energy. It wouldn't be until he carefully applied the lipstick (several different shades for contouring) that she would bring to life her creation, emerging like a butterfly from its cocoon.

Marilyn's personal secretary, May Reis, who had accompanied her from New York the previous day, announced the arrival of Sydney Guilaroff. He was going to style Marilyn's hair.

Guilaroff, a Canadian discovered by Joan Crawford, had become the most famous hairdresser in Hollywood. And Marilyn wanted nothing but the best today.

Marilyn, now in her movie-star persona, was gay and witty, laughing and joking with Guilaroff. As he put the finishing touches on her hair—a pageboy coiffure—there was a sharp knock at the front door of the bungalow.

Mae opened the door and Spyros Skouras, the head of Fox Studios and the man who had master-minded the day's event, came rushing in. A tall, imposing, yet fatherly figure, with thinning white hair and black glasses, the Greek Spyros had been a champion of Marilyn's since her first contract at Fox, recognizing her special genius.

"You just *have* to be on time," he lamented to Monroe.

Marilyn, still in the tattered robe, but looking quite lovely, smiled. "Don't worry," she said slowly, drawing the words out.

He groaned. "That's what you always say."

"The longer you stay here, the longer I'll be," she responded sweetly.

Spyros sighed, turned on his heels, and marched out, slamming the door.

Then came the dress, a little black-net number, rather transparent in the bosom, leaving nothing to the imagination. Perhaps it was too revealing for the occasion, but so what? She had to live up to her reputation. And, besides, how often would she get to meet the Premier of Russia?

The State Department had told Marilyn that Nikita Khrushchev wanted to see her on his visit to the United States. Her! Little Norma Jeane Mortenson from the orphanage that nobody had ever paid any attention to. They said he had seen pictures of her at the American National Exhibition that had opened in Moscow in July. And so Spyros cooked up the idea of throwing a luncheon for Khrushchev at Fox Studios when the Premier stopped in Los Angeles on his cross-country trip. While Marilyn wouldn't be the only star in attendance, she would certainly be the brightest.

"We have to go," Mae told Marilyn.

The chauffeur pulled the sleek black limousine up to the bungalow. Marilyn, along with Mae, got in, and they began the ten minute drive to the studio lot on West Pico Boulevard.

When the limo arrived, the parking lot was almost empty.

Marilyn plunged into despair. "Oh, we're late!" she moaned. "It's all over."

Mae shook her head, and patted Marilyn's knee. "No, my dear, we're early. The others haven't arrived."

Marilyn brightened. "Well, what do you know about that! I *am* on time."

Inside the studio commissary, which had been converted into a banquet room, a dozen or so reporters milled around, anxiously waiting for the event to start. When Marilyn entered the room, they froze, so shocked were they to see her early. Then pandemonium broke out as the reporters rushed her, firing questions. She stood her ground and smiled.

"Did you come from New York just to see Khrushchev?" one reporter asked.

"Yes," she responded. "And I'm very happy to be here."

"Do you think he wants to see *you*?" asked another, a small man with a thin mustache and long pointed nose.

Marilyn studied the man's weasel-ish face for a moment; she made a habit of remembering new enemies. "I hope so."

"Where's your husband?" the enemy smirked. "Didn't *he* want to meet Khrushchev?"

All eyes were on her, pen tips to pads, ready for her answer.

"Mr. Miller," she said pleasantly, "couldn't come because he has a new screenplay to finish, one that I'll be starring in."

Actually, her husband could have come, and had wanted to, but after much deliberation had decided that, due to his past trouble with the House Committee on Un-American Activities, he had better not. The press might skewer him.

He was right.

Now others were arriving, movie stars like Elizabeth Taylor, Bob Hope, Debbie Reynolds, Frank Sinatra, along with dignitaries and some of the most powerful businessmen in town. Five hundred people had been invited to the banquet honoring the dictator of Russia.

Marilyn moved to her appointed place near the head table.

The crowd stirred . . . and parted like the Red Sea as Nikita Khrushchev stepped into the room.

He was a short, rotund man, bald, except for a silver fringe of hair rimming pointed ears like an elf. His face was round, with an upturned nose and several chins; his eyes were hard black marbles. He was wearing a light tan suit, cream-colored shirt, and brown shoes.

Flanking Khrushchev was an entourage of perhaps fifty people: translators, bureaucrats, and agents from the FBI, CIA, and KGB.

Trailing behind the entourage came the mayor of Los Angeles, Norris Poulson, his lips a thin tight line. Marilyn wondered if something had gone wrong at the airport, because Khrushchev was scowling, bushy eyebrows knitted together, thick bottom lip protruding.

Then across the glittering panorama of jewels, furs, and suntans, Khrushchev spotted Marilyn. His face exploded into a grin. He rolled toward her like a tank.

She stood from her chair, chest heaving, lips quivering in an open smile, and extended one hand. He grasped it with both of his hands, which were soft and hairless.

A hush fell over the room.

In perfect Russian, Marilyn welcomed him to the United States and to Hollywood. She told him that a cat and dog could live together in harmony, and that they must strive to do so. And she said it was an honor to meet him, correctly pronouncing his last name, Crew-*shove.*

He beamed, and two gold teeth winked at her as a smile split his face. Standing next to the Premier was his personal translator, a handsome young man whose name tag read: Oleg Troyanovsky. The translator looked at Marilyn, impressed.

Khrushchev then spoke to her in Russian, and Marilyn nodded at what he said. But she really didn't know exactly what he was talking about. Oh, she knew some of the words, because her former coach, Natasha Lytess, was Russian, and often had spoken the language. But it was Marilyn's friend, the great director and teacher, Michael Chekhov—who had studied at the Stanislavski Moscow Art Theatre before he defected—who had taught her the little speech, which she had practiced for hours on end.

Impulsively, for it had not been planned, Marilyn leaned forward and kissed Khrushchev's chubby cheek.

The crowd hooted, and laughed and applauded.

The Premier blushed. But Marilyn knew he was pleased.

Chair legs screeched as everyone took their seats. Khrushchev, at the head table decorated with little Soviet and American flags, was seated between Erick Johnston, President of the Motion Pictures Association, and Spyros Skouras.

After a brief welcoming by the mayor of Los Angeles— Khrushchev again scowling—the luncheon was served: Chicken Kiev, corn, and red roasted potatoes.

Through the clatter and chatter of the meal, Marilyn could hear the Greek-born Spyros talking to Khrushchev, telling him (through interpreter Oleg, who was seated on the other side of Spyros) that he, too, had once been a poor shepherd boy, but had risen to great power under capitalism. Khrushchev turned his bullet eyes on him, and spoke tersely in Russian. Said Oleg to Spyros, "And *I* have risen to great power, but under communism!"

Spyros dropped the conversation.

Suddenly an aid of Khrushchev's rushed up behind the Premier and handed him a note.

Khrushchev took it and read the note. His face turned crimson with fury. He pushed back his chair, nearly toppling it over as he stood, fists balled, body shaking, and he slammed those fists on the table, spilling drinks, making the china jump.

Everyone froze. Marilyn gasped. Something dreadful must have happened.

Waving off his interpreter, Khrushchev spoke in thick English with a quavering voice. "I have come to this town where lives the cream of American art. And just imagine, I, a Premier, a Soviet representative . . . " He paused, shaking his head, his face growing dark. "Just now I was told I could not go to Disneyland. I ask: Why not? Do you have rocket-launching pads there? I do not know. Is there an epidemic of cholera there or something? Have gangsters taken hold of the place that can destroy me? Then what must I do? Commit suicide? This situation is inconceivable. . . . I cannot find words to explain this to my people. *I want to go to Disneyland!*"

The guests looked on with amazement.

Spyros, his face a combination of embarrassment and concern, stood. "Mr. Khrushchev," he said solemnly, "our first concern is your safety. And the Secret Service could not guarantee it at Disneyland. Even your own KGB could not guarantee it. . . . Now, we have a lovely show for you next door on the sound stage. . . ." He turned to the audience, "Everyone, please join us."

The banquet room began to buzz again, as people whispered, some snickering, at the spectacle they'd just witnessed. Khrushchev, looking weary, was ushered from the head table, and the crowd started to get up, and file out of the commissary. Soon the room was empty.

Except for Marilyn, who hadn't moved from her chair.

She felt sorry for Khrushchev. His trip to the United States was not going very well. The papers had been full of his blustering outbursts and out-right threats. She understood his frustration. She knew how the press could twist your words and turn against you....

Upset, Marilyn got up from the table and wandered off to the bathroom.

She was straightening her dress in a stall, and about to flush the toilet when the bathroom door opened.

Male voices trailed in.

Mortified, she froze, realizing that in her self-absorbed condition she had gone into the wrong bathroom. It wasn't the first time this had happened to her.

She stood motionless in the stall.

Water ran in the sink.

"Sivodnya vyechiram."

"Dva chisa."

A hollow laugh. *"Da svidaniya, Khrushchev."*

Through the crack of the door hinge Marilyn could see the men, two of Khrushchev's uniformed KGB agents. One wore thick wire-framed glasses, the other had a pockmarked face.

The man with the bad complexion shut the water off, and they left, their boots slapping the tiled floor. The bathroom door opened and whooshed shut.

Marilyn backed up into a corner of the stall. She had understood the words the two men spoke, and those words sent terror rushing through her.

Tonight. Two o'clock. Good-bye, Khrushchev....

She stayed there for a long time, trembling, eyes wide.

It was well after midnight, and Nikita Khrushchev was in bed in the Presidential Suite on the top floor of the Beverly Hills Hotel. Exhausted, but unable to sleep, he lay in his silk pajamas staring at the ceiling in the darkness.

The civic dinner that evening at the Ambassador Hotel had gone even worse than the luncheon at Fox Studios. For the second time the mayor of Los Angeles had insulted him.

The first time was at the airport. The mayor had had the gall to give him—the Premier of Russia!—a paltry one-sentence introduction. It was quite clear to everyone, Khrushchev included, that the mayor held nothing but disdain for the dictator.

Nikita had a nice speech he was going to give when he came off the huge Tupelov jetliner, about how happy he was to be in Los Angeles and what he hoped to accomplish there, but after the mayor vilified him, Khrushchev read only one sentence from *his* notes before sticking them angrily back in his pocket.

Then at the Ambassador Hotel dinner, that *vyesh brakovanaya* mayor had again denigrated him by stating pompously, "You shall not bury us, and we shall not bury you. But, if challenged, we shall fight to the death to preserve our system."

Khrushchev, holding a prepared speech on California weather, disarmament, and how Los Angeles smog resembled the cold war, stood up, ripped the pages of his speech in pieces, and threw them at the mayor. "I want to ask you," Khrushchev had shouted with a pointing finger, "why did you mention that? Already in the U.S. press I have clarified that—I only meant communism will outlive capitalism. I trust that even mayors read."

The audience had nervously laughed.

Khrushchev went on, "In our country, chairman of councils who do not read the press risk not being reelected."

The audience applauded.

But the approval came too late. For the Premier had removed one of his brown shoes, and began pounding it on the table.

"I have come here with serious intentions," Khrushchev hollered, "and you reduce the matter to simply a joke. It is a question of war or peace, of life or death! Well, it took me twelve hours to get here, and it will take me just twelve hours to go home."

Then, to make matters worse, a reporter had yelled, "Where were you when Stalin was murdering innocent people?"

Khrushchev had refused to answer such an ignorant question. Of *course* he had supported Stalin, even worked for him. To oppose Stalin would have meant certain death! How *else* could he, Khrushchev, have survived to reach the top to change conditions. Hadn't he then thrown out all of Stalin's men after the dictator's death? Hadn't he then denounced Stalin and everything that butcher stood for? Wasn't he trying improve life for the Russian people? These American reporters were so stupid!

Nikita, lying on the bed in the Presidential Suite, hands behind his head, felt as close to depression as he'd ever come. If the egotistical Americans weren't concerned about disarmament, then so be it. The Russians had nuclear rockets aimed at every one of their major cities . . . and they could aim more and more. . . .

A tap, tap, tapping caught his attention.

Nikita sat up in bed and listened. The sound was coming from across the room.

He reached for the Tokarev Model 30 under his pillow, but the pistol wasn't there.

The tapping persisted.

Nikita got out of bed and cautiously moved toward the noise, which was coming from one of the windows. He peered through the darkness of the room. There was a young girl on the other side of the window, out on the fire escape. The fingers of one of her hands was tapping on the glass.

He came closer to the window. Could it be . . . ? No, his eyes must be failing him. Yes, it was! Marilyn Monroe!

Quickly he unlatched the window and drew it up wide.

She was crouched on the fire escape, wearing American blue jeans, and a plaid blouse tied at her waist. Her hair was tousled, a tangle of blond curls, her face void of any makeup.

In the moonlight, she was more beautiful than the glamorous photos he had seen of her in Moscow. She looked like a young fresh-scrubbed Russian peasant girl. To gaze on her beauty made his heart ache.

"You have to get out of here!" she whispered. "Something terrible is going to happen." The girl seemed terrified.

Nikita smiled, flattered that the great American movie star was concerned for him. "What could happen?" he laughed. "Over one hundred people are on this floor to protect me."

"Then how did I make it up this fire escape?"

His smile faded. He crouched down to face her.

Quickly she told him about the two KGB agents in the bathroom.

"Please," she pleaded, "it's almost two o'clock. You must come with me. . . . I rented a car." She reached out with both hands, grabbed onto his pajama top, and tugged.

Should he believe her? He studied her face. Yes. She was telling the truth. Where *was* the guard on the fire escape? And where was the pistol that he'd left beneath his pillow shortly before retiring?

Nikita stood up, and snatched his tan trousers from a nearby chair, pulled them over his pajama bottoms, then plucked up his brown shoes.

"Hurry, hurry, hurry!" Marilyn cried from the window.

Shoes in hand, Nikita climbed through the window, and swiftly, agilely followed Marilyn down the fire escape, even as behind him he heard the splintering of the door to his locked room, and the unmistakable *snick, snick* of a silenced gun, as bullets chewed up the bed where fortunately, thanks to Marilyn, he was not lying.

Nikita and Marilyn jumped from the last few steps of the fire escape as another bullet zinged off the metal railing. Hand in hand, they ran through the foliage on the hotel grounds. As they rounded a bush, Marilyn, in the lead, stumbled and nearly fell over a body sprawled on the grass.

She stifled a scream with her hands.

Nikita, breathing heavily, looked down at the Russian in uniform, lying faceup, a small black hole in the middle of his pockmarked forehead. "The guard on the fire escape," he said flatly.

"He was in the bathroom!" Marilyn whispered.

"Where is the car?" Nikita asked urgently.

"This way!"

Parked near Marilyn's bungalow was a blue 1959 Buick. They ran to it, and climbed in the front seat, Marilyn behind the chrome wheel, Nikita next to her.

Marilyn started the engine and drove rapidly off the hotel grounds, turned left on Sunset Boulevard, and sped away.

"Where are we going?" Nikita asked, looking at Marilyn. Her face was wet with tears.

"Somewhere they'll never think to look for you."

"Where?"

"Disneyland."

Jack Harrigan was dreaming that Allen Dulles, head of the Central Intelligence Agency, had given him a promotion, when he was rousted from his bed.

Ralph Krueger of the Secret Service had burst into the CIA agent's room, which was down the hall from the Presidential Suite, shouting that Khrushchev was missing, turning Harrigan's pleasant dream into a nightmare.

It was a little past two in the morning.

Harrigan, who made it a habit of wearing his clothes to bed during cross-country junkets, flew out of his room, and down the corridor toward the Presidential Suite, cursing as he ran.

Security had gotten lax, and he blamed himself for it. In New York, twenty thousand men—CIA, FBI, KGB, state and local police—were on hand to protect Khrushchev when he had first arrived. In Washington, DC, the number dropped to ten thousand. Then in Des Moines security dwindled to five thousand. And by the time the Premier reached Los Angeles—the last leg of his trip—only a few hundred men or so stood between the dictator and disaster. They had been lulled by how well things had gone, and seduced by the California climate.

Harrigan had argued with his superior that of all the cities, Los Angeles posed the greatest threat for an assassination attempt, because of the influx of minorities, and harboring of kooks. But his boss turned a deaf ear.

Now, rushing toward Khrushchev's room, Harrigan wished he had argued harder.

Harrigan entered the outer room of the opulent suite, stepping over the body of the Russian agent who had been guarding the Premier's bedroom door that night. The right lens of the man's thick wire-framed glasses was shattered, leaving a black bloody hole where his eye should have been.

He went into the bedroom, passed the splintered door. Feathers littered the mattress, the pillows shot to shit. But there was no sign of blood anywhere.

Ralph, who had woken Harrigan, spoke hoarsely in his ear.

"There's another dead Russian out in the bushes."

Harrigan stared at the open window, its brocade curtains billowing gently in the autumn night breeze.

It looked like a kidnapping, but then, why the bullet-riddled bed? Was it an assassination attempt gone awry? If so, then where was Khrushchev?

Another KGB agent, a brawny man with a blond crew-cut, rushed up to Harrigan.

"Do you know what this means?" yelled the KGB agent.

"Not yet," Harrigan said.

"*I* do! It means war between us! Annihilation! The end of civilization!"

Harrigan grabbed him by a lapel.

"Pull yourself together, man," the CIA agent said through clenched teeth. "Maybe that's exactly what somebody—whoever is behind this—*wants* to have happen."

Harrigan released the lapel, and the KGB officer blinked, embarrassed.

Harrigan took command. "We've got to contain this," he said to everyone in the room. "Secret Service fan out on the grounds. KGB stay put . . . we already have two dead Russians."

Then to Ralph Krueger he instructed, "Get me the surveillance tapes of this room."

In the dead of night, Marilyn drove south on the deserted Santa Monica Freeway to Disneyland. The amusement park, surrounded by acres and acres of orange groves, had opened just four years ago near the town of Anaheim.

She exited the freeway and onto an asphalt road that led to the park.

Nikita leaned forward, peering through the windshield, trying to get a first glimpse of the extraordinary attraction.

They had been silent during the twenty-five-minute drive it took them to get there, Marilyn going over and over in her mind what had happened. Nikita, she assumed, had been doing the same.

But now he seemed unconcerned, just an anxious kid waiting to get to Disneyland.

"Is locked," he said disappointedly, as they passed by the dark entrance, its front gate shut tight for the night.

"We can get in through the back," she replied, and drove on, past the huge asphalt parking lot on their left.

The road curved around the property, which was protected by a chain-link fence. But now the fence ended, giving way to thick bushes and trees. At the back of the park was a dirt access road— the employee and service entrance—which took them inside. Soon the road forked. Marilyn stopped the car. To the left was Tomorrowland. To the right lay Adventureland. Straight ahead was Fantasyland.

Marilyn drove straight ahead.

They sat in a large teacup at the Mad Hatter's Tea Party, the whirling ride of colorful cups on saucers now still. Across the way, Mr. Toad's Wild Ride was deathly silent. Everything looked surreal and spooky.

Marilyn shivered, and not from the cool autumn breeze. Dust swirled on the dirt floor of the midway, carrying off candy wrappers. A crushed Mouseketeer hat lay discarded on the ground. Evidence that people had once been there.

It was as if the bomb had dropped, and she and Khrushchev were the only ones left alive. As if beyond the orange groves, Los Angeles was gone, destroyed in one horrific second, leveled, a pile of ashes and bones. . . .

"I'm frightened," she whispered.

Nikita took her hand in his. "I also am frightened," he said. But his voice was strong, and she took comfort from that.

"It just *couldn't* have been us," she said, referring to the attempt on his life.

"America hates me."

"But those men were yours."

"Working for you."

Marilyn shook her head. "No. They didn't expect to die. It was someone else who double-crossed them."

"Who?"

She thought for a moment, then said firmly, "Red China."

Nikita laughed. "They are fellow communists. Comrades."

"Don't be so sure."

Nikita turned toward her, eyes narrowed. "Why do you say that?"

"Because. I have found, in my life, it is the people I trust most who hurt me." Marilyn leaned toward him. "Who would benefit if we killed each other? Ummm? Who would then rule the world?"

Nikita's smile seemed amused at her speculation. But his eyes were not; they were hard and cold.

They sat in silence.

"I read the speech you gave in Moscow to the Twentieth Congress after you took over from Stalin," she announced. "I read all of it."

His mouth dropped open. "Even *I*," he said astounded, "do not have a complete script of that speech, speaking for six hours from my mind. Where did you get it?"

"From the State Department."

He stared at her.

"I could probably get you a copy," she offered.

Nikita smiled wryly. "We are first in space. But in espionage . . ." He shook his head.

"I told them that if I agreed to meet you, I just had to read it. I just had to know."

"Know? Know what?"

"What was in your heart."

He said nothing.

She touched his hand. "Your anguish was genuine," Marilyn said softly. "It made me cry."

He looked away from her.

Marilyn sighed and gazed up at the stars.

"Dostoevsky said Mother Russia was a freak of nature," she said. "Maybe that's why I identify with her, because that's what people say about me."

Nikita looked back at her. "Then the people are *wrong*," he said, almost angrily. "You are the most beautiful, intelligent woman I have ever met."

Marilyn looked into his eyes, which, for the first time, were neither cold nor hard.

"But I," he said, his voice nearly inaudible, "must be a freak to you."

Marilyn shook her head slowly. "That's one thing men never seem to understand about me," she said sadly. "It's not what's on the outside, it's what's on the inside that counts."

She moved closer to him and whispered. "I think I know how to make the cold war a little warmer. . . ."

And she kissed him. Softly. Sweetly. And her world began to spin.

She opened her eyes, and realized that it wasn't the world that was spinning, but rather the teacup, and them within it, going faster and faster, the centrifugal force throwing them roughly together, the safety bar not latched.

A shot rang out and part of the rim of the teacup exploded, showering them with plaster. Nikita pulled her off the seat and down to the bottom of the whirling cup.

A second shot shattered the wall of the teacup, and it fell away tossing Marilyn and Nikita onto the wooden floor of the ride, like a pair of dice being thrown out of a tumbler.

The floor, which was also spinning, but not nearly as fast as the teacups, made it impossible for Marilyn to stand, dizzy as she already was. She could only crawl on her hands and knees toward Nikita, who was also trying to get to his feet.

Across the wooden floor of the ride a figure in black approached, maneuvering around the whirling cups, a high-powered rifle tucked under his left arm. With his right hand he pulled an automatic out of a shoulder holster, and aimed the weapon at the Premier of Russia.

Marilyn screamed.

The expression on Nikita's face was not one of fear, nor acceptance, but a combination of resolve and courage typical of the Russian soldier he once had been.

With tremendous force, Nikita threw one of his heavy brown shoes, smacking the assassin square in the face.

The assassin reeled backward, yelping in pain, dropping the

rifle, and Nikita seized the moment to charge the man, and they struggled in a violent embrace as the revolver went off. . . .

Jack Harrigan, behind the wheel of his black sedan, sped along the Santa Monica Freeway. Ralph Krueger, his face a steel mask, sat in the passenger seat.

Behind them, other sedans carrying FBI, CIA, and KGB agents, and squad cars from the local police—their domes flashing—followed at a reckless pace.

The surveillance tape of Khrushchev's room turned up an interesting, and unmistakable, voice: Marilyn Monroe's, just moments before the sounds of a silenced gun being repeatedly fired filled the tape.

Harrigan knew Monroe was staying in one of the bungalows and raced over there. The lights were on and Monroe's personal secretary, wringing her hands, spilled what she knew the moment Harrigan stepped into the room. Marilyn, fearing an assassination attempt, had taken Khrushchev, and was hiding him at Disneyland.

Harrigan couldn't believe his ears. Damned if that dizzy blonde hadn't saved the dictator's life!

Harrigan's hands on the steering wheel where clammy; a bead of sweat ran down his ruggedly lined face. He hadn't voiced a real concern to the FBI agent sitting next to him: that finding Marilyn's secretary alive in the bungalow was a bad sign. That meant that the assassin didn't need the information. Because he—who ever "he" was—was already following Marilyn.

Harrigan prayed they wouldn't be too late. . . .

He brought the sedan to an abrupt stop in front of the entrance to Disneyland. The other cars screeched to a halt behind him. Car doors slammed as the agents and police got out of their vehicles. Quickly they formed a semicircle around Harrigan, who stood planted in front of the locked gate.

"We're going in in three teams," he said, raising his voice for everyone to hear. "Each team will be comprised of police, FBI, CIA, and KGB. We'll split up at the end of Main Street. Team number one will go to the left; team two, to the right. Team three will continue straight. We'll all converge at the back. Any question?"

No one said anything.

"Okay," Harrigan said. "Somebody break the lock. And for God's sake, let's not shoot at each other. . . ."

Main Street, a replica of turn-of-the-century Victorian storefronts, was eerily dark as Harrigan jogged along in the lead, eyes darting from doorway to doorway, half expecting the assassin to jump out; the other men followed him, stirring up the dusty street.

Harrigan signaled silently for the teams to split—to the left and right—while he pressed on ahead with his men.

He was crossing the wooden bridge of Sleeping Beauty's Castle when the wind delivered a scream. A woman's scream. Marilyn's. Harrigan broke into a run, drawing his gun from his shoulder holster, racing ahead of the others, into Fantasyland, hurtling over hedges, then careening down the midway toward the source of the scream, coming to an abrupt halt at a chest-high chain-link fence that surrounded a ride called the Mad Hatter's Teaparty.

Near the center of the spinning ride, Khrushchev struggled with a figure in black. Monroe was on her hands and knees crawling to reach a rifle a few yards away, when a shot rang out.

Harrigan, gun in hand, vaulted the fence, his heart in his throat.

Then the assassin fell away, slumping to the floor, and Khrushchev stood alone.

Strong hands reached down and helped Marilyn to her feet. It was the man who had jumped over the fence.

"Jack Harrigan, Miss Monroe. CIA," he said to her, then asked, "Are you all right?"

In shock, she barely nodded.

The ride was slowing now, coming to an end, and dozens of men swarmed around them.

Khrushchev, who seemed undaunted, asked Harrigan, "Who is this assassin?"

Harrigan looked over at the figure, lying vacant-eyed beside a teacup, a hole in his chest, blood puddling as if the teacup had spilled. "Wong Chan. Our man in Hong Kong lost track of him a few months ago."

Marilyn looked sharply at Khrushchev. "See," she said, her eyes wide, "I told you. Red China."

Khrushchev nodded solemnly.

"Let's get off this damn thing," Harrigan suggested.

As they exited the ride, Khrushchev said to Harrigan, "Maybe we could help one another."

"How do you mean, Mr. Khrushchev?"

"We are first in space. You are first in espionage. Perhaps we could share some . . . information." There was a twinkle in Khrushchev's eyes. "Besides," he continued, "I believe we get many of our secrets from the same people. Why don't we combine forces and cut down the bill?"

Harrigan smiled. "I think that's a fine idea."

Out on the midway, Harrigan put a hand on Marilyn's shoulder.

"I think you know," he told her, "that we—hell, the whole world—owes you a great debt. If it hadn't been for you . . ."

Marilyn put the fingers of one hand to his lips to quiet him. "I only did what any good American would do," she said, and meant it.

"If there's *anything,* anything at all you want . . ." Harrigan offered.

"There *is* something," she said.

Harrigan cocked an eyebrow. "Name it."

"Mr. Khrushchev would like to see Disneyland."

And she smiled.

And Harrigan smiled. "We'll have this park up and running if we have to get Walt Disney himself out of bed."

Khrushchev grinned. "Then, I get to see Disneyland?"

"You get to see Disneyland," Marilyn and Harrigan said together, and laughed.

Khrushchev turned to Marilyn. "Where should we go first?"

Marilyn thought a moment, then looped an arm in his. "Why don't we go over to Tomorrowland and see what the future will bring?"

AFTERWORD

When I was in elementary school in the 1950s, we used to sing, "On top of old Smoky, all covered with snow, I saw Davey Crockett kiss Marilyn Monroe." I don't think I really knew who she was.

As a teenager in the early 1960s, I squirmed in my theater seat with embarrassment, watching the voluptuous Marilyn cavort in a see-through dress in *Some Like It Hot*. Only years later, in the 1970s, did I rediscover that movie, and her unique comedic talent, which led me to more of her movies, and eventually to every book I could find on her. (I don't remember the day Marilyn Monroe died; I was in junior high in a small town in Iowa.)

What fascinates me the most about Marilyn Monroe? The fact that, unlike Brigitte Bardot—who was the same person off as on the screen—Norma Jeane completely invented Marilyn Monroe. And the orphaned Norma Jeane was determined not to let anything stop her creation. . . . Not love, not money, or even death itself.

—Barbara Collins

DESTINY

BY PATRICIA WALLACE

 THE ACTION ON the blackjack tables was heavy for a Tuesday night. Weeknights, even in July, weren't all that busy as a rule, but from the moment she pushed out the day-shift dealer, Giselle had been pitching cards at a jam-up pace.

Of course, with a movie crew in town, many of these customers had come hoping to catch a glimpse of Clark Gable or Montgomery Clift. Or Marilyn Monroe, who hadn't arrived yet, although filming had started yesterday.

Whatever drew them to the tables, Giselle was running hot, with the house winning almost every hand. That would keep the pit boss happy, and a happy pit boss meant the odds were favorable that she'd be assigned to a high limit table, where all it would take was a single high-rolling "George" to make her night.

The pity was, there weren't all that many Georges—the fond name given to generous tippers—while there seemed to be an endless parade of so-called fleas.

As a dealer, Giselle lived on tips, which meant that, like Blanche in *A Streetcar Named Desire,* she depended very much on the kindness of strangers. . . .

Her landlord, quite naturally, did not. He wanted his eighty-five dollars of rent in full and on time. The power company had a similar attitude. As for the phone company, she'd gotten a final disconnect notice in Saturday's mail, and if she couldn't pay up by Friday, she'd have to rely on two tin cans and a piece of string.

But at nine o'clock, three hours into her shift, she'd collected only three dollars and seventy-five cents in tokes, two bits at a time.

When her relief showed up for the dinner break, she gladly stepped back from the table.

"Should I be wearing a flea collar?" the relief dealer murmured as they changed places.

"Wouldn't hurt," Giselle sighed.

"Aren't you eating?" Etta Mae asked as she sat down.

"Who can eat? It was a hundred and four today; I lose my appetite when it's this hot." Giselle slipped her shoes off and reached under the table to rub her right heel. It might look easy, but standing and pitching cards eight hours a night was hell on the feet.

Etta Mae shook her head in disbelief, hacking away at a piece of fried chicken. "No wonder you're so skinny. A girl needs sustenance, honey."

"Maybe later."

"Wait a minute," Etta Mae said, frowning, "don't tell me you're skipping dinner 'cause you're broke again?"

"I'm always broke," Giselle admitted, "but this time it really is the heat."

"That's Reno for you. Freeze your butt off in the winter and fry all summer long. And if that ain't enough"—Etta Mae waved a fork at her—"there's slot machines looking to suck every last dime from your purse."

"You know I don't gamble, Etta Mae."

"See that you don't start. The only thing that'll ruin a woman faster than a game of chance is hooking up with the wrong man."

Giselle smiled. Etta Mae was at most ten years older than her, which meant Etta might be all of thirty-three, but she clucked and fussed over the younger girls like a mother hen.

"Speaking of the male species," Etta Mae said, licking gravy off her fingers, "how's your Jimmy?"

"He's not *my* Jimmy," Giselle said, perhaps a shade too quickly. Alarmingly, she felt her color begin to rise and cursed her fair complexion for revealing every emotion she ever had.

"Maybe not, but he wants to be," Etta Mae observed slyly. "He's a keeper, Jimmy is. A real cutie pie. A girl could do a lot worse."

Her face felt as though it might burst into flames. "A girl could do worse *if* that girl was looking to get married, which I am *not*."

"Oh, that's right, I forgot. You don't believe in marriage."

"It's not that I don't believe in marriage, it's just not for me," Giselle said, lifting her chin in defiance. "It's 1960, Etta Mae, and these days, a girl doesn't have to get married to be happy. I'm not *settling*, like my mama did. I don't plan to be tied down with a husband and kids; I want more in my life than a house with a white picket fence. I want a . . . a career."

"You're still having Hollywood dreams?"

"It's not just a dream," Giselle insisted. Seeing the pity in Etta Mae's eyes, she went on: "It's what I *have* to do. I have talent, everyone says—"

"I know you do, honey," Etta Mae said, reaching across the table to pat her hand. "Trouble is, you can't cozy up to your talent on a stormy night."

At 2:00 A.M., Giselle headed for the time clock to punch out. Her heart thudded so hard when she saw a piece of pink paper clipped to her time card—had she been fired, and if so, what was she going to do?—that her hands shook as she opened it to read.

The Misfits casting call was centered at the top of the page. Her name had been penciled in on the blank line below that. The text read:

> *Please report to the lobby of the Mapes Hotel, Wednesday morning, July 20th, at eight o'clock sharp. Expect to work 3–6 days, at $10 per day. You must bring your identification card to the set to work.*

Stamped at the bottom of the page in bold black letters was NEVADA STATE EMPLOYMENT SERVICE.

"Is this for real?" she asked wonderingly. She read the notice over and over again to convince herself that it was, oblivious to her coworkers' curious stares as they punched out and headed home.

It took a dozen readings before she began to believe in her good fortune—and to trust that the words would not disappear from the page if she looked away.

"This is it," she said to the empty hallway. "The beginning of my acting career."

After a restless night, Giselle was the first extra to arrive at the Mapes lobby, well before 8:00 A.M.. She felt a little tired, but she'd had three cups of strong black coffee this morning, and had taken a fifteen-minute shower, standing under the cool spray of water until she was wide awake and shivering.

Even so, she didn't care to tempt fate by sitting in one of the plush cushioned chairs in the lobby. Instead, she paced back and forth, as unobtrusively as possible, both to stay awake and try to calm her nerves.

She hadn't expected to be nervous. After all, this was her big break. Ever since Miss Beechum's drama class in high school, she'd known that it was her ultimate destiny to be on the silver screen.

Of course, this wasn't a speaking part, but Miss Beechum had told her she had *presence* when she played Wendy in *Peter Pan* her junior year, and if she could convey the essence of her character without uttering a single word, someone—maybe even the director, John Huston—was bound to notice.

Ten seconds of camera time, and she'd be on her way. She'd move to Hollywood and wait tables if she had to—she'd done it before and could do it again—or whatever it took to make ends meet while she sought her fame and fortune.

Other girls had done it.

Norma Jeane had done it.

She could do it, too.

Her first hour in show business and already she'd nearly gotten run over by the Overland Limited train.

The scene being shot was of Clark Gable saying good-bye to a divorcée who was going home to St. Louis after shedding her husband in a Reno courtroom. The extras had been herded down to the

Southern Pacific train station to mill around in the background, and in the confusion and excitement of the big moment, Giselle somehow ended up on the wrong side of the tracks.

The problem was that in reality, the Overland Limited was going west, to San Francisco. In the movie, the train was supposedly heading east.

Striving for the inner truth Miss Beechum had proclaimed as essential to an artist's craft, and absorbed in centering her character in the act of meeting a friend at the station, she found herself south of the tracks.

When the real morning train arrived from Chicago at roughly 8:25 and she was decidedly off-camera, Giselle felt the tears well up in her eyes.

Use the emotion, she told herself as she hurried toward the caboose, intending to cross behind the train. *Feel it. You're late, because you've had awful, dreadful news. A death in the family? No, better yet, a death in* her *family. That's it! But you have to be brave. Your heart is aching, your very best friend is arriving on the train and you have to meet her. You have to tell her the terrible news that her dear Aunt Sylvia is dead. . . . Good, that's good. Go with it.*

Unfortunately, she went with it just as the train began to back up, startling her and causing her to stumble so that she narrowly avoided being squashed as flat as a new penny on the silver rail.

She nearly wet her pants.

Even Miss Beechum, in all her glory, would have trouble using *that.*

Luckily, no one else seemed to notice, although when she joined the other extras a minute later, still wobbly in the knees, the wardrobe mistress took one look at her and ordered her over to makeup.

"You could use a little rouge, sweetie," the wardrobe mistress said, eyeing her critically. "You're as white as a ghost."

The rest of the day passed uneventfully in comparison. Mostly it seemed to be hurry up and wait; after a second brief scene near the train station with Eli Wallach and Mr. Gable, the cast and crew had moved lock, stock, and barrel to the quiet "boardinghouse" where Marilyn's character, Roslyn—awaiting a divorce of her own—was rooming with Isabelle, played by Thelma Ritter.

In actuality, the two-story frame house belonged to the Reno chapter of the USO.

For this scene, Giselle had changed into blue denim pedal pushers, a white blouse and saddle shoes, and pulled her hair back into a ponytail. She was supposed to portray a teenaged girl walking by the boardinghouse as Eli Wallach, whose character was a mechanic, drove up to have a look at Marilyn's Cadillac convertible.

Giselle practiced the walk half a dozen times, acutely aware that the camera angle meant she would be filmed from the side and back. It wasn't the easiest thing in the world to put personality into the mundane act of walking when all anyone would ever see was the back of your head, but she did her best to spice it up by swinging her hips . . . until the young assistant director told her to knock it off.

"In case you haven't noticed, this isn't a war movie," he said. "That means there's only one bombshell allowed, and you ain't it."

"Yes, sir," she said meekly. It wouldn't help her career to be noticed for the wrong reasons.

Between takes, she and the other extras tried to keep from baking their brains in the blistering, hundred-degree sunlight. Standing in what passed for shade, they watched in amazement as a grip battered the brand new Caddy, inflicting dings and dents with a sledgehammer.

Giselle sipped what tasted like her millionth cup of black coffee, and made a face. The stuff was potent enough to strip varnish with, and it made her sweat, but so far it was doing the trick, keeping her awake.

She *did* have a headache, though, and every blow of the sledgehammer reverberated dully inside her skull. "Why are they doing that?" she asked no one in particular.

The man standing beside her glanced at her. "The story is that guys keep bumping fenders with Marilyn, hoping they can strike up a conversation."

"Really?"

"I kid you not." The man, who appeared to be in his forties, had slicked-back hair and a pencil-thin mustache on his even thinner upper lip. He looked her up and down with obvious calculation. "Are you an actress?"

A creep-alert warning went off in her head, but there was no telling who this guy might be; the place was crawling with Hollywood types. "Yes, I am," she said modestly, and—she couldn't help herself—fluttered her eyelashes.

"I thought so." He slipped his hand into his jacket pocket and extracted a white business card. "The name's Bentley, C. J. Bentley."

Giselle took the card, half expecting to see an oily stain on the corner where his fingers had touched it. All that was printed on the card was his name and a phone number. That was kind of strange, she thought. "Are you with the film company?"

"I'm a talent scout," Bentley said, lowering his voice. "Can't put that on the card, you understand, or they'd be chasing me down the street. Hell, before I wised up and took my address off the card, they would actually camp out on my doorstep."

"They?"

"Wannabes." His eyes shifted from left to right and back again, as if checking to make sure no one was listening. "You wouldn't believe how many people want to be in pictures. Some of them get a little desperate after awhile. But I know talent when I see it."

"Do you mean . . . me?"

"Yes, indeed." He leaned toward her, his Brylcreemed hair glistening in the sun. "And I happen to know a producer who's looking for just your type."

For a moment, Giselle thought she might swoon.

"He's doing a film down in Mexico—Acapulco, to be exact— and he needs an ingenue to play the, uh, the love interest. A fresh face is what he's looking for, along with a certain, shall we say, innocence?"

"I can play innocent."

Again he gave her an appraising look. "Yes, I think you'd do nicely. . . . What's your name, my dear?"

"Giselle." She took a deep breath, hoping to clear her head of the fuzzies. "I don't know how to thank you, Mr. Bentley—"

"Call me C.J., but you don't have to thank me. After all, it's my job and"—he smiled unctuously—"my *pleasure* to assist young actresses in any way I can. And you know, I believe I have the script for the movie in my hotel room at the Riverside. If you're interested, you could maybe come by some night and—"

And what was never clarified because the assistant director called her name.

"You're up," the A.D. said.

At six o'clock, Giselle stepped up to the blackjack table and began shuffling the deck. She hadn't slept in more than twenty-four hours, and had never been this tired in her entire life.

Exhaustion weighed on her, making her arms and legs feel leaden and slightly numb. At the same time, she was aware of a peculiar tingling in her muscles, very much like her entire body had banged its funny bone.

It took a conscious effort to deal the cards. The simple math of the game required her total concentration, to the point that she couldn't comprehend what the players were saying to her unless they spoke slooooowly.

Making small talk was essential to making tips, but tonight, even that was beyond her.

Worse still, she was running ice cold, breaking with almost every hand.

The pit boss, of course, noticed her table was bleeding red chips, and that earned her an early push from Florence, the casino's tourniquet of choice.

"Something wrong?" Flo whispered as Giselle surrendered the cards.

"It's not my night," Giselle said, and hurried off to splash cold water on her face.

When she returned to her table fifteen minutes and two cups of coffee later, the players were nearly beside themselves with excitement.

"Did you see her?"

"Who?"

"Marilyn Monroe! She just walked by!"

"Marilyn?" Giselle looked in the direction the players were pointing, but all she could see was a crowd of men—and wasn't that typical?—moving toward the front of the hotel. "Marilyn?"

An older woman with a mouth like a prune leaned forward confidentially. "She's no Jean Harlow, but in person, she *is* a knockout."

Giselle smiled wanly. "And I missed her."

"Isn't she staying here?"

"Yes, but—"

"Ahem," a voice said from behind her.

Without looking, Giselle knew it was the pit boss checking up on her and—aided by the rush of adrenaline in her veins—she quickly began to deal the cards. Somehow she managed to deal herself a blackjack two hands in a row, and as she scooped up the second round of players' bets, she sensed the pit boss had skulked away. Breathing a sigh of relief, she settled into the game.

Thirty minutes before her shift ended, Jimmy showed up wearing his Sunday best, a tan Western shirt with mother-of-pearl buttons and white piping, brand new Levis with a heavy silver-and-turquoise buckle, accessorized with a black Stetson and cowboy boots.

That he had showered and shaved before coming by was evident in the fact that his dark hair was still wet, the razor nicks on his chiseled jaw, and the nearly overpowering scent of Old Spice aftershave.

"Hey, stranger," Jimmy said, sitting at the seventh position, directly to her right.

"Hey, Jimmy."

He tossed a twenty-dollar bill on the table, and said, "In silver, please."

Giselle cut four stacks of silver dollars, five to a stack, and pushed it across the green felt to him. "Good luck, sir."

"Good luck, she says," Jimmy stage-whispered to the only other player at the table. "You think she really means it? 'Cause I could use a little luck right now, if you catch my drift."

The player, a man in his sixties who'd been knocking back complimentary shots of tequila all night, squinted hard at Jimmy but didn't answer.

Giselle flashed a "so there" look at Jimmy and dealt the hand. "I thought you weren't coming to town until the movie people left."

Jimmy shrugged and smiled, showing his dimples. "Changed my mind. I figured I'd better keep an eye on things."

"An eye on *me,* you mean," she said, taking a peek at her hole card. It was a ten and she had a seven showing, so she'd be standing pat.

"That, too." Jimmy took a hit, and lined up three sevens. "Twenty-one the hard way."

The other player had eighteen, so she paid them both, scooped up the cards and started shuffling the deck. As she did, the tequila drinker gathered his chips, tipped her a dollar, gave a shaky salute, and walked away without saying a word.

"It's just you and me now," Jimmy said.

"And in twenty minutes, it'll be just you," she said, feeling cross. "*I'll* be going home."

His smile crinkled the corners of his too-blue eyes. "I could go with you—"

The prospect of being alone again with Jimmy in her apartment sent the blood rushing to her face. After the last time, when he'd—

When she'd—

When they'd—

Giselle blocked those thoughts from her mind. "Not a chance, Jimmy," she said.

He ducked his head, one of his patented "Aw shucks" moves, then reached across the table and ran a finger down the back of her hand. "You sure?"

"I'm positive." She pulled her hand away before he noticed that she was trembling. "You aren't as irresistible as you think."

"I'm not?"

Out of the corner of her eye, she saw the pit boss approaching, and said loud enough for him to hear, "Your bet, sir?"

Jimmy slid five dollars into the circle. "I bet you're going to marry me."

Furious, she glared at him, but dealt him the ace and queen of hearts.

"Blackjack, darlin'," Jimmy smiled, watching as she busted, hitting a fifteen. "I win."

"Not always," Giselle said.

On Thursday, Giselle caught a glimpse of Marilyn as the actress arrived to shoot her first scene at the boardinghouse with Kevin McCarthy playing her soon-to-be ex-husband. From a distance, Marilyn looked young and vulnerable and, Giselle thought, a little sad.

The very notion that the most beautiful woman in the world might be sad made Giselle want to cry.

It was the lack of sleep, she told herself, that had her on the verge of tears, but all the same she was aware of an intense longing . . . for what, she didn't know.

You know, a voice whispered.

Startled, Giselle looked around, expecting to see someone standing nearby.

But there was no one.

By Friday at noon, she had slept only seven hours over three days' time. Sitting on the lawn across from the movie boardinghouse, her skin felt tender, stretched tight, and her eyes burned. The tingle in her body had transformed into a persistent, bone-deep ache.

She also developed a shuddering aversion to coffee and switched to Coca-Cola as her source of caffeine, which she almost inhaled in the heat of the day.

All she had to do, she reassured herself, was somehow make it through the night. There was no filming scheduled over the weekend, thankfully, although on Monday she had a call-back for a scene at Harrah's Club, which would be closed for the occasion.

Of course, she still had to work tonight—and Saturday night—but she could at least sleep straight through between her shifts.

Giselle had never seen such heavy action in the two years she'd been dealing as there was that Friday night. The casino floor was packed tight with people, most of whom were vying for a spot at the tables. There were so many players encircling the craps tables that a fist fight broke out between a couple of cowboys who each had laid claim to the same tiny space.

The air conditioning was no match for the throng of gamblers, and it seemed almost as hot inside as out, the air stifling and reeking of booze, sweat, and far too much cheap perfume.

There were a couple of star sightings, of Montgomery Clift being ushered through an awed crowd, of Arthur Miller in black-tie going out for a late dinner—without Marilyn—and, later still, of Marilyn herself.

Surrounded by her entourage, Marilyn seemed distant and fragile, a little girl lost.

The evening wore on.

Loud as it was in the casino, there was no way to make conversation with the players, so Giselle followed the supreme maxim of her profession: When the going gets tough, dummy up and deal.

As bad luck would have it, she ended up pulling three hours of overtime.

At five-thirty Saturday morning, she finally made it home, and collapsed fully clothed onto her bed. The last thing she heard before she fell asleep was a wistful female voice: *Don't you just hate to sleep alone?*

The doorbell rang. And rang. And rang.

Giselle groaned, and raised her head to look at the clock on her bedside table. Eleven o'clock. A.M. by the looks of it, with sunlight filtering through the venetian blinds.

The doorbell rang again.

"Go away," she mumbled, face in the pillow.

Whoever was at the door began to knock. A minute or so of polite knocking that gave way to pounding. Loud pounding, sure to disturb the neighbors.

Although her muscles were in the wet noodle stage, she somehow managed to get out of bed, running a hand through her hair and straightening her blouse as she staggered to the front door. Along the way, she looked for a weapon she could use if the doorbell-ringer turned out to be the masher her mother had always warned her about.

It was Jimmy, holding a small bouquet of wild flowers. He tipped his hat when she opened the door. "Good morning, gorgeous."

"*What* are you doing here?"

"I tried to call, but your phone's disconnected—"

She had a dim recollection of receiving a past due notice, but she was too tired at the moment to care. "It is?"

"Sure enough. The thing is, I wanted to apologize for the other night. I'm not usually that cocky—"

"Yes, you are."

"Well, I don't mean to be." He put a hand on either side of the door frame and leaned in, as though he might kiss her . . . but he didn't.

Why don't you kiss him? the voice whispered.

Giselle frowned. "How did you do that?"

"Do what?"

"Get that voice inside my head."

Jimmy blinked as though dumbfounded. "What voice are you talking about, Giselle?"

"Her voice," she said irritably. "Marilyn's voice. However you're doing it, I don't need anyone putting thoughts in my head."

They're your own thoughts, honey.

"Cut it out, Jimmy," she said, "I'm too tired to play games." She was reaching for the door to slam it in his face when she saw C. J. Bentley coming up the walk, resplendent in white slacks and a plaid jacket. "What now?"

There was a terrible, awkward moment as Jimmy and Bentley sized each other up, Jimmy straightening to his full height of six foot two, and squaring his shoulders in an oddly endearing way.

Bentley, who stood a good seven inches shorter than Jimmy, brushed past him as if he wasn't even there. "Top of the morning, my dear. I'm glad I found you."

"How did you—"

"I have my sources," Bentley said, flashing his oily smile as he sidled his way into her front room. "It's better if you don't know."

Hooking his thumbs through his belt loops, Jimmy stepped forward. "Well, I'd sure like to know who's been giving out the lady's address—"

"I wanted to see you," Bentley said, pointedly ignoring Jimmy, "because something has come up, urgent business that I simply must attend to. I'm flying back to Hollywood this afternoon."

"So soon?" In her mind, her career sprouted wings and headed for the window.

"Regrettably, yes. But"—Bentley pulled an envelope from his inside jacket pocket and gave it to her—"I have something for you."

His hand, soft and moist, lingered a moment too long on hers, and Giselle knew in that instant what the price would be to have C. J. Bentley discover her.

A pretty girl has to be careful. Men always want something, honey, even the good ones. And you can't always tell them apart.

Except she could, this time. With Bentley watching her expectantly and Jimmy glowering in silence, she opened the envelope and peeked inside.

It took her sleep-deprived brain a minute to register what she was seeing. "A bus ticket?"

"To Hollywood," Bentley said, beaming. "I would have booked you on the plane with me, but I had a bad night at the tables and ... well, you know how it is. Anyway, when you get into town, give me a call—"

"Get into town?" Jimmy interrupted. "Town as in Hollywood?"

Giselle felt his eyes upon her as she fumbled with the ticket, noting the fare was one-way to Los Angeles, departing at nine o'clock this evening. "But it's such short notice ... I'm not sure ..."

"What's going on?" Jimmy demanded.

"Jimmy, I ..."

"Is there a problem?" Bentley inquired solicitously. "Have I misunderstood your intentions? Because I was under the impression that you wanted to audition for the, uh, the ingenue role."

"I did, I mean, I do, but—"

"Which is it? I spoke to the producer and he's eager to meet with you, but if you're not interested, there are other girls—"

"It's not that I'm not interested, Mr. Bentley—"

"C.J."

"—it's just that this is all so sudden." Giselle glanced at Jimmy and saw a storm brewing. "Can I think about it for a day or two?"

Bentley laughed, not at all kindly. "Opportunity is knocking, and you've got to *think* about whether to let it in? I must say, I'm surprised."

"So am I," she said, feeling heartsick.

"I guess you'll have to decide whether you want to be an actress, or deal cards for the rest of your life. Either way, the clock is ticking, my dear. Speaking of which"—Bentley glanced at his watch—"I have a plane to catch."

Stricken, Giselle watched him walk away, taking her dreams, her *destiny* with him.

The room swayed, and she leaned against the door, closing her eyes. If she didn't catch the nine o'clock bus to LA, there would be no Hollywood premieres, no spotlights sweeping the night sky to draw her devoted fans to a darkened theater, no waiting in breathless anticipation for her name to be called at the Academy Awards.

If she wasn't on that bus, the closest she would ever get to the movies would be a double feature at the El Rancho Drive-In.

"Giselle? Are you okay, honey?"

His touch sent a shiver through her—he was so gentle for a big man—and she reluctantly opened her eyes. "I don't know what to do, Jimmy."

"It has to be your decision." He brushed the hair out of her face. "As much as I love you, I can't make you stay if your heart's set on going."

"It was until . . . oh, I can't think straight. I don't know what's wrong with me."

"There's nothing wrong with you," Jimmy said, in a husky voice.

The clock stopped ticking and the rest of the world faded into the background, like a water color back-drop on a Hollywood stage. The only sound Giselle heard was her own heartbeat.

Jimmy kissed her.

It had snowed late in the afternoon, and the pavement was icy, but with Jimmy's strong arms to hold her, Giselle made it to the box office of the Granada Theater. She stood by as he bought two tickets to *The Misfits.*

Looking at the poster, she thought it sad that Clark Gable hadn't lived to see the movie, although some people said filming in the rugged high desert in the summer heat had hastened his death.

But heat wasn't all bad, and maybe that was his destiny, as this was hers.

"Ready?" Jimmy said, coming up behind her and kissing her neck.

"As I'll ever be," she said, taking his arm. Now six months pregnant, she walked with the grace of a wildebeest, but Jimmy didn't seem to mind.

Inside, waiting for the curtain to rise, she felt a flutter of nerves at her film debut. It wasn't at all like she'd expected, sitting anonymously in a Reno theater with a small pillow in the middle of her back, but somehow that was okay.

"Want to save these?" Jimmy asked, handing her the ticket stubs.

"You bet," Giselle said, tucking them away as the lights went down. She knew exactly where to put them . . . in her keepsake box, next to the pink casting call sheet and the bus ticket she hadn't used.

AFTERWORD

Always a film buff, even as a child I spent most Saturdays at the local theater, sitting in the dark, watching all kinds of marvelous wonders on the screen. Although I dearly loved being scared half to death by *The Wizard of Oz* and *The War of the Worlds*, I also took notice of Marilyn Monroe, the most beautiful actress, who also happened to be—I thought—very funny, intentionally or not.

When Marilyn died on August 5, 1962, I was twelve. My sister and I were staying for a few days at a friend's house in Scotts Valley, California. I remember Mrs. Hill serving us breakfast (oatmeal with brown sugar and raisins) and telling us that Marilyn Monroe had died. She didn't tell us how Marilyn had died, but regardless, it was stunning news, which I hoped wasn't true, knowing even at twelve that rumors weren't always true. Sadly, this one was. Later that day, we went to the beach in Santa Cruz, and I forgot about the grown-up world.

In the years since, I've seen Marilyn countless times in most, if not all, of her films. My admiration for her deepened with every viewing. My daughter, Christina, is a fan too, perhaps as a result of all those lazy weekend days when Mom would insist on watching *The Seven Year Itch* or *Bus Stop* one more time. . . .

As I researched "Destiny," I remembered very clearly that whenever Marilyn was on the screen, I couldn't take my eyes off her. I knew her mannerisms, the range of her smiles—from sweetly uncertain to that knock 'em dead, megawatt knee-buckler—and, of course, her walk. And yet somehow, she always remained . . . elusive. An image on film, caught but not held. Fleeting. Ephemeral. And beautiful still.

—Patricia Wallace

THE HOUSE THAT NORMA BOUGHT

BY T. J. MacGREGOR

(1)

THE STREETS OF Palm Beach are paved in gold, like the road to Oz. The expensive shops glitter in the glow of the street lights, the shiny cars are as sleek as bullets. I wouldn't mind living here, I think Mom and I would be happy.

But tonight she isn't thinking about putting down roots. Tonight she's all tight and anxious, smoking too much, her face hard as glass. We're circling the restaurant where we're going.

"Checklist," she says.

"Shoot."

"How long are we in line before you say you have to use the restroom?"

"Less than five minutes."

"What's the maximum number of people?"

"Six, including the maid."

"When we leave the restroom, which way do we turn?"

"Right, toward the side exit."

Mom beams. "Good, button. Anything else?"

"Yeah. If there are eight or nine people in the restroom, we can stall up to five minutes to see if any leave."

"And if no one leaves?"

"We walk."

She parks our rusty Buick half a block away and we get out, a mother and daughter in search of a late dinner. She glances at her watch, Mom does, to time how long it takes us to get from the car to the restaurant. She's real precise. You have to be in this business.

You also have to look right and we do. We're dressed real nice, Mom in a pretty summer dress and flats, her hair blond tonight and piled on top of her head in some fancy do. She's wearing her green contacts, has padded her hips and belly, and stuffed her bra with Kleenex. It adds about twenty pounds to her appearance.

I'm disguised, too. My curly hair is even curlier than usual, thanks to the heat here in Florida, and is a shade darker than Mom's. I pulled it back with barrettes and put on this silly little hat with a bow in front that I bought for fifty cents at some garage sale. My dress is frilly, with lace and stuff, and I hate it. My shoes are new, black patent leather shoes with a strap that fits over the top of my feet. They squeeze my toes. I'm sure I already have blisters on my heels.

But I can stand almost anything if it's temporary.

So we go into the restaurant and Mom gives her name to the hostess. Taylor, Marilyn Taylor. It's a combination of Mom's two favorite actresses, Elizabeth Taylor and Marilyn Monroe. She used it a few months ago when we were in New York, working the big hotels. My name tonight is Annette, my favorite Mousketeer.

We wait by the wall. The place is packed with rich people, the ladies in their silks and diamonds, the men in suits and gold. You could gag on the confusion of odors in the air—expensive perfumes and aftershaves, expensive foods, the sudden rush of warm sea air when the door opens. It makes my head spin. I don't feel so good.

I tug on my mom's hand and tell her I need to use the restroom. The man in front of us hears and gives me a snotty look, making it real clear that he thinks kids my age shouldn't be seen or heard at this hour. He's wearing a black tuxedo with a carnation on the collar. I hope the stupid flower wilts before the night is out.

Mom is cool, we've done this routine before. She slips an arm around my shoulders and we slide out of line and head down the hall to the ladies' room. This part can be tricky, the timing has to be just right. The restroom has to be far enough from the dining room so that if anyone screams, it won't be heard. Four in the bathroom is the ideal number and that includes the maid who hands out tiny bars of soap and fresh towels. Oh, the other thing is there has to be a second way out.

We're sure of the first and last conditions, we've been watching this place for weeks. It's the in-between stuff that makes me nervous.

(2)

I step into the restroom first, Mom is right behind me. It's big, this room, everything seems to shine: the gold faucets on the marble sinks, the clean bright tile walls, the crisp hand towels that the maid gives you when you leave the stall.

I move along the row of stalls, supposedly looking for one that's vacant, but what I'm really doing is counting feet. Eight with the maid. Two too many. But Mom signals me to go into one of the stalls just the same. We'll give it a few minutes, see how many leave.

I latch the door and put my feet directly in front of the toilet, so if anyone peeks under it'll seem that I'm sitting where I'm supposed to be sitting. But of course I lean forward, my head almost touching the floor, and take a new count of the feet.

It's amazing what you see from this angle, almost upside down, blood rushing into your eyes. The shoes, the ankles, and all those purses resting ever so quietly against the floor.

The feet two stalls to my right are leaving. So are the feet to my left. We may be in luck. I count to ten, cough to let Mom know I'm coming out, and flush the toilet. The handles are gold, I like that, I like how it feels against my skin.

When I step out, the maid hands me a towel; it's fluffy, wonderfully warm, and smells like August up north, when the woods are filled with green. I go over to the sink and scan the room in the mirror. We're down to five, four right out here with Mom and me, one still in a stall.

Mom catches my eye, winks. That's the green light. I turn on the water and Mom heads for the door, digging into her purse. When she reaches it, she turns, gun at her side, hidden in the folds of her dress. A stall door is opening, Mom and I both see it, the fifth woman coming out.

She's got very black hair that curls stiffly to her ears, red lips, these incredibly sad eyes. For a second I feel sort of bad for her, I don't know why, she's just another rich woman with diamond earrings and a wad of cash in her purse. But I feel bad, okay? It throws my timing off a little. Mom is over there by the door, coughing and clearing her throat, trying to get my attention. She's real nervous, biting at the side of her thumbnail, frowning, her eyes flicking back and forth, signaling me to get on with it.

I turn on the gold faucets. Mom raises her arms, the gun aimed at the center of the room. "Good evening, ladies. Please don't make a sound," she says, her voice echoing against the tile walls. "Don't make me use this gun."

The five women are frozen, like figures in a photograph. I can tell nothing like this has ever happened to any of them before. I walk over to the maid, take the basket of towels from her paralyzed hands, dump the towels on the floor. Then I turn and face the other women, smiling my best kid smile, which is supposed to put them at ease.

"As Annette comes around with the basket, you will deposit your jewelry into it," Mom says. "You will hand Annette your wallets. You will please keep your mouths shut. If we're clear on that, ladies, please nod your heads."

Five nods.

I head over to the woman at the sink closest to me, a plumpo who probably owns a yapping poodle and gives everybody grief. There is sweat on her forehead, she is panting, she may have a stroke before we're finished. Her dimpled hand fumbles with the diamonds dangling at her ears, drops them into the basket. A thousand bucks easy. Except that Mom and I don't hock the jewels. We hide them in the trunk of the car. It's the cash we're interested in.

And plumpo is emptying plenty of cash into the basket. Fifties, hundreds, then the wallet. I don't want her stupid wallet and pluck it out. I hand it back to her and she smiles a fat old lady smile then slumps against the sink, dabbing at her face with a towel.

The next woman is real nervous. She's younger than plumpo, in her early twenties. "I . . . I . . . don't have much jewelry."

I do my kid smile again. "The watch is okay. And whatever you've got in your wallet."

"Sure, okay, my wallet." A wad of tens.

I move on to the lady with the black hair and the real sad eyes. She holds her wallet over the basket and shakes the money into it. Twenties, fifties, hundreds. The bills tumble fast. Her eyes hold mine as the money falls out and something flashes between us, something that makes me kind of nervous, like maybe Mom and I have made a big mistake.

I back away from the lady with the black hair, back toward Mom with her gun. "We're finished," I say.

Mom doesn't argue with me. She knows I have a feel for these things. If I say we're done, then we're done and that's it. The night's take has been pretty good and I really don't like the way the lady with the black hair is looking at me.

I dump the contents of the basket into the nice leather bag Mom carries slung over her shoulder. While she is talking to the ladies, thanking them for their cooperation, I open the door a crack, peer out.

We're clear, the hall is clear, we've got a straight shot to the side exit. But plumpo decides to be a heroine and lunges for me. She figures she's going to grab me around the neck and force Mom to put down her gun.

But my Mom is fast, very fast and very smart. She throws her left arm around the brunette's neck, jerking her back so hard she loses one of her heels, loses it the way Cinderella lost her pretty glass slipper. Plumpo stops dead. Mom waves her gun around so the ladies know she is serious, that she will do major damage to the brunette with the sad eyes if anyone moves.

No one moves.

No one breathes.

You will wait, Mom tells them, until the brunette returns to the bathroom, everyone clear?

Nods all around.

I sniff the air, just to be sure. Fear has this certain stink that you always recognize, once you've gotten a whiff of it. It's part rain, part blood. And I smell it now. These ladies are scared, they'll agree to anything.

(3)

We escape into the hall, me in the lead, Mom and the brunette behind us. I glance back just once to see the lady between us, Mom so close behind her I know the gun is stuck in her back. She doesn't look scared, just sort of startled.

We reach the door, I push it open, Mom shoves the brunette outside. She hobbles along in one shoe, then kicks it off without missing a beat and keeps moving forward. So far, she hasn't said a word, hasn't screamed, hasn't done anything some of the ladies have done over the years.

There was this one real southern lady at the Tutweiler Hotel in Birmingham a few years ago who lost it bad as soon as we were on the street. She dropped to her knees and started praying hard and fast to Jesus even though Mom had the gun to her head.

Another time, in Greenwich Village, this beatnik lady in black tights pulled out a funny cigarette as we were hurrying up the street, lit it, and handed it to Mom. Before too long, she and Mom were yukking it up, flat out hysterics, and we ended up in the beatnik's apartment above a coffee house. She went on the road with us for about a year, until she met some guy out in Frisco and got married.

But the brunette hasn't said a word.

She doesn't even seem to feel the heat. It's usually not this hot in Florida in May; this is an August or September heat, hot enough so that I've been dreaming of Canada, some pretty place like Vancouver. But Mom isn't thinking about the heat, she isn't thinking of anything except getting to the Buick as fast as possible.

She hurries the brunette along the street. "Listen," Mom says to her. "We're only taking you as far as the car, then you're free. But if you scream, if you make any fast moves before then, you're dead."

"I understand the rules," the brunette says.

"You look familiar to me," Mom remarks. "Have we met before?"

The brunette laughs softly. "No, we've never met."

I sense something about her that's a little off, but I don't know what it is. That's the problem with these feelings of mine. They come up from someplace way down inside of me, rising like stuff from the bottom of the ocean, and when the light hits them they are changed, different, not what I thought they were.

Sirens shred the air, the ladies back there in the restroom obviously didn't follow Mom's directions. We walk faster, the Buick in sight now. It looks pretty bad, parked crookedly at the curb, under the street light, the back fender loose, rust eaten through it like a cancer. But hey, it's home. The trunk is jammed with what we own.

Mom talks all the time about the day we'll settle in somewhere and live regular lives. She's got the spot picked out, a small town in upstate New York somewhere, a cottage on a lake. The schools are good there, she says. We could have a life there. But she's been talking like that since I was in kindergarten and we left the Army base where we lived with my dad. Even though she says he isn't my real dad, he's the only dad I remember and there are times when I miss him a lot.

The sirens are louder, very close now. Mom throws open the passenger door and shoves the brunette in the back. "Change in plans, sorry. You'll have to go with us a ways." She thrusts the gun in my hands. "Watch her, button."

Seconds later, we're pulling away from the curb, the Buick's engine roaring like some caged and terrified lion.

(4)

I'm aiming the gun at the brunette, she doesn't seem to notice it. She's running her hands over the torn seats, picking up my dolls, touching the little suitcase where I keep their clothes.

Street lights flash past the windows, the shriek of sirens fills the car. Then half a dozen cop cars race past us, headed in the opposite direction. In the spill of their lights, I notice the silver fabric of the lady's dress, how it shimmers, how it hugs her breasts, her hips, her narrow waist. I notice the curve of her chin, her pretty, painted mouth, and those eyes. She's sad, this lady is, a deep down sadness that nothing can touch. I want to put my arms around her, hug her, tell her it's going to be okay.

The cop cars shrink to bright red dots behind us. The brunette looks at me, at the gun, at me again. "What's your name?" she asks.

Funny, how I suddenly don't know what to tell her. I'm Annette tonight and last night I was Holly. Two weeks ago I was Suzanne and a year ago in New York I was Beth. In kindergarten on the base, I always knew who I was. Grace, named after Grace Kelly, another one of Mom's favorites.

"Gra—"

"No!" Mom snaps. "You never give your name."

"I have to call you something," the brunette says.

"Marilyn and Annette," Mom replies. "That's what we're called. Who're you?"

"Call me Norma." Once again I feel this weirdness about her. She's no more a Norma than we are Marilyn and Annette. She's running from something, too. "So what's next?"

Mom and I look at each other and I know she's thinking what I am. This Norma person is sort of like that Greenwich Village beatnik who joined us for awhile. But I don't lower the gun. "What's next," Mom says, "is you count the take, Norma."

Mom hands the leather bag to me and I pass it back to Norma. She unzips it, dumps the money on the seat, and begins to count. Lights dance across her face, I realize how incredibly pretty she is and wonder if someday I might look like that. Right now, I don't feel too pretty. My real hair, which is the color of dirty water, is thick and curly. My body is pole thin, boobs are a couple years in the future. I have matchstick legs. My nose turns up at the end. But what the hell, I have nice teeth and that counts for something, doesn't it?

"Three thousand six hundred and change," Norma announces.

"Goddamn," Mom breathes. "Very good."

"Do you want the money back in the bag?" Norma asks.

Mom nods and murmurs something about how good the take was. The excited edge to her voice worries me, I know what it means. I know that she'll wake up tomorrow ready to pull another one. She'll be puffed up with confidence, she'll believe we're better than we are, that we can't get caught. It happened before.

In Denver about a year ago, we had a fabulous take one night and the next day Mom decided we were going to hit this restaurant. We got out by the skin of our teeth and Mom sank into this blackness where I could barely reach her. It lasted for days, our bill added up, we couldn't pay it. We finally had to drive forty miles to hock some jewelry. We've never been back to Denver.

We've been to Aspen, though, Aspen in the dead of winter, the pretty town with all the rich skiers on the white, white slopes. I liked Aspen just fine, but I was two years younger then, just nine, and maybe if I went back today I wouldn't like it as much.

I think there are probably places like that in Norma's life. I think maybe we have more in common than we know.

(5)

A hotel room somewhere in Coral Gables. I'm studying a map to see just how far we drove, Mom is sipping warm scotch from a glass and glances frequently out the window. Norma is standing at the closet, also sipping from a glass of scotch as she goes through Mom's clothes.

Mom always unpacks as soon as she gets into a room, she thinks we're going to be in one place longer than we are. She's an optimist.

"Marilyn" says Norma, "I hope you don't mind my saying so, but blue isn't your color. And you've got an awful lot of blue here. I think you'd look better in more of this."

She plucks a dress off a hanger, one of Mom's summer outfits, a nice little number that's pale green linen, a suit with a pillbox hat to match. "The First Lady favors pillbox hats, you know. This is very stylish. And the green will do great things for your eyes." She walks over to Mom, the dress held high, like a promise.

Mom sits up straighter, the glass of scotch at her mouth, her eyes on the suit. "You really think the color is okay?"

"Definitely."

Norma stops in front of Mom, who reaches out to touch the fabric. "Could I wear it to the Breakers?"

"Of course you could. It would be perfect for their Saturday night buffet."

They've obviously been talking about this when I haven't been in the room. I'm pretty sure they're referring to tomorrow night, Saturday, May 26, as the night to hit the Breakers.

It's only the fanciest hotel in Palm Beach, we've driven past it, a tremendous hotel smack on the Atlantic. There are golf courses, penthouses, and people so rich that if we do this right, this could be the last job we pull. I could retire at the age of eleven and have a normal life.

I set down the map and stroll over to where they are, but they don't seem to notice me. They are deep in conversation about the color of the suit. "Will any of my clothes fit you?" Mom asks her.

"I think that white dress will," Norma replies. "Do you have any white shoes?"

"Yeah, somewhere in my suitcase. What size do you wear?"

They talk back and forth for awhile, like sisters who have suddenly discovered that they like each other. They hurry over to the closet, they laugh, they play dress up. I enjoy seeing Mom like this, acting like a regular lady, no mania, no black and terrible mood where she is unreachable.

The possibility of a normal life suddenly moves much, much closer.

(6)

Sirens wake me during the night. The cops are looking for us, I heard it on the news. But there wasn't any mention of Norma. Why not? Surely the ladies in the restroom must have mentioned that we took a hostage. Maybe the cops figure we let her off and she fled. Or they think she's dead. Or maybe she's someone very important and they don't want her name in the news.

I get out of bed, careful not to wake Norma, who is sleeping with her head at the foot of my bed. I nearly trip over the empty scotch bottle and go over to the window. I peer out through the curtains, into the parking lot.

Quiet, everything is quiet. There are trees at the edge of it, a row of poinciana trees. Although I can't see the blossoms now, I know they are blood red, that when they fall to the ground they shrivel up but don't lose their color.

I think Mom and I are a bit like that. It's just a feeling I have, that even though we're rarely what we seem to be, there's some basic quality that we never lose. I am thinking about that when Norma comes up behind me so quietly I don't even know she's there until she whispers, "Thanks. I never had a chance to say that."

She is wearing one of Mom's baggy T-shirts, her black hair is mussed, her makeup is gone, and you know what? She's still pretty. It comes from her eyes, I think, wells up inside of them like the feelings do inside of me. "Thanks for what?" I ask.

She shrugs, her eyes are fixed on the trees just beyond the parking lot. "You gave me the perfect excuse to escape a dinner I didn't want to go to."

"Were you with your boyfriend?"

"We were supposed to meet there." That sadness springs into her eyes again. "He's not really my boyfriend. He's . . ." She shrugs. "I don't know what you'd call him. Things haven't been going too well with us. What about you? How long have you and your Mom been on the road?"

"Six years."

"What about your school work?"

"Mom teaches me. She used to be a teacher on the base where we lived. I'm two grade levels higher in everything."

"How come you left the base?"

"Mom and Dad argued all the time." That's only part of the truth and although I want to tell her the whole truth, I'm afraid she'll think I'm weird. "She was sure he'd come looking for us, that's why we move around."

"You're lucky you have the freedom to move around like this."

"You don't?"

She combs her fingers back through her hair and shakes her head. "Not really. You and your mom gave me the chance to take a break from my life."

"Is your life that bad?"

She thinks about this, her sad eyes swimming with emotions I can't identify. "Not bad. Just . . . difficult sometimes."

"Can you keep a secret, Norma?"

She leans close to me, smiling, those eyes fastening on mine. "Honey, you wouldn't believe some of the secrets I've kept. Your secret is definitely safe with me." She makes a cross over her heart and holds up her hand. "Cross my heart and hope to die."

"When we were living on the base, I had to go to the hospital once a month for all these tests. It was real bad. I used to beg my dad not to make me go, but he always said it wasn't up to him. That's when he and my mom argued the most."

"Were you sick or something?"

"No. I've never been sick."

"Then why did you have to go for tests?"

"Because I'm different. I'm a hybrid."

I blurt it, the first time I have ever told my secret to anyone. Norma frowns, she doesn't get it.

"A hybrid is a cross between two different species," she says.

I nod. She laughs, reaches out, and strokes my cheek. "You look normal to me, Annette."

"Inside I'm not normal."

I tell her the story my mom has always told me, that I was part of an experiment that took place between 1953 and 1955. The agreement that made this experiment possible was between the government and some outer space people who wanted to cross breed. My dad supposedly volunteered my mother for the experiment. He got a promotion and she got me.

Norma doesn't laugh, doesn't tell me I'm nuts, doesn't react the way I thought she might. She seems to be thinking it over. "Do *you* think you're a hybrid?" she finally asks. "Or do you believe it just because your mother says it's so?"

"I don't know. I don't remember any of the tests, but sometimes I feel like I'm different from other people."

"Then, honey, we've got plenty in common. I feel that way most of the time." She slips her arms around me, hugging me fiercely. Her scent is different, although I'm not sure how. I feel afraid for her, the fear like some old piece of food that has gotten stuck in my throat.

"We're a couple of hybrids, you and me. That's *our* secret. Now c'mon, let's get some sleep, huh?"

(7)

When I wake up Saturday morning, Mom and Norma have bought takeout and are eating breakfast and chatting over coffee. I like the soft twitter of their voices, the sudden bursts of their laughter. It makes me feel like we're a family, that maybe Norma is my long lost aunt or something.

But suddenly I'm aware of their actual words, that they're planning the heist tonight at the Breakers, who will do what, how we'll pull it off. I get up and walk over to where they're sitting. Mom's eyes are bright and excited, she hugs me good morning and pulls up a chair so I can join her and Norma.

"I'm going to be the driver tonight, button. Same routine, except the car's going to be right out front when we leave. Norma and I think the take will be substantial."

"Enough so we can retire?"

Mom, still smiling, says, "Well, I don't know about that, but . . ."

"I'm not going to do it unless we can get enough to retire, Mom. I don't want to do this anymore."

Her smile thins a little. "I, uh, didn't know you felt so strongly about it, honey."

"Then you haven't been listening." I push away from the table and walk into the bathroom and shut the door.

When I come out, Mom is gone and it's just Norma and me. She is standing at the window, smoking a cigarette. "Is twenty-five thousand enough?" she asks without looking at me.

It sounds like a fortune, but what do I know? "Enough for what?"

She looks at me then, smiling slightly. "Enough for two people to live on until they decide what to do."

"I don't know."

Norma stabs out her cigarette, grins, tells me she'll be back in a little while. My mother, she says, just walked across the street to buy some hair color and will be back in a few minutes. "You mind staying alone?"

I shake my head and sit at the window, watching as she hurries toward the lobby.

Mom returns before Norma does. She's all hyped up about tonight, ready to turn herself into a redhead or a brunette, ready to do whatever it takes. "As soon as Norma gets back, we're going shopping. For clothes, button. For clothes."

"You like her a lot, don't you."

"Don't you?" For a moment or two, Mom looks worried. Even though she doesn't say it, I know she wants to hear about any feelings I have concerning Norma.

"I'm afraid for her," I say.

"Afraid how?"

"I don't know. Just afraid."

Mom's eyes hold mine for a moment longer, then she just nods and goes back to mixing the hair dye.

(8)

Without a doubt, the Buick is the saddest-looking car in the parking lot at the Breakers, not the sort of car driven by people who will attend this buffet. Mom parks as far away from the front door as possible and is biting at her lower lip when she turns to Norma and me.

"Are you sure you want to do this?"

"Positive," Norma says, primping in the mirror, putting on fresh lipstick, a little more mascara. She tightens the scarf that covers her hair. She's been wearing it since she emerged from the bathroom in our motel room. "Give us thirty minutes, then pick us up at the front door."

"Let's synchronize watches," Mom says. "I've got five after nine."

Norma glances at her watch, nods, looks down at me. "You ready, Annette?"

Not really. My throat is very dry, my hands are sweaty. I'm more nervous about this job than I've been about any of the others.

"Ready." I sling the strap of my purse over my shoulder, kiss Mom quickly on the cheek, and slide out of the car behind Norma.

Mom drives off, the Buick rattling and spitting smoke. Norma and I walk into the lobby dressed like movie stars, in clothes she bought us during our shopping spree. She hasn't removed the scarf from her head and I'm beginning to wonder if she's bald or something under it. Maybe she was shaving her head when she was in the bathroom so long today. Maybe she's more of a hybrid than I am.

We walk through the tremendous lobby toward a side hallway where the banquet rooms are. I hear music, people in evening clothes spill out of doorways, ice tinkles in glasses. Men and women in crisp white uniforms move through the crowd balancing trays of drinks and hors d'oeuvres.

We help ourselves to food from the trays. I notice how people look at Norma, like they recognize her from somewhere. One man in a tuxedo hurries alongside her and says, "Excuse me, may I have your autograph, Ms. Monroe?"

Norma laughs, touches the man's arm. "That's awfully nice of you, sir, mistaking me for her. But I'm just here for dinner." Then she and I continue on down the hall, weaving our way through the crowd.

I look at her more closely now. "You do kinda look like her."

"Yeah, people have said that. I wouldn't want to be her, though." She takes my hand, gives it a quick squeeze, and doesn't let go. "Just think of all the things she can't do because people know what she looks like. Because people recognize her. She can't go shopping like we did today, can't walk into a restaurant for lunch like we did, can't even stroll to the corner drug store."

"But she's rich."

"And lonely," Norma said. "Everyone wants something from her, so she doesn't know who her real friends are. And I just bet she never has the chance to spend time with a neat kid like you."

"I don't feel so neat."

"Take my word for it, hon, you are." We turn down another hall, she checks the time. "Let's stop in the ladies room."

It's fancier than the bathroom at the restaurant last night, huge as a living room, shiny marble floors, white wicker doors on the stalls, and probably gold-plated toilet seats. And it's absolutely empty, not even a maid handing out warm towels.

Norma sets her purse on the counter, removes a fat envelope, and crouches down so we're eye level. Maybe it's my imagination, but her eyes don't seem quite as sad tonight.

"Listen, hon. I think you and your mom are pretty terrific, okay? But your mother has some, uh, well, sort of funny ideas about this hybrid business. All this moving around just reinforces this idea she's got in her head that your dad or the government or whoever is looking for you. I'd like to make it easier for her to get over that idea and easier for you to find an ordinary life." She hands me the bulging envelope. "We'll tell your mother we had an excellent half hour working the banquet room, okay?"

She winks, straightens up, and I just stand there, stupidly, with the envelope in my hand. I know without looking that it contains $25,000. "But . . . but . . ."

"Better dump it in your purse, hon. We've got to head out front. Your mom will be pulling up in a few minutes."

I quickly empty the envelope into my purse, bills tumbling out, fifties, hundreds, five hundreds, more money than I've ever seen in one place in my life. My purse bulges so badly I can't zip it shut. My hands are shaking when we leave the restroom. Norma looks at me once, laughs quietly to herself, and grasps my hand.

As she does, the feelings surge. "They're going to write books about you." I blurt the words, blurt them just as I did when I told her about the hybrid business. She stops and stares at me, her bright red lips slightly parted. "Don't trust the brothers, they're loyal only to themselves and to each other."

Her mouth opens wider, but no words come out. I want to shut up, but the feelings keep surging, sliding up my throat and charging into the air like wild horses. "Don't be home in early August."

That's it. The feelings dry up. Norma is motionless.

"I'm sorry, I didn't mean to . . . I . . ."

"It's okay," she says quickly, softly, and takes my hand again. "Let's get out of here."

(9)

Mom drives, her eyes as huge as dinner plates, and keeps looking down at my purse and shaking her head, like she doesn't quite believe it. Norma, sitting on my right, chatters on about the wallets we lifted, the purses we dipped into.

"I just couldn't believe it, Marilyn, all these men and women carrying so much money."

"A third of it's yours," my mother says.

Norma shakes her head. "No, you keep my third. Just promise me you'll settle in somewhere for awhile. This daughter of yours needs to go to school, to have a normal life."

Mom glances over at her and something passes between them, I can feel it, an understanding too deep and complex for words. "I know just the place," Mom says. "There's this town in upstate New York . . ."

Her excitement leaps from her skin and into the air in the car. Norma nudges me and we both smile.

(10)

"Right here? You want me to let you off here?" Mom exclaims.

"This is fine," Norma replies.

Mom and I are both staring at the high gates of the beachside estate. Mom stammers, "But this is where the . . ."

"Right," Norma says quickly, then leans over and hugs me tightly, whispering, "Take care of yourself and your mom."

And while she is hugging me, while my arms are wrapped around her and a lump sits in my throat, I see her body in a dark room. I see figures moving through the room, rearranging certain things, tidying up, yes, that's the phrase that sticks in my head. *Tidying up.*

I don't know what it means.

She moves away from me and leans across me to hug Mom. Then she slips out of the Buick. As she walks through the headlights, she whips off the scarf and shakes her thick blonde hair, running her fingers through it. "My God," Mom whispers.

"She sure looks like Marilyn Monroe, doesn't she," I say.

Mom just keeps staring.

The iron gate is yawning open now, dogs are barking, but no lights have come on. Norma turns toward the car and wiggles her fingers, blows us a kiss, then vanishes through the gates, into the abyss.

"You think she lives there, Mom?"

"No." She puts the Buick in gear and pulls away. "The president's mother lives there."

"President of what?"

"Of the United States."

(1 1)

And now we live in the house that Norma bought, live on a lake in the Adirondacks with three dogs, two cats, a hamster, and a hundred ducks. Mom has gone back to teaching, I'm six years older, we're doing okay. Mom has her bad days, she has her good days. I don't get feelings anymore.

Norma and the brothers she shouldn't have trusted are all dead. That drives me a little nuts sometimes, she would have been better off with us. I am haunted by my last memory of her, how she blew us that silly kiss, then walked through the open gates, where the blackness swallowed her.

T. J. MacGregor, center

AFTERWORD

In August 1962, I was fifteen and living in Caracas, Venezuela. There had been political turmoil for some time—bombings, rumors of an imminent overthrow of the government. Grocery store shelves were practically bare because of a run on food and supplies. Many American families had moved back to the States. I was preparing for boarding school in Massachusetts and spending the last days of summer with friends I wouldn't see until Christmas.

Most of the American parents weren't allowing their kids to walk to and from each other's homes. So we hung out at a club in Caracas that had a swimming pool and tennis courts. The club stood on a hill overlooking a neighborhood called Las Mercedes. From the front railing, I could see the magnificent mountains that surround Caracas, the narrow, shaded streets of the neighborhood where I had spent all of my life. We were there the day I heard about MM's death.

A group of us were watching a procession of military trucks and tanks on the autopista—an interstate-equivalent that ran through and around the city. We watched, I remember, with a collective, silent dread that each eruption of violence would radiate from the heart of the city and touch our lives in ways we weren't prepared to face just yet. Most of my friends were, like me, the children of American oil company employees and we felt a special passion for Venezuela and for Caracas in particular. We were bonded by our common experience as Americans living abroad, we didn't want it to end.

As we stood watching the military vehicles snake through the shimmering light, someone turned and pointed at the TV that was on in the snack bar. MM's face filled the screen as a Venezuelan broadcaster announced that she was dead, an apparent suicide.

I remember how my stomach tightened, the dread hardening into a knot of certainty that her death somehow spelled the end of an idyllic childhood for me. A year later, my dad took early retirement and we left Venezuela forever.

—T. J. MacGregor

DROWNING IN THE RIVER OF NO RETURN

BY J. N. WILLIAMSON

 SHE WRIGGLED OUT of her skirt first, knowing the fact that she wore no underwear would get their complete attention. Her yellow sweater came off at the full extension of her arms raised above her blond head because she knew how much higher and more prominent her breasts looked that way.

Then she stared down, wide-eyed, at the men fanned out across the incredible bed that seemed to stretch from horizon to horizon, each of them also naked. They all demonstrated their attentiveness by simultaneously saluting, though none of them touched fingertips to foreheads.

"Let's not do anything yet," she said, climbing in. "Just hold me close."

And they did, man after man, embracing her warmly, fondly. They were oblivious to the indications of desire supplied by their bodies. It was wonderful, except—Marilyn wasn't sure for a moment her eyes were not deceiving her—

Except another young woman whom she knew was hovering weirdly in the air to her right, looking accusingly at her. There was also disapproval in the expression, her lips were moving as though she was trying to say something important.

Marilyn opened her eyes wide and sat up straight, alone in her bedroom, wondering why Mother—if that's who the woman was—had had to show up just when an army of warm, accepting guys had been behaving so *nicely* in her dream.

Her gaze fell to a personal horoscope and forecast she had been leafing through before she dozed. Neatly typed, it lay face up on the floor beside the bed, the line she was reading showing her birth-date—June 1, 1926—and the line beneath it saying the Sun and Mercury were in Gemini that day, thirty-six long damn years ago. The astrologer had said she was moved around a lot as a kid, and would always be restless because she was smarter than anybody understood.

Then why aren't I smart enough to even know what day *this is,* she wondered, suddenly panicky and getting up—*or whether it's day or night?*

The lights had been left on all over the house and the curtains were drawn, the blinds down. She snatched up an unsorted newspaper she found in the front room to solve part of the mystery: "Saturday, August 4, 1962," Marilyn read aloud, force-feeding the data into her woozy brain. So was it evening? Later?

Running on bare toes to the closest window, she peeked around a curtain.

Blackness, except the hooded eye of the moon squinting back. A recollection of peeping through a mesh-covered window at the orphanage when she was nine and a half flickered in her mind (Why had Mama had to be schizo, and did she ever look out in the hope of somehow seeing her little girl?). "What's with this walk down Memory Lane, you idiot?" she asked herself, and decided to get busy at something.

She put a stack of Sinatra records on the stereo, always privately charged up by protective Frankie's intimate voice, maybe more so than she was by the man himself. Mournful sounds from the first album made her frown, disappointed. She'd hoped it would be Francis with Basie or Hefti, but it was the first song of his "Only the Lonely," without a swinging tune anywhere on it. "Crap!" she said, started to flip the little reject doodad—

Stopped, seeing that dirty glasses and ashtrays crammed with smoldering cigarettes were all over the room. Folks had been there earlier that night, apparently a number of people. *Then why don't I remember any of 'em?* she wondered, trying briefly to recapture a face, a body, a voice.

But she spotted a mostly-full bottle of booze of some kind and a glass that wasn't totally filthy, poured and took a pull without bothering to see what she was drinking. Then she spied a clock, partly hidden by a sports jacket some guy had left behind. She checked it out, found it was hours until dawn, and padded unhesitatingly toward the bathroom in quest of her sedatives. "Norma Jeane has t'have sleepy pills t'go sleepy-bye," she sang, carrying her glass and bottle with her. Thirty-six lousy years old and can't even remember the time, or who came for a visit. It definitely had not included the little brother, the dandy little crime buster! Resting the booze and glass on the countertop beside the lavatory, she rummaged in the medicine cabinet until she found the right pill bottle. "I s'pose I'm not good enough for him"—she sat on the toilet seat with no need to fumble with clothing—"now that he's saving half of America, and busting the other half!"

She giggled, shook out two pills and washed them down with a swig from her glass. "Whoa, horsie," she reminded herself, sitting straight up to pee, "gotta watch *that!* One more overdose and the career is down the toidy too!" Lord knew it was rocky enough now.

Her thoughts episodic, she tore off some tissue squares. Weird how Mother seemed to show up just when the dream was going so well. Not that it was her fault, of course, unless she'd figured out how to have astral whatyamacallit. Marilyn was reminded of her horoscope and decided to read it again while she was dozing off.

Rinsing her fingers, the pretty blonde caught sight of herself in the mirror and did what she knew millions of men would have enjoyed doing: She gave a close visual inspection to her nude and world-famous self.

Her hair certainly wasn't "tousled" right now, which some guys had told her they dug, it was a wreck. Besides that, her darker roots were showing. Marilyn glanced down her body, realized she needed bleach again for that hair, wasn't in the mood to risk another infection. Her gaze rose once more to her face with the complexion that marvelously never seemed to let her down—not yet—and opened her eyes as widely as possible both to conjure innocence and, magician-like, to misdirect her own attention from fine lines under the eyes. "Not bad for an old bag," she said aloud, then made a face and refilled her glass from the bottle she had brought along.

But when she looked back into the mirror, it was in the direction of her torso, and Marilyn instantly straightened her back, then thrust her breasts forward while her elbows and forearms were pinched in on her ribs. The image of herself before the age of twenty-one, photographed for a calendar that made her fifty bucks and them gadzillion thousands, was imprinted on her memory because she'd stared at it in a mood of awe. Her left arm wasn't even raised but her nipples had been perfectly centered, and tilted up, like all her aspirations. Now, they had appeared for the first time to her to be headed slowly downward. She was starting to sag—her bottom too, she concluded, posing sideways—she was convinced of it.

Frankie's voice from a different album flowed through the open bathroom door in rueful agreement: "Just Look at Me Now!" Yet it didn't *matter* with him, or Joe, or even Jack or Bobby—they were guys, they'd look goddam *distinguished* at sixty or seventy. Frank could probably sell a gold album when he was seventy-five! Arthur would write plays and get them produced when he was white-haired all over!

Norma Jeane, the three syllables seemed to be spoken from a corner of the mirror and, simultaneously, from behind the still most desirable woman on earth. She started to look for the face (if any), then grabbed her bottle and glass and hurried from the bathroom as if she truly had somewhere to go. The voice—if any—had sounded maternal, firm, filled with warning, and Mama was none of that. And the only older women she could recall who had the faintest interest in her had wanted her in their beds, as if striking before their husbands got around to begging.

Perching on the edge of her mattress with her booze left on a bedside table, Marilyn wondered what her forecast said about the next day—today, really, since technically it was already Sunday, August fifth. But it had slipped off to the floor, and when she sank to her knees to retrieve it, other images of herself in that posture came to mind. No one had ever understood how she felt about it—kneeling naked before some guy, and many of them over the years. It had created in her imagination the picture of herself as neither grown up and big, but foreshortened; a half-child, half-kewpie doll who was being only partly used and, in return, was accepted. One-hundred percent needed at that moment. In a way she'd never known more power than she had on those occasions upon her knees. Once, pertly, merely joking, she had told a guy, "That's enough, let's go dancing," and the expression of horror on his face made her believe he might have been happier to hear his house was on fire! How could a girl have more power than that?

Marilyn stretched out on her back, the astrological report held at arm's length overhead *(Who had this forecast erected for me, anyway? Men are always so eager to erect things).*

She remembered reading in the past that Gemini people wanted very much to think for themselves, even when the facts contradicted their opinions, and did so with such versatility that pinning them down was like trying to catch hold of a ghost. They needed to be different from their parents—"How true!" she exclaimed—and Mercury, the thought planet, exaggerated all that when it, too, was in Gemini. "Your senses are all wildly alive," this report said, "and you drink in whatever excites you intellectually."

Yawning, Marilyn glanced down at the next planet discussed, Neptune, seeing it referred to as "the influence of your dreams, illusions, and spiritual unconscious." "NEPTUNE IN LEO: You want to be admired and win approval, and behave as openly and warmheartedly as possible, to fulfill your dreams. Unfortunately, this means other people take advantage of you...."

True, true, true! she mused. That was why she'd begun posing for a photographer, believing nobody would ever notice anything about her, except, maybe, her good looks. Then the folks at Fox saw what they called her "flesh impact," and here came the hours on her knees—"like a wind-up toy they got started by sticking dicks in my mouth instead of coins." Well, the coins had finally come, too, she reminded herself.

"VENUS IN ARIES: How your senses and commitments are cultivated to please your birth moon," the report went on, "and in Aries, it's very personal and makes you want relationships in which you and your partner do everything for each other. You are extremely independent and bold. You don't care what people who aren't close to you say when they're critical." *But everyone gets picky sooner or later,* Marilyn thought. Joe wanted her to quit if her career wouldn't let her be a lady. And those who couldn't care less about that believed they could teach her better ways to dress, be on time, walk, stand up, or even screw!

She got to a sitting position to take a sip and not drip on her tummy—"Slowly, girl, baby sips," she cautioned herself—and peered down to the next part of her horoscope reading. Even with so many lights on she was having trouble focusing, but she had no idea where her glasses were.

Frank sang "Call Me Irresponsible" from the front room and, though she barely made out the words, it seemed to Marilyn an admonishment. She picked up a handful of coins from the table next to the bed and threw them at the open door as if the singer had been standing there.

"MARS AND URANUS IN PISCES: From birth, the influence of the opposite sex and your own actions have worked with the planet of unexpected change to thwart your basic Sun in Gemini interests," she read. Drawing the horoscope nearer made it easier to figure out. "Pisces is the most emotional sign, that of raw feeling. Mars here causes you to brood, doubt yourself, and behave impulsively. You need more rest than you often get. Uranus here gives you intuition but also both good and bad hunches, and an urge to learn more about yourself. But what you learn won't always bring you happiness, or peace of mind."

Blinking slightly from eye strain, Marilyn stopped reading for awhile, shoved herself to her feet, and realized she was about to cry. "Men have screwed things up since my birth!" she paraphrased the astrologer sarcastically, making a wobbly beeline for the telephone. "No shit, Sherlock!" Once she'd dreamed that the daddy she never saw, Mr. Edward Mortenson himself, left Mama because he looked like Clark Gable and just couldn't be confined by one woman and a baby girl. But when she was getting married the first time at sixteen and needed to have her birth certificate, she learned the truth: Empty-headed little Norma Jeane was just a bastard. Daddy hadn't *had* to stay home, because he wasn't part of their home. Instead, he drove off on his motorcycle—and got himself killed on it when she was three.

As for that part about her needing more rest, Marilyn mused as she sat down again and opened her phone directory, she hadn't been able to get a good night's sleep since then. Why did the assholes think she kept taking sedatives? Did they believe she was too stupid to know what they were supposed to *do?*

None of the first three people she tried to reach on the phone answered, but Marilyn had a great many names and numbers in her little red book and the determination to keep trying. Finally, one of her ex-husbands answered, sounding irritable and out of it.

"For God's sake, Mar," he said after she'd spoken, "don't you know what time it is?"

She pulled herself erect in a mixture of dignity and willingness to play. "It could just be it's for *His* sake," she said solemnly. "As for the other question, time is relative—in fact, it's becoming a *close* relative quite recently. And besides, I've lost my watch!"

There was no reply. An instant later, she knew there would not be one, because he hung up.

"Have a nice life," she said, slamming down her phone and jumping to her feet. "You bastard," she added, retreating to her astrological report.

Instead, she remained afoot, pacing restlessly as she tried not to focus on the son-of-a-bitch who had once turned her ear crimson with his frequent phone calls and the whispered bullshit that kept her listening even when she was due on the set. "For about a nickel I'd wake him again and tell him off in no uncertain terms!" she threatened aloud. But all the terms were uncertain now and nobody stepped forward with a nickel.

Don't call folks and bother them, honey, said the firmly maternal voice Marilyn had heard in the bathroom—or, she realized when she turned quickly to find the source of the speaker—her head. Did it sound like Mama in her good moments or maybe the way she herself might sound when she was—?

Off balance, Marilyn sat heavily and unexpectedly in her bean-bag chair, still clutching the horoscope analysis. She looked down to clear her head and her gaze fell on her bare thighs, her legs spread due to the way she had lost her balance. The first new thought passing quickly through her mind was that the thighs were getting fat.

But she straightened her legs and changed her mind. Knowing just what she was doing, she put the tips of her fingers between them, lightly touching herself. Memories stirred. She had made the mistake once of telling somebody she considered having sex with most men she met, and of course they'd made a big deal of that. All she'd meant was that she was introduced to a lot of handsome guys and she wondered what they would be like, in the sack. Didn't everyone do that, automatically?

Hell, even the shrink she had been seeing almost every day lately had looked shocked when she told him of the dream she kept having as a girl—the one about taking off all her clothing in church, at which point nearly everyone clapped. Was it her fault the stupid shrink asked if she had any "recurring dreams?"

She hadn't told him of the dream of stripping in the Oval Office to the applause of the President's Cabinet.

Withdrawing her hand, she made the mental note to check out what sort of day this one was going to be and went back to her horoscope:

". . . MOON AND JUPITER IN AQUARIUS: The former triggers your instinctive likes or dislikes, your feelings you can't quite express to the world. In Aquarius it is where it is for the U.S. itself, both caring about the underdog and that which is dangerously inventive or different. It made you want to cast an image of yourself that isn't totally 'you'—but puts you ahead of the times—and to find happiness by satisfying the common urges you can handle. Jupiter adds self-confidence accumulated in just those areas mentioned. In them, nothing is too important for you to tackle, but there's also the risk of building castles in the air. Try to be more realistic to balance your airy air-sign personality. . . ."

Marilyn sighed, read the lines about the moon's influence again. A series of pictures of how often she had chirped "Okay" to everything from moving in with somebody for "awhile" and caving in to nice older men, to getting impulsively married, reeled through her brain like old-fashioned film scenes denoting a passage of time. Maybe the star-gazer was right, maybe she had been unrealistic to daydream of becoming the First Lady. But Jack was a Gemini person too, and she'd always heard Geminians were a sort of split sign, subconsciously looking for the other half of themselves! So they could go ahead and *be* the twins that were drawn as their picture.

Frank's voice reached her ears once again and she dimly recognized a ballad, "Lost in the Stars."

"SATURN IN SCORPIO." This was the final birth factor covered before the daily forecast or predictions section started, Marilyn knew. She had paid more attention to the latter since she got the astrology report, figuring she couldn't do much about the crap going on when she was born anyway. Besides, she'd skimmed the stuff concerning Saturn—planet of demands, delays, rewards and punishments, it was called—and a single line she'd read stuck with her: In Scorpio, Saturn was the source of her far-flung sexual appeal—but also *all* the elements of sexuality in her life. Something about that had scared her and she had never quite been able to digest the rest of the description.

Even now, in this late-night/early-morning, no-time aloneness, she discovered she wasn't yet ready for the next part or for the day's forecast. Rising, she went back to the phone table for her drink and the bottle, her perfect bottom rolling in a manner still capable of gripping the attention of almost any heterosexual man. But now it was because she was unsteady, getting drowsier by the second. She considered phoning the shrink to say she chose the astrologer's advice to sleep in, go for the Z's; but her maid was supposed to come clean up the dump, and Lena was bound to wake her anyway.

Yet that had a happy sound to it, too, Marilyn thought brightly, pouring more booze into her glass. If she mixed too much alcohol with the sleepy pills, there'd be someone there to snap her out of it! Drinking up, she added more to her glass before weaving a path back to the bed to read until she dropped off.

Flopping down belly-first, head toward the foot of the bed with the horoscope turned to the right page and on the floor, she forced herself to concentrate on the paragraph concerning Saturn in Scorpio.

"Saturn here squares your independent Neptune as well as your pair of Aquarian planets," the astrologer had written, "and all squaring aspects *thwart* and *block* in a mutual or 'both ways' sense. So your Saturn in the most intense and yet security-requiring sign sometimes harms your moon-driven self-image, and your confident, friendly deeds of an experimental nature reduce your feeling of security or stability. Don't forget I taught you that Neptune governs drugs and alcohol."

The description, Marilyn realized, slipping her fingertips under her chin to ponder, was so accurate it was spooky. She remembered getting modeling jobs after a photographer said she was "voluptuous," and divorced her first husband, Jim. Folks never got it that it was because she had badly yearned to earn some money of her own. Then there were all the men who *seemed* nice, had power, and didn't expect her to do anything she hadn't already done—but afterward, somehow, she felt as if she wasn't truly important enough to be anything but sexy. The next line in the horoscope made her giggle a little, even if it was basically true: "Scorpio squaring Aquarius makes you bite off more than you can chew."

She flipped pages to the forecast for whenever she got up, her mind at a sort-of crossroads between fixity on what she was reading and a foggy tuning-out of everything else happening in the world.

"*Sunday, August 5.* This is a day when your past comes hauntingly to life," said the astrologer, "because the Sun now in Leo squares your Scorpio Saturn." That was interesting, she thought, considering how she was already reviewing so many events in her life. "Two planets currently in Virgo also oppose your two Pisces planets, and that can imply both serious risks and, with your birth Uranus one of them, unplanned-for interruption to your actual safety." Marilyn distantly heard a voice—the one she'd heard all night—say, *Pay attention, girl, heed what he's saying.* "Even your emotions and fortune can meet with conflict today with the Leo Sun opposing your Moon and Jupiter. My advice is to remain calm and moderate, and see only those you trust implicitly. Stay home until August 6th."

There—she'd read all of the report, through today! Who said she couldn't finish anything? Only detachedly conscious of the advice she had just read, she allowed the document to fall from her fingers to the floor. For a long while now Marilyn hadn't been sure—most of the time—whether she drifted into sleep, or passed out. All she knew was that she hoped she would experience the nice, safe, drowsy sensation of hovering midway between awareness of the world and the universe of not-knowingness—or, if she was lucky after she was unconscious, one of her favorite dreams of approval.

And this minute of her life was the snug-as-a-bug hovering, so she smiled like a contented little girl, as aware as any star that she was doing it. A small, functioning corner of her movie-mind wondered if she continued smiling after she was asleep, and she hoped so.

Frankie sang the musical question, "How Little We Know?," so loudly Marilyn knew she wasn't dreaming. Opening her eyes, she wondered for a fraction of a second if he had come for a little late-night visit.

She shoved herself up at arm's length from the bed, realizing Frank was not the kind of idiot who would let himself in to someone else's house and begin singing at the front door—certainly not with an entire orchestra! But how had the volume been turned up so loudly?

The phone rang as if it had a heart attack as its goal. Its sudden, shrill ring was a jarring noise that jangled Marilyn's nerves as much as her thoughts—more so because between the cranked-up stereo, the screeching telephone, and the combination of pills and booze she had ingested, it was impossible for her to do more than respond to the commands.

Standing to go answer the telephone required greater effort than she could remember, and crossing the bedroom floor to it gave her the impression of swimming in molasses. Heading there on baby steps, she arrived and just leaned on it a few seconds to clear her thoughts. All that came through just then was a realization that Frankie was singing "Witchcraft" now. She nodded to the singer, for how she felt at this instant was as if someone had cast a spell on her, turned her into a damn *zombie* and—

The phone's ringing stopped. Sounds like somebody stumbling, maybe swearing, filtered through Sinatra's impeccable phrasing and Marilyn looked quickly toward the bedroom door. The phone rang again, jerking her head around so she could face it, so she could reach down, pick it up and stop that much of the confusing chaos going on. "Hullo, hullo?" she said into the mouthpiece. "Who's there?"

"Marilyn, it's me. Thank God you answered! Why didn't you answer my other calls?"

She knew at once who it was, the accent reminded her of only one other person on earth, but this voice was higher. But what other calls? "I was kind-of asleep." She wanted to brush back her hair but she was afraid to try to balance on one hand and arm; she didn't want to sit down, because something—or someone—deep inside her head was telling her she needed to be ready for an awful moment of some kind (*Serious risks to your actual safety/Pay attention now*). "Are you in town?"

"I'll be on a plane after we hang up. Listen, you're in terrible jeopardy, Marilyn. I learned some gangsters—hitmen—know where you are. I'm afraid they're headed for your house."

Her lips formed the two syllables of "hitmen" without her actually saying them. "Why?" she managed to ask, wishing she could really wake up. "*Why?*"

"It's a long story," he answered, and sighed. He had to give her a staccato reply; she would insist on some explanation. "If you tell the press about your connections with my brother and me, the Mafia boss thinks the media will also find out about an old arrangement between our father and him. Besides, he's the one who asked Frank to introduce you to Jack." A nervous laugh. "The don is Gemini, like you, but not nearly so beautiful. Just get out of there." A breath. "Go to the hotel—you know which one—immediately. I'll find you."

She nodded, fragments of it getting through. "I was just mad when I told someone I'd go to the press if you guys weren't nicer." She glanced down at her unclad body. "I can't just leave, like *that*," she complained. (*You need more rest/Norma Jeane, heed what he's saying.*) "What time is it?" she whispered.

"Get *out*, dammit!" he shouted in her ear. "I simply can't involve the authorities in this, so just *leave*. Do it *now*, Marilyn!" And he hung up.

She put the phone down on the stand instead of the cradle and turned in a full circle, never this frightened before and never so bewilderingly groggy. "I've never met any hitmen, not a one." *(Gemini looks for its missing half/The don is Gemini.)*

"Where did I put my clothes?" Marilyn asked the yawning bedroom door, beyond which the rest of the house had fallen ominously still. The nice guy who'd phoned to warn her, the awareness came out of the blue—one of the brothers who had given her the dream of someday being a First Lady—had celebrated his birthday last November. He was Scorpio, then; like where her Saturn was. *(See people you trust/stay home until August 6th.)* "I used to have lots of clothes, but now I don't know where."

She teetered back to her bed, and her drink, as if walking a tightrope. Her spirit yearned tremendously for sleep; rest, peace and quiet; no terror. Accomplishing her goal, Marilyn took only a small sip to be a good girl, then curled herself on the bed in a neat foetal ball.

Frankie sang—too loudly for a lullabye—"Put Your Dreams Away."

The men came into the bedroom in a silent rush, the strange things they required for this particular job held efficiently in their hands, ready for work, oblivious even to the beauty of an unclothed young woman. One of them put the phone back in its cradle.

They didn't really have much more to do, but they were real pros and did their chores thoroughly anyway.

AFTERWORD

I think many dark crimes were committed against this poor woman.

As for Marilyn Monroe reading a personal horoscope report and forecast in these final hours as I depict them: I rarely mention it since my full-time writing career started thirteen years ago, but I served as editor-in-chief for an astrology publisher in my twenties. I even started my own mail-order astrology company (with my wife, Mary) and operated that for several years. Of course, I don't know if Marilyn had a personal horoscope, but it doesn't sound too far-fetched to me. I assure you that the horoscope I briefly interpret in my story is handled very accurately. So are the "predictions" that the (fictitious) astrologer supplied her with for the day she died.

Yes, I do believe any astrologer would have warned her of danger on August 5, 1962. I just don't know if one did so.

—J. N. Williamson

DEAR MOM

BY JILL M. MORGAN

 DEAR MOM, the letter began.

Jeffrey tore the page from the cheap tablet and balled it into his fist. He couldn't look at the words, couldn't think about how she'd abandoned him as an infant, sentencing him to the life he'd led. All her fault.

Mothers had no right to desert their kids, especially not to go to Hollywood and become famous. She hadn't cared about him. So what if she'd only been seventeen when she'd given birth to him, just a kid herself. Didn't matter. He had no sympathy for that scared, pregnant girl, or for the movie star she was now.

He was the abandoned baby. He'd lived the life she'd given him, shuffled from one foster care home to another, to juvenile hall, to the streets . . . and now it was time for payback.

Jeffrey started the letter again. He had to be careful. If she knew what he intended, she'd find a way to stop it. She was rich enough to hire people to protect her. She'd push him away again, throw him out of her life. Throw him out of her death. He had to make sure that didn't happen.

> *Dear Marilyn Monroe,* he wrote on a clean sheet of paper, *I have seen every one of your movies. I keep a framed photo of you in my room. Your face is the first thing I see when I wake up, and the last thing I see before I go to sleep. I won't forget what you've done for me—not ever.*
>
> *Your fan,*
> *Jeffrey*

The letter was like all the others he'd sent to her in the last year. She hadn't answered a single one. Of course, living on the street, he didn't have a postal address. That wasn't important. The important thing was she hadn't found him, hadn't recognized her son when she heard from him, hadn't rescued him from this miserable life.

For that, he was going to kill her.

The day was gray and threatening rain, unusual for Los Angeles. Jeffrey had to stop writing when a new gust of wind-driven leaves and prickle balls pelted the ground where he sat beneath the tree. His shelter didn't protect him from harsh weather. He shivered in his thin shirt. No T-shirt; no underwear; no socks.

He did have a gun. He'd found it on a hillside where he camped one night, probably thrown away after a robbery, or murder, he liked to imagine. He often thought *he* might have been the one who committed that murder, liked to pretend it was real, but he knew it wasn't. Still, the gun belonged to him now, and it was loaded.

Sometimes, when days were hard to endure, like this rainy one, he held the gun in his hands and let himself think of his mother— Marilyn. He wanted her to know who he was before he pulled the trigger. That was important. She should realize he was her son, the one she'd abandoned so long ago. She should feel regret for her action, maybe ask him to forgive her . . . then he'd blow her head off.

It wasn't so much that he wanted her dead; he just wanted her punished. She had hurt him and had to pay.

His last foster mother, back when he was eleven, had been a big fan of Marilyn Monroe. She bought movie magazines every time she went to the market. She dyed her hair to look like Marilyn's, and told Jeffrey anything he wanted to know about her favorite star.

"Her name isn't really Marilyn, you know," she'd told him. "It's Norma Jeane."

He'd acted as if he didn't care, barely seeming to listen, but he *had* listened. He remembered every detail, when and where she'd been born—June 1, 1926, in Los Angeles, California—the name of her first husband—Jimmy Dougherty—and how old she'd been when she got involved with Hollywood—sixteen. He remembered, because he'd known from the first time he saw a picture in one of his foster mother's movie magazines, he'd found his real mother.

As he got older, he made finding her the focus of his life. That focus became even clearer when he ran away from the last foster home the state provided for him, and after his time in Juvenile Hall. At eighteen, the state had discharged him from their tender care. He was responsible to no one anymore, least of all to the mother who'd deserted him.

That was two years ago. Twenty was a lifetime away from eighteen. Twenty had learned what life was like on the streets. If he had hated his mother for the miserable life she had given him as a child, he hated her even more for the life he lived now. He had nothing, no one, and would never amount to anything. All because of her. He thought about Marilyn all the time . . . and about how much he wanted to kill her.

The wind blew harder. The idea of writing a letter seemed less pleasurable. He wanted to be somewhere inside, somewhere warm and beautiful, like her house. The more he thought about it, the more he wanted to be there.

I have a right, don't I? I should have grown up in a fancy house like hers. She owes me.

He started walking. Brentwood was a long way from Hollywood. He managed to survive on the streets in Hollywood, selling whatever he could steal, when there was anything worth stealing, and selling himself when there was nothing else. Most of the time, it was himself.

As he walked, wind pushing at his back, he remembered all the quick fumblings in the dark, remembered, and wished he could cry. He had stopped crying when he was eight or nine. People didn't care. He'd learned that, and begun to hate, instead.

"Hey, buddy! Want a ride?" yelled a friendly-sounding voice.

Jeffrey turned and tried to see the beefy-looking man in the white pickup. Grit and dust blew into his eyes, making it nearly impossible to see. He trudged a few feet closer to the car, head down, walking into the gust. He was at the car window before he saw the man's eyes. Mean eyes, reminding Jeffrey of the fat, sweat-smelling guard at Juvenile Hall.

"Get in," said the man in the truck. One pointy tooth bit at his bottom lip, showing nervousness or excitement. Jeffrey didn't know which. Didn't care. It was a ride, and out of the wind.

He opened the door and slipped into the passenger seat. The

truck smelled of cigarettes and whiskey. The old dude had been drinking. Not such a bad thing, considering what Jeffrey had in mind for him. It might make things easier.

"Bad day to be out on the road," said the porker.

"Yeah."

"Want a drink to warm you?" the man said, handing Jeffrey the bottle of Old Crow.

He took a swig. They liked it when he drank with them. All those guys in cars and pickups, they felt more comfortable if both of them were loaded.

Jeffrey didn't need booze, he was already loaded. His hand touched the gun tucked into his waistband at his back. This guy might live or die. It was up to him. If he drove Jeffrey to Brentwood and dropped him off to see his mom, then everything would be all right. If he tried anything else . . . Jeffrey *wanted* to see if the gun really worked.

"You into guys?" the old man asked, giving him a look.

"No."

"Sure about that?"

Jeffrey was very sure.

"Cause I was thinking," said the man, "I know a place we could stay for the night. It'd be good to get out of this damn wind, wouldn't it?" The truck was still in neutral. They weren't moving.

Now, Jeffrey gave him a look. "I'm going to Brentwood."

"Brentwood!" He laughed. "You think you can get more money up there? I'll give you money."

"I don't need your money. I'm going to see my mother."

The man nodded his pig face, studying Jeffrey, as if deciding about something. "I don't think you've got a mother in Brentwood at all. I think you're on the road to make a quick buck from men like me."

He reached his thick, bread-maker arms toward Jeffrey, arms that looked as if they had kneaded dough a thousand-thousand times. He put his hand on Jeffrey's jeans, high up on his left thigh.

"You'd better get your hand off me."

"I don't think so," said the man, reaching higher on Jeffrey's leg, "not till I'm—"

The barrel of the gun touched Pig-Face's nose. When Jeffrey pulled the trigger, the guy's whole head hit the driver's window and splattered like a smashed watermelon, oozing red juice and pinkish pulp. It was beautiful.

The man's feet were still twitching when Jeffrey kicked him out the door. His body landed hard. Jeffrey was shaking inside, but it felt good. Exciting. He had stood up for himself and won. That was the great part. This old guy dead on the road, that was nothing.

There were some rags in the back of the pickup. He used them to mop up the worst of the gore from the driver's seat, side window, and windshield. He tossed out the whiskey bottle. Didn't need it.

The keys still dangled in the ignition, the truck idling at a throaty purr. He considered the possibilities. Probably not a good idea to be driving a dead man's truck. Especially with smeared blood and brain matter all over it. *And on me.* Jeffrey's face, hands, and shirt were flecked with blood. Which meant he couldn't walk to Brentwood. He'd have to drive. A flash of fury spiked in him at the trouble Pig-Face had caused.

He shifted gears and drove right over the man. Reversed, backing over the body, shifted, and drove over him again. Now, he felt better.

It was nearly dark. That was good. Less people would notice the smear on the windshield. He rolled the driver's side window down to hide the coating of blood. Couldn't see through it, anyway.

His plan was simple. He'd drive as close as he could to Brentwood, ditch the truck somewhere, and walk the rest of the way home in the dark. He could shower and change clothes at his mom's house. She wouldn't mind. He felt sure of that. His hand touched the gun at his back. Very sure.

Brentwood was a gated community. A uniformed guard stood at the entrance, allowing cars to pass through the gateway, or directing them to turn around. Jeffrey could imagine what the guard would say to him, even if he explained he was only going to see his mother. The guard wouldn't understand.

Jeffrey thought about killing the guy. The idea tempted him.

Walk up to the guardhouse and put a bullet through the man's fore-head. He liked the way heads exploded. He considered it. *No, too many people would notice that.* As much as he wanted to use the gun again, he'd better wait until he saw his mom. After all, he was here to pay her a visit.

The wind had stopped blowing, as if Brentwood was too refined for flying grit and dust. Jeffrey had ditched the truck on a side street a mile down the road. Getting past the guard meant he had to climb a high earthen bank of foothill, then scale the brick wall into the gated community.

His mom was making it hard for him. She could have left a pass for him with the guard, but he knew she wouldn't have been thoughtful enough to have done that. Never thought of how much trouble she caused him.

If somebody heard him climbing the wall, they'd call the cops. If the cops found him, they'd see the blood and maybe they'd find the dead guy on the road. All over the road. Jeffrey would be back in jail. He wouldn't be sent to juvie this time. He'd be sent to state prison, where there were lots of men like Pig-Face just waiting for young guys like him.

He had to be quiet. Being quiet was something Jeffrey had learned how to do long ago. Mean-faced foster dads with leather belts liked quiet. Juvenile Hall guards liked quiet. Homeless shelters liked quiet, too. After a lifetime of learning, he knew all about being quiet. He climbed the wall, barely making a sound.

On the other side of the wall, it was a Magicland opened up. Ex-pensive estates were sheltered like islands on the green sea of their lawns. Trees and flowers decorated the lavish settings, like some-thing out of a beautifully illustrated children's book. This was where the rich lived, in these private little islands on the Brentwood Sea.

This is where he *should* have grown up. His mom's home was one of these. She took care of a house, a front lawn with fancy flow-ers and big, showy trees, but not her own kid. Not him. Him, she threw away.

Anger slipped over him like the cold raindrops slipping under his collar and down his back. Some things had to be made right. If he let her get away with it, then he could never think of that little kid again, the boy he'd been, and remember the pain in those eyes. He'd be responsible for keeping the pain there, because he'd failed the kid . . . like she did.

It took him a long time to reach his mom's block. He'd been careful, hiding when cars passed by, keeping out of sight when people were in their yards. It wasn't too difficult. The folks of Brentwood didn't spend much time in their yards. Not like the cities where Jeffrey came from, places where men and boys stood on street corners and waited for something to happen, or for drugs, or for somebody to mess up.

Kids lived on those streets, maybe locked out, maybe hiding from a whipping, or waiting for one that would happen when the old man came home. Kids roamed the street like vicious little dogs, dangerous if you looked funny at them, hungry, lonely, past caring for the families in their houses. Jeffrey didn't see a single kid on the streets in this town. Not one.

He found her block.

It was late. People were sleeping in their beds. The rich in this town were having pretty dreams in their pretty houses on their pretty islands in the big Brentwood Sea. Wake up time. He was the nightmare, the thing she'd forgotten.

The wall was easy to scale. He dropped onto the patio and glanced around. A pool, he'd expected that. The house was smaller than he'd imagined. The pool was nice, but it had started raining and he was wet enough. The sliding glass patio door was unlocked and slightly open. He pried off the screen and pushed the door open far enough for him to step inside. He was dripping rainwater on her hardwood floor. A puddle formed where he stood.

He felt the *rush* now, a shudder running through him like electric current. He was going to see her. Any minute, he'd open a door and there she'd be—his mom. That scared little kid, the one who'd stupidly waited for her to come back, looked around the rooms as if this was the night Mommy would return. Inside, he called out to her, *Mommy, Mommy . . . where are you?*

Mommy didn't want you, Jeffrey thought, silencing the brat.

He stepped into the hallway, noticing the two doors at the end of the passage. Bedrooms. One would be hers. He moved in soft-footed steps, each one bringing him closer to his past. Moving forward, but going back. Remembering his nights alone, without her, abandoned.

Which door?

He chose the one at the very end of the hall. More space. It would be the biggest. Probably hers. She liked her comfort.

He turned the handle, careful to put his shirttail between the skin of his palm and the doorknob, leaving no prints for anyone to find. The doorknob turned easily. With one small push it opened and he stepped inside the bedroom.

Dark surrounded him. Thick curtains were drawn to block any glimmer of light. Plush carpet muffled his steps across the floor. There was no sound other than his own breathing and the slight crush of his footsteps on the well-padded carpet. No sound. Not even . . .

He found a lamp and switched on the light. The sight was stark, vivid, and glaring. Marilyn—Mom—lay sprawled half in and half out of her bed. Her satin nightgown was sultry pink, clinging to her body and slightly twisted by her position, falling over the edge of the mattress. Her head lolled limply, as though she'd dropped something on the floor and was looking for it. But her eyes would never look for anything again. They were wide open and unseeing.

The phone was off the hook, and a spilled vial of prescription drugs were scattered in tiny pills across her nightstand. A glass of clear liquid—not water—was beside the vial. Gin? Vodka? Booze and pills. *Not a good combination, Mom.*

He touched her, the first time he'd touched his mother since . . . well, since she'd given him away. How long ago? It wasn't a warm response. Her skin was cold. Her face was grayish purple. Not a pretty sight.

"Dammit!" Jeffrey swore, worn out with frustration at this unexpected turn of events. How the hell could she be dead when he'd come all this way to kill her? "You never give me a break, do you, Mom?"

He wasn't too worried about someone coming into the room. He had the gun. This was his time with his mother. A son ought to have that right, shouldn't he? *Damn her,* he thought again. *Always thinking of herself.*

That's when he noticed the folded notepaper dropped on the floor. It looked as if it had fallen from her extended hand. *A note for me?* he wondered. How had she known he'd be here?

> *Johnny,* it read, *I can't go on after what we've done to our child. I only did it for you, but now you're through with me, as if I meant nothing. What about our child? Do you think I could ever forget? I love you, and I loved our baby.* The note was signed, *Forgive me, Marilyn.*

Jeffrey read the words over and over. This was the only letter he'd ever had from his mom, even if it wasn't exactly written to him. It was *about* him. She hadn't said his name, but she'd called him, *our child.* Tears welled in his eyes.

She'd thought of him, after all. The whole thing made sense, finally. Somehow, she'd known he was coming to this house tonight, known he planned to kill her, and took her own life to prevent him from murdering his mother. She'd done that for him.

It was the *only* thing she'd ever done for him—no, she had given him birth; he guessed he had to count that. Still, it was a big thing, giving up her life to help him. If he'd killed her, he might have wound up getting arrested, might have gone to prison. She'd saved him from that. It was kind of nice when he thought about it. Touching.

He tucked the note into his pocket. It was his now. Whoever she'd meant to receive this, whoever *Johnny* was, he could go hang. Jeffrey was walking out of the room, leaving the light on, when he realized. *Johnny* was his dad. Had to be. She'd said so in the note.

The anger he'd felt toward his mother found a new target. No wonder she'd given him up. *I only did it for you,* the note had said. Dad had wanted it.

Jeffrey took one last look at Mom and walked out of the room. Tears were streaming down his face, as if he'd been to a real funeral and heard all the pretty words a preacher would say, and the way mourners would come up to him, shake his hand and say, "She loved you, son." The whole scene was right there in his head, like a sad movie. Mom's last.

He walked out of the room and down the hall. From another area of the house, Jeffrey heard the tinny sound of TV voices. *Someone still up?* He tiptoed along the corridor, bringing the gun from his pocket. He could shoot somebody. He might miss because tears were still flooding his eyes, but he could take aim and shoot.

He released the safety. Ready.

The room, a den or small office—he wouldn't think of it as a family room—was bathed in the soft light of a TV screen. Asleep on the sofa was a dark-haired woman. The TV was turned to a news station showing an earlier broadcast.

Jeffrey kept his gun pointed at the dark-haired woman's head, but his attention was distracted by the scenes on the screen. It was the president, smiling as if the whole world were a funny story and he was telling it.

Jeffrey stepped closer to the set, listening to the words. "The president has always been closely linked with Hollywood. Those actors and actresses who supported his candidacy and who have now become welcome guests of the White House include Frank Sinatra, Peter Lawford, Sammy Davis, Jr., and other stars such as Marilyn Monroe. Few Presidents have had Happy Birthday sung to them in a more impressive fashion."

A film clip followed of Marilyn Monroe, dressed in her slinky best, standing at a microphone and singing in a slow, temptress voice, the words of the song. It was sexual, intimate, and very revealing of their personal relationship.

"John Kennedy is a president with attachments to Hollywood," said the commentator, "and clearly, Hollywood has formed its own attachments to him."

Johnny. Of course.

It was simple, deciding what to do. All this time, he'd been blaming the wrong person for his abandonment and the ruining of his life. Mom had loved him. She'd said so in her letter. She wasn't to blame. He forgave her everything. As it turned out, he was glad he hadn't killed her.

Jeffrey backed out of the room, keeping the nose of his gun

pointed at the head of the dark-haired, sleeping woman. Time to leave. He retraced his steps to the sliding glass door, still slightly open, and walked through the opening and out into the yard. The rain had stopped. He climbed over the wall and dropped to the other side.

Brentwood was asleep. Mothers and dads were in their beds, some of them dreaming, some just sleeping, one of them dead. He knew something the whole town—no, the whole world—didn't know. Marilyn Monroe was dead. That would be news . . . tomorrow.

For tonight, Jeffrey concentrated on getting away from this area. When Mom's body was discovered by the dark-haired woman, police would be all over this town. He'd be gone by then.

He knew exactly where he was going. It would take a little while to make plans and get things ready. He was patient. His moment would arrive. His act of vengeance had been denied him tonight. Mom had protected him, in her own way.

But, what about Dad?

Marilyn Monroe was born in 1926, and died in 1962. John Kennedy died the following year.

AFTERWORD

I was at home with my parents in Atwater, near Los Angeles, when I heard on the news that Marilyn had died. School was out for the summer. I was fifteen, probably putting a lot more thought into my upcoming junior year of high school than giving any consideration to Marilyn Monroe. And yet, I remember my parents watching the news with avid interest, my mother especially. My mom bought movie magazines and liked to keep up with the latest news about superstars. She had very little interest in the modern actors so popular with my age group. They didn't count as real stars. Marilyn did. I saw sadness in my mother's eyes as she watched the scenes on TV of Marilyn's death. I remember how much coverage there was on television, and in the news, and realized that so many people were touched by her loss, as if in some personal way. They felt they knew her, perhaps in the same way my character felt he knew Marilyn, in the image he'd created for her. I remember the nation's sorrow on the day she died. It struck me that she must be more than I had understood of her, and because teenagers like romantic tragedies, I took her then and there to my heart.

To me, the one word that best fits Marilyn is "poignant." I remember her most as the waif-faced woman-child, seemingly lost and long-ing for love, still a legendary beauty, but her eyes saying she'd waited too long. Maybe it was that image of a lost child that inspired me to write "Dear Mom." In writing the story, I compared all the abortions Marilyn was reputed to have had with her often-stated wish to have a child, which I believe was genuine. I came up with a woman who caught at life with one hand and pushed it away with the other. I wanted this tragic character to find happiness, but knew she wouldn't. That's where the idea for the young man of my story came from, the abandoned child who believed he was Marilyn's son. Why not? It was part of the tragedy of her myth. Who better to have for an image of the young mother who abandoned you than Marilyn? My feelings about Marilyn changed during the writing of my story only in that I now consider what her life meant to other people, how it affected them.

—Jill M. Morgan

MISTRESS FAME

BY BILLIE SUE MOSIMAN

*ame will go by and, so long, I've had you,
fame. If it goes by, I've always known it was
fickle. So at least it's something I experienced,
but that's not where I live.*

—Marilyn Monroe, conclusion of taped
conversation published in *Life*
(New York, August 3, 1962), the day that Monroe died

 "I PROBABLY SHOULDN'T have said that in the interview. I'm always saying things that get me in trouble."
I sat across from Marilyn where she lay prone on the sofa, a damp cloth covering her eyes. She had been crying. Again. She wasn't so beautiful when she wept. Her eyes were puffed and her color mottled with splotches of wine. It always broke my heart to see her cry. Her unhappiness made her naturally golden aura fade to a watery muddy brown. I was so glad I had been sent to guide her away from here. She couldn't take much more before shattering like a porcelain doll dropped on hard concrete.

"What can they do to you for being blunt and speaking your mind, kill you? You worry too much," I said, trying to be of help.

"Don't even say things like that!"

She was screeching. It hurt my ears. I covered them, to hold down the volume. "Now, now . . ."

"You're supposed to help me, not make me more upset. You know I'm already scared to death of Bobby and John. I'm scared of the studios. I'm scared of . . . scared of living."

I couldn't get up and touch her to let her know how much I

cared, how sorry I was for setting her off. I have no solidity, being a minor spirit from an outer realm. I had been dispatched with the usual orders: Carry her over. Don't wait too long. Be swift and merciful.

She did not know my purpose, of course, and I would not tell her until she was ready to hear it.

Spirits who can coalesce from the ethereal to the corporeal are on a higher plane than I have achieved—or might ever achieve, to be truthful. The higher beings can't be bothered with chores like the one I'd been given. It is left to those like me, the lower, less busy, and, ultimately, more compassionate spirits, to ready souls for the dark.

"Fame is a mistress with a whip," I said, hoping to make her understand. "You courted her and she came. But she's harsh and unrelenting. She cares nothing for how you deal with her gift. Surely you knew that."

"I didn't know anything," Marilyn said, her voice breathy now and sad. "I've been dumb, so dumb all of my life. I wanted fame, but so does everyone else in Hollywood. I don't know why it has to be the burden it's turned out to be. What's a sex goddess to do with her fame when she's closing in on forty?"

"You're just thirty-six, Marilyn. You're not an old woman. You're still one of the most extraordinary women in the world." Why did she not know it? Her own blindness had created at least half her troubles.

She pulled the damp cloth aside and stared at me with a quizzical expression. When Marilyn looked straight at me—for she rarely does it, I think she's too afraid—she melts my heart. There's such longing in her that it fills a room like the scent from several bouquets of fragrant, freshly cut roses.

"Why do you call me Marilyn? Why don't you call me Norma Jeane?"

"Norma Jeane was the girl you used to be. Marilyn is your best name, your real name."

"Does anyone else see you?"

I shook my head. "No, just you. I've come just for you." This was as close as I've ever explained my real reason for being here. She won't yet understand my words, mistaking me to mean I've come just to be her personal guide when I really mean I have come to take her away from the world.

"Do other people ever see spirits? Maybe I've made you up. Maybe I've really lost my mind. Oh God. Oh God."

"Hush now, take it easy. I'm as real as you, Marilyn. I'm sure other people do see us. They just don't discuss it in public, not unless they enjoy reputations as psychics or clairvoyants. And no, you haven't lost your mind."

"That's what everyone thinks, though. They treat me like I'm mentally ill and that turns me into a bundle of nerves so I don't know what I'm doing. I know I'm difficult to work with. I know I demand too much, but my last movie was *The Misfits*! I had to act with Gable, for pete's sake, him and his bad breath and his stinking ego. That movie premiered two years ago and I don't think I'm going to be offered anything much from now on.

"People treat me so bad. I don't know why. I never deserved to be treated the way I have."

Tears welled in her eyes again even as she stared at me. She pulled the cloth over her face and I waited, giving her time to find her calm center again.

"You're tired, Marilyn. You've spent your life fast and it's tired you."

I thought from the long silence that she had dozed. After a few minutes she finally heaved a sigh and said, "I didn't know any other way to spend it. I had to work hard and fast or I would have been left behind. I never could have found any fame at all."

She was right, of course. Some people luck into the Mistress and others have to chase her skirts for a ride. Marilyn had to race for fame. It had tired her out, literally, caused her to grow ill, mentally and physically, made it appear to her colleagues that she was a quarter horse so that they expected more from her than she had to give. Poor Marilyn had been meant to be an old-fashioned buggy hauler. She didn't have the constitution to keep up. She had fallen behind so many times now that the race was over.

She just didn't know it yet.

I had been dreaming of Marilyn as a young girl, the Marilyn

who had all the dreams and enough enthusiasm to fuel a hydroplant, when she abruptly sat up on the sofa and flung the damp cloth to the floor at her bare feet.

"I'm going out," she said. "Don't follow me this time. I want to be alone."

"You're in no condition . . ."

"Don't tell me what condition I'm in! Who are you to tell *me* what I can or cannot do? I'm the star here. I'm the real person. You're just a . . . just a . . . ghost!"

She stumbled from the room, leaving me sitting in the easy chair. She had drunk too much and rested too little. She was distraught and hanging by a thread to sanity. She was always alone these days. She didn't have to flee from me to find solitude. Everyone had deserted my poor Marilyn long since. They couldn't fix her life any more than I can, who can blame them for wandering away? Sometimes you just have to let go, cut all ties, and let your friend or lover dangle over the abyss.

Wherever Marilyn went, she would not find the peace she sought. Wherever she went, she took all her psychic baggage with her. In her heart she knew there was no escape, but she tried to pretend otherwise.

I moved into her bedroom and found her sitting on the side of the bed, head in her hands.

"Marilyn, don't go out."

"I can't find anything to wear," she said, her voice muffled. "My stuff's at the cleaners or it's dirty. I can't go out in dirty clothes."

"Stay here with me. I love you. I'll do anything to help you."

"Will you hand me that bottle of sleeping tablets?"

My heart leaped. She must know my true purpose. She was coming closer to recognizing that tonight she would leave life behind. I would have to explain nothing to her.

"Here," I said. "Help yourself."

She took the bottle from the air where it floated and she unscrewed the cap. She looked up at me hovering above her. "Tell me about death."

"I can't because there is no death. I've never seen its face. It's a myth man believes because he can't see into the beyond."

"Then tell me about what it's like where you come from."

She needed courage and this was her way of asking for it. "It's quiet, Marilyn. No phones ringing, no schedules. No fame and the repercussions of that fame. No physical being to keep in shape and save from running to fat. No faithless lovers who use and discard you. No politics to play, asses to kiss, lies to tell. No insulting B-movie parts to turn down. No friends who betray you, no envious enemies, no worries to weigh you down."

"That must be heaven. Is that what heaven is like?"

"There's no name for it, there's no reason to name what makes up reality."

"Then there aren't any streets paved in gold or heavenly mansions or a throne with God sitting in it, angels at each side?"

I would not lie to her. I shook my head. "Fairy tales," I said. "Although the truth is even more majestic."

She poured out a handful of sleeping pills. She bowed her head like a penitent to contemplate them.

"I'll get you water." I hurried to the bathroom and ran tap water into a glass. When I returned, her mood had changed once again. She was always mercurial and unreliable, but this turnabout surprised me. I thought we were so close to the end.

"You might be a demon trying to lure me to hell. Suicide's a sin." She scowled at me and even bared her teeth. I expected her to growl like a trapped animal willing to fight to the death rather than be captured.

I sighed to hear her take this tack, though I wasn't surprised. I am one of the suicide brigade and I wouldn't have been sent to Marilyn if she wasn't supposed to end her own life. Now I had to convince her there was no sin involved. At least half of my clients had to be finally convinced of the rightness of their decisions. I had a lot of practice at it.

"There is no such thing as sin."

"Isn't there? Then murderers, the greatest sinners of all, must go to heaven too." She threw back her head and laughed a caustic laugh that made her sound mad. "No retribution, no hell, no burning lake of fire. The final indignity to all victims everywhere."

"There is no such thing as heaven or hell, I told you that."

"I don't understand!" She flung the empty medicine bottle at me and it went through, striking the wall behind to bounce off onto the floor. "You're a liar and a fake. You're a figment of my imagination. I only see you when I'm drunk. I'm not going to listen to you."

She dropped the handful of tablets on the bedside table and scrambled under the disheveled covers. She pulled the sheet up over her head. I set the water glass next to the tablets and went to the corner to stand and to wait.

We had time. Let her pout.

"Wha . . . ? Where am I?"

I moved from the shadowed corner to her bedside to look down at her. It was discouraging to see how far Beauty had fallen. The roots of her fine blond hair needed a bleach job and there were a few spidery wrinkles at the corners of her closed eyes. The pillow was gray-damp where a small trickle of saliva had dripped from her open mouth. She smelled of sleep and sweat and despair, a sharp but not unpleasant odor. She had been talking in her drunken sleep. Suddenly she sat up, probably sensing I was nearby.

"Oh, it's you." She rubbed sleep from her eyes.

"How do you feel? You've been out for four hours."

"I have a horrible headache. Jesus, it hurts." She struggled into a sitting position. The straps of her slip fell down each shoulder and I could see the tops of her naked breasts rising as she breathed. Never had there been a more spectacular example of female flesh. If she had not been so needy, she might have found a way to sit next to a world leader and could have orchestrated the world. Much of her potential had gone unplumbed.

"There's water here," I said, thinking she would remember the sleeping tablets.

"Thanks." She reached over and took the glass to down the liquid in it. I took the glass from her and went to refill it. This was not working out as easily as I had thought it might. I'd been with her for two months already and she seemed no nearer to closing out the books than when I first appeared to her.

"Damn, that made me sick to my stomach. I probably should have taken a shot of bourbon instead."

I had a plan. I'd only implemented it twice before, but it had worked marvels. It seemed I had to do something to help Marilyn, something more than I had done so far. If I failed in my job I'd be earthbound until my subject either turned a corner and embraced life or finally gave it up altogether.

"I'll give you a glimpse of what it's like," I said softly.

"What what's like?"

"The other side. The long sleep."

She narrowed her eyes. Billy Wilder would one day be quoted, after her death, saying that she was the meanest woman he ever knew. He would not be far wrong, but where he would go amiss was in the fact that Marilyn Monroe used her meanness and the hardness of character to protect the vulnerable kernel that was her ragged soul. Without using her wit and a measure of cruelty, she never would have found Mistress Fame at all. Many before her had been made of softer stuff, and they had all floundered.

Of course, another comrade spirit would guide Mr. Wilder away one fine day and he would regret what he'd said about dear Marilyn.

"What are you saying?" she asked. "Or maybe I should say, what are you offering?"

"A tour. A brief one. You can decide then whether you want to stay here, living on, or come with me for good."

"I get it now. Finally I get it. You're the Death Angel and you've been sent to fetch me."

I made a dismissing sound in my throat. "There is no such thing. I'm just one of many; I'm not any special spirit. But it's true I've been sent on a mission to . . . show you the way."

"How could I visit death and come back?"

I pointed to the sleeping tablets heaped on the bedside table next to the refilled water glass. "You don't take enough to make it permanent. You take enough to make you sleep the sleep of near death. I promise to bring you back for your final decision. No one can *make* you stay dead unless that's what you want, Marilyn."

She turned aside her head. Her gaze focused on the middle distance where she tried to see into the hazy future. "I might make more movies. I might make one where I really shine. I'm not too old. I'm not too much of a ruin yet. I have a few friends left."

"I wish you believed that," I said gently.

She began to cry. "I wish I did too."

"Then shall we go away for just a little while? Take that tour? I'll bring you back, I promise."

"Fuck it, fuck everything," she said vehemently. She grabbed approximately half the pile of tablets, sloshed the water glass getting it to her mouth, and gulped down three and four pills at a time, her fierce eyes steady on my face. Was she doing it to spite me or herself?

I smiled benevolently. She had the heart of a lioness. She was truly a goddess sent to travel the Earth. I loved her more than anyone I had ever guided over, my lovely Marilyn, my queen.

"It's dark."

I had her by the hand, able to touch her spirit with my own now. I led her forward through a passage. "It won't be long," I said. "Keep faith with me, don't be afraid."

"I'm not afraid," she lied. "How can dead people be afraid?" She trembled like a skinny pine in a storm wind.

"You're not dead. You're just visiting, remember? It's not far now. See ahead how the passage opens out into the beyond?"

"Oh God."

I squeezed her hand, lending her strength and hope. The passage wound around a curve, narrowed, then widened a few feet, the walls retreating, and there we were on the brink, facing the mighty void. Even I, familiar with that void, hardly dared to breathe when faced with it once again after my sojourn on Earth.

"See it? Do you feel the beauty? Do you hear the silence?"

She stood poised at the lip of the passage, her face smooth as a child's face, her spirit still now as a woodland pond.

"I don't know what to say. It's so . . . empty."

"This portion of it, yes. I'll take you to where you can see the Creation."

I stepped out into the void and brought her along with me, tugging her forward. We moved as spirits move, instantaneously to where I wanted to go. We crossed vast endless eternity in a blink.

We stood in the Nowhere next to the being I called the Master, having no name for that which was father to every atom, every thought and action.

"Oh Jesus, who is it, where are we?" Marilyn cried.

"Look to your right," a spectral voice said to us.

Marilyn swiveled her head right and saw the blackness, the empty endless. "There's nothing there," she said, her voice piping and high with alarm.

"Now look to your left," the Master said.

Now she would see it! She turned to look and flinched, her hand tightening like a vice on mine. "What is it? What is that?"

"That is all that ever was or will be," came the answer. *"One time I flicked all that from the tips of my fingers the way a man who has dipped his hands in water might flick off the droplets. It came from me, from my body, and it shall return to me in full."*

To our left lay the Creation, the place where Marilyn came from and where I had come from long long ago and the place from whence all living matter originated. It lay in an oval bubble, encased in a transparent film, surrounded by the void. Inside the egg-shaped bubble swirled multicolored planets and suns. Myriad universes teemed, alive with motion and blinking, sparkling light. Stars winked out, black holes sucked in whole streams of celestial bodies, novas burned bright, then dimmed.

"Where are the souls of the dead, where did they go?" Marilyn asked, awed by the sight.

"The dead are there, above the living, but inside that place. Nothing is ever lost. The dead too will return to me one day."

"Do you intervene there? Do you listen to and answer prayers?"

"I'll have no more to do with it until the time I take it back," said the Master. *"The Creation is on its own and has been from the beginning."*

I felt peace descending into Marilyn the way it had me when I first came here. All anxiety fled, taking with it heartbreak and grief and despondency. Her spirit relaxed in acceptance of what was and what would be. Neither of us could see the entire Creator, for this being stood alone in the void, more gigantic by a thousandfold than the Creation, larger than anything man had reason to even imagine. We stood next to this being, down below, but no one had ever seen his face, and I doubted any of us ever would. We and our kind and the material matter of all the worlds that made up the Creation were but an afterthought. Our petty day-to-day concerns and even our deaths were not the Master's affair.

Yet he was here, always present when I had to bring someone who needed to see the truth.

I moved away, taking Marilyn with me back to the passage and then through the thin membrane into the world of the living. She gasped, her chest jerking spasmodically as she entered into life, sucking air that seared her lungs, and made her cough. Her eyelids fluttered and she groaned. Finally, she opened her eyes and she remembered where we had been.

"Well?" I wondered what her choice would be. Surely her troubled life was not the place for her, but would she now understand that?

"Hand me the rest of the sleeping pills."

I scooped them up and deposited them into the palm of her outstretched hand. My spirit soared, lifting me from the bedside. "Fame will follow you into the beyond," I said. She knew I told her the truth. She knew I could see into her past and into the future of the physical world.

"You need not worry that you'll be forgotten. Twenty years from today, fifty years from today, a hundred years, and the world will remember you. Fame will never desert you. It will only grow.

"They'll write books about your life and tell stories about your passing. Young women will continue to idolize your beauty and men will hang your picture on their walls in order to fantasize dreams of true love. You'll have more fans than you ever had before. You'll be loved, Marilyn, the way you always wanted."

She took the tablets, arching her neck to swallow, wincing as they went down. She drank all the water and set the glass on the table.

"Take my hand," she said. "Lead me away again. Tell me how much they'll love me. Tell me how much they'll care."

Her lids drifted closed for the second time and I hovered above her until the time came when I could coax her spirit out and away for the last journey home.

At the entrance to the void I said, "You were wrong, what you said to that interviewer from the magazine."

"What did I say?"

"You told him you had experienced fame, but it wasn't where you lived."

"I remember now. I thought it would make trouble for me. People twisted my words."

"The truth is Fame is where you always lived, Marilyn. The Mistress loved you dearly, though the cost was great and the life you lived short."

"I don't care about any of it now. It all seems . . . so long ago."

We stood for several moments or lifetimes or eternities, holding hands, looking out and down into that black heart of emptiness. I could tell this time she was not afraid.

"One more leap and we join the stars," I said, leaning over to kiss her cool dry cheek.

She grinned for the first time since I'd known her, her smile a bright twinkling star lost in the glory of the galaxy.

AFTERWORD

I always thought Marilyn Monroe was one of the most beautiful women in the world. I thought she was underestimated, talented, and stuck in the role of sexpot when she had ambitions to be a real actress. I didn't change my mind when writing about her. There was something about Marilyn beyond her mystique as a Love Goddess. She was a tragic figure, larger than life, a real star.

The summer Marilyn died, I don't remember the event or what I was doing. I was a junior in high school and so I was probably off swimming in the creeks in South Alabama. I don't think I'd seen a MM movie for some years. She influenced me most when I was younger and I saw her movies at the drive-in with my parents. I remember my parents didn't think much of her acting, but even then I could feel that behind the acting in the films, she was a suffering kind of individual who had dreams that weren't being fulfilled.

—Billie Sue Mosiman

MARILYN MONROE ON 165TH STREET

BY LINDA MANNHEIM
(FOR ABBY)

 WHEN SILVIA WAS a little girl, her sister used to scare her to tears by telling her Marilyn Monroe was coming. Their mother would be off cleaning someone's house, and Silvia would be sitting on the dirty carpeting in the living room, cutting shapes from construction paper, lost in thought. And maybe Maria would spot her like that, through the glass-paned door. She would choose just that moment to burst in and scream, "Run! Run! Marilyn Monroe is coming!"

And Silvia, the fear stopped up in her throat, would drop her blunt scissors to the ground and go running down the long, dark hallway, nearly sliding on the speckled linoleum in her half-off socks. She would hide behind the smelly wool coats and the old leather shoes in the front closet, and Maria would call to her, "Don't come out yet! Marilyn Monroe is still here!"

Silvia would stay there, quaking with fear and sobbing softly while Maria watched *The Carol Burnett Show* and *Mary Tyler Moore*. That was how I found them when I went downstairs to their apartment and Maria opened the door. The TV was on, and next to the couch there was an open box of Capt'n Crunch. Maria looked at me like she was all pissed off that I'd interrupted her show and was waiting for me to explain why I'd come so I could leave again. Silvia's sobs came softly from the closet. "My mother said to tell you that your mother called, and she wanted me to tell you that she can't come home for another hour more, and she said that you should take the chicken out of the freezer and go put it in a bowl of hot water now," I reported, with the plodding efficiency of an undertaker.

Really, I did not want to speak to Maria at all, but because her family's phone had been disconnected, I was assigned to convey messages to Maria's family that came in on our phone. I decided that conveying these messages or talking to her during emergency situations did not really constitute "speaking" with her. But I would never say anything nice to her or the mean girls in hot pants she hung out with in school. "How come Silvia's crying?" I asked.

"Because she's stupid," Maria said, tossing back her dark wavy hair that fell down to her butt.

"You're stupid," I told Maria. "Your platform shoes are the stupidest shoes I've ever seen."

"You better go," Maria said, glaring at me, as she backed off to the kitchen. "You better get out of my house."

From inside the closet, I could hear Silvia sob, almost inaudibly, "Marilyn Monroe. Marilyn Monroe."

I opened the closet door, which was hard to do because all the layers of paint along the doorframe sometimes made it stick. But once a crack of light made its way into the darkness, Silvia started to scream, then she collapsed into a series of sobs. "Honey," I asked, pulling her out into the dim hallway light. "What's wrong?"

She held onto me in that way that little kids do, their weeping all getting under your skin and right into the cavity of your chest so that it becomes all the weeping you ever did too. "Marilyn Monroe is coming," Silvia explained, in a little gasp.

"What?" I asked, lifting up Silvia and letting her cry into my shoulder. "Who's'at?" I asked. "What? Marilyn Monroe. What's she? She's just an old movie star, right? She's not even alive anymore, I'll bet you."

"She's dead," Silvia confirmed, tears still running down her face. "She's a ghost."

We had to go to Westchester to see my Uncle Carlo perform with his band. I'd seen them before. It was stupid. My Uncle Carlo would make his hair all greasy and comb it back so it looked just like the hair that all the men had on the old TV shows we watched. All these people were my parents' age and would wear really ugly clothes, like poodle skirts and little tight pants that were too short. On the way there, I sat in the back seat of the car and looked out the window resentfully, asking my parents how come we had to do this, and what was the big deal? It was nostalgia, my mother explained. I would understand when I got older. But I knew that I never would. I would never like bobby socks, which were too much like the socks I had to wear when I was little. And how come they always started cheering when the band played "Wake Up Little Susie" and "Rock Around the Clock"? What was wrong with all of them?

This time, there were all these striped awnings set up outside, and the air smelled like beer. We sat at a round white metal table and I drank eight Shirley Temples. Afterwards, on our way back into the city, we stopped at Caldor's Department Store. I wandered over to a corner of the store where, on a table, someone had arranged all these copies of a book called *Marilyn*. A blonde lady, slightly dazed-looking, lips parted, stared at me from the book's cover. I wondered if this was Marilyn Monroe and flipped open the jacket to find out it was. This was an entire big book about Marilyn Monroe. I looked at the price. My parents would never get it for me. I took off my sweater and tried to bunch it up around the book so that no one would know I was hiding anything inside. This was 1973. Out in places like Westchester then, there weren't tags that sent off theft detectors. Security guards didn't follow you around the way they do now. It was amazing what you could get away with. Once, in the Woolworth's on 181st Street, my cousin and I carried out a red beanbag chair and never got stopped. Things were there for the taking then.

At home, I looked at the book with my back to the door, hunched over it as I sat cross-legged on my bed, so if anyone came in, they couldn't see what I was reading. Marilyn Monroe was supposed to be beautiful, but I didn't think she was beautiful. Her hair looked tired like my mother's, pushed into strange shapes that weren't right. She was too heavy, wasn't slinky the way I thought actresses should be. And that mole on her cheek, was that a beauty spot? I'd heard women call them beauty spots on TV, seen them draw the dot on with an eyebrow pencil. Why was that supposed to be beautiful? I had a feeling this was something my mother would tell me I would understand when I got older, but I knew that I never would.

Marilyn Monroe was walking across a beach, a short, white terry cloth robe around her, her legs covered with sand. Was that sexy? You could keep the sand off your legs by getting back in the water and then putting on flip flops and drying off as soon as you got out again. Didn't she know that? Marilyn Monroe was putting her arms around a tree, elated at something, but I didn't think it was real elation. Marilyn Monroe was standing above a subway grate, her skirt blowing up as she grinned with glee. Didn't she know you should never ever stand or even walk on a subway grate? You never knew when they would cave in, and then you'd be down there, all mush on the subway tracks. Why were they taking pictures of her doing these things?

Then I looked at a picture way in the beginning of the book. Marilyn Monroe was standing in a pair of blue jeans and shirt made out of bandannas. She was smiling, and she didn't look all spaced out. Her hair looked normal. It was brown, and wavy, and tied back, just the way Silvia's was. So that's how come people said she was beautiful, I thought.

I would have to show this book to Silvia, show it to her so she would know Marilyn Monroe was nothing to be afraid of. She would see that once Marilyn Monroe was a pretty girl, and then she turned into a woman who looked as weary as our mothers. Everything about her would seem completely familiar.

I read through the book to find stories I could tell Silvia about Marilyn Monroe. Her name wasn't even Marilyn Monroe, but Norma Jeane Baker. She was in an orphanage for a while and had to bathe in water that some other girls had bathed in first. Someone shot her dog. She got married when she was sixteen, five years older than me. I didn't want to tell Silvia these stories. I leafed through the pictures again. Marilyn Monroe getting out of a pool, one arm and one leg slung over the swimming pool's lip. Marilyn Monroe clutching a sheet to her chest while she kissed an older man with a mustache. What was wrong with everyone? Why did they all want to look at pictures like these? How come they showed her like she was gonna walk out naked any minute instead of just showing her naked and getting it done with?

"You should come over to my house later 'cause I got something to show you," I told Silvia, in the schoolyard during lunch. She was playing double dutch with some other little kids.

"What?" Silvia asked.

"You come on to my house after school today," I told her. "But don't bring your stupid sister."

"Okay," Silvia said.

Once school was done, after Silvia dropped her books and her lunch box downstairs, she came up to my apartment. My parents were both at work, so no one else was home. Silvia stood in the living room, her big eyes all expectant, and I told her, "Wait right here."

Then I went and got the book. She stared at the lady on the cover, asked me, "Who is that?"

"That's Marilyn Monroe," I told her.

For a second, her lips turned down with fear.

"Don't be scared," I told Silvia, bringing her closer. "She's just a lady. See?"

I put the book on the coffee table and turned the pages while Silvia stared. Marilyn Monroe in an evening gown. Marilyn Monroe pushing her shoulders forward as if she wanted the person taking her picture to go away, but was too polite to say so. Marilyn Monroe drinking champagne with an old man, a white-blonde tuft of hair falling on her forehead. I said to Silvia, "Marilyn Monroe."

Then, near the end of the book, a picture of a man whose face was folded in grief. Joe DiMaggio, I read. Once, when I'd heard a Simon and Garfunkel song about him, I asked my mother who he was, and she told me he was a fantastic ball player, that he played right across the river in Yankee Stadium. "Where did he go?" I asked her.

"What do you mean?" she'd asked me.

"Did he die?" I asked. I told her about the song.

"Laura," she said, shaking her head. And then the doorbell rang so I'd never gotten to hear what her explanation was.

Now, as Silvia and I bent over the book, I read that Joe DiMaggio was married to Marilyn Monroe once, and that last picture was taken at her funeral. I read that you were supposed to see the grief of the entire nation in his face.

The doorbell rang. Quickly, I hid the book under the couch and went to answer the door. It was Maria. She had on blue eye shadow and kept flicking her hair back while she stood. "You better come downstairs," she said, looking past me, to Silvia.

"Marilyn Monroe isn't a monster," Silvia said accusingly, her small chin in the air.

You could see something taken from Maria, her eyes tightening. "You don't get downstairs, Marilyn Monroe is gonna get you, and the boiler man who lives in the basement is gonna get you too."

"Liar," Silvia accused. "Laura showed me the book, and now I know that Marilyn Monroe wouldn't come get me, 'cause she's just a lady like Mami is."

I stood against the wall, my arms folded, and smugly smiled.

"What book?" Maria asked.

"This book," Silvia said, walking back to the living room and pulling the book out from under the couch. Maria and I followed and watched Silvia struggle to get the heavy volume onto the coffee table.

Maria kneeled before the table and leafed through the book slowly, staring at the pictures: Marilyn Monroe as a tiny bride, a veil shaping her face into a heart; Marilyn Monroe sitting on the floor in a filmy red gown, looking as if she's trying to talk down someone who's going to hit her; Marilyn Monroe stretched out naked on a red satin sheet, like a woman who's doing nothing more than showing what a woman's body looks like in profile.

Maria flipped back to the book jacket and saw the price. "You stole this," she whinily accused.

"Did not," I told her.

"Did too," she said back. "I'm gonna tell everyone unless you let me take it to look at."

What could I do?

The truth is, Maria did give me back the book when she was done looking at it. And then I read some. And then a curious thing happened. Me and Maria and Silvia, we all started talking about it, about that book. And then Maria found some more books about Marilyn Monroe, so we started talking about those too. It wasn't like Maria changed or anything like that. She was still one of the snotty girls at school. And when she knew something about Marilyn Monroe that I didn't, she must've thought she was the biggest thing in the whole wide world, like Marilyn Monroe had told her this stuff personally. She read more stuff about Marilyn Monroe than I ever would, and then she told us all about this TV show that was going to be about Marilyn Monroe too. Maria wanted to go to Anita Navarro's house to watch it because Anita Navarro had a color TV. I hated having to be with Anita and Maria too. Anita kept touching up her nail polish during the show and the air smelled bad from it. We were supposed to watch Marilyn Monroe sing "Happy Birthday" to President Kennedy. "Ladies and gentlemen," the announcer said. "The late Miss Marilyn Monroe."

"Oh my God," I said, lurching forward. "That's so weird! She wasn't even dead yet."

"She didn't get there on time," Anita said, shaking her head while she finished the last nail. "Get it? They were making a joke because she was late." Then Anita turned to me and stared, eyes popped wide as if she wanted to see why I was stupid.

Maria angrily said, "Shhh." She sounded so much like her mother that, for a minute, I was scared.

Marilyn Monroe sang "Happy Birthday" to the president in a little, breathy voice. It was just the regular birthday song, nothing special about it. "This is so weird," I proclaimed to Maria and Anita and Silvia, when the song was done. "How come they wanted her to do that? How come she was supposed to put on that dress and get on stage just so she would sing the birthday song to him? If they were having an affair, how come she didn't sing it to him at home? How come she sang all funny like that? Is that supposed to be sexy or something?"

Further evidence that people who lived during the 1950s had a bizarre sense of what was attractive and what was fun.

*   *   *

The first time I saw Marilyn Monroe in real life, she was walking
down 165th Street toward St. Nicholas Avenue. She was wearing a
white halter dress, just like the one she wore when she stood over
the subway grate and her skirt went up. She walked fast, the gray
July air kissing the skin of her upper arms and shoulders. The men
hanging out on the stoops called out to her. She just smiled and
kept walking. I couldn't follow her. I wasn't supposed to go down to
St. Nicholas Avenue by myself. It was one of the few warnings I listened to. Dos Puertas was on St. Nicholas Avenue, the bar where
Maria and Silvia's father got shot. I hung off the side of the steps to
my building and watched Marilyn Monroe disappear as she turned
the corner. Then I ran upstairs to tell Maria what I'd seen.

It was when I got to the part about Dos Puertas that Maria's face
broke, and she said, sharp-voiced, "You lie, Laura."

"You lie," I said back. "You think you know everything."

"Stupid," Maria told me. "Marilyn Monroe is dead, and even if
she was alive, she wouldn't come here!"

That night, I lay in bed thinking of all the things I could have
said back to Maria Cuellar. Of course Marilyn Monroe had come
here. How else could they have filmed her with her skirt getting
blown up over a subway grate? She'd lived in New York once, hadn't
she? Everyone did sooner or later. They were all there, on that island
with me. But I knew what Maria meant. She meant I was stupid to
think we'd see any of those people where we were. She meant Marilyn Monroe wouldn't come uptown.

I hooded the lamp next to my bed with a blanket and looked at
the book again: Marilyn Monroe sitting in front of a palm reader's
storefront in a peasant blouse, her hand cocked up in imitation of
the painted palm behind her; Marilyn Monroe in a bathtub, her
head and legs sticking out from the bubbles, her expression asking,
Is this okay?; Marilyn Monroe in a black sequined gown, caught in
mid-air during a jump, her face turned to the camera as if she wants
to know why she has to do this.

Then I looked out the window at the purple and gray night, a
few people leaning against parked cars, and a brown Lincoln with

New Jersey plates gunning up toward Broadway. The only light came from the bodega on the corner, its boxes of plantains and Puerto Rican grapes out front still, and, inside, its cut melon surrounded by flies and dried ham sliced into portions too small to be good for anything. It was open all night. The cashier there once whapped Maria's chest with a long stretch of tape from the cash register. He'd be doing what he always did that night, keying numbers in as he moved the food from one side to the other, wiping the dust off the top of soda cans when people complained 'bout the dirt. And Maria, she'd be upstairs doing her nails again. Everything would go on same as it was before for them, but not for me. Nothing was the same. Out there, somewhere, was Marilyn Monroe.

"Come with me," I told Silvia, the next day. "She may come again."

When we sat down at first, the cement steps were too hot to stay on, so we stood sometimes. And Maria stood with us. "But don't think I'm waiting to see Marilyn Monroe," she told us. "Because I'm not. Because she's dead, and I'm not too much of a fool to know that like you are, Laura. But I was gonna be here today anyway. So I'm just here. That's all it is."

Two o'clock came, and there was no Marilyn Monroe there. I shouldn't have told anyone, because what if she never came again? We bought those icies that cost a nickel and get squeezed out of a tube. The acid tang hit the back of my throat and I coughed. "Don't you go coughing on me," Maria screamed, jumping back. The blue icies were the best; we all got blue tongues. We were waving our tongues at one another when she came again: Marilyn.

This time, she was wearing a black sequined gown, and the strap started to slide off her shoulder. She stood where she was, wiggling slightly, as she pushed the strap back up. The men across the street went crazy. One screamed for water, said, in Spanish, that he was getting too hot. Marilyn said to him, in her breathy little voice, "I like it hot." Then started walking again, wiggling as she went.

Maria was drop-jawed, her eyes big. Silvia's chin was clenched in triumph. Marilyn Monroe had come, but Silvia had not succumbed to fear. And I was not awestruck to stillness this time. I ran after her. I followed Marilyn Monroe to where she was turning the corner at the end of the block. When I got down to St. Nicholas Avenue, I stood stock still on the west side of the street. I turned and saw Marilyn Monroe keep going down the sidewalk, through the crowds. I watched as she disappeared in the Dos Puertas bar.

I ran back to my building and stopped off at Maria and Silvia's house to tell them what I'd seen. Silvia went right back to watching *I Dream of Jeannie* as soon as she opened the door. Maria was in the kitchen, her face as dry and tight as the mean fourth-grade teacher's.

"You're not supposed to go there," she said accusingly, before I could even tell her what I'd seen. She swallowed as if there was a small, hard candy stuck in her throat, and continued making thin, gray hamburgers.

"I didn't go there," I responded, adamantly. But Maria didn't seem to believe me, so I said again, "I didn't go there. I just went down to the corner, and I watched her go into the bar."

"Which bar?" Maria asked, looking at me as she squeezed a chunk of hamburger with one hand. Of course, she knew which bar.

"Dos Puertas," she forced me to say.

"Aye!" she screamed. "Stupid!"

"I didn't go there," I screamed back.

"You go and I'll tell your mother on you!"

"I didn't go there," I repeated. I backed away from Maria and the Formica table with its aluminum trim. "I only came down to tell you your mother called, and she said she's gonna be late and you should put the french fries in at twenty to six."

Maria stared at me, her eyes popped wide and burning dark. "I'll tell on you," she warned once more.

"I didn't do nothing," I said again.

Marilyn Monroe walked past in next afternoon's yellow sun, her hair burning white blonde in the heat, dark glasses obscuring her eyes. She had on a big white shirt and black pedal pushers. She carried a beige bag by its looped strap. This time, when the men called after her, she didn't turn and she didn't smile. She just kept walking on ahead, grim-faced, tight-lipped. Then she turned to me, and said softly, "Hello." And she almost smiled, but she kept walking. I watched her go, watched the seams of her pants shift with her angry wiggle, then I realized I could try to catch up with her and talk. I had to hurry. I tore from my place by the stoop and felt a hand close on my wrist, got yanked back, into the shadow of my Uncle Carlo. He felt his unshaved face with his free hand, squinted, and asked, "Where you going, Laura?"

"Nowhere," I told him.

"Where you going just now?" he asked. "You're not going to talk to that lady, hah?"

"No," I told him.

"She's crazy," he told me. "Sick in the head. You stay away from her. Understand?"

I nodded. Carlo let go of my wrist.

I should have asked someone for protection, something to make the bad things stay away. That's what I thought as I walked down to St. Nicholas Avenue, my heart growing bigger and bigger as I neared the bar. It was very hot, and I kept bumping into people on the street when I tried to get south. Traffic moved slow around all the double parked cars, horns honking and music coming from the store with all the eight-track tapes in the window.

When I first stepped into the Dos Puertas, it was dark and cool and quiet. Yellow shapes swam before my eyes and I couldn't see. An oakey beer smell filled the air.

A man's voice asked, "What do you want, boy?"

A breathy voice said, "That's not a boy. That's a little girl."

Ever since I'd gotten my shag haircut, people kept thinking I was a boy.

"Are you Marilyn Monroe?" I asked the breathy voice.

My eyes adjusted. The yellow bars floated away. I saw her sitting there at one of the tables, smoking a cigarette. She was still wearing her dark glasses, just like I heard movie stars did. She didn't have to answer my question. I knew it was her.

"What do you want?" the bartender asked, polishing glasses.

"Shirley Temple," I told him, walking to the center table where Marilyn Monroe sat. We were the only people in the bar. I put my hands on the back of one of the empty chairs and waited for the bartender to get me my drink, but when I looked up at him, he just continued to wipe the glasses and grin, like he knew something I wasn't ever going to know.

"One of yours?" the bartender asked Marilyn Monroe.

"What an awful thing to say," she told the bartender, her voice thin and flat now.

The bartender nodded and grinned even wider while he held a glass to the light.

"It's time to go," he told me. He had a quiet voice with a hint of threat in it. The quieter he got, the more trouble you were in. I knew this because my Uncle Carlo was the same way.

"Let's go," Marilyn Monroe said, stubbing out her cigarette and gathering her things up.

" 'Ey!" the bartender shouted, putting the glass and towel on the bar.

She gave him a curt smile and shimmied out the swinging doors backwards, motioning for me to follow.

Out on street, she stood completely still in the crowd, as if she didn't know where to go. People moved around us as if we were lampposts that had suddenly sprung from the ground. "What are we doing?" I asked Marilyn Monroe.

"Tell me where you live," she said.

"I can't go there now," I pleaded. "I need to talk to you. That's why I came to the bar."

She moved a piece of foamy, frothy hair that kept falling in her eyes, as if by stroking it, she would learn the answer of what to do. Then she started to walk again, with purpose.

"Where are we going?" I asked.

"To my apartment," she said.

"Where's zat?"

Still marching ahead, not even turning to me, she answered, "Haven Avenue."

Marilyn Monroe had posters of herself all over her apartment. They were curling against the wall from the humidity, pockmarked and torn at the corners from being hung with tacks.

Marilyn Monroe said, "I'll be back," when we arrived at her house. Then she disappeared into a room behind a door that had grown fatter than its frame from repeated coats of paint. I sat on the windowsill above the fire escape and watched the boats move slowly down the wide, black Hudson River. I could hear the water running in the bathroom, and the click of a bottle being put on a sink. When Marilyn Monroe came into the dusty, empty living room, her face was caked heavily with makeup, but it didn't cover the purple bruise near her eye.

She leaned to take a box of blue-tipped matches off the coffee table, then struck one to light her cigarette. Blowing a stream of smoke in the air, while I straddled the windowsill and watched, she asked, "Will your parents worry if you're not home?"

I shrugged and told her, "They work."

"My mother worked," Marilyn Monroe said, plopping down on the couch and tipping her cigarette ash into a kidney-shaped ashtray flecked in orange and gold. "She worked two jobs once to try and get us a house."

"Are you really Marilyn Monroe?" I asked her.

"What do you think?" she asked me, smiling her sad smile.

She was supposed to be dead, of course. But grown-ups were wrong about many things, didn't want you to believe in anything, were always talking about how hard a place the world was and how, when you grew, you would learn the same. Maria was exactly a little grown up, always telling me I should learn things weren't as good or magic as I thought. Maybe I would be able to prove them all wrong. Or maybe, as Uncle Carlo said, she was a crazy lady.

I told Marilyn Monroe, "I don't know."

She answered, "I don't either."

I swallowed. Maybe what she meant was, she was really Norma Jeane. I hoped that was what she meant. I hoped she wasn't crazy.

I asked, "What happened to your eye?"

"I'm going to have to leave," she answered, absently straightening an afghan that hung on the back of the couch.

"You mean leave for good?" I asked.

"What's your name?" she asked, sweetly.

I told her.

"Laura," she said, saying it the Anglo way and nodding with approval. "I have to go very soon. You can come with me while I pack my things up."

"How come you have to go?" I asked, following after her fast as she went into the bedroom. It was a mess, looked the way mine did when my mother used to yell at me to clean it. The bed was all rumpled. There were piles of clothes here and there, beaded sweaters balled in a chair, slinky skirts in heaps on the floor. Marilyn began to sort the clothes.

"I saw a book on you," I told her.

"Which?" she asked, stopping as she leaned with a skirt in her hand.

"The big one. The one that just came out."

Her expression tightened. Her eyes grew hot. "That one," she said. Her voice came out a little huskier.

"Don't you like it?" I asked.

"I can't stand that man," she told me.

"Who?" I asked. "The guy who wrote it?"

"Have you read anything else of his?" she asked, shaking her head. She held up a blouse then. "I have too many like these," she said. "Do you want it?"

It was a white silky thing, with a nipped-in waist. I would never have chosen anything like it. But Marilyn Monroe was offering it to me. I told her, "Thank you."

She stared at me for a second. "You have nice eyes," she told me. I said, "Thank you."

"And if you used makeup," she said, taking out her compact and putting powder on my face, "you could look very pretty."

I didn't like wearing makeup. It made my face itch and I didn't like the smell. But when Marilyn Monroe patted my face with the powder puff, made me pull my lips back so she could slick lipstick on and then told me to kiss a tissue, I felt like she was painting on love.

"We have to do so much to be pretty," she sighed, icing my eyelids with white shadow. She told me, "Look."

I saw myself in the mirror. I wasn't pretty. The corners of my mouth turned down and I thought I would cry.

"You *are* pretty," Marilyn Monroe told me. "But a girl can't always see it."

She pulled me close to her and gave me a hug. I smelled her perfume, her makeup.

When she let me go, she told me, "I'm going to get a drink."

I looked at the clothes and things on her dresser while she was gone. There were lacy slips and lipstick tubes, compacts and slinky skirts, stained blouses and, everywhere, books. There were stacks of books by the bed, old and leather bound, paperbound and dog-eared; *The Brothers Karamazov* and *Down These Mean Streets, Letters to a Young Poet* and *I Know Why the Caged Bird Sings*. She came back in carrying a glass of champagne and a glass of Coke, handed me the Coke. "What did you want to ask me?" she wanted to know.

"How come you sang 'Happy Birthday' to the president?" I asked, after searching in my mind for questions I'd had but coming up blank.

"To Jack?" Marilyn Monroe asked, sitting on the floor and sipping champagne. "It was his birthday," she laughed. "He was my friend."

"How come if you were having an affair, you didn't just sing to him at home?"

"We were just friends by then," she said. And suddenly, her face got very sad and she looked away. "What songs do you sing?" she asked.

I sang "Philadelphia Freedom" for her, and she told me I had a nice voice. Then she sang a song for me that was from a movie she made, something about diamonds and friends. And then she was all packed up. She tripped a little on her heels.

"It's time to go," she told me, when she had her suitcase in hand, her sunglasses on, and a scarf tied under her chin.

"Where will you go?" I asked.

"The next place," she told me.

"But you haven't seen Silvia yet," I said.

I explained who Silvia was, how she had been afraid of Marilyn Monroe, but wasn't anymore. Marilyn Monroe looked outside, to the sun that would soon dip down and melt into New Jersey's chemical plants. "Please," I begged. "Will you come to my house with me?"

She agreed that, if I ran on ahead and got Silvia to come on downstairs, she would stop on her way to the subway and meet Silvia.

I didn't tell Silvia what I wanted her to come downstairs for. She came though, and then Maria was on her way back from the park and was there too when Marilyn Monroe walked up the street, shifting her heavy suitcase from hand to hand. She knelt down before Silvia and asked her, "Are you Laura's friend?"

Silvia nodded.

Carlo came up behind us, and hollered, "I told you that lady is crazy. Stay away!"

Silvia's lower lip quivered.

Marilyn Monroe glared at Carlo, then told Silvia, "There's nothing to be afraid of."

She rustled Silvia's hair, then rose. Carlo stood with his arms folded as if waiting for her to go. I thought I heard him say, under his breath, that she was a rotten *putona,* but I never saw his lips move. I thought Marilyn Monroe heard him too and was pretending she hadn't. She put her sunglasses back on, picked up her bags, and walked away. Without saying a word, Maria and Silvia and I walked after her to the subway. As she passed the groups of men along the street, they hooted approvingly or hollered meanly. I was a little afraid and a little sad and when I looked at Maria and Silvia I could see they were too. Even Maria showed it.

The men screamed: Princess! Mama! *Putona!*

Marilyn Monroe whirled around and told us, "You don't have to follow me, you know."

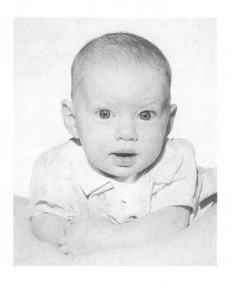

AFTERWORD

Like the narrator of my story, I grew up in North Manhattan during the 1970s and first heard of Marilyn Monroe as a result of the tremendous hype surrounding Norman Mailer's biography. I didn't understand why so many grown-ups were fascinated by her. My impression of Mailer's book, though I wouldn't have been able to articulate it this way then, was that he was a dirty old man who viewed Marilyn Monroe as an inflatable doll with a troubled past. The text of the book made me queasy, and most of the photographs left me unmoved.

It was only as an adult, viewing Mailer's book again for the first time in twenty years, that I looked closely at Marilyn's face in the photos and saw how often her expression didn't match her pose. Gloria Steinem's book, which I read to research this story, brought Marilyn out of the realm of icons for me, and made me see her as one of many women alive in the 1950s, trying to do the best she could with the limited number of roles (in life) she was taught were possible. I think that all women, thirty-five years after Marilyn's death, in some way touch the boundaries that constrained her. I once might have said Marilyn

Monroe embodied the status quo, but Steinem's book made me see the ways she also tried to subvert it. I came away from reading it with a feeling of kinship and affection for Marilyn, as well as a tremendous amount of respect.

—Linda Mannheim

THE CHILD STAR

BY MELISSA MIA HALL

 "NOVEMBER 22 IS just another day to me. For my grandmother it would've meant death if she hadn't already been murdered. I know, that's not fair. Nobody will say my grandmother was killed, I mean, nobody knows she was a mother. Like it didn't matter.

"I could say that I'm her reincarnation or that her spirit speaks through me. Yeah, I'm channeling Marilyn. Right. Jesus. Him, too. I don't know. But—just look at me. Don't I look just like her? I'm going to be a movie star. Right? Yeah, like everyone will love me and stuff and I'll stop doing it for food. Sure. Why the hell not? Things happen. Ha—"

The girl swallows a big gulp of air. If she'd been out in the unseasonal rain outside Hugo's on Santa Monica, she'd be a drowned bird. As it is, she does smell like wet feathers. He knows it is probably just some weird cologne, meant to conjure passion and instead manufactures sick obsession. Wet feathers and muck. Grope me—jump me, but why don't you take a bath first. Jeremy stares at his tape recorder. He lifts his fifth cup of coffee to his lips. Dark Kenyan beans. His teeth are almost chattering. He swallows.

"It's a death thing, a death wish, not just blonde ambition, whatever that means. It's not about cone bras or diamond rings in my twat or in my nose. It's about being beautiful, so beautiful no one can see you. It's about disappearing into somebody's Barbie doll fantasy. I mean, what's really wrong with that. I saw a talk show where this nut had herself made over into Barbie's image. But was she a nut if that made her happy? What do you think? You're the smart guy, right?"

She touches her very short, very platinum blonde hair. She looks at her Miracle bra uplift and scratches the mole which or may or may not be painted on. She does look like the Mmm-mm girl, a very young and very desperate Norma Jeane, an almost-Marilyn, doing tricks for a meal, but discreetly and with a wild horses-have-to-do-it trembling smile and a small, nervous laugh.

He shuts his eyes for a second, the dimple in his left cheek appearing as his mouth spreads into one of his irresistible smiles. He knows it's that way. He's had a way with females since he sucked his mother's breast for the first time. Will he suck this thing's breasts? Only a C cup. They're not as big as Marilyn's were, he's sure of that.

"Is it still on? Is it working?"

The smile slips away. His eyes are wide open and checking the quiet tape recorder. "Yes, go ahead. It's still on."

"Are you sure? This is an exclusive. I've never told anyone. I'm giving you the God's honest truth. My dad would kill me if he found out. He has never gotten over it all."

"Your father."

"Yeah, Marilyn was his mom."

"You're absolutely sure of this?"

"Sure." She looks so vulnerable. He remembers a fifties photo of Norma Jeane-cum-Marilyn as a cornfed, glam-cum-farmer girl. A smile streaks across her features like a comet, then her eyelids drop in a seductive pose. Her shoulders lift defensively. "You believe me, I know you do."

"So how come your dad has never come forward?"

"It was a secret, stupid." Her lips are too red, too glossy. She has never touched her coffee but she has finished her very large mushroom omelet and two glasses of water and a glass of orange juice. Now she plays with her napkin, twisting it into interesting shapes. "You don't tell secrets."

"Why are you?"

"Oh, it wasn't a secret to me. I always knew. Dad just didn't want anyone else to know. It was so—embarrassing."

His neck is stiff. He needs three Extra-Strength Tylenols or something a lot more powerful. He watches an over-the-hill rock star stumble in, accompanied by a pouting has-been supermodel and two exhausted hangers-on. They seem disappointed that no one appreciates the allure of their questionable star qualities. A waiter greets them cordially and leads them to a distant table.

Jeremy wishes he hadn't picked this girl off the street. He wishes he'd interviewed the African American hooker with the great legs. He just needed one more interview to finish his article on LA hookers "post Earthquake/post fire," and there she was, looking so young and true, reminiscent of all those fantasy Hollywood blondes.

"I'll do anything you say for one hour—if you'll just feed me." That's what she'd said when he requested an interview, standing on the street, in front of Frederick's of Hollywood, of all places. Jeremy had sensed an air of off-kilter oddness about her even then. It had turned him on, in fact.

She'd motioned toward the Musso and Frank Grill. Jeremy had just shook his head, leering slightly at her breathlessly short skirt, tartan pleats flying. "Let's go to my neighborhood."

When they got closer and closer to West Hollywood. "You gay?" she'd said, looking a little faint. What had she gotten herself into? Jeremy could not help laughing. "You scared? Gay men are not boogey men."

"But a lot of them are sick. Not sick in the head, you know, but sick. Are you sick?"

"I don't have AIDS, if that's what you mean." Jeremy was taking her to Hugo's for a late breakfast. She'd looked so hungry.

There you were. "And I'm not gay. I'm hopelessly sad and vaguely heterosexual. I don't want sex with you. I want words."

"Well, you know I never do it for just money. Just when I'm hungry. I have standards," she had said.

There you are and here they are, still at Hugo's. Jeremy remembers Marilyn had done the same thing. She had to eat and she didn't have enough money half the time. Jeremy's stiff neck grew some frozen hairs. What had he gotten himself into?

She opens her pretty mouth and her soft voice gets lower. "You know, I could've sold my story to *Hard Copy* and made a mint. But you just looked so right. I could tell you weren't a John. You know, we could go to your place. You could take care of me, for awhile. You're not married, right? You're not with someone, are you? I bet you know people. Producers and stuff. Am I right? You're in show business. Are you really a screenwriter, looking for a story? I'll be your story. You'd like that, I bet."

He feels her leg touch his.

"How old are you?"

"Young. But old enough."

Jeremy is thirty-five. He is old enough to know better. And young enough not to give a damn. Suddenly he finds he does. He's been trying to make it, really, really make it, as a writer out here in LA all of his life. A string of dead-end writing jobs had led him to try journalism. But he has never given up on writing that one spec script that would land him out in the writing ozone—the BIG LEAGUES, where you could curse Oliver Stone, and make fun of Joe Esterhas, Jeffrey Katzenberg and Mike Ovitz, chew the fat with Steven Spielberg and date Barbra Streisand. Oh God. This is it.

He can smell it.

He can also tell there's a slightly sour note underneath her cologne. Or is that his own smell? A panicky sweat dampens his shirt. *I'm melting. Get me out of here. It's not worth it. I can write commercials. I can write travel brochures. My computer is crashing. I'm crashing.*

But the movie'll be great. He can see it—the car swerves on the wet LA streets. She whimpers incoherently, trying to hold on to the door handle. Suddenly the car hits a Miata at a busy intersection. Her door isn't locked and in her excitement, she opens it and falls out like a doll. She hangs for a second, then flies out into the street.

Our hero regains control of the car, but maybe it's too late for the young hooker who looks like a young dead movie star—Jeremy, you've gotten yourself into a helluva situation here. She's just a kid with a lot of makeup on. You don't want to do this. But what is he doing? Making money. Making ideas work. Sell your ideas, they're worth something.

The rain has stopped. He surveys the steam rising. The pavement seems to shimmer and dance with gold coins and pieces of silver. Paul Simon's old song "Diamonds on the Soles of Her Shoes" pierces the air. The aging model, all of maybe twenty-seven, has brought her portable CD player. The waiter says something that makes her turn it off abruptly. Jeremy finishes his coffee while the girl waits. Their eyes are on each other alone. Anyone watching them would think they are lovers or soon will be.

A sharply dressed woman passes their table. She waves at her waiting client or friend; in this town you can never tell.

"I'll need proof."

He'll have to do research. *Does that mean I have to get into your pants? Is she wearing panties?*

"Where do you live? And—what did you say your name was?" Some journalist. He had a degree in film, not newspapers. His hands sweat. He wipes his palms and waits.

She has power. For Jeremy, all women have power. Power to take over, organize, reorganize, his life too many times. He's been celibate for over a year or more since his last girlfriend, Susan P., refused to use birth control. He doesn't want children in his life right now. It's not like they don't have their place. It's just that he doesn't want them in his place. At least, not yet.

"That's a secret and I didn't tell you my name because you never asked."

"So I'm asking."

"Let's go to your place."

Jeremy now wipes the back of his neck where unfrozen hairs drip rivulets of water. She is no longer a slightly overweight Kate Moss with dyed blonde hair. Now she is the spitting image of a dead actress the entire universe still dreams about and gossips about as if she were still alive. Her sexuality is more brazen than Madonna's and more vulnerable than Cindy Crawford's. And it's right in front of him like a platter of rich desserts. Take a bite.

"Please."

He nods and, wordlessly, they leave the restaurant. The sun struggles through clouds and smog. His dusty Honda suddenly looks like a Porsche, a golden chariot taking them to Paradise.

"I just moved in," he says as they go into his condo. The security system is on the fritz. She fingers the blank screen. "Cool," she whispers.

The only real furniture is the complex entertainment system he had installed the week before with the money he made from writing a few episodes of a forgettable morning TV show.

She plops on the pillows he uses for chairs.

"I'm having a sofa custom-made in Brentwood."

"Do you ever watch *Melrose Place*?" She stares at the huge blank TV screen. "I really love Heather Locklear."

"No," he lies. Her legs are wide open. She's not wearing panties. Ever since Sharon Stone did that he's found it a sign of immaturity. It's not a turn-on. He heads to the bathroom. He runs cold water. His hands keeps splashing water on his cheeks. His nose drips. He wipes his face with a hundred percent cotton towel. She won't go away. He asked for this. He wants this. And he has condoms, plenty of condoms, stashed away for the proverbial rainy day. His hands shake as he selects one from the shelf.

He goes outside and sees that she is stark naked. Her breasts are so white. Her whole body is white. Not a hair on her except down there. He says "Down there" aloud.

"Grandmother liked to be naked. It's the way God intended us to be. I want to walk naked down the street. I want to be free. Why don't you take your clothes off and let's talk some more."

He is afraid to do that. He keeps waiting for a pounding on the door. The police. The next door neighbor. A TV crew from some news show. Barbara Walters or David Letterman. Somebody. Can't look at her. He looks at the bulge in his pants getting bigger. The embarrassment is outweighed by his excitement.

"You can't be too careful these days," he says feebly. "I like to get to know someone before I have sex with them. I don't do prostitutes." *So what is this girl, Jeremy? Research. Sure.*

She covers her breasts with the corner of a pillow and straddles another, as if she's at home. "I'm not a prostitute. They thought my grannie was, but she wasn't either. I think you believe me. You look like you believe me. But you also look like you think I might be crazy."

Her buttocks are sweetly curving and tempting to contemplate. Jeremy goes to the coat closet and pulls out a raincoat. "Cover yourself, please," he says, politely. Manners are important, that's what his mother always told him. She would not approve of young women lolling about naked on his floor pillows. They belong in his bed. He smiles. *She doesn't have any wrinkles. Guess she uses sunblock or she's just too young.*

They could go upstairs. They could throw caution to the wind. A wind's kicking up again. He opens a window and lets it in.

"Why don't you tell me your name or your father's name?"

"Some things are better not shared."

"How much do you want?" He sits beside her. "I'm sick of this shit. Either tell the truth or get out of here." His hand grips her thin soft arm a little too tightly. She has simply draped the khaki raincoat around her shoulders like a stiff shawl. He looks at her and wants her. He decides to fish around for the condom he's hiding in his trouser pockets. Just in case. It is painful.

"She was right. About men and stuff. I've read everything I could about her. Daddy didn't know. I did it in secret. It wasn't her fault, you know. She was just a kid. It's not in any of the books, though. They just hint about it, here and there. But none of them knew what really happened.

"A living hell. Do you know what a living hell is? She was just a little girl." She lifts her shoulders again in that gesture that Jeremy found so seductive, so Marilyn. Despite his best efforts, his left hand reaches out and cups one of the free breasts. His mouth trembles.

"Go on," he says, his other hand reaching down to fondle a place lower down. "Keep talking."

Her eyes seem moist like a Disney cartoon character. Bambi lost in the woods. She opens her arms and the raincoat falls off.

The wind enters the room again, hitting the blank TV screen and toppling a pile of CDs. "I've been there, in a living hell. Daddy says I was born there and the way I figured it, I was just walking in my grandmother's footsteps.

"But I didn't have a baby. Dad said I can't get pregnant if I don't have periods. You know, if you have a baby when you're almost a baby yourself, it can do something to your female parts. I wonder if that's why she could never have a baby again. That bitch made her give the baby up. She didn't want to. Daddy never got over it. You know it's not good when you're not wanted. Daddy says he was wanted, by some good county people. But Norma Jeane was not wanted. Not really. You don't have to do research to figure that out."

He unzips his pants. His clothes fall like rain. She says nothing while he kisses her. He is not supposed to do this. He knows better.

It just feels so good. He feels huge, defiantly masculine. She grows smaller and smaller in his hands. She screams.

He rolls off of her. Minutes roll by and the wind moans.

Blood on the pillows. She was a virgin, a fucking virgin. It had been hard getting in. And he forgot the damn condom. Jeremy stands shakily. "Do you want something?"

She looks like she's dead. Jeremy sees the discarded tape recorder on the floor. What is her name? *He's blown the interview. The driver's door has been blown, as well. Jeremy, our hero, is now the villain. He flies out into the street and is run over by a champagne-colored Porsche. He is dead.*

It's a secret.

"Hey, are you okay?" She's ruined his floor pillow. "How old did you say you are?" She has to be at least eighteen. Maybe seventeen. He chews his lower lip. She suddenly looks like a child. He remembers Jodie Foster in that old Scorsese film. The one with De Niro. "Are you talking to me?" That one. Such a good little actress. "What's your name?"

Her eyes are shut. Her breasts look deflated. A B cup? Her makeup is smeared. The red lips are gone. Pale pink lips part. "Norma, just Norma."

"Stop dissing me."

"What's that mean? Is dissing like pissing?" Her eyes are wide open, mascara smeared and red. She has been crying soundlessly, like a silent movie child star. Not Shirley Temple, but a Gish girl, made up to look younger than she is. Or maybe Mary Pickford? No, Jodie Foster. Not Marilyn. And yet, Marilyn. He believes she is the real thing. She is Marilyn/Norma Jeane's granddaughter.

"Do you think you got me pregnant? My period's not regular yet."

Jeremy wants to commit suicide. "How old are you, Norma?"

"Almost twelve."

Nausea rushes him to the bathroom where he vomits copiously. Mostly coffee. And sin. Original or venial, he's not quite sure since he hasn't studied catechism since elementary school in Philadelphia. It wasn't his fault. She tricked him. Listerine takes care of the sour taste. He returns to the girl. She has dressed herself. "I'm sorry about the pillow," she says.

Jeremy thinks about calling the police, turning himself in. He thinks about going to Brazil or France. What if her father is some movie mogul? What if he's a policeman? He thinks about Woody Allen.

He thinks about dying.

"Should I call your father?"

"That's how old my grandmother was when she was raped."

"I didn't rape you!" Jeremy babbles. He says something else softly, something he can hardly register himself. "You raped me—" *Very feeble excuses don't film well. Our hero spins around, flailing his underdeveloped arms. They are distinctly flabby.*

"I want to be pregnant. I want a baby. I want someone who will love me. You think, well, your mom and dad, see, they are supposed to do that. They don't just give you away and all. They keep you. My dad was forced from his mama's arms and I've been forced from his, see?"

Jeremy doesn't see. His head spins around and connects with the corner of his entertainment center. He falls to the floor and stares up at the ceiling. The cracks are never-ending. He wants her to leave, just leave and never come back. *Please roll the end credits.*

"I'll be your baby."

Jeremy can't scream, he can't afford it. He sees her for the first time, really sees her.

"What do you think it does to a kid to have a kid? You're not going to make me leave, are you? Will you let me stay, will you, please?" Her eyes are dark, pleading. Her small frame shakes. "My father is dead. He had a heart attack and I don't have any place to go to. Our landlord says I owe them three months back rent. Dad said you can't get blood out of a turnip. All I know, I can't go back there. This way they don't know where I am and who's to care? They don't care. I'm sure they've taken our stuff, what we had, anyway. We didn't have any money. Do you know what it's like to not have any money? I'm so hungry all the time.

"Daddy always said I look just like her but he didn't want me acting like her. Am I acting like her? It's all I got. I look older than I am. I started growing breasts at eight. I can't help it."

She keeps leaning over him. Jeremy is afraid. He is more afraid than he has ever been in his entire life.

"Will you take care of me?"

This is his spec script. This is his ticket out. *I'm sorry but this isn't right for us. It will never play in Cincinnati or in Amarillo. Who cares what they're watching in those places? It's Seattle, right, that counts, or maybe San Diego?*

"I'm good at acting. I know I could be a star. You could help me. Will you take care of me? If I am pregnant, may I keep it? I'll let you name it if it's a boy, but if it's a girl, can we name it after her?"

"Norma or Marilyn?" Jeremy says slowly.

"No, Jean, after Jean Harlow. Grandmother would think I look like her. You know, a girl's looks are her fortune. That's what Daddy used to say."

A sin. A sinner. Jeremy begins to pray silently for deliverance. He hasn't prayed since he was twelve. What was that like, being twelve, almost grown with almost grown thoughts and childish fears? *I want my cup with blue stars—wasn't that in* The Haunting, *a horror movie his mother used to love? Julie Harris and Claire Bloom. He'd hated that movie. But he'd watched it over and over, morbidly curious and tantalized by the silvery images. He'd even read the Jackson book once. Because of that cup with blue stars. Or something like that. And the dread and foreboding of predestined calamity.*

The heart wants what it wants and then some. He thought she was so much older. The shame pushes him up to his haunches. He sits like a dog, panting. The child star has gone to the kitchen to rattle pans and search for food in his almost empty larder.

He could adopt her.

AFTERWORD

I was a little girl at the time of Marilyn's death. Marilyn was my Barbie doll with the platinum bubble hairdo. Her crazy breathy voice made me laugh. I remember being surprised when I found out she was dead—what was it—ten years later. In researching her life for this story, I focused on her childhood and adolescence. I became convinced she was molested, perhaps on multiple occasions. Her early life was a nightmare. Marilyn is a poster child for all the children who fall through the cracks.

Marilyn told friends she had a baby once that her "guardian" had forced her to give up. So much was stolen from this child/girl, I believe it could very well have happened. At the least, Marilyn's childhood innocence was taken from her.

Whether she was murdered, committed suicide, or was the victim of a medical rescue gone awry, Marilyn Monroe/Norma Jeane remains a symbol of all that is wrong with the way we treat beautiful people. As she struggled to be defined as an adult artist, Marilyn also struggled to find satisfying relationships, but was caught in the web created by early childhood traumas.

She was a Goddess. We demanded for her to be a Goddess, or, at the least, the persona of my bubble-haired Barbie. She just wanted to be loved for herself.

—Melissa Mia Hall

THE COST OF FREEDOM

BY PETER CROWTHER

*arilyn Monroe in her little spike
heels reeling through Niagra Falls*

From "To the Film Industry in Crisis"
by Frank O'Hara (1926–66)

One

THE DARKNESS SWALLOWED the change without him noticing it, replacing the lonely, winking towers and the frustrated howl of police cars and ambulances hunting the streets in feral packs with one- and two-storey housing developments and the constant drone of a stream of top-forty music on the Chevy's radio. The inside of the car was like a hospital operating theater, a sterilized area that somehow existed outside of the mainstream reality. For Docherty, that reality was a long stretch of road, a sentence of Kerouac-like proportions punctuated only by occasional information signs, lit up by the oncoming headlights like exclamation marks.

Docherty shifted in his seat and shook a cigarette out of the packet on the dash. He licked the end once and then slid it into the corner of his mouth, considering not lighting it but just driving on into the oncoming lights while he chewed on the filter. Maybe that would have the same effect as the nicotine. Then again, maybe not. He decided not to try and pushed in the lighter beside the radio fascia.

As Steely Dan's "Reeling In the Years" faded, the lighter clicked out. Docherty removed it and held it against the Chesterfield, pulling on the smoke. In a deep voice that hinted of the Plains, the DJ told him the time and bemoaned the loss of all the great bands. "Ah, Walter Becker and Donald Fagen . . . what did you *do*?" He finished off, drawing out the last word like a stretch of taffy and blowing out his own smoke into the solitude of his studio. "That was the great Steely Dan "Reeling In the Years," brought to you people of the night by Station WVLK. I'm Johnny-Ray Di Phillipo . . . and you're not."

The mournful wail of Neil Young's harmonica intro to The Stills Young Band's "Long May You Run" cut through the darkness. "This is for all you people who're on the move this September night," Johnny-Ray moaned. "It's a lonely world but we can hack it together. All we gotta do is *keep* moving."

Docherty blew smoke at the windshield and watched it hug the glass in stringy wisps.

Neil Young sang about trunks of memories.

Docherty glanced to the seat beside him, taking in the sloppily-wrapped brown paper packages, one large and flat, covering the whole seat, and another smaller one lying on top of it. A glimpse of white material fluffed at one of the bigger package's corners, where the paper had not quite overlapped. He looked in the rearview mirror and saw the box on the back seat, and the jumble of clothes lying inside it like a bunch of colored clouds. It looked like a thrift store donation.

Trunks of memories.

He looked back at the road, his mind drifting back to another September while the headlights of the oncoming cars washed across his blank expression.

He is six going on seven years old, listening for the first time to a story from his mother. Over the years, she will tell this story many times, each time embellishing it with a little more pizzazz, a little more decoration. But though the story will change slightly around the edges over time, the center will always remain the same. That's the beauty of a good story, she will tell him many years later.

The story starts off in a magic kingdom, she says. Like Oz, he supposes, from the movie. He loves movies, loves the make-believe . . . though his mom will only let him watch certain movies. But this isn't a happy magic kingdom. It's more like a prison.

A prison? Like in the movies, with George Raft and Humpy Bogart and James Cagney? he asks. She laughs and says kind of, telling him it's Humphrey, not Humpy. He nods and says the word—*Humph*rey—quietly to himself and then settles back next to her on the sofa and listens.

In this magic kingdom, she tells him, there are many magic people. These people are magic because they create fantasies—like fairy stories, she adds—for all the other people.

She stops and takes a sip of her drink. His mom always has a drink by her side. She continues.

But of all the magic people, there is one who is the most magic of them all. A princess.

A princess? he says. Like a queen?

Something like that, she answers, and tousles his hair. He responds, moving his head against her hand like a cat wanting to be stroked. She tucks her legs up on the sofa and pats her lap. He lays out along the sofa and rests his head in her lap. His mother takes thick folds of his hair and wraps them around her fingers, tugging gently and smoothing it out. He feels sleepy and warm and safe.

His mom's voice lilts and drifts as she continues the story, picking her words real careful.

The princess is unhappy, his mother tells him, always crying. She's lonely even though she's always surrounded by lots of people.

This doesn't make much sense to him and he tells her, the words tumbling out over his chin and into her lap, like warm soup he can't hold in his mouth.

She tells him it's always loneliest in a crowd. The princess wants her prince but he can't come to her.

Why not? he asks.

Because the prince is a very famous man—the most famous man in the whole land—and, worst of all, he already has a wife.

Oh, he thinks, his mouth forming the word silently.

This princess was very, very famous. But her fame made her unhappy and lonely. Her unhappiness made her look for company: first she looked to a great athlete to make her happy; and then she looked to a great storyteller. But, though each of them made her forget her troubles for a while, they couldn't make her truly happy. And then she met the prince.

Slipping slowly toward sleep, he thinks of a man in shining armour. The man looks like Robert Taylor—who, his mom once told him, she had met once upon a time—and he carries a white shield with an eagle on it.

The prince and the princess fall very much in love.

His mother's voice takes him closer to sleep.

And because he is so very, very powerful, this prince, he works out a plan to make the princess happy. The plan involves making all the people in the magic kingdom think that the princess has died.

He opens his eyes. He doesn't like the sound of this part. He asks his mom if this is a happy story or a sad story. She says for him to wait and see.

He keeps listening with his eyes open for a while.

Well, she continues, the prince has a friend called Billy who looks after law and order in the land where the magic kingdom sits. And one day he and his helpers find a lady who has died. This lady is the down-and-out spitting image of the princess, she says.

Wow!

Yes, and so the prince's friend Billy takes the dead lady to the princess's house in the magic kingdom and makes pretend that she's the princess.

All of the kingdom is sad when they hear that the princess is dead. But, of course, she isn't dead, is she?

No, he answers sleepily.

And the prince, well, he sneaks the princess away from the magic kingdom to a faraway place where she can be happy. But she tells him she can only be happy if he comes with her.

Where is the faraway place? he asks.

Oh, it's a—she hesitates—a farm. A hidden farm.

Like with geese and cattle and stuff?

His mother laughs. No, not a farm like that, she says, taking another sip of her drink. This farm is big—not really a farm at all; more like a mansion—and covers many, many acres. In his mind's eye he sees The Ponderosa, from the *Bonanza* television show.

Anyway, she continues, still twisting his hair in her hand, the princess begs the prince to come and join her. But he can't, although he does give her a present.

Yeah? What kind of present?

Oh, the most wonderful present she could ever have, she says, her voice going all drifty and soft. He gives her a baby.

He frowns. Where does he get the baby from?

He doesn't get it from anywhere, she says. He makes it, makes it in the princess's tummy.

Oh.

And then . . . His mother's voice starts to falter. And then a terrible thing happens. A bad man—a *very* bad man—comes along. One day, when the prince is visiting with the people, the bad man climbs to a high building and he shoots the prince.

Does he kill him?

Yes, yes, he kills him.

Why?

He hears her take another drink. Nobody ever finds out why, she says, because another man—a man who loved the prince very much—takes the law of the land into his own hands and shoots the bad man.

Dead?

He feels her nod. Dead.

Dead. The word washed around his head as a truck's horn sounded beside him, dopplering from and back into the distances that stretched out on the highway in front and behind the Chevy.

A rest area sign came up. He indicated and moved into the exit lane.

Two

The girl had a hell of an overbite but was otherwise pretty. She sashayed along the aisle to Docherty's table, gave him a toothy smile and handed over plastic, wipe-clean menu. "Hi," was all she said.

"Hi, yourself." Docherty managed around a handful of nuts from the small tub on the table.

"What can I get you? Coffee or a beer?"

He glanced at the menu. Burger seemed to be the specialty of the house. The only way they didn't seem to serve it was raw, but he figured they'd do it if he asked for it. "I'll have . . ." He ran his eyes down each side. "Give me a coffee—black—and—" He checked the sandwiches listing. "And a schlemiel"—*Eat it—you'll feel like one!* the menu boasted—"but hold the dressing."

"It'll be dry, sir," the girl said, raising her eyebrows in an *are-you-really-sure-you-wanna-do-this?* expression.

He held out the menu. "That's okay. I'm as wet as I need to be."

The eyebrows did a double-take before the girl, looking just a little flustered, accepted the menu back and told him that was no problem. He nodded and watched her walk away from him to the swing doors at the end of the bar. He looked around at the other "people of the night." There were seven apart from him. And the girl. And whoever was in the back putting together his sandwich— sliced turkey, salami and swiss cheese on pumpernickel.

Out in the parking area there were three cars and a small truck—an eight-wheeler—all with Connecticut plates. As he stared into the darkness, the girl brought him a cup of coffee and a small, metal bowl of chopped salad in sweet vinegar, then laid out napkin, knife, and fork by his clasped hands. He watched her reflection in the window, walking away from him into the ghost of a diner backroom.

He pulled out a cigarette and tapped it on the table, slid it into his mouth and lit it. The smoke tasted and felt good. It even looked good, rolling against the window and the distant two-way call of the highway. It was as though it fell in between distances, forming a barrier . . . a cushion against what was now and what was to come. Something familiar amidst the strangeness. Something that he could recognize and depend on.

Docherty stared into the night and remembered.

He didn't remember when he had first learned who his mother really was. Nor his father, for that matter. It was like he had always known it. Like race memory.

On Sunday, August 5, 1962, his mom had told him, piecing to-gether fragments of memory over the years so that it made an almost-sensible full cloth, two cops had made a left out of Glendon

Avenue into Wilshire Boulevard. It was a little after two in the morning, the time that people were closest to death and you could hear the graveyards whispering in the wind.

On the sidewalk a little way up the street, lying spread-eagled on her back, was a woman. She was talking to the moon and coughing up blood, his mother told him, much, much later. Then she had smiled and taken a sip of coffee before adding, I've done that, too.

She told him that the cops who had found the woman almost rang it in that it was her, but the woman was talking in Spanish so they guessed it wasn't. By the time the ambulance arrived, the woman was probably dead, but they loaded her inside anyway and took her downtown. LAPD Chief William Parker had called up Docherty's father to say that the impossible had happened. They had found a ringer. But they had to move tonight.

Within two hours it was all done.

At the instruction of Twentieth Century–Fox publicists Frank Neill, John Campbell, and Arthur Jacobs, his mom made calls, enigmatic calls, to several friends and acquaintances. None of them took the calls seriously. But then they hadn't expected them to. It was like groundwork, recollections that people could dredge up the following day amidst guilt and hangovers.

Then she had been bundled out into a limousine while two of Billy Parker's men brought the dead woman up to his mom's room. Billy later destroyed all the police documents on her death except for a thick bundle of heavily censored papers which he eventually released in the 1970s.

What followed had been a nightmare, she told him, even though she had not been directly involved. Does *he* know? she would ask, when she read statements in the daily papers. Does *she* know? But it got so that nobody knew who did know, so everyone kept quiet. She was dead, and that was all there was to it.

Florabel Muir, crime reporter with the Hearst corporation, requested details of calls his mom had made, only to be told that such details were gone, possibly destroyed. The *Herald Tribune*'s Hollywood reporter Joe Hyams received a similar story from General Telephone citing "men in dark suits and well-shined shoes" as having confiscated the records.

Suspicions and stories were flying fast and furious but, amazingly, they were actually helping the situation. Because these were not stories about maybe she wasn't really dead but rather that she had been murdered. Five days later the LA County coroner released the cause of death as being barbiturate poisoning—unspecified quantities of Nembutal and chloral hydrate were mentioned—and that it was probably suicide. It was all over, bar the shouting. But there was plenty of that.

The funeral was a difficult time for her, his mother told Docherty. Seeing and hearing about all those people who had meant so much to her at one time or another, watching them suffer when she could simply say, *No, it's okay. I'm alive. Here I am, see.* But she couldn't do that, not after all they had gone through.

But while the theory that she had been murdered had helped his mother, by covering up the truth, they weren't helping his father. *With me out of the way,* she told him, *all of the people who really had it in for your father tightened up the screws. The most consistent and evil of these was FBI head man J. Edgar Hoover who had decided to spread all kinds of lies about me and your dad's brother, hurtful things that could only succeed in destroying your dad's reputation.*

But it all died down eventually, she told him. They couldn't get him fair and they couldn't get him dirty. When she told him this, her eyes glistened like jewels in water. And then she said, So they had him killed.

The girl slid a heaped plate onto the table and said, "There you go, sir. If you need anything more, just give me a call. Enjoy your meal now."

Docherty stared at the sandwich. Then he pushed it away from him and stubbed out his cigarette. He placed a ten dollar bill beneath his cup and walked off into the night.

Three

Just above New Milford, the Housatonic River valley narrowed sharply and U.S. 7 left 202 behind, along with all the minimalls, the factory store outlets, and the dark loneliness of the night. On either side of the road, steep, wooded hills rose up amidst thick loosestrife down by the river's banks, purple in the early light of the sun.

Docherty saw occasional egrets and herons—even went through a working covered bridge in West Cornwall—while the road beckoned him onward, greedily.

By the time he reached Southfield, having drifted along a winding, pretty road past isolated farms and in and out of tiny, twisting valleys, Docherty had smoked a half dozen cigarettes and ached his way through a lifetime of memories.

He was almost up to date.

In his mind, he picked up the telephone on the second ring.

"Jimmy?" the voice croaked, nearly all of its familiarity gone.

"Mom?"

"Listen to me, Jimmy," she said. "I'm not well. And I mean *not* well at all. Do you understand what I'm saying?"

"Mom, what's the matter?"

"No time to talk about it now. I need to see you. Can you come down? Like, today?"

And so he had gone. Left New York bound for the past, memories clogging his head and his throat like swollen bread, and fluttering in his chest like they had a life of their own. Maybe they had.

He got to the farm in time to spend almost an hour with his mother before she died. In that time, she told him how much she loved him and how much she had missed his father. Told him how she was looking forward to seeing him again. But . . . and it was a big *but:* Would he do one thing for her? Sure, he told her. Just name it. She had sighed then, like a huge weight had been lifted from her chest. He had marvelled at how beautiful she still was. Even with her hair brown and bobbed, just the way it had always been all the time he had known her; even with her glasses and her schoolma'am clothes; even with her cancer, nibbling at her insides in a final feeding frenzy.

Just name it, he told her.

So she had named it. A simple request but needing almost herculean effort. A theft. Promise me, she asked him. Promise me that you'll bring it to me and have them dress me in it. Your father always liked that dress, she told him, and I guess I just want to be in it when I see him again. Will you do that for me? she asked him. Sure I will, he told her.

Twenty minutes later she was dead.

That was three days ago.

Two days ago, powered only by love and adrenaline, he had slipped into the caravan-sized locker in Ann Strasberg's Manhattan warehouse and stolen as much as he could carry. He figured that to take several items, and not all of which related to his mother, he could cover the real reason behind the theft. So, in addition to the white dress she had asked him for, Docherty took clothes belonging to James Dean, Montgomery Clift, Marlon Brando, and Paul Newman. And he took one other item of his mom's . . . for himself. A skintight dress she had worn back in 1962 when she had sung "Happy Birthday" to his father.

The following day—yesterday—he had been sitting at home, making plans to go back and bury his mother in her favorite dress when the telephone had rung.

"Hello?"

"Is that James Docherty?" an elderly man's voice inquired.

"Yes, it is," he said.

There was a pause. "James, this is your father."

Four

It was early afternoon by the time he hit Route 57, driving northwest from New Marlboro to Hartsville, passing by lakes too small to be named and with not a single fast-food joint to be seen anywhere. And that went ditto for strip malls, billboards, and even telephone wires.

At Hartsville he turned east on 23 to Monterey before switching to north at West Otis, where the road dropped down a steep hill and took him through thick woods before flattening out into a land of immaculate farmhouses, overgrown meadows, and rolling cornfields. Heading for Tyringham.

On the telephone, after telling Docherty things that only his true father could know, his father had told him that he would tell him everything when he saw him, but basically, this is the way things had happened.

He had intended to leave his wife and his office for Docherty's mother. Hell, he said, didn't the King of England do the very same thing? Docherty said that he guessed so. But, his father had drawled on in the same clipped Massachusetts twang that he had heard from the radio broadcasts and the countless newsreels he had watched, telling him that things had been getting a little hairy "out there." Docherty hadn't exactly been sure where "out there" had been, but he let it go. Hell, he had been too brain-shot to say anything. So he had just listened.

And listened.

It was like a plot from a cheap novel. It involved subterfuge and deceit, lies and counter-lies. He told Docherty that, although it was far from being common knowledge, it was not unusual to use a double in an open-car drive situation. It had never been something that he had gone in for particularly but, this time, he had been concerned. He hadn't had any real reason to suspect anything, just a feeling of uneasiness that made him say, repeatedly, he didn't want to go to Texas. And it had paid off. Once it was done, he realized that he would never be able to feel safe again.

Docherty had said, And my mom? I suppose you were concerned for her safety, too? Absolutely, came the reply after a short pause. Absolutely. Anyway, he went on, there weren't many people who knew about it and so we decided to let it go at that and call it a day.

Call it a day? He had made it sound like a nickel-and-dime gambler throwing in a bad hand. Made it sound easy. Oh, it was complicated, his father reassured him. Very complicated. But, I had reached a point where all I wanted was my freedom. Can you understand that? he asked Docherty. Docherty said, Yes, he could understand that. Then his father had said that he had simply decided it was in everyone's best interests to stay dead. And the fewer people who knew that, the better.

Docherty had nodded to the emptiness of his room.

He had listened to how his father had made sure that his mom received sizeable payments from his estate to ensure she had a good life. He already knew about these. Had known about them for almost twenty of his thirty years. He had thought what a good man his father truly must have been.

Then he wondered why his father had called.

I know she's dead, he said. I've followed her progress all the time. Yours too. I knew she was dead almost as quickly as you did. And, at first, I thought that that was that. His father cleared his throat before continuing. And then I read about the Strasberg warehouse theft? He phrased the statement like a question and then waited for Docherty to say something. Docherty remained silent.

Was it you? he asked. Docherty saw no reason to lie.

I guessed it. You did well, he said.

Mom said she wanted to be buried in the white dress, Docherty told him. You know the one?

His father sighed. I know the one. From the *Itch* movie, right? Docherty said, Right. She remembered you liking the dress—I *loved* that dress, he interrupted—right, Docherty said. Anyway, she wanted to be wearing it when she saw you again.

His father said, Oh, God, and fell silent for almost a minute. Then he said, Thank you for telling me that. That's okay, Docherty said, keeping his voice even and steady, trying not to let the white of the knuckles in his hand holding the receiver spread out into his words.

Well, aside from passing on my condolences, Docherty's father said, my reason for the call is to ask you for a memento. A memento? Docherty repeated. Yes. I'd like the other dress you have, the one your mother wore when she sang to me that time back in 1962. You have that, don't you? I have it, Docherty told him.

And so they arranged the meeting.

Five

Tyringham Road ended in Lee at the tail end of the afternoon, with the sun showing lazily through the golds and reds and browns of the trees that lay thick on the surrounding hillsides. From here, Docherty could drive on to take in Edith Wharton's home, the Norman Rockwell museum, and the Red Lion Inn. But he chose to pull left on an old track that led down to a stream that lay in the shadow of Route 41.

The old man was leaning against a tree, drinking in the last remnants of the day. When Docherty's car pulled up, the man stood up straight and waved once before starting toward the car.

Docherty turned off the engine and lifted one of the brown paper-wrapped packages from the front passenger seat. He stepped outside, hoisted the package under his arm and slammed the car door.

"James," the old man said, holding out his arm. Even from where he stood, by the car, Docherty could see the man's eyes. They were filled with tears. He supposed that kind of thing was easy for a politician. Or a prince.

Docherty walked forward, saying nothing until he stood in front of his father. Then he held out the package.

The old man took it and held it to his chest.

"You don't look too much different," Docherty said, forcing a smile. "The slap-top probably helps, though."

His father gave him an easy smile and rubbed the weathered skin on the top of his head. "Natural," he said. "Shaved it at first, but it's been this way of its own accord for more than twenty years."

"Suits you."

"Why, thank you."

"Did you miss my mom?"

The old man shook his head. "You wouldn't believe," he said in a voice that was midway between a whisper and a wheeze. "There were times, James, many, many times, when I thought about all the enjoyment she gave to me. And, in those times, I couldn't help but think of all the enjoyment I missed out on."

Docherty nodded and reached into his jacket pocket. "I think you should have thought not of what my mother could have given to you, but rather what you could have given to my mother."

The old man frowned.

Docherty pulled out the .38 and fired once. The bullet hit the old man square in the chest, its impact lifting him from the ground and setting him down back beside the tree he had been standing against when Docherty had arrived.

He walked across and felt for a pulse. There was none. He pulled the wrapping paper from the dress and crumpled it into a ball. Then he walked back to the car and tossed it inside. Minutes later, he was heading for Lenox where he would take Route 41 and head back along the westerly edge of the Housatonic valley.

On the way back, he realized that they had been right all along. There *had* been a second gunman.

The cost of freedom is always high—but Americans have always paid it . . .
—John F. Kennedy

AFTERWORD

I always thought that Marilyn was terribly underrated.

Sure, she was a great-looking woman, but she also had an excellent sense of timing and a natural feel for comedy acting, which never seemed to be given full rein. (Interestingly, I do not recall being attracted to her sexually—rather, I had the hots for Hayley Mills. . . . Looking back now, I wonder whether my parents were putting something in my food.)

Like so many entertainers, Monroe gave freely of herself and never received the kind of support and guidance, which—as a result of her tragic situation and that of people like Garland, Presley, Hendrix, and so on—is now rightly recognized as being of tremendous importance.

Loneliness must surely be one of the most distressing factors of stardom. As I researched the various books on her life and her career, I was increasingly convinced that all she ever wanted was a little friendship and affection. I doubt that she got it in any great measure. When she died, I was just thirteen, so I must confess, regretfully, that her death had no real impact. In those days—and at that age, of course—death did not seem to touch you as strongly as it seems to do today. I wish it had meant more to me.

And so, I set about trying to give her a little bit of something that she may have sought, while leaving the way open for some timely retribution. "The Cost of Freedom" is an unashamed what-if fantasy that is my own way of saying, "bad luck, kid," while at the same time offering an answer of sorts to one of our most enduring riddles.

—Peter Crowther

THE FOUNTAIN STREET GHOST

BY CATHERINE DAIN

 "IF ANYBODY WOULD dream about a visitation from Marilyn Monroe, Bobby would. But I still think holding a séance is a little silly." Faith had to pause for breath. The angle of the Kings Road slope was too steep to climb while talking. "I should have had you drop me off."

"It's only three blocks. That isn't worth taking the car out of the garage for, when I'd just have to put it back in and then walk by myself. You know there's no place to park around here on Friday nights. The overflow from the House of Blues lot takes up everything for miles," Michael responded. "Besides, only this block is uphill. The two blocks along Fountain are flat."

"And then we reach the stairs."

Michael glared and kept walking. Faith hurried to catch up. They had almost reached the end of the block, and Fountain was level as promised.

Turning the corner didn't change the scenery. Both West Hollywood streets were overbuilt with beige, gray, and white condominiums partially covered with massive shrubbery. The California bungalows that had once graced the area had been deemed an inefficient use of expensive real estate a couple of decades before. Aesthetics loses out to economics every time, Faith thought. She didn't say it because she was conserving breath for the stairs.

"Bobby thought the apartment was haunted even before the dream about Marilyn Monroe's ghost," Michael said. "And he denies he was asleep. He hired Frankie Fallon to conduct a séance only because he's hoping for confirmation. I don't think that's the least little bit silly. Marilyn did live in the building, after all, which may be the only reason it's still standing. So many people willing to pay premium rent to follow in her footsteps."

"Or whatever," Faith sniffed.

"Is that a polite way of saying that you don't understand the MM mystique?"

"I do understand. Marilyn was a tragic figure, and some disturbed persons find that romantic. I just don't happen to be one of them."

"I hope you're not going to tell Bobby you think he's disturbed."

"Bobby knows very well what I think of him, and my opinion doesn't bother him in the least. I'm sure he also knows that inviting me to a séance confirms it. Why—even if there are ghosts, and I don't believe in them for a minute—why would ghosts talk to Frankie Fallon? Especially the spirits of the stars." Faith stopped at the foot of the stairs leading from the street to Bobby's apartment building. "I'm glad they saved it, for whatever reason. It ought to be an historical monument, if it isn't already."

"I thought you were coming with an open mind."

"I'm doing my best," she sighed, grabbing the railing.

Ornamental urns flanked the steps. The patches of lawn on either side were neatly trimmed, and the L-shaped stucco chateau beyond seemed newly painted white. White scrollwork outlined the second-story windows, which had been further adorned with tiny round decks and white iron grills. Ivy geraniums mixed with gloxinia spilled between the bars, the red and pink flowers appearing especially bright in the early evening glow. The summer sun wouldn't set for another half hour.

Faith knew they were small decks rather than large window boxes only because she had squeezed onto one of the two off Bobby's living room. Before the high-rise had been built around the corner of La Cienega, the view must have been classic LA, all the way to Catalina on a clear day.

Another set of stairs inside the building took them up to Bobby's apartment. Faith paused again at the front door.

"The exercise is good for you," Michael said. "You must have put on ten pounds in the last six months."

"Have not," Faith snapped. "I've allowed myself a slight weight gain, but it's been ten pounds spread over a year and two months."

"Spread is the word for it."

"I'm not an actress anymore, and the worth of a therapist isn't judged by her waistline. Fortunately."

"Just what I was going to say." Michael smiled enough to take the sting out of it.

"Are you supporting the cultural imperative?"

"Not at all. I don't think anyone should be judged by appearance, you know that, whether it's Madonna or Sylvester Stallone. Or Marilyn Monroe's ghost, for that matter. And I wouldn't choose either a therapist or a friend based on buffness. As long as you're comfortable and healthy, weigh what you like."

"Thank you." Faith decided not to give him the satisfaction of admitting that sometimes she still worried about how she looked. "That's why so many actresses have eating disorders, you know. They're under so much pressure to stay unnaturally thin that they react by bingeing. One extreme to the other. No sense of moderation. In anything."

The wooden stairs creaked as they climbed.

"How wonderful that changing professions changed your personality. Too bad MM didn't see the light and get out while there was time."

"You're being flippant, but it's true. Getting out of the business—and dealing with the ego problems that come when the attention is gone—has a remarkable effect on one's mental health. At least it was good for mine."

Michael didn't answer. Faith was momentarily annoyed, until she reminded herself that she didn't need his validation.

He lifted the black iron knocker on the apartment door and let it fall.

The burnished oak door was opened almost at once by a young man with shaggy blond hair and a surfer's tan. He wore a brocade vest over a collarless white shirt and jeans, as if undecided about the nature of the occasion he was dressing for. His face was as smooth and bland as a banana-nut muffin.

"Hi, I'm glad you're here." Bobby ushered them into a large, sparsely furnished living room that seemed even emptier because of the cathedral ceiling.

A Swedish modern conversation group that looked straight from the Ikea showroom, complete with striped area rug, faced a white stone fireplace. Michael and Faith each took one of the low chairs.

"Traci called to say that Frankie is running a little late, but they'll be here. Do you want wine?"

"Yes," Michael said.

"Who's Traci?" Faith asked.

"Traci Sloane. She's Frankie Fallon's assistant. And she drives him everywhere. Don't you watch the show?"

Bobby tossed the question over his shoulder as he headed through the dining alcove to the kitchen. The dining room table had been covered with a white cloth. A brass candelabrum with five white candles waited under the chandelier. The setting sun had glazed the room a soft, rosy pink.

"I don't think I get that channel," Faith called after him.

"It's on channel nine," Michael muttered.

"You must tell me the night and time." Faith clasped her hands under her chin and smiled.

"You didn't have to come."

"Yes, I did. I've never been to a séance."

"Here we are, darlings." Bobby set a bamboo tray with a bottle of Chardonnay in an ice bucket and three stemmed glasses on the round coffee table. A plate held a wedge of Brie wreathed with crackers.

"Tell me about your dream," Faith said.

"I wasn't dreaming, I swear it," Bobby answered, handing her a glass. "I was lying in bed, awake, when I heard a woman sobbing. The sound seemed to come from inside the room. And then a blonde in a white halter dress floated through. She glanced over her shoulder, and I saw it was Marilyn."

"Sobbing?" Faith asked.

"Well, no. But the sobbing had stopped by then. For that night, at least. I've heard it several times since."

"Have you checked with your neighbors?"

"Really, Faith. What am I going to do? Start knocking on strange doors, asking, 'Excuse me, but do you cry in the middle of the night?' " Bobby punctuated the line with his glass, almost spilling the wine.

"You've lived in this building for five years. How can your neighbors be strangers?"

"He didn't say strangers," Michael said. "He said strange."

"I sit corrected." Faith turned back to Bobby. "Don't you know your neighbors?"

"Only by sight. We nod on the stairs, that's all. But even if the sobbing is a neighbor—and if it is, why is it always at three fifteen in the morning—that doesn't explain the vision." Bobby neatly skinned the top off the Brie and smeared some on a cracker.

"Well, if the vision only appeared once—"

Faith broke off when she heard the door knocker.

"I wasn't dreaming," Bobby said as he got up to answer it. "And I saw her twice. Then when Frankie Fallon mentioned speaking to Marilyn's spirit on his television show, I simply had to invite him over."

"Hello, dear souls!"

A short, frail man with a halo of wispy red hair swept into the room, followed by a healthy looking blonde half his age.

Faith and Michael stood while Bobby made the introductions.

"Faith!" Frankie Fallon exclaimed, kissing her hand. "What a wonderful name! Your parents must have had a beautiful vision for their daughter to have named you Faith."

"Thank you," Faith said politely. "I chose the name myself."

She wasn't sure she wanted her hand kissed, but she let him do it anyway. His skin was so white it was almost translucent, held together by a webbing of blue veins and fine wrinkles. There was so little flesh underneath that Frankie seemed halfway to mummification.

"Even better, dear soul." He looked up at her with large blue eyes that seemed to be focused on another dimension. "Even better."

As Frankie moved on to inspect Michael, Traci Sloane grasped Faith's hand firmly. Traci's skin seemed especially tanned and solid after Frankie's fragility.

"I'm Frankie's assistant," she said.

Faith wondered if Traci wore all that jewelry on television. The left ear wasn't bad—just a gold half moon with pearl and lapis dangles—but the right ear had a cluster of gold stars hanging from the lobe, plus three small hoops running up the ridge. Three gold chains and a rope of pearls decorated Traci's pink T-shirt. A trendy floral skirt fell almost to her sandals. Faith reminded herself that she wasn't a consultant and kept her mouth shut. She managed a closed-lipped smile.

"Would anyone like wine?" Bobby asked.

"No, no, dear soul," Frankie said. "Not until after the séance. Alcohol attracts too many entities, and we may not want them all."

"What does that mean?" Faith asked.

Frankie did his best to focus his blue eyes on her, and Faith found it hard to believe he hadn't consumed the major part of a bottle before he left home.

"Like attracts like," Frankie said. "And spirits attract spirits. That's why so many creative people—actors and writers and artists—become caught by the distilled and fermented kind. They're always surrounded by the ones who have left the flesh, but are still drawn to certain pleasures."

"Are you saying actors drink because they're surrounded by ghosts who still like the taste?" Faith asked.

"Crudely but wisely put, dear soul." Frankie nodded gently, as if he couldn't remember how to stop. "Creative people are always more sensitive to the presence of the dear departed ones who remained tied to this realm. Many admit that their best ideas come from outside themselves."

Faith sniffed.

Frankie smiled benignly, still nodding. "Although saying these beings remember the taste might be more precise. They can only sense the fumes in their present state. And then there's an amplifier effect, like an echo in reverse. The more one drinks, the more spirits one attracts, and the more spirits one attracts, the more one drinks.

Sometimes it becomes hard to remember who is in control. Which is why we will call the spirits before anyone takes another sip of wine."

He held out his arms to gather them in. Traci moved ahead to check out the dining room.

The rosy sun had faded to gray. Traci pulled a lighter out of her shoulder bag and lit the candles.

"A round table would have been better," she said. "Bobby and I can sit on either side of Frankie, but that means Faith and Michael will have to hold hands across the table."

"And we will all do that," Frankie said, "as soon as we have washed our hands. I want a clean connection."

"The bathroom is down the hall to the left," Bobby said. "But it'll be quicker if those who don't have to use the facility for other purposes wash in the kitchen."

Faith took the kitchen. She wanted to stay as close as possible to the dining room. Since Traci used the kitchen sink as well, she was able at least to keep her in sight. Faith began to wish she had inspected the table when she first arrived. But she didn't really think Bobby would rig a séance for her benefit, and neither Traci nor Frankie were left alone in the dining room.

Faith was reasonably confident that nothing would happen when the others returned to the dining room.

They sat as Traci had directed, Frankie at the head of the table, with his back to the kitchen, Traci and Michael on one side, Bobby and Faith on the other.

"Take hands, dear souls," Frankie said, reaching for Traci and Bobby. "And shut your eyes."

Faith felt awkward, stretching her arm across the table for Michael's hand, but she managed. She didn't like shutting her eyes—that was giving an opening for someone to set something up—but she did as told.

The soft, clean hands in hers seemed to form a water seal, bonding her to the circle.

"We ask for a cone of white light," Frankie said. "We ask that only spirits of goodwill come within this room. We would like to speak particularly with the entity who was once known as Marilyn

Monroe. Give us a sign when you're here, sweet spirit."

Faith opened her eyes to slits and tilted her head to check the others. Everyone was sitting with head bowed and eyes closed, presumably holding hands.

A faint breeze wafted across the room. Faith saw the candles flicker. She struggled against a rush of anxiety, but it faded as the flames steadied. Michael's eyes popped open.

"Thank you, sweet spirit," Frankie said. "You can all open your eyes now, or leave them closed, as you wish."

Traci and Bobby opened their eyes. Frankie stayed with his head bowed a moment longer.

"I have the spirit of Hedda Hopper," he said, finally opening his eyes. "She wants us to know that Marilyn won't be coming tonight because there is someone in this room who doesn't adore her. Marilyn didn't like to attend gatherings where one person didn't adore her when she was still in the flesh, and she sees no reason why she should do so now."

"Oh, God, Faith," Bobby moaned. "I knew I shouldn't have invited you."

"I can leave," Faith snapped.

"No, no, dear soul," Frankie said. "The circle is formed. Hedda can tell us everything we need to know."

"Has Marilyn been here?" Bobby asked.

"Yes, dear soul. Hedda says that Marilyn's spirit has indeed visited this building where she once lived."

"Does she want something from me?"

Frankie was silent. Faith was annoyed to realize that they were all trying to hear whatever Frankie listened for.

"Hedda says that Marilyn's visits do not concern you directly, although she is pleased that you cared enough to invite this humble channel." Frankie was staring at a spot on the far wall of the living room. Faith fought the urge to turn around to check for ghosts.

"Is she here for the crying woman?" Bobby asked.

"Hedda believes so, but she says she has no information on that entity."

"Why not?" Faith asked.

Bobby glared at her.

"Some things are not revealed to us, dear soul," Frankie said. "But Hedda does have a message for you. She says your grandmother Myrtle, who wanted to be an actress in life, is enjoying the company of many from the Hollywood community now that she has passed on. Burt Lancaster is especially fond of her, and Myrtle is happier than she dreamed possible."

"What?" Faith was so startled that she would have dropped hands if Bobby and Michael hadn't held firmly.

Frankie ignored her. "Myrtle is pleased that you pursued her dream, even though it didn't quite work out as you wanted, and she hopes that your new career will be rewarding. She says you will have a new client soon."

Faith was too stunned to respond.

"Does Hedda have a message for me?" Bobby asked.

"Yes. Marilyn is so pleased with you, that someday, when you need a prayer answered, she will see that it is granted."

"Wow!"

Faith kept her grip on Bobby's hand.

"Hedda has another message for one in our circle," Frankie said.

"I hope this one is mine," Michael said.

"Yes, dear soul. The message is from your grandfather Thomas. Thomas knows that the Lord takes care of the lilies of the field, and will surely provide for you, but he nevertheless wishes you would devote more time to your psychotherapy practice. He reminds you that you have gifts that are needed by others, and he hopes you will make use of them."

"At least that was good advice," Faith muttered.

"Hedda has one last message for the company, this one from James Dean. He says you are all three very talented people with the potential for great success, as long as you don't drink and drive."

"More good advice," Michael whispered.

The candles flickered in a new breeze.

"Another spirit wishes to speak with us. Jean Harlow says that she does have information about the crying woman." Frankie nodded at something in whatever unearthly realm his eyes were focused on.

"How did Jean Harlow get into this?" Faith muttered.

"Jean Harlow felt a kinship with Marilyn, and occasionally checked on her while she was living here. She still maintains some contact with the building because she finds it so entertaining," Frankie answered. "Jean says the woman is married to a musician, and the reason she starts crying at three fifteen is that if he isn't home by then, he isn't coming at all."

"That makes sense," Bobby said. "Although crying about it isn't going to do her any good."

"Why doesn't she just leave him?" Michael asked.

"Jean says it's a karmic tie from a past life, and the woman isn't able to change the pattern without help. She says that's why Marilyn has allowed herself to be seen in this building, to draw attention to the situation and get help for the woman. Marilyn hopes one of you will interfere."

"That's for you, Faith," Bobby whispered.

"Why does Marilyn care?" Faith asked.

"Hedda says that Marilyn is improving her chances for a happier incarnation next time by doing occasional good deeds while her soul is in energy form. This crying woman is one of her projects," Frankie replied.

"Celestial community service?" Michael asked.

Everyone ignored him.

The candles flickered one more time.

"Hedda says good-bye for now. And so does Jean." Frankie continued to stare in the general direction of the living room wall a moment longer, then blinked and smiled at each of them in turn. "Are you happy, dear souls? You can break the circle if you wish."

"Thrilled," Bobby replied. "Would anyone like wine now? Except Traci, who's driving."

"We would love to spend some time with you, dear souls, but we have another engagement this evening," Frankie said, patting Bobby's hand with the one that had been holding Traci's.

"Don't blow the candles out," Traci said. She stood up and rearranged her shoulder bag. "Let them burn to the stub if you can, otherwise snuff them."

"I'm so grateful," Bobby said, dropping Faith's hand to double the clasp with Frankie. "I hope we can do this again."

"Any time, dear soul, any time."

Faith and Michael stayed in their seats as Bobby showed the medium and his assistant to the front door.

"Well?" Michael asked.

"I'm sure it's all explainable," Faith answered.

"Then explain it out here," Bobby called from the living room. "And don't blow the candles out."

Faith was tempted, but she refrained.

"Didn't you have to pay him?" she asked, after they had regrouped by the fireplace.

"Credit card over the phone when I made the appointment," Bobby said.

"If he's such a good psychic, you'd think he could sense the deadbeats," Faith said.

Michael tried to shush her, and Faith regretted the comment. A true psychic would indeed ask Bobby for a credit card in advance.

"How would you explain the breeze?" Bobby asked, ignoring her comment.

Faith took a sip of wine. It was a little too warm, but drinkable. "Some kind of air pump in that shoulder bag, triggered by Traci's foot under the table."

"And the names? I gather you did have a grandmother named Myrtle."

"He could have gotten my grandmother's name from records somewhere. Everything's on the Internet now."

"Everything but why the woman cries," Bobby replied. "I don't know why you have to tear down the curtain, Faith. Why can't you just accept that we aren't in Kansas anymore?"

"Where's Kansas?" Michael asked.

Both Faith and Bobby glared, and he shrugged his shoulders.

"Sorry," he added.

"Wherever we are, I don't believe ghosts are hanging around to give us advice," Faith said.

"Then I think you should stay the night." Bobby stated it firmly, punctuating again with his wine glass. He licked off the few drops that fell on his wrist.

"What?"

"Oh, for God's sake, Faith, that isn't a proposition. You can sleep wherever you like, as long as it isn't with me. But I think you should find out for yourself what's going on," Bobby said.

"I agree." Michael nodded, clearly enjoying the situation. "I think you should stay and find out for yourself. After all, Jean Harlow said Marilyn wanted someone to interfere."

"Frankie said, you mean," Faith said, ready to argue.

"Frankie said Jean said Marilyn said," Bobby chanted.

"Faith, you know you want to," Michael said.

By the time the bottle of wine was gone, Faith had decided they were right.

"I'll stay out here, in one of the chairs," she said. "I don't want to fall into a sound sleep. I want to be alert."

"Call me tomorrow and let me know what happens," Michael said, kissing her on the cheek.

"I may have to call sooner than that—my car is in your garage."

"Take a cab home if it's before ten. We'll have lunch, and I'll get you back to your car."

Bobby saw him to the door.

"You don't have to amuse me," Faith said when he returned.

"I'm just picking up the glasses," he said. "And then I'm going to snuff the candles. I have Tetris on my Nintendo, if you want to amuse yourself."

"Do you have a book?"

"I have a week's worth of the trades, plus the current *Dramalogue*."

Faith shook her head. "I don't do that anymore. I'll just sit here and brood until morning."

"Suit yourself."

Once Bobby had gone to bed and the lights were out, Faith understood how the apartment could inspire visions of ghosts. Pale light from the high windows cast shifting shadows on the walls.

If there is a ghost, she thought, it ought to be Peter Cushing's.

But it was Marilyn Monroe who danced at the periphery of her mind, just out of reach. Faith was wide awake, certainly, when she tried to focus on the haze in the corner, inches beyond the moonglow. How sad she felt, how sad that she couldn't quite see.

She almost jumped out of her skin when a hand touched her shoulder.

"I thought you weren't going to sleep," Bobby said.

"I wasn't asleep."

"You were. I had to shake you. You haven't heard the crying, have you?"

"What—" Faith started, then stopped. She hadn't heard it consciously, but that had been the source of her own feeling of sadness. The sobbing.

As she listened, the low sobbing crescendoed to a high wail, filling the room.

"It must be the woman downstairs," Bobby said. "I've tried to figure out where the sound is coming from, and it has to be rising through the heating vents."

"Well, time to meddle."

"Are you sure you want to?"

"No, but I think someone should—if I were crying like that, I'd want someone to help me. And so I guess I have to try to help her." Faith struggled out of the chair and stretched her stiff legs.

"Your grandmother said you were going to have a new client soon."

"Frankie said that. And it was a safe prediction, since he didn't say how soon."

"Well, good luck. I'll be waiting."

Faith ran her hand through her hair and thought about a mirror and some fresh makeup, but a new wail set her moving toward the door.

The hall was quiet and dimly lit. Faith moved quickly down the stairs.

She leaned her ear against the door directly below Bobby's and thought she could discern muffled sobs. She rapped the iron knocker sharply, and the sound stopped. While she was trying to decide whether to keep knocking or leave, the door opened a crack, held by a chain.

Faith caught a glimpse of a single puffy eye and then the door slammed shut.

She lifted the knocker and let it fall one more time.

"I thought you might want to talk," she called.

She had started back down the hall when a woman's voice stopped her.

"Wait—don't leave yet."

The woman standing in the doorway had the anguished look of an abandoned child. Dark hair hung limply around a red, swollen face. She hugged a stained flannel bathrobe close to her thin body.

"I'm sorry," she said. "For a minute I thought you were Marilyn's ghost. But you're too old, and your hair isn't blond enough, and she never appears in her frumpy period, the way she looked when she was married to Arthur Miller. I guess you have to be real."

"Marilyn's ghost?" Faith was too stunned to comment on the rest of the woman's reaction to her.

"Yes. I've seen her several times. She lived in this building, a long time ago."

"I know Marilyn lived here." Faith stared at the woman, not certain how to continue.

"What did you want?"

"A friend of mine lives upstairs. We heard you crying, and I thought you might want to talk. I'm a therapist."

The woman wiped her eyes with one hand, then looked at Faith again. "Maybe I do want to talk. I don't know." She shivered for a moment. "Not now. Do you have a card or something?"

"Upstairs. I left my purse upstairs."

"Stick it through the mail slot. Maybe I'll call you."

Faith was trying to think of something more to say when the woman shut the door.

Bobby had kept his promise to wait up. He even fixed Faith a cup of tea while she called a taxi. She told him briefly what happened.

"Do you think you'll hear from her?" he asked.

"I'll have to wait and see," she answered.

By the time she met Michael for lunch the next day, Faith had more information.

The woman had already made an appointment to talk.

"Why did she decide to trust you?" Michael asked.

"She had asked Marilyn's ghost for help, and for a moment she thought I was Marilyn's ghost, answering her prayer. Then she realized I don't look much like Marilyn Monroe." Faith decided not to mention the word frumpy. "She still thinks Marilyn's ghost answered her prayer."

"Are you ready to revise your opinion of Frankie Fallon yet?"

"Not really. I asked Lily—that's the woman's name—if she had ever heard of him, and it seems that she had called him one night after hearing him mention Marilyn's spirit on his television show. Probably the same one Bobby saw. She told Frankie that she was praying to Marilyn's ghost." Faith put on her glasses to study the menu, but she could feel Michael staring at her.

"Are you suggesting that Frankie Fallon set all this up to make it appear as if Marilyn Monroe's ghost was answering Lily's prayer?"

"I think it's possible."

Michael put his hand on the menu, so she had to glance up at him over the top of her glasses.

"If you're truly convinced he's a bad wizard, then you have to admit he's an awfully good man, at least when it comes to providing for the lilies of the field."

"Your grandfather mentioned them."

"Frankie mentioned them."

"I remember. Let's eat."

"And the ghost?"

"Maybe it wasn't a ghost." Faith gently removed his hand. "Maybe it was an angel. Who knows?"

AFTERWORD

I heard that Marilyn Monroe was dead on Sunday afternoon. A friend called me, crying, to pass on the news that Marilyn Monroe had committed suicide the night before. I was stunned and puzzled and, at least to some extent, despairing. If Marilyn Monroe couldn't find love and happiness, what hope was there for the rest of us?

I was living in New York that year, studying acting at Neighborhood Playhouse. I thought Marilyn was funny and charming and sexy, and if she wasn't taken seriously as an actress, well, so what? Neither was anyone else except for Katharine Hepburn and a few old Brits. I envied her fame—especially when it brought her the opportunity to sing "Happy Birthday" to President Kennedy. (I didn't envy Jackie Kennedy. And I still have trouble believing that only people in the entertainment industry knew of her husband's escapades.) I wondered what it would be like to be Marilyn Monroe, and still to fall victim to the dark night of the soul.

Since then, she has become my own private metaphor to describe the difficulties that uncommon women have in maintaining relationships: Marilyn Monroe was home alone on a Saturday night when she killed herself. (Where have you gone, Joe DiMaggio?) Arguments that she wasn't really alone or that her suicide might have been abetted only beg the question. Marilyn Monroe had no "significant other." And who were we women in 1962 unless we were with men?

With that in mind . . . what would Marilyn's ghost be doing today?

—Catherine Dain

FANTASY

BY EILEEN DREYER

 FANTASY WAS THE kind of place that existed to validate its own name. Tucked away between a boutique and gelato shop at the edge of the rehabbed section of downtown, this latest in trendy clubs carried its neoned name above the door like a sweeping purple invitation. A promise. A certainty. All your dreams fulfilled here. All your mistakes made invisible.

The booths were black leather and the partitions smoked glass. Soft jazz drifted on cigar smoke from the back room, and the bar, which wrapped its way along the front glass wall, around the open brasswork elevator that lifted clientele from the earth to the third floor dance-and-pool parlor, and up three steps to the cordoned-off private section, was actually a backlit saltwater fish tank that was staffed by beautiful, silent, smiling tenders in tuxes who alternated shaking exotic drinks with shaking food over the exotic fish that spun in endless neon patterns along the wall.

Fantasy was expensive, it was soft-spoken, it was dark. It was where every Friday evening at five, just in time for Fantasy's version of happy hour, Martin Johnson pushed through the brass and glass front door, meandered over the mirror-black floor where beautiful people talked in hushed, important voices over vodka martinis, and up to one of the black-and-chrome barstools that lined the tank.

If one took the time to look at Martin out on the street, one would think that Martin Johnson didn't have the imagination to feed his illusions in such a high-brow place. Martin, in the light of day, was average. Average height, average hair, average eyes. Martin was the kind of person who could pull off an armed hold-up in broad daylight in front of a convention of police officers and get away with it, because the description would have come out average, brown, and brown, with no remarkable features. Martin's clothes were even unremarkable. Every Friday, at exactly the same time, in exactly the same plain gray suit. If anybody ever frequented Fantasy, like they did local neighborhood bars, they would have picked up on this.

The bartenders did. But the bartenders were paid to overlook things like that. They simply greeted Martin like a new customer each time, asking his preference, even though they knew it would be the same—bourbon and sweet soda—and listened attentively to his small words as if never hearing them before.

Part of the fantasy, of course, was to be someone you weren't. Someone mysterious, someone handsome and dashing. Someone desirable to the other half-frantic customers who hid their uncertainties behind dark sunglasses on a dark floor and their insecurities beneath everything from JCPenney to Armani.

For Martin Johnson, the pattern never changed. He never talked to anyone on the floor, since the floor crowd tended to be the impatient ones. He sat at the bar close to where the elevator whirred and clanked up and down so he could watch the people lifting their way from soft seduction up to pulsating arousal and back down again. He ordered his drink from the same bartender, asking him his name each time and smiling in greeting, and watched the room as if he were James Bond scouting the area for possible enemy activity.

He usually stayed two hours and two bourbon and sweets, and sometimes he would be lucky enough to strike up conversation with one or two of the women who preferred the community of barstools to the isolation of the floor. Inevitably, each time, Martin ended up walking alone back out the front door with nothing on his arm but his sleeve and his slacks lighter by at least a couple of twenties.

The bouncer thought he was weird, but then, it wasn't the bouncer's job to cull weird out of the mix. The bartenders thought he was harmless, and the fish seemed to like to nudge along the glass right by where his wingtip-shod foot swept a continuous arc for the two hours he was there. And every once in a while, every long once in a while, he actually got a woman interested for more than a few minutes.

It happened that way on the second Friday of the month. Payday, the bartenders figured, because Martin was spending, and the two women who perched themselves on side-by-side stools with almost identical skirt-hitching movements were accepting.

"Come here often?" Martin asked in his quiet, unprepossessing voice, just like he always did.

The bartender splashed bourbon into a smoky indigo glass and waited, just like always, for the reaction.

There was a blonde and a redhead to choose from, the redhead thin and edgy with a grin like the grill of an old Nash, and the blonde round and soft and blessed with a breathy giggle.

"Never," they said almost in unison, then grinned and giggled.

Placing the cocktail napkin on the glass bar with the precision of a geisha performing a tea ceremony, the bartender cast a casual look around the bend to where two other bartenders were watching. One held up five fingers. The other held up ten. Martin's bartender nodded, taking the odds against Martin as he laid Martin's second highball just a little off-center on the napkin and watched Martin unconsciously reposition it as he zeroed in on the blonde.

Martin liked blondes, especially ones who could rub across a barstool like a chamois doing car windows. Martin had never scored with one. The bartender had hope, though. One of these days, Martin was going to abandon that loser line of his and actually come up with something workable.

"We've heard so much about it," the blonde offered, sipping at her frozen daiquiri and taking a wide-eyed look around. "It's really . . . hot here, ya know?"

The redhead nodded and leaned closer to Martin, who leaned a little away. "Hot," she said on a whisper that had the unfortunate sound of ground glass.

"You . . . come here much?" the blonde asked Martin.

He nodded and sipped at his drink. If this took long enough, the bartender knew, Martin would need an uncommon third. If Martin blew it, the cost of the drink would still cover the bets. If Martin finally figured out the trick, the bartender could damn near retire on his winnings.

"It relaxes me," Martin said.

"Oh," the blonde answered with a knowing nod that barely moved her moussed and sculpted hair. "Us, too. We've been under such stress lately, ya know?"

Martin leaned closer. "What do you do?" he asked, offering a quiet smile that seemed to make the blonde wiggle even more.

"We're executive assistants," the redhead said. "At a very big law firm."

Which, in the Fantasy lexicon, translated into receptionists. The bartender resupplied his fruit sections and Martin smiled.

"But that's just till we can . . . break in," the blonde said. "You know. We're actresses."

Not one of the three saw the bartender grin as he created art out of lime slices.

Martin was nodding. "Actresses," he said, considering the blonde with her lazy eyes and dimpled chin. "I bet you're really good. I bet you are."

"*You* must be really successful," the redhead broke in, her voice edgy with being ignored. "If you come here all the time."

Martin finished his drink right on schedule and turned to the bartender.

"Another round, please, Matt," he requested. "For the ladies, too."

The ladies cooed. Both of them. Martin only smiled at the blonde, but neither seemed to take note, as if they were two halves of the same science project.

Matt refilled the glasses and fed the clownfish that were nudging Martin's soles and eased back into the shadows to wait for the almost inevitable third act to this farce. Come on, Martin, he thought. Surprise me. Use some *real* imagination here.

"I do all right," Martin acknowledged, swirling the liquid in his glass to make the ice clink. Behind him the elevator sighed to the floor to pick up another group of dancers.

"You going to tell us what you do?" the redhead asked.

"I should probably let you guess," he answered.

The bartender shook his head. Here they went.

"I bet I know what you do," the blonde offered, motioning to him with her glass.

Martin's eyebrows slid north. "Bet you don't."

They all smiled, recognizing the conduit for the evening. From fantasy to game to outcome.

It was game time, and the blonde buffed the stool with her butt as if working up ideas like static electricity as the redhead grinned with gleaming teeth.

"Oh, she's really good at this," she said. "I bet she wins."

"What do you bet?" Martin immediately asked.

Both women giggled. "You name it."

"You take me home," he challenged brightly, color flaring high on his sallow cheeks.

"Home?" the blonde echoed in a high, childish tone, her eyes ages older than her voice. "But what would we do?"

Martin leaned a little close. "I'm sure we'd think of something."

"And if we win?" she challenged, her tone suddenly softer, earnest.

He shrugged. "You name it."

The blonde didn't even look around her for inspiration. She just smiled, and the redhead sat back for the ride.

"Your house," she said. "Our rules."

Even the bartender was impressed. He'd underestimated all three of them, especially Martin.

"You're on," he said.

Maybe, the bartender thought, completely intrigued now, Martin would pull this one out of the fire.

The blonde held out her hand. "Deal."

They shook, and it looked like an act of foreplay.

"Priest," she said, without even letting go.

Martin laughed, a soft, controlled sound. "Nope."

She tilted her head for consideration. "Hmmmmm. Something . . . quiet. CPA."

"Never."

"Dentist."

"Not even warm."

"We never lose," the redhead assured him.

"You're about to," Martin said.

The bartender waited, almost hoping against hope that for once Martin wouldn't blow it.

"Nurse."

"Insurance salesman."

"Teacher."

They guessed for twenty minutes and for twenty minutes Martin told them they were way off. The bartender actually got a fourth drink out of Martin, along with a good tip.

"Give up?" Martin asked for the fifth time.

"How 'bout a hint?" the blonde asked.

"Sure," Martin agreed readily. "It's classified."

"You're a *spy*?" the redhead shrilled.

"Not exactly."

The bartender, frowning in disappointment, started clearing up. Game, set, and match. Damn. He could have used that extra cash tonight.

"A military guy?" the blonde ventured.

"Nope."

"What else is classified?"

"Oh, lots of positions."

"Here? In town?"

"Give up?"

It was almost all over now, the bartender thought as the two women consulted each other with sparkling eyes.

"This had better be worth it," the blonde said.

"Oh, it is," Martin assured her, leaning very close. "I have a fantasy job. And only you will know what it is."

They giggled together. "Oh, okay."

The bartender grabbed the three remaining glasses before the women could heave them.

"Well," Martin confided, leaning close. "I work for the secret service."

Both women stared. "So?"

"So," he said. "I'm the man in charge of watching Marilyn Monroe."

Both women blinked. Down the bar, the other two bartenders grinned like IRS auditors with Willie Nelson in sight.

"You're jokin', right?" the redhead asked.

Martin shook his head. "No. I'm telling you, this is all secret. Really secret. I shouldn't even be telling you."

Like he'd told every other blonde he'd cornered on that barstool, the bartender thought in disparagement.

"You watch Marilyn Monroe," the blonde retorted with some spite. "The Marilyn Monroe who's been dead since 1962. That Marilyn Monroe."

Martin scooted even closer, so that his chin was just about due north of her considerable cleavage. "She's not, ya know. The government had to get her out of the way. She was going to completely tear apart the Kennedy presidency."

"So, they like, what? Put her on an island with Elvis?"

"She died of an overdose!" the redhead snorted.

The bartender counted the seconds now before all three barstools would be empty. By now, he had this down to a science, and damn it, Martin hadn't disappointed him yet.

"That's what you're supposed to think," Martin assured her, his voice the utmost of conspiratorial whispers. "The government and the Mafia worked together to set up her death, only she never died. My job is to keep her in control."

The blonde seemed to have run out of words. The bartender didn't blame her.

"You're nuts," she finally managed, suddenly sounding just a little frightened.

"You don't believe me?" Martin countered. "Come on home with me. I'll show you."

The blonde grabbed the redhead by the arm and pulled her off the stool. "Yeah, you'll show us, you jerk. You just leave us alone, okay?"

"What about our bet?"

"I think you're taking this place just a little too seriously, bud. We live on a real planet, ya know?"

"But you didn't guess."

"And you didn't even guess that we're really Martians scoping

out the club scene on earth for a little spring break time. Go to a
Star Trek convention, you geek!" She yanked on the blonde again,
and started moving. "Come on, Norma."

The blonde flounced.

"Norma?" Martin echoed, his eyes lighting.

The blonde spun on him. "Don't," she commanded, a finger in
his face. "Don't even start. And *don't* follow us out the door."

"Doesn't it just figure," the redhead was grousing as she tugged
her friend along after her across the highly polished floor. "Our first
try at this place, we don't get a fantasy, we get a friggin' nightmare!"

Giving the tiniest of sighs, Martin watched them go. The bartender, constrained by good manners and a tougher employment
policy, still couldn't keep his silence another Friday evening.

"They're right, ya know," he said. "You should take that line to
an *X-Files* Encounter Group. It's just a little too much for this
place."

Martin shrugged agreeably and dropped a last ten dollar tip on
the counter where the electric yellow and purple fish circled lazily.
"I guess so," he admitted, and walked on out of the bar.

The night outside was humid, the western sky still molten with
the setting sun. It was early yet, especially for a Friday night. Pulling
out his car keys, Martin walked over to the corner parking lot where
Porsches nestled cheek and jowl with Cherokee wagons and a van
or two. Martin's keys unlocked a sedate blue sedan. He climbed in
and headed away from the smoke of a dark bar.

By the time Martin got out of the gourmet-to-go place, the sun had
slid beyond the horizon, taking any of the breeze with it. The sky
was still a thick red, and the trees hung listless in the evening air.
Traffic crawled and horns blatted in syncopated frustration. The
real world. The tired, anxious streets outside Fantasy. Martin nestled his bags of food into the empty passenger seat and steered
through the increasingly upscale streets until he reached the one
with privacy fences and privacy gates and towering chimneys behind lush trees.

The one into which he turned was white brick and old and rambling, with soft lights and a high brick fence separating it from the neighbors. Martin didn't even seem to notice the opulence as he climbed out of the car, as he trudged up the walk and settled his key into the side door and let himself in.

He didn't really notice the quiet elegance of the rooms that surrounded him or the shudder of blinking lights on the security panel in the wall as he punched in his code. Martin slipped out of his suit jacket and went about setting out a table with linen and crystal and china and candles. He carefully set out the food in warming dishes and culled a rose or two from the fresh arrangement in the echoing front hallway for his budvase. And when all was finished, he pushed the set table along on its wheeled legs back to what he considered the family room.

The house was quiet. The neighborhood was quiet. But as he inserted the key into the door of the west wing of the house, Martin heard the chatter of a subdued television on the other side. He smiled.

"Martin?" the voice asked as he pushed his way into the dimly lit apartment decorated all in white. White carpet, white couches, white piano. White bed across from a television turned to an old black-and-white movie.

"Good evening," he greeted his guest. "How are you?"

She turned to face him with young eyes in an old face. "I thought I could see Bobby tonight," she objected in soft, breathy tones that belonged to a child.

"I told you before," he said. "Tonight he's sitting with Jack. I thought just you and I could have dinner tonight, Marilyn."

"Oh, thank you, Martin," she smiled. "I'd like that. And you can tell me all about yourself."

Martin smiled back and sat down, just as if he were settling onto a barstool. "I'd like that very much, Marilyn. I really would."

AFTERWORD

I'm not as interested in Marilyn Monroe as I am in the image of Marilyn Monroe. I'm fascinated by whom we choose to be our immortals. She was quixotic, charismatic, and, in spurts, talented. I wonder if it wasn't her vulnerability more than her beauty that still speaks to us after all these years. I wonder if the appeal isn't simply that she's another of the Young Dead Club. Would Brando be seen differently if he had died in James Dean's car? Would Marilyn have lost most of her mystery if she'd lived long enough to bore us with half a dozen ghosted autobiographies and a long term on *Hollywood Squares*?

Because I wasn't into film yet, and because my parents weren't at all, I barely remember her death. I was ten years old, so music and sports were much more interesting to me (ask me how I felt about Timmy McCarver that summer, and you'd get a completely different answer).

I do find it interesting to note that if she were alive today, Marilyn Monroe would be considered too fat to be beautiful. And that's too bad, because she had a supremely female figure.

—Eileen Dreyer

HER BIGGEST FAN

JOHN A. DAY

 HAROLD BROWN SHUCKED his coat in the entryway. He bounced upstairs, flipping on lights as he passed up the dark paneled stairwell and into the upstairs hall. In his left hand was a cardboard tube. And in that was his latest acquisition—the coming attractions poster from *Gentlemen Prefer Blondes*. This wasn't entirely a legal possession.

He turned into the first room at the top of the stairs. This small room held his narrow bed, with wagon wheel headboard and footboard—and his collection. The walls were plastered, sometimes overlapping, with pictures of Marilyn. Most were publicity photos (with the form letter response to each of his 256 letters) and magazine covers he had clipped from the film fan magazines, or movie posters. A life-size cardboard cutout of her in a swimsuit stood by his unmade bed. Rows of china plates and tumblers, her picture imprinted on their surfaces, leaned against the wall on a shelf above his bed. And behind his Tom Swift books, two shapely Marilyn dolls.

After an acquisition, he usually spent hours finding the right spot for it. Then he would remove one of the older keepsakes, carefully press it between sheets of wax paper, and lay it with the others in one of his cedar chests. In the bare spot he would pin his new prize. Inevitably he ended the evening by studying the photo or poster, first up close to memorize the tiniest details of her face, then from his desk while he pasted articles about her in one of several bound volumes, and lastly from his bed. He left the desk lamp on so that as he fell asleep his final sight would be of her.

Tonight he couldn't summon the usual enthusiasm. He remembered his mother, who hadn't approved of his collection, often saying that she should "throw out this trash with the trash."

Maybe now Mother would approve of him, now that he was going to make something of himself, now that he would soon be Marilyn's husband.

He laid the unopened cardboard carrier on his bed and went down to the kitchen.

He made a bologna and lettuce sandwich on white bread. Sandwich in hand, he stepped from the linoleum of the kitchen floor and down the wooden steps into the basement.

A bare bulb, hanging by a thin electrical cord from the ground floor beams, lit his workshop. Formerly the laundry room, he had converted it into a workshop after his mother's death. Here he had built *the* machine. So far, he had told no one what he had built, so he hadn't given it a name. To him it was simply *the* machine. As always, the shape of the machine, a giant rotating drum encompassing a smaller rotating drum within a rigid steel framework, reminded him of a snake swallowing its own tail.

The idea for the machine came to him while he was washing clothes one night shortly after his mother's death. He had pulled his clothes from the dryer and folded his socks as Mother had taught him—left over right and then rolled into a ball so they wouldn't become separated in his dresser—when he noticed a dark sock was missing: a dark sock with vivid pink and yellow plaid argyle around the ankles. So he searched the clothes hamper and the path from his bedroom to the basement. He searched the dryer, the washer, under the washing machine, finding only a large dust bunny and a dried-up rat wrapped around an ancient box of rat poison. He didn't find a dark sock with vivid pink and yellow argyle across the ankles.

He remembered Mother had always joked that the dryer ate clothes. At least, he always thought she was joking. Now he wondered—would it eat again?

He returned the clothes to the dryer. A half hour later, when it stopped tumbling, he counted the clothes. This time a blue sock with green and red zigzag stripes, threadbare at the heel but still wearable, had disappeared.

Another man, he supposed, would have counted the loss of two of his favorite socks as a warning to go no further. Somewhere inside him, however, a cruel voice whispered. *What's it all for? Empty desolation and then one day you die.* He decided to continue until he was naked, if that was what ended this experiment.

Happy for the first time in months, he fed clothes into the dryer. Later, when the drum tumbled to a stop, the clothes stuck together with heavy static. The arms of his shirts and legs of his pants clung to each other like desperate lovers. And like jealous lovers, the clothes defended their union against the invasion of his hands with bright sparks of static electricity as he carefully separated them. His count confirmed another sock and one of his boxer shorts had disappeared and could not be found. Not in the dryer. Not on the floor. Definitely not at home. Just gone.

Astonishing. While not a physicist, he still understood that mass couldn't be destroyed. It could be converted to energy, but he doubted that a dryer contained enough energy to even begin such a process. Perhaps the clothes were removed, not destroyed, sent to some other place or time. Harold paced the small basement. Perhaps the clothes slid into another world like Earth. Maybe even identical to Earth. Yes, he decided, that seemed right. And maybe we slip into this other dimension or into a number of nearly identical dimensions, but we never realize anything has changed because everything is exactly the same, except perhaps that "potato" is spelled "potatoe" or you slept on your right side instead of the left.

That explained so much—all the trivial inconsequences of life, the tiny fumbles and strange coincidences. Inexplicable mood swings or sudden twists in conversation—the invisible switch of people so similar, done so smoothly, that no one remarked on the difference.

The rotation of charged particles within a heated steel drum is a dimensional transport, he realized with a thrill. Then another thought, deeper and more devious, struck him. *If there are other dimensions with carbon copies of myself*—and he shuddered as he imagined hundreds, perhaps thousands of sad, moping Harold Browns watching her movies, writing dopey fan letters, all of them desperate and longing—*if there are thousands of me, perhaps there are thousands of her.* Marilyns by the thousands, each a little different. And the last, final, heart-stopping thought: *Surely among thou-*

sands of Marilyns, one can be for me. Perhaps somewhere Marilyn, moved by a lonely fan letter, reached out to the man who wrote it, seeing in the long delicate prose his devotion, his strength and honesty, and had fallen in love. Perhaps somewhere he and Marilyn were man and wife.

He began to construct a device that could, by rotating static charge, propel him into another world.

Surprisingly soon, he clicked on the right combination of rotating steel, heat, and tumbling wool to send any number of odd things out and away. An old shoe, a skate key, a ragtime 45 that he never listened to much anymore—all went away. He tested animals in it first, to ensure his safety: a bird, a cat, a dog—captured with food on his back porch, then secreted inside the house. They all tumbled for a moment in blind panic within his machine and then, as he watched in delight, they spun away, fading like fog from a winter windshield.

Harold believed he had solved the final obstruction—the secret of catching the machine up in its own tumbling static charge so that it transported itself into another dimension, but he hadn't tested it yet. He knew it would work, just as he knew *how* it would work. He would picture where he wanted to go (his favorite fantasy: Marilyn in a bathing suit. Sometimes rising from her private pool, the water glistening on her bare flesh and the wet fabric of her suit stroking her like a second skin. Sometimes bending over him as he rested in his chair by the pool, her breasts teased by gravity, urged by gravity to spill out the top of her sleek suit, while she asked him with concern if he was too hot and if she should bring him a cool drink. Sometimes the fantasy was simpler, and they laid side by side on pool chairs, while he watched her out of the corner of his eye, seeing her golden body and her face coyly hidden by a large broad-brimmed hat). His mind, imagining her in this way and acting as a kind of autopilot, would deliver him to her.

That was the idea, untried so far. Tonight would be the ultimate test. He wasn't sure if it would work, but frankly didn't care. To be with her he would suffer anything, he would do anything.

Harold set the external timer for five minutes. He thought that was enough time to bring him to her—it shouldn't take long. His palms itching with anxiety, he crawled into the metal belly of the beast, curled into a ball, and slammed the circular glass door shut. The machine smelled of steel and ozone, of sweat and fur and animal fear. He felt cramped and claustrophobic. *What if I don't go anywhere, but just fade away and cease to exist? What if there really aren't other worlds? What if there's just an empty fog?* A primordial fog where nothing had ever existed or ever would. Outside of time, outside of space, a nothingness that went on and on into eternity. Perhaps he would be stuck out there. *Would I live on forever? I would go insane.* The kitchen timer he had fixed to the machine's control ticked like a maniacal time bomb as it counted down to zero.

It rang loudly and the cylinder began to rotate. He braced himself, feet against the far wall, his back against the other as he rolled up, poised for a moment at the top of an arc, then turned upside down. *This is it! No going back now!*

Hot air blasted him. Static lifted the thin hairs plastered across his head. The basement flip-flopped: one moment upright, the next upside down. He was queasily reminded of a game he had played as a child when he would spin like a top until he couldn't stand any more. Afterward, for long minutes, he had felt the earth spinning under him, swaying beneath him as if on some giant pivot. He remembered the power he had felt then, to know that he could move the world. Now he gulped as he turned over again and again. Will alone kept his dinner within his churning stomach.

Outside the machine, a fog had swallowed the basement. *Just like I thought! I bet if I open the door I'd fall into nothingness forever. Or the fog will enter and devour me. Whichever way, I won't be happy. Nothing ever goes my way.*

The fog darkened and he couldn't see his feet above his head. The fog hadn't been nothing, he knew now. A diffuse light had spread so smoothly through it, that it had seemed almost like no light at all. The darkness outside was true nothingness. He cursed the foolishness that had led into oblivion. *I am like the animals I captured with bait and sent away into darkness, I followed my dream of her into death. Now there is nothing left of me, but regret.*

At that moment, his spirits at their lowest, the timer chinged and he stopped tumbling. He settled within the drum, dizzy and confused.

It was dark outside the porthole, without a single light or reflection. Suddenly claustrophobic, he shoved against the door and fell out as it opened easily.

His face struck something hard, rough. He stroked it in dazed pain, feeling aggregate rock and dust under his fingers. His fingers encountered wood, the first step of a stair. At the top of the stairs he saw a thin band of light under a closed door. He climbed the steps and flipped a light switch by the door.

Looking down, in the sudden glare, he saw a basement with a wooden bench to his left with a tumble of tools and jars full of discarded screws. Along the back wall a rack of paint-stained shelves held several tins, their exteriors stained with the colors of their contents. His machine hulked in the corner. With a thrill of déjà vu, he recognized the basement. His basement, as it was before he had scrambled it and turned its contents into a workshop to manufacture his machine.

"I don't understand. I shouldn't be *here*. I should be in Marilyn's house," he said aloud. He should be where he had pictured himself—by her pool, not in his own basement. *Did I tumble for a while and then emerge back in my own basement? Did I travel across time instead of across dimensions?*

In the kitchen, beyond the closed door, he heard a gentle rustling. *How far back in time am I? Is Mother still alive?*

With shaky hands, he cracked open the basement door. He saw his kitchen, as it had been months ago, with the black-and-white linoleum sparkling clean and the countertops free of the clutter he had accumulated. A man, dressed in brown slacks and brown leather shoes, stood at the sink with his back to Harold. He fashioned a sandwich from mustard, bologna, bread, and lettuce. A growing bald spot crowned the back of his head. This was a side of himself he had never seen before, not so clearly. He didn't know that his bald spot had grown so large.

"Harold, is that sandwich ready yet? I'm about to starve up here!" A woman called from upstairs. Harold's head whipped around, recognizing the voice immediately: Marilyn's. He felt sharp relief. So the machine had worked after all! The other Harold yelled back upstairs. "I'm almost done!"

This was the moment he had planned for. There had to be a Harold here for Marilyn to marry and there was only one way to remove him. Harold looked around the basement and spotted a large steel wrench. He climbed down the stairs and hesitantly picked up the wrench, reluctant to take this final irrevocable step—to strike this other and take his place. It wasn't something he enjoyed, it was something he had to do, to take Marilyn as his wife. He strengthened his resolve and crept up behind the man. He brought the wrench up over his head.

At the last moment, the other man sensed something, for he turned and Harold smashed the wrench into his forehead. Blood spurted across the counter and splattered the white bread and mixed like ketchup in the mustard. He crashed to the floor. Harold stared at the ruined face so like his own. It was like looking into the future: One day his face might be smashed too, and this is how he would look. Harold didn't care for it.

"What was that noise? Are you okay?" Marilyn called again. He frowned, her voice didn't sound exactly like it did in the movies. It was rougher and deeper. He reminded himself that she was acting in her movies and her voice might not sound exactly the same in person.

"I just tripped," he said, hesitantly. *Do I sound like himself? How do I sound here?* "I'm all right."

The other wasn't dead. He moaned as Harold dragged him down into the basement. He laid him in his machine, then threw the switch that sent him tumbling away. The last sight Harold had of the other, his eyes opened large as dinner plates as he began to rotate. Then he and the machine faded away.

"Sayonara, sucker," Harold said. "She's all mine now."

Marilyn yelled again. "Jesus, Harold! How long does it take you to make a damn sandwich?"

She sounded impatient and that irritated Harold. *How dare she be impatient when I've waited my whole life to be with her. Living in Hollywood, she's become spoiled. She hasn't been taught respect. I'll just have to set some ground rules and be firm. Teach her to honor and obey.*

Upstairs, he tossed the bloody sandwich into the trash and pulled a couple of fresh slices out of the bread bag. He spread mustard on one, layered bologna and lettuce between them, and laid them on a plate.

"Coming, Marilyn," he yelled.

"What did you say?"

"I said I'm coming!" Geez, was she deaf? He felt disturbed and grumpy. This wasn't coming out like he planned. First almost puking his guts out in the mad dryer, then seeing his own face smashed in, then this house and Marilyn—they weren't at all what he expected.

At the top of the stairs, he saw the light under Mother's bedroom door and was shocked as he thought that Mother was somehow impossibly alive after all. Then, with a prickly sense of unease, that he and Marilyn slept in Mother's bed. *What would Mother think?*

He chided himself. *You got what you came here for. Stop quibbling at nambly details! Go get her!*

Marilyn on satin sheets in a satin gown—that's what I should image. Her gown tight across her delicious hips and breasts. Her hair spread across lacy pillows. And she's pouting—her lips trembling— because I'm late with her sandwich.

He opened the door. A woman, sitting at a makeup table at the room's far side, twisted to look at him. She wore a tattered chenille robe with tacky flowers appliquéd on it; underneath it, her body was thick and sagged like an old worn couch. Dirty brown hair was rolled on orange curlers the size of juice cans. Her eyes were worn, tired, sad; they looked like they had seen every rotten thing ever done. A cigarette twitched in her mouth as she cursed him.

"Jesus, Harold! How long does it take to make a goddamn sandwich? Bring it over here before I starve to death."

His mouth wobbled. That voice. Unmistakable as ever, but in this dumpy body? The plate and sandwich fell to the floor, the porcelain smashed into a thousand pieces.

"Marilyn?" he asked. "What have you done to yourself? You look horrible!"

Her eyes squinted angrily. "Marilyn? Who the hell's Marilyn? Some girl you've got on the string? I swear Harold, I've about had it with you."

His knees wobbled and he sat on the bed before he fell. "Marilyn? It is you, isn't it? My God, what happened to you! You're so . . . so . . . plain."

"What happened to me? What happened to you? You go down into the kitchen to fix me a sandwich and you come back babbling. What happened? Did you trip and hit your head?" She stepped in closer and sniffed. "Have you been hitting the bottle again?"

He smelled cigarettes on her breath. Her eyes brimmed with some great loss. In her eyes and in her voice were all that remained of the Marilyn he knew.

"This is wrong, all wrong," he said. "You're supposed to be beautiful and rich. We should be in your mansion in Hollywood, not this dump. Jesus, Marilyn, what did you do? Did you get kicked out? Lose your contract? Was it drugs?" He had read about some pretty wild parties in the fan magazines. They hadn't specifically mentioned drugs and alcohol, but it was pretty clear. He could read between the lines. "What was your last movie? Was it *Gentlemen Prefer Blondes*? *Seven Year Itch*? *Some Like It Hot*?"

She stepped back, eyes wide with horror. "Movies? I don't know what you're talking about. You're nuts."

He jumped up and grabbed her and shook her like a rag doll. Her curlers popped free and flew across the room as her head whipped around. "Think, damn it, think! You've got to have made *some* movie!"

"Stop it, Harold! You're hurting me."

His thoughts scrambled over the movies she had made when just a starlet, when her parts were mere walk-ons. "Damn it, Marilyn! What was your last movie? Tell me!"

"I haven't been in any movies! I don't know what you're talking about," she cried. Her hair hung low over her face. "And stop calling me that name! You know damn well my name's Norma Jeane! Stop calling me Marilyn!"

The blood drained from his face. Norma Jeane was nobody. A girl eager to make it big, but nothing until her first movie. Nothing!

She had never gone to Hollywood. Never become famous. He laughed at the irony. Of course she was nothing—why else would she marry a nobody like him? And he had taken the place of the poor schmuck who had married her—the guy should be grateful Harold had separated him from this!

"Well, I'm not nobody, do you hear?" He shook his fist. She shrunk away. "There are thousands of you! Hundreds better than you, you miserable wretch. It's not too late to change all this. I'll start over, form a clearer picture, and I'm going to keep trying until I find the real thing."

Harold stumbled from the room. He had to get into the machine again. In an infinite number of universes, in an infinite recombination of events, somewhere he was married to the glorious Marilyn Monroe.

He entered the kitchen and strangled a shriek as he saw a body laying on the floor—his body—it was unmistakable even with blood pooling on the linoleum by its head. But that was impossible, he had sent the body away. What was it doing here again?

He heard a whisper of motion and turned to see himself charging from the living room, a bloody wrench held high above his head like a Japanese samurai, an insane grimace on his face that he had never seen before in any mirror. The impossibility of it froze him for a critical microsecond—if that was him on the floor, then who was charging him? He threw up his arm as the other hit him. Pain shot up his elbow. His arm flopped uncontrollably against his side as he backed away from this madman.

The other swung the bloody wrench again. Harold stepped back into the doorway of the cellar.

Another body slumped at the top of the stairs; he saw it too late and he stepped on its arm. It slid under his foot and he tripped. The body rolled with him as he tumbled head over heels down the stairs. He felt something snap within him as he somersaulted down.

When the initial shock had passed, his eyes opened into darkness. The only light came from the door into the kitchen above him. By this wan light, Harold saw that the body entangled with him was yet another Harold. His head swam with pain and confusion. *Another one? But then who did I send away? And who was on the kitchen floor? And the madman with the wrench?*

It struck him suddenly that in an infinite number of universes, with innumerable chances for Marilyn Monroe to marry a nobody like him, there must be other Harolds who, like him, were lonely voyeurs at *her* movies, who hoarded her photos in the screen magazines, who dreamed of holding her in his arms, and who constructed mighty machines in dark basements to travel into her space.

Something stung his eye. He dragged his hand across his forehead and felt his hair sticky with blood. He laughed, then choked as a sharp pain stabbed him in the lungs. Didn't he know exactly what he looked like now? Hadn't he seen himself after a blow to the head?

He fought unconsciousness.

A hum filled the air and the darkness turned a deep ultraviolet blue. The blue grew brighter as brilliant sparks lit the corner of the room. By the light of artificial lightning he saw five other mammoth machines. Another machine materialized. This one was slicker than the others, the edges smoother, more polished, as if it had been made on an assembly line instead of by hand.

The door in the latest machine opened and a woman climbed out. She wore a miniskirt and a short-sleeved blouse in some silvery material. The blouse had a vaguely military cut and an emblem over the breast. She wore high-heeled silver boots and her hair was platinum blonde. Her face was beautiful; the face that Harold had crossed an unimaginable void to be with.

She gripped an odd-looking pistol with a wide-mouthed bore and looked capable of using it.

The stairs creaked as the Harold with the wrench stepped over him; the bloody tool clutched in his hand. He stared at the woman. "Marilyn," he whispered.

"All right, Harold. That's far enough," she said. "You've done enough damage today. You can't go around bashing people on the head and hope to take their place. We won't allow it."

The door to the newest machine opened again as a man in a trim gray jumpsuit stepped out. He had an emblem similar to hers on his military cap. Turning back to the machine, he assisted a man in brown slacks and brown leather shoes to step out who had a white-bandage-wrapped head.

Harold stared at the newcomers. The one in the bandage was the man he had struck and sent away. And the man in the uniform, his head near the other as he helped him out of the machine, could be his identical twin.

Bloody-wrench Harold looked at the two Harolds, side by side. His face turned purple. He screamed and raised his wrench high as he dove for them. Marilyn's gun made a soft *fuht* noise and a little dart appeared in his neck. He wavered on his knees, then crashed down. Her expression didn't change. She might shoot down mad Harolds every day, Harold thought, then wondered, as he looked around at the collection of conscious and unconscious men, if that might not literally be true.

"You boys have been busy today. Our travel board lit up like a Christmas tree," she said. "And then this one"—she waved her gun at Bandaged Harold—"flew off the board like a rocket, heading into nowhere. Did *you* send him on his one-way trip or was it one of these other guys?"

He stared at her. *To win you I would do anything.* He said nothing.

"No matter. We're sending all of you home and we're going to smash your machines."

They loaded each Harold in the machine which had brought him, then attached a guidance device to the exterior that would also destroy the machine minutes after it brought them to their home dimension. They woke each Harold and explained this clearly to him before sending him away.

He watched them as they worked, saw the way their hands touched casually as one handed a tool to the other and the unspoken communication of their eyes. There was more than a working partnership between the two.

Marilyn brought a first-aid kit. He breathed in sweet perfume while she examined the wound on his forehead. A plastic nameplate pinned to her breast pocket read SGT. N. J. BROWN. He wished he had the strength to touch her. While she attended him, her partner carried Bandaged Harold upstairs and tried to calm his wife.

They returned Harold himself in their own machine since his had been left behind somewhere in the voids of space-time when they rescued Bandaged Harold. They dumped him in his basement with an admonition to never build another machine; they would be watching and would not be so easy on him if he was caught a second time.

He sat on the bottom step of the basement stairs, staring where the machine had vanished in a fuzzy blue spot.

He remembered her cool hands on him as she had wiped the blood from his forehead, her face so near he could have kissed her merely by stretching out his lips. One Norma Jeane old, her life wasted in frustration; the other young, strong, everything his dream had been without the glamour and fame. Both married to him.

He turned to the workbench where the remnants of his earlier experiments lay and surveyed what work needed to be done.

AFTERWORD

Marilyn died when I was very young, so my memories of her are from her movies. I've long been interested in collectors and their collections. James Dean, Elvis, Marilyn—people obsess over these stars long after their deaths, and I wanted to tell the tale of the ultimate obsessed fan.

What, after all, would complete a fan's collection, but the ultimate object herself? Marilyn.

—John A. Day

O, VIRGINIA

BY STEPHEN GALLAGHER

 I GREW UP on those stories where the circus comes to town. You know the ones. It's always a circus or a travelling fair, and the people who came with it are always somehow *other* and scary. A small and placid community gets all shaken up, the town's suddenly full of magic, and everybody's life is changed and made mysterious.

I don't know why those stories meant so much to me. I read them in books I got from the library, but they might as well have been taking place on Mars. Our town had a visit from a circus twice a year, and it was nothing like that.

Ours was a circus and travelling fair combined. It was family-owned, with the same name appearing on the show posters, the booths, and the sides of the clapped-out wagons that brought it all in. They pitched on a rubble-strewn croft and they stayed for four days at a time. When they went, the croft reverted to a parking place for lorries and haulage vehicles. During those four days and nights, crime rose, drunkenness increased, and the streets all around were measurably less safe. There was a concentration of lights like an electrical storm. There was the noise of old pop records, played at a deafening level that was way beyond the limits of the equipment.

Naturally, for an eleven-year-old it was a magnet.

It was magic of a kind, I suppose. Not the magic of the stories, but a sweaty, oily, ugly kind of magic. Mine wasn't one of those stable, self-contained little communities, it was an industrial suburb in the North-West of England. And the show people weren't in any sense ethereal. My memory is that the rides were all supervised by medically classifiable morons, and the sideshows by change-counting fishwives with hands like tree bark.

A couple of times I went on my own, but mostly I'd go with Otto. Otto was a half-German boy, an oddity in the school, and I expect that this was part of the reason why we were friends. While the fair was in town, we'd go just about every night; we scrounged what money we could and pooled it and made it last, but even when our money was gone we still went along anyway. We'd hang about. Walk around. Watch. Occasionally some of the people who ran the stalls would tell us to get out of the way of the paying customers, but mostly we were invisible.

We'd stand outside the Wall of Death, and we'd watch the walls shake as the motor bikes went around inside. That was when we couldn't afford to go in. The Wall of Death was one of the few attractions where they didn't turn us away because we were too young. They wouldn't let us into the knife-thrower's show, because they made this big thing about how the woman who stood there would have to take most of her clothes off to make her the least possible target so she could avoid the blades. Crowds of young drunks would suddenly develop an animated interest in the knife-thrower's art.

Otto and I were still in short trousers. We weren't even tall for our ages. Over the past three years' worth of visits we'd been frequently rebuffed. When we tried to get into the freak show, it was the same kind of story.

The woman in the pay booth looked down on us and said, "How old are you two?"

"Eleven," Otto said.

"Twelve," I said, lying.

"Can you see that?" the woman said, and she pointed at something that was pinned up in the booth beside her. Obediently, we looked. It was one of those joke car number plates and it read, RU21.

She said, "What does it say?"

"It doesn't say anything," Otto said.

So now she pointed to the letters and numbers, one at a time. "It says are . . . you . . . twenty-one. Are you?"

I was ready to slink off, but Otto was genuinely puzzled. "Why does it say that?" he said.

"This is a show for grown-ups. And you're little kids. So bugger off, boys, and don't mither. Come back when you're older."

Crestfallen and embarrassed, we retreated to a distance.

"Rotten cow," Otto said.

"Yeah," I agreed, unable to think of anything of equal daring.

We went to look at other things, but we kept coming back to the same spot. I can't speak for Otto, but even the outside of the freak show had a terrifying fascination for me. It was basically a lorry, but the shape of it had disappeared because fold-out sides and add-on pieces had turned the whole thing into a shanty building. Lurid sign-writing on the sides, more vivid than it was accurate, read: ABBOMINATIONS OF NATURE. FREAKS AND MONSTERS.

And, most mystifyingly, PARTS OF THE STARS.

For a while, we watched people going in. Then we watched them as they came out, and we tried to read their expressions to get some idea of what they might have seen inside. Most were talking, or looking ahead to whatever it was they were planning to do next. It was as if the show had already passed from their minds and left no impression. But not everyone was like that. There were quite a few nervous gigglers, mostly girls with their boyfriends piling it on. Odd ones—and these were the ones who caught my imagination—emerged and slipped off into the night, faces pale and dismayed.

What had *they* seen?

And what exactly was the meaning of that expression they wore? It wasn't just the susceptible ones. Some of them looked like quite hard types. It was as if they'd been hit with something they'd never even imagined they could feel. I can't describe it. They looked suddenly fragile.

Disarmed.

Otto wanted to see if we could peek into the circus, so I went along. There was an open flap at the back where the acts came and went, and sometimes you could get an angle and see a six-inch-wide slice of the action for nothing.

The circus wasn't much. An aunt took me, once. There appeared to be three performing families and they swapped around and helped in each other's acts. I counted four horses, three camels, and one sad-looking elephant. The trapeze family had a certain glamour, but that was helped by distance. The man who did the catching got drunk and picked fights in local pubs while the two women, awesome in flight, looked flat-footed and stocky when you saw them shopping in Tescos. The circus had no band, just an amplified Hammond organ, and there were rumours about the organist that small boys like us were never supposed to hear.

Neither of us could see anything, and Otto finally had to concede that we were wasting our time, and then it started to rain so we moved to another part of the ground.

Now we were close to the knife thrower's tent, where there was a man who kept up a constant come-along drone over the loudspeaker system. The knife thrower was up there on the forestage in his fringed jacket, and there alongside him was his moll who promised to take her clothes off. This was no dream girl. Only in retrospect do I realize what she actually looked like: a hardened, tired, working-class woman with bottle-blonde hair that didn't match the color of its roots. The two of them were just disappearing inside.

It must have been the middle of a slack evening. I suppose that the pitchman must have been aware of us hanging around all night because suddenly, over the loudspeaker system, we heard, "All right then, lads. Do you want to see the show?"

We blushed, we panicked. Yes, he was looking our way; and just about everyone in the fairground, we imagined, would be able to hear him calling to us.

"We're just waiting to meet someone," I called out, and we backed off further.

"We could have gone in, then!" Otto said to me a couple of minutes later, furiously and under his breath. I pointed out that he hadn't shown any noticeable courage when the offer was being made.

I realized that, somehow, we'd gone full circle and we were back at the freak show.

The rain had started to come down heavily now, and we were cold. We'd no gloves, but we dragged our pullovers down over our knuckles. Avoiding the mud, we found a bit of canvas to stand under.

From here, we could see all the misspelled publicity and the amateurish paintings on the sides of the boards. All right, so we couldn't get in. But speculation was free.

Otto said, "If a calf's got two heads, how does it know which way it wants to go? I mean, do they both have control of everything?"

"It could be that one of them's just like a passenger," I suggested. "Otherwise they'd have to work something out and I don't think cows are all that bright."

I was keeping one eye on the people coming out. Not so many of them, now. Apprehensive though I was of what might be inside, I started to envy them. They'd *seen*. Their score in life was higher than mine. I felt a kind of rage against my limitations. There was somehow no dignity in being so protected.

One came out with his head bowed, and I could have sworn that he was in tears.

After some further discussion about the coordination of six-legged sheep, I suddenly said, "What I'm wondering is, what does it mean by Parts of the Stars?"

Otto got smug. "I know that," he said.

"How?"

"I just do. It's pieces of famous people's dead bodies. If you're famous and you die, they don't just bury you like they do anyone else. They make you have this special operation."

"What's the point of an operation when you're dead?"

"It's not like an ordinary operation. They cut you right open so everything comes out," Otto said, with an all-encompassing gesture that made the entire process only too vivid. "Then they cut the top of your head off with a saw, and get your brain."

"What for?"

"It's the law. My grandmother got all upset because they wanted to do it to my granddad."

"Your granddad wasn't famous," I said, thinking that I'd spotted the flaw and that this was all turning into an enormous con on Otto's part.

He wasn't fazed. "You don't have to be," he said. "But if you *are* famous and you die, you get it done to you for certain."

That was it, I'd bought it now. My imagination was hooked, and I started to get into the swing of it.

I said, "Imagine not being dead, and waking up while they're doing it."

"If you weren't dead when they started, you'd be dead afterwards."

"What's the point of it?"

"It's so they can look at everything and work out what you died of," Otto said with assurance. "They have doctors who don't mind that kind of thing. Everything they take out doesn't get buried, it gets put in jam jars in stuff like vinegar. They only bury the part that's left over."

I said, "What kind of things are you talking about?"

"Brains," Otto said. "Eyes." I imagined people lining up to get into heaven, reamed out and flip-skulled. Daylight shining through the holes where their eyes had been. If they had such a thing as daylight in heaven.

But Otto wasn't finished yet. He lowered his voice. "Rude parts," he said.

My heart did a somersault.

"Titties?" I said in a breathless, anguished whisper.

"Of the Stars," said Otto. Then he said, "And, you know what I heard they've got?"

I waited.

He told me.

After that I looked across at the freak show with renewed angst and interest. Rain had more or less settled in for the night. Drops of it were sizzling on the hot light bulbs. The fairground was emptying, and some of the stalls were already closing up. Someone with a pole came along and lifted some of the overhead canvas, and a couple of gallons of rainwater hit the ground only yards away.

They closed up the freak show, then, and Otto and I finally gave up and went home. We had to walk home in the rain, because we were pennies short of our bus fare. I got shouted at for getting my hair wet and my clothes soaked through. That night I slept deeply, and I dreamed of the Parts of the Stars.

The next day was a school day.

During the lunch hour, Otto and I went to the pie shop and then took the pies down to the canal. We sat on a bench and ate the pies, and then we screwed up the white paper bags and shied them at the ducks on the murky, reed-clogged water. The ducks squawked and made a fuss because they thought the bags were bread, but then they quickly lost interest.

"You can see the circus and the fair from the bridge," said Otto.

The intention was that we'd just go to the bridge and look. I don't recall the exact sequence, but I know it was inevitable we'd end up at the fairground. By then we had about fifteen minutes of the lunch hour left, and I was optimistically thinking we'd have plenty of time to get back, even though it had taken us the best part of half an hour to get down there.

It all looked quite different in daylight. It was just as tacky, but with none of the redeeming excitement. Dead bulbs hung on their lines. The sideshow stalls had been emptied of their cheap soft toys and plaster ornaments.

Otto said, "The Wall of Death's gone."

I'd felt that something was missing, and I saw that he was right. There was a bare churned-up space where the Wall of Death had been, the shape of a raw O still imprinted on the ground. They'd struck it and moved on already. It wasn't even the weekend, yet.

Looking around now, I could see that some of the other attractions had been partly dismantled. The cars had been taken off the Spider, and its legs hinged up in the middle. There was no roof on the Waltzer. They were longer fairground rides, but more visibly machines on trailers.

Free-standing metal barriers had been put across to close off the area, but there was no one around. It was lunchtime, after all. The fairground workers were probably over in their caravans, which from here looked like a gathering of wedding cakes.

"The freak show isn't locked," Otto said.

He was right about that, as well. There was a big padlock on the entrance door of the shanty building, but the hasp was turned back and the padlock was hanging open.

"Fancy a look?" Otto said.

"We'd get done," I said.

"Not if we're quick."

Otto didn't even wait. He slipped around the barrier and walked straight across the open ground toward the freak show. I didn't move. He stopped by the door and turned to look back at me. We had one of those silent arguments over a distance, all mouthings and exaggerated gestures. I was trying to point out to him that we were in school uniform; even if we were spotted and ran, we'd be traceable. He didn't get it. He carried on not getting it for a while, and then he opened the door and went in.

My heart was hammering like a drum filled with stones. I was convinced that Otto was about to be caught. It was perfectly possible, even probable, that someone was working inside; but I heard no bellowing, no shouting, nothing.

Inside me, something seemed to burst. Before I even knew what I was doing, I ran over and went in after him.

The shanty had a canvas roof, and the light inside was like the light in a tent. The floor creaked as I stepped in and closed the door behind me. I was working out my excuses. I was taking my cat to the vet's and I saw it run in here. I'd heard someone shouting for help. Something. Anything.

I looked around.

My first feeling was of an enormous sense of cheat. There was a two-headed calf, all right. It was a photograph, pasted onto a board. Almost everything was a photograph, apart from the tallest and smallest people in the world, who were life-sized but incredibly lousy painted figures on hinged sheets of hardboard. In a display case there was a pair of tiny boots and something that appeared to have been stuck together out of a dried fish and a monkey. In a frame behind that was a birth certificate for the oldest man in Britain. It was on shiny photocopier paper that had faded to the point where only parts of it were at all legible.

Something snorted behind me, and I almost hit the roof. I turned around. In a waist-high pen was a sheep with matted wool. It was a live one, but it seemed to be kneeling. When I looked more closely, its front legs were oddly bifurcated so that a pair of spare and useless hooves stuck out behind.

This, presumably, was the six-legged sheep. It wasn't six-legged at all; it was just desperately, sadly crippled. It made a scrabbling sound as it hitched itself around in the confined space. Coordination would never be a problem for it. The poor beast couldn't even stand.

And then I heard Otto call out in a whisper, "They're down here."

He'd come around a corner, and was beckoning me down into the back part of the shanty. He disappeared out of sight and before following him, I looked at sheep again. Its eyes were dull, and it had no interest in me. It didn't appear to have any interest in anything.

It was darker at the back of the building. Set apart from the rest of the non-show, this section led to the exit. I saw shelves. I saw jars.

"Parts of the Stars," Otto said proudly, as if they were here to prove him right.

I wasn't looking at the parts of the stars right then. I was looking at the Medical Mistakes that began the section. Mostly these were plaster casts of deformities, but there was one big jar with a tiny, drowned-looking body squashed up into it. It looked like a baby mouse before its fur grows and its eyes open, so pale that you could see the entire map of veins through its skin. It was floating in murky fluid and it was heartbreakingly human.

Then there were more jars. They weren't jam jars at all, they were far too big. Otto seemed to have come straight to these and to have noticed nothing else.

"Look," he said.

I looked. He was pointing to a half-gallon container with its lid sealed all around with sellotape and a handwritten label that read, in big block capitals, THE PENUS AND TESTICCLES OF ERROL FLYNN. Down in the bottom of the jar was something that looked at first like a bowel movement, and at second glance like an oversized gherkin.

I looked at the next one. BOGEY'S LUNG. I remembered my dad saying that Bogey had died of lung cancer. My mother had almost run from the room. Cancer was a word you only whispered, back then, and never in the presence of children; it was like the name of one of the major demons.

The object that was supposed to be Bogey's lung resembled a stiff, cooked liver. The next jar had the same murky fluid but nothing obviously in it. No label, and just a residue of sludge at the bottom.

I said, "What's that supposed to be?"

"Bogey's bogies," Otto suggested, and we had a cackling fit that for me was made even more intense by my terror of being heard.

I moved along, and looked at some of the others. Some of the subjects dated way back, and a lot of the so-called stars I'd never heard of. All the time, I was tensed for the slightest noise from outside. As far as sound was concerned, the walls were so flimsy that there might as well have been no barrier between us and the rest of the world.

Otto was skipping everything, looking only at the labels until he found what he was looking for.

"It's here," he said excitedly.

I moved to join him. On the top shelf, just out of reach, was THE VIRGINIA OF MARILYN MONROE.

I said, "What's a virginia?"

Otto said, "I think it's another name for . . . you know."

I peered.

"I can't see anything," I said.

"Reach it down."

I was startled at the very suggestion. As if we weren't criminals enough!

"No," I said.

"You're soft, you," Otto said scornfully. "I'll do it."

"You'll get us both killed!"

"That's the only thing that would shut you up from whining."

He stretched up his arms to reach it down. Otto had begun to outgrow his school blazer and it was a size too small, so the sleeves rode up to somewhere around his elbows. They stayed there as he lowered the jar.

The object inside the jar bobbed as the fluid tipped. Clouds rose inside as years-old sediment was disturbed. I looked around, terrified, but I couldn't bring myself to leave. I had to see.

"It's like piss soup," Otto said, holding it up before his face and inspecting it closely.

He gave it a shake.

I think they were old confectionery jars, the kind with the plug-in glass stopper for a lid. The stopper just sits there, held in by its own weight. The lid had been sealed into place with sellotape, but the sellotape had dried out completely until it was brown and crackly, like insects' wings. As soon as the surging fluid hit it, the lid flew off.

The stink was incredible. The stuff showered onto the floor and with it slithered something about the size and color of a rotten banana peel.

"That's it!" Otto said excitedly.

I was horrified. Otto had put the jar aside on the floor, and was crouching over the mess on the boards. How he could even breathe the air without keeling over, I don't know.

I was trying not to cough, because of the fumes. It wasn't vinegar, it was something else.

"I don't want to see," I said, with my own breath catching in my throat.

"You've got to!" insisted Otto, as if his own experience wouldn't be validated without someone else along.

I could see more than I needed to from where I was standing. The jar exhibit resembled a piece of brown leather, like one of those ancient sandals they dredge up out of a peat bog. Part of it had bristles, like pork rind. I didn't want to look any closer. If it genuinely was what it purported to be, I suddenly wanted to see it even less.

It wasn't the reaction I might have expected to have. I mean. The Virginia of Marilyn Monroe. A boy could only dream.

But these weren't the kind of dreams that I wanted.

The stink was indescribable, and it was getting even worse.

"It's melting," Otto said, incredulously.

He was right. Exposed to air, the object was deliquescing before our eyes. In less than a minute, it was slime.

He stood up. Our eyes met.

"Come on," I said.

We burst out of the exit door running. I don't know if anyone saw us, and we didn't stop to see. We didn't even slow until we reached the canal and then, even though we were a good ten minutes late for afternoon school, we had to slow to a walk.

Otto seemed exhilarated. I remembered the reactions we'd observed on people emerging, the only evidence on which we could try to gauge the emotional temperature of what lay inside. It was only years later that I was to realize that whatever was in the shanty was emotionally neutral. It was the interior architecture of the people that governed their reactions.

Otto was high. My timing was bad, and he looked at me as I was wiping my eyes on one of my sleeves.

"You fucking baby," he said. But not just with the contempt I would have expected; there was a certain wonder in his tone as well.

"Shut up," I said.

Nothing more was said after that. We could each incriminate the other, so probably nothing would be. We braced ourselves for terrible consequences, but none came. One of the girls complained about the strange smell in the French classroom that afternoon, and asked for a window to be opened. Even that might have been for some other reason, although I don't honestly think so.

The next time I was in the library, I looked up Virginia in the dictionary. It puzzled me, because it was a place in the United States and not a part of the body at all. Otto talked about our exploit a few times, but I never encouraged him and after a while we let the subject drop.

The next year, we went again. The knife thrower didn't return in that next season but the Wall of Death and the freak show were there, both unchanged and as dilapidated as before. We hovered outside the freak show for a while, and then we decided to try it on. Our voices had dropped in the course of the year, which I suppose meant that a couple of other things had dropped as well. There was someone different in the booth, a teenager who looked as if he only shaved once every couple of weeks, and then only to take the tops from off his spots. He took our money and let us in without a murmur.

Everything was the same, even the sheep. It shuffled and it stared into nowhere. A few other people were in there with us, trying to make the most out of a lousy-value deal. Otto and I went straight through to the Parts of the Stars.

There they were. Errol's tacky tackle. Bogey's bogies.

And there, at the end, in the same jar, in fluid that wasn't noticeably fresher than the rest; magically restored or somehow otherwise replaced, The Virginia of Marilyn Monroe.

I suppose we should have drawn the obvious conclusion, but we didn't. I think we still assumed it was real. Trust and gullibility are things that we're born with, and they can take time to unlearn. Perhaps we can only absorb one of life's big lessons at any given moment, and I'd already had one of mine when my heart had moved in a way that I could never have imagined before, and that I would never afterwards forget.

That's my excuse, anyway. I can't think of any other way to explain without shame how, for the rest of that year and for some time thereafter, I went around holding the awed conviction that our experience had been an authentic one and that when it came to Virginias, every woman had a minimum of two.

AFTERWORD

I wrote a couple of paragraphs on the subject of how and why I came to write "O, Virginia," and then I had to throw them away. There was nothing wrong with them, as far as they went. But they rambled on about fame and the dark downside of living a life that becomes myth, and they didn't get to the point.

The point is that I once saw a photograph of Marilyn Monroe sneaked by someone in the mortuary after her autopsy, lying with her hair scraped back and the sheet under her chin, looking nothing like herself. If it hadn't been for the caption, I'd never have known who it was. I wasn't a fan. I think even now I can name with certainty only one movie that she appeared in (unless I think for a while, and then I can get to three or four).

But the picture made me feel sad. It was the kind of sadness in which for a moment you sense the interconnectedness of everything. Writing the story was an attempt to explain why. If I didn't manage it there, I've got no chance of doing it now.

—Stephen Gallagher

SOMETHING'S GOT TO GIVE

BY JANET BERLINER AND
GEORGE GUTHRIDGE
(WITH SPECIAL THANKS TO STEVEN LEVI)

1993

THE HOUSE LIGHTS come on and Victor walks on-stage at the Dunes. The audience rises to its feet. He can see them, smell them, feel them. "Brava, Marilyn," they scream.

"Bravo!" a few of them shout, directing their kudos to the man whose virtuoso impersonation so captures her essence that they feel her presence even after she has been dead for more than thirty years.

Most of the time, even Victor does not think of himself as anything but Marilyn. He has allowed her to age. Her hair, like his own, is white, her hands as laden with wrinkles as any septuagenarian's. The public loves the honesty. Every show is a sellout, often months in advance.

He has kept her alive for them since the death of Norma Jeane Baker.

Tonight, he will let her die. When he removes the trappings, it will be for the last time.

There is a new element abroad amongst the audience, something tangible and horrific. Victor hates it. He feels as if he is not only mocking the dead but also the dying. An hour or two after the show ends, tradition will die for him, and for Las Vegas.

The Dunes will close its doors.

Exactly one month later, tourists and locals will crowd the streets with their cameras, waiting in a bittersweet October twilight to record the implosion of the hotel. Some will dance in celebration of the new; others will cry, remembering a time when The Dunes *was* Las Vegas.

The implosion will take seconds; the building of a new hotel and showroom will take years. When it reopens, it will do so without him. He is too old to tour, too old to wait.

Since the beginning of his career, Victor has been Marilyn even when he is not onstage. His suite at the Dunes is a duplicate of her home, ersatz where hers is the real thing, but exact enough that only an expert would know that hers were antiques, one of a kind, while his are perfectly designed copies, like the radiant-cut emerald-shaped cubic zirconia ring on his finger—an exact replacement for the diamond ring she wore in *Some Like It Hot*, indistinguishable to the naked eye.

Victor smiles almost shyly at the audience—her smile. He is afraid, like she was most of her life, but he performs, and the audience, as always, clamors for more as the curtain comes down. The stagehands prepare for the encore, the final act of this final show. At every other performance, Victor has played this last song as the late, forgotten Norma Jeane Baker, in pale lipstick and a mousy wig. This time, he returns to the stage in the red dress and strips before a silenced audience.

Gone are the chorus girls and the muscular male backup with glistening chests and electronic guitars, explosions, tendriled smoke. The stage is empty but for a street lamp and a bus-stop bench with Marilyn's famous flying dress poster on it. Only the face isn't Marilyn, it's Norma Jeane.

Quietly, Victor-as-Marilyn begins to sing. The song is the Hollies hit he added to the repertoire a decade ago: *"Some day my name and hers,"* he sings in Marilyn's breathy, sensuous voice, *"are going to be the same."*

Slowly, using a few pieces of makeup he has been clutching in his hand, he transforms the image on the poster back to Marilyn. Then he leans sideways to kiss her full on the mouth and the curtain falls one last time. He takes no more bows.

Tears stream down his face. He can sense the tingling in the audience's hands as the applause rings on and on.

A stagehand brings Kleenex.

Victor goes to the dressing room, brushing by and thanking well-wishers who touch his hand and shoulder, kiss his cheek. The dressing room is empty except for a Marilyn who, surrounded by tiny flame-shaped lights and the sepia photos she treasures, greets him from the makeup mirror. *Give 'em hell, kid,* his fellow septuagenarian Sinatra wrote on the glass, in her lipstick, a month ago. *We're the end of an era.*

1962

Victor Schafle had been working Vegas for half a dozen years, first as a stripper with a little hooking on the side, then with moderate success doing the Marilyn gig. He considered auditioning for the part of her double in *Something's Got to Give* to be something of a joke, and was more shocked than anything else when he got the job. As it turned out, he beat out several hopefuls with better boobs and every bit as ready to lie down for the job because casting knew the director preferred a quick wit and a hard ass to starry-eyed pussy.

Dressed in his Marilyn casuals, he arrived at the lot early, and was pleasantly surprised when the guard did a double-take, looked at his watch, and waved him through with "Hello, Miss Monroe. Nice to see you." On the set, people brought him coffee, opened doors, made small talk about subjects they assumed he understood.

When shooting was about to begin and the real Marilyn had not yet arrived, Victor had no choice but to tell everyone who he was. He felt anger directed at him, as if he and not Marilyn were the one who was late. Cukor, the director, swore loudly and ordered the shooting to commence.

Marilyn never did show up that day. Victor took his day's pay happily, and used part of it for a taxi to her house in Brentwood. He told himself it was to introduce himself and to check on her well-being, but he knew he was just another tourist come to gawk at the high wall and stand of eucalyptus trees that shielded the mock-adobe hacienda at the end of the cul-de-sac.

A housekeeper opened the door as he was about to knock. Bird-like and bespectacled, she prattled about the high cost and low quality of the broccoli at the supermarket, finishing in a voice closer to that of disciplinarian than employee: "I covered it with melted Swiss, so I know you'll like it," and insisted that Victor sit down and eat.

"You seem awfully quiet tonight, dear," she said. "Everything all right on the set?"

His mouth full—he realized he had not eaten all day—Victor nodded, hoping she did not see his trembling.

The next hours were bliss. Eunice, resplendent in black hat and coat, announced that she was going out for the evening. Marilyn was not home, and he assumed ownership of her house, intending simply to stay there until he heard her coming and then slip out of the back door.

Alone in her domain, he opened her dresser. Fingering her silks gave him an erection, and he wished he had strength enough to slip into a teddy and lie on the bed. Maybe pop some of the pills whose plastic bottles, arranged according to height, were lined up like toy soldiers before the mirror. He wondered what it would be like to have Marilyn's former husband Joe DiMaggio touch him; he had always loved baseball—men with big bats and hard balls, as his friends liked to say.

Deep in fantasy, he did not hear Marilyn until she stood in the foyer saying, "Eunice? Eunice?" He hardly had time to hide before she entered the bedroom and collapsed across the bed with a hard-breathed "Oh, God," then jackknifed her body, pulled off her heels, and tossed them against the blackout cloth that covered the window. "Bastards," she said, "but we're beating them, aren't we, Norma Jeane. We're on the downhill side now. Payback time."

Looking groggy with exhaustion, she sat up, legs hanging off the bed, staring down as she wiggled her toes in her nylons. "Bunch of vampires," she said. She blew a breath up from her lower lip and dragged herself over to the vanity, so tired she was barely able to hold her head up as she peered into the mirror. "Let me sleep, Sister," she said. "Just this once. I can't go back to the set when you've got me feeling like this."

She stood, wavering, stripped off her top, and reached around to unzip the skirt. He waited, heart in his throat, for her to put her things away and discover him in the depths of her closet, wondering if it would do any good to throw himself on her mercy. There could be no excuse for his being there.

But she merely dropped the things on the floor and slumped again onto the pink vanity chair. Eyes pinched shut, head in hand, she felt around like a blind person, located a ballpoint, and slid a steno notebook over close to herself. She lifted her eyelids slightly and began listlessly to write, her wrist so limp he wondered how she could hold the pen much less maneuver it.

The pen fell.

She ran her fingers through her hair and leaned close to the mirror as if half expecting it to support her. "Just a couple of randy-mandys, is all. I need them, Norma Jeane. I have to get some rest."

From a bottle she shook out two burnt-orange pills that looked like cough drops, stared at them in her palm as the fingers of her other hand searched out glass and crystal decanter. She poured, swallowed the pills. Suddenly, her facial expression changed. She looked plain—almost ugly—as she grabbed bottles and yanked off caps, all the while glaring at the mirror.

"This is what it t-takes, M-Marilyn?" she stammered angrily. "This is it? This is always it! *I* w-wouldn't need any of it, I c-can t-tell you that." She let the water run in her bathroom sink and scrubbed her face until every last trace of makeup was gone.

It had all happened in the space of a few moments. Victor held his breath, watching the split personality at work and wondering what was going to happen next. He knew that Marilyn was Marilyn again when, from beneath the vanity, she pulled out a half-empty fifth of champagne, opened capsules, and dropped the contents into the bottle. Lifting it in a toast and smiling, she said, "Bedtime cocktail! To your health, Norma Jeane!"

The stammer had gone. It was apparently part of the Norma Jeane persona, Victor thought, watching her down the champagne and drop the bottle onto the carpet. The remainder of the contents trickled into the fiber. "Warm as a honey-filled balloon," she murmured.

Her eyes snapped open and abruptly she gripped the pen and began writing—printing, Victor saw—all concentration now. She kept her gaze on the paper. Riveted, it seemed to him. As though she feared to look in the mirror. Then she rose, jaw tight with anger, and held the page toward the mirror.

"You l-like it, M-Marilyn?" she hissed. Her cheeks looked angular and stark, and her eyes had narrowed to cruel slits. She jammed the pad against the glass, covering the reflection. "You out-on-a-limb b-bimbo!"

Letting the pad fall, she swept the pill bottles from the counter. "And d-don't you d-dare make poor Eunice pick them up in the m-morning," she stammered, stumbling toward the bed. She pulled off her slip, pitched it against the wall, and lay down on her stomach, arms extended, gripping the sheets. She was crying, her back rising and falling.

After a time her body went slack, her breathing regular but for intermittent sobs—crying in her sleep. Victor tiptoed from the room, feeling a mix of pity, exhilaration, and remorse, as if he had witnessed the First Lady pick her nose, heard the Queen fart. It left him feeling guilty, yet quickened his pulse.

He slipped back into his high heels, grabbed up the small carry-all bag he had left under the Formica dining table, and was reaching for the doorknob when someone knocked. He froze. The knocking grew louder.

"Get that, will you, Eunice?" Marilyn called out thickly from the bedroom. "Whoever it is, tell them Marilyn's had enough of their business for the day." Her door slammed shut.

Victor glanced around for somewhere to hide, then decided the best concealment was openness. Get rid of them before they questioned his being there. Tell them the truth: Marilyn was sleeping, she'd phone them in the morning. Her insomnia was no secret; they would understand.

Cukor entered. His thinning hair, square glasses, short-sleeve shirt, and sleeveless sweater made him look more like an accountant than a director. His mood swings were as well known as his predilection for slim young men. Whatever ebullience he usually fostered was gone. His mouth turned down at the corners and his upper lip was hard-edged against his teeth.

"Where were you today?" he demanded, glaring through his glasses.

On your set, Victor started to say, but Cukor interrupted him before he could find the words.

"And I don't want to hear about migraines. I've got migraines of my own. From scheduling around you, Marilyn. The budget's so out of whack my wallet's grown teeth and is biting me on the ass."

"Tomorrow," Victor managed. He wanted to say, I'm sure she'll be there tomorrow, but his throat felt so tight he couldn't speak. Of all the people to find him here! He wondered if anything would appease the director should he realize the truth. He wondered what Cukor liked in bed.

Cukor pointed a finger as might a schoolmarm. "Don't let me down."

Whatever was constricting Victor's throat released. "Promise," he said, and then could not help himself. "I promise," and added, flashing his eyes, "George."

He took hold of the door and let his body language talk.

"You get some sleep," Cukor said. "Be on time tomorrow."

"I will. Promise."

"We're paying you a lot for this one," Cukor said, backing outside. "Don't forget it. You want Fox to go on upping the ante, you've got to . . ."

"Put out?" Victor blew him a kiss and shut the door the instant the director's wingtip brogue was off the stoop.

After he heard the director's car drive away, Victor felt more alive than he had in years. He phoned for a cab and soon had his eyes closed, his head against the seat-back as the taxi wended among the tangled lanes. Dreamily, he wondered if it would be possible, highly unlikely but maybe just possible in Hollywood, where dreams came true at least on celluloid, that he could be Marilyn in the morning, everyone marveling at her acting in the reunion-with-children scene, done in a take or two, certain to survive the cutting room. Ah, for a few seconds of film!

For the briefest of possible moments, he wondered what it

would be like if she died and he had to finish the film for her. Then the realization of his foolishness seized him. "Stop!" he cried out, grabbing the cabby's shoulder.

The man eased the car to curbside. "Get yo' hand off'n me, you shrieking queen," he said into the rearview. "You ain't no Marilyn Mon-roe."

Victor handed him a twenty, took off his shoes, and ran back toward Marilyn's. Eunice was home, her DeSoto in the drive. He changed behind the house, in the shadows of the eucalyptus, dumping everything from the bag and sticking in the heels, wig, skirt, blouse, padded bra, perfumed panties. He did his best with compact, Kleenex, and moonlight to remove the makeup, then pulled himself into a Hawaiian shirt.

How could he have been so stupid, trying to play out a pipedream! He might pass for Marilyn, but as soon as she arrived on the set the charade would be discovered. Yes, his little subterfuge with Cukor had worked, but what if the director mentioned being at the house? Even if she attributed her confusion to the drugs, things would likely add up—wrong.

There was only one thing to do. Convince Marilyn she had met Cukor.

He checked the compact, slicked back his hair, straightened his shoulders, and presented himself at the front door.

Eunice answered. "Here to escort Miss Monroe to the set," he said.

"At this hour? Are you crazy? And where's the limo?"

"Came by taxi," he said. "I'm supposed to make sure she gets in the limo, in the morning." He showed her the pass he had received upon exiting the lot earlier in the evening.

"Then come back in the morning." She started to shut the door.

He lifted his bag, showing he was prepared to stay the night. "Please." He gave her his Audrey Hepburn tragic-innocence smile. "Miss Murray, help me. I'll sit out on the street if I must."

She relented, giving him the spare bedroom. When the limo came in the morning, he found himself seated in the back with Marilyn. She was wearing a headscarf and leaning against the door, handkerchief in hand, regarding him through dark glasses even though dawn had just broken.

"Of course I remember talking with George," Marilyn said, when he asked her. "Just after . . ."

"As I said, just after Eunice came back. I was in the living room. . . ."

"Spying on me, of course," she said. "You think I don't know that Eunice is in my psychiatrist's employ? You think I don't know that she goes out in the evenings to report about me?" She crossed a leg at the knee and went back to staring out of the window, her chin on her palm.

What a fool he'd been last night, Victor thought. He would have to tell her the truth, or some of it, at least. She would find out anyway when they reached the lot. Besides, confession was good for the soul—though whose soul, he didn't know.

"Actually, I came out to meet you," he said. "But you were already in bed."

He told her as much of the truth as he felt was necessary, about having been hired as her double and why. Her reaction surprised him. She simply folded her arms and stared at the roof of the car.

"At least there won't be two blonde bimbos on the set," she said flatly.

It occurred to him that perhaps he had been wrong about his hiring, too. With Marilyn, the studio used brunette doubles, adding wigs only at the last moment. He had heard that she had temper tantrums if other blondes were at a shoot, that like many actresses she didn't want lookalikes around. Now, remembering how she had fallen apart in front of the mirror—how it had triggered a switch with the Norma Jeane persona—it occurred to him that her reasons were far more complex.

Seeing a lookalike was like seeing herself in a mirror. And she hated mirrors. They scared her.

"I wouldn't miss a day, not an hour, if it weren't for the goddamn press and the lawyers and," she dug in her purse and pulled out nasal spray, "and this sinusitis." She tilted her head, sprayed, sniffed. "That, and my damn period. Endometriosis, the doctors say. Doctors! Jesus, you can't imagine the pain."

"I know just how you feel." He leaned forward in sympathy, al-most, *almost,* putting a hand on her knee.

"Sure you do." She laughed with a kind of adolescent delight. "You must not be a spy. Even they're not so dumb as to hire a snitch who would say something that stupid. What did you say your name is?"

He blushed at his faux pas, bumping his fingers together to show his helplessness. It was hardly his fault that he'd been born male. "Victor," he said. "My name's Victor."

"Victor," she repeated. "I like that." She held out her hand. "Okay, Victor, I'll forgive you, if you'll forgive me for that rude com-ment."

He gladly shook her hand.

That day they did the reunion-with-children, scene 33, she even more magnificent than he had imagined he would have been. Her control, both acting and self, amazed him. But despite her profes-sionalism, despite her energy and the real tears she shed when her character reunited with two kids after eight storyline years, there were problems. While she hugged the children, Cukor found her smile more gratitude than genuine, simplistic, simpish, always something wrong. There were whispers that she was too maternal. A pool sprang up about her miscarriages and abortions. Eleven was the operative number. Some said higher.

"I don't want to ride home alone," she told him at the end of the day. "Come with me."

"You're sure?"

"I don't trust any of those bastards. At least you're not one of them." She signaled for the limo. "They don't think I know what's going on, but I do. Fox manufactures rumors about my stability, then it fosters the rumors, all so that son-of-a-bitch Cukor and the other cutthroats can have an excuse not to pay me what I'm worth."

She slid on her sunglasses with a gesture of angry resolve, but the moment she closed the car door her body appeared to collapse. "I must finish this shoot, Victor. I can't miss anymore."

She was trembling. On the way home she remained silent as she tried to write in her steno pad, but ended up saying, "Damn, damn!" and stabbing the paper with her pen. She tied on her headscarf—almost like a shield, Victor thought—and stared outside, biting her lip, her eyes moist with frustration.

At her house door she took his hand, a gesture of girlish innocence, and invited him in; she took his hand again when Eunice informed her of the calls: lawyers, her publicists, the IRS, Peter Lawford to remind her of his *you can't miss this one* party.

"I need . . . sleep," she said in a voice filled with desperation.

"You need food," Eunice said.

"Have Victor bring something in." She kicked off her shoes and, in stockinged feet, stumbled into her bedroom.

Tray in hand, he found her softly crying, huddled over her vanity. "Norma Jeane is at me all of the time, pushing me to be what she wants to be." She shook her head sadly. "My life just keeps running me. Like now. I need rest. I need to finish the picture. I don't want to go to that party, but what choice do I have?"

Victor felt so sorry for her that he reacted without thinking. "Maybe there's a way you can rest . . . and still go," he said. She looked at him in such hopeful confusion that something stirred in him, something he had thought buried beneath the avalanche of his years of hustling. She was so shrewd and yet so fragile, such a pro and such an innocent. He loved her.

"Close your eyes," he said.

"I'd love to. For a millennium."

He reached into her closet and changed quickly into the first evening gown he could find. "I won't try to do the makeup in a hurry, so just imagine that part," he said, adjusting the blonde wig he'd selected from her collection in the closet where he'd hid the night before. *One of hers.* The thought thrilled him.

She appraised him without humor, without anger. "You don't look like me at all," she concluded.

"But they think I do," he said, sitting down on the bed.

He told her of his confrontation with Cukor, and of how he had eaten the broccoli and cheese Eunice had prepared for her. She pulled a face, laughed, and agreed to let him attend the party in her place while she stayed home and slept. If the hoax was discovered, she decided, she would insist it had been her idea.

The prospect of the intrigue perked her up, as if, despite her absence, she would be in control. She quickly prepped him on whom to avoid, what small talk to engage in, how to keep conversation down to news on the set. When he was able to dismiss Eunice for the evening, Marilyn was convinced. Like a child playing dress-up, she helped him choose his outfit, his jewels, his makeup. She even called a taxi for him.

Cinderella could not have experienced anything finer, Victor decided, as he offered a cheek to directors whose feet he would gladly have kissed hours before, linked elbows as he shared champagne with Lawford and Kilgallen, felt the brush of Bobby's lips on his knuckles.

He returned to Marilyn only to find that she had not lived up to her half of the bargain. She was curled up, groaning, in a fetal ball on the bedroom floor.

"Miss Monroe?" he asked hesitantly.

When she did not answer, except to continue groaning, he leaned down and touched her shoulder.

She rolled over, face red and contorted with anger, and began beating at his chest. "I want out, g-goddamn you! You hear m-me? L-Let me go!"

Her fury shocked him and he fell back, as much in surprise as from the physical hammering.

"You c-can't keep me l-locked up forever!"

It was not so much the look on her face or the words themselves that made him realize what had happened, but rather the stammer.

She was not Marilyn, nor was she speaking to him. Something—the drugs, alcohol, anxiety—had triggered her and now she was Norma Jeane, speaking to herself. Her *other* self. Her *Marilyn* self.

She tried to get up, but couldn't. He poured her a glass of water and held her as she gulped, stabbing a finger toward her vanity and the array of prescription drugs that lay tumbled upon its surface.

"Which one?" he asked.

"All! Whatever! A-Anything. S-something, goddamnit!"

Victor's own drug use had never been physician-directed. Hers, however, clearly was. The labels represented a dozen doctors. Dubiously, he shook several pills into his palm.

She crawled toward him on hands and knees and picked up the champagne bottle which lay where it had rolled the night before. Ignoring him, she swigged down a handful of pills, fighting with the prescription bottles to find another type she wanted.

Capsules spilled across the vanity.

"Norma Jeane hates this stuff," she said slowly, with no trace of a stammer. "Norma Jeane hates me." She sat up ramrod-straight on the carpet, with her head held high. "She wants to kill me, you know, but I won't let her. I've got to . . . got to . . . finish the picture."

With that, she tumbled over and lay with her face buried in the thick pile of the carpet.

Victor looked down at the sad, crying creature whom, he realized, he had loved long before he had ever impersonated her on a stage. Perhaps because he had been so intimate with her these past two days, he understood her dilemma, one she herself did not comprehend. Insomnia, endometriosis, sinusitis . . . those were only symptoms of a deeper disease. The real pain came from Norma Jeane Baker, the stuttering, mousy, sexually fearful woman who was trying to destroy the Marilyn persona she had so laboriously created.

Marilyn tried crying herself to sleep in Victor's arms. Neither of them slept, so the next day on the set was a disaster. She barely remembered who she was, much less her lines. She did not even react when Cukor resorted to screaming.

In the evening she had to entertain, her home this time, but she was afraid to leave her room. Still, a Marilyn emerged who was articulate, graceful, witty, wise—all she had been at the best of times—and as midnight neared she managed to ease even the socially slow out of the door. Only one person had asked about the whimpering from the bedroom. "Mafia," she said in a stage whisper. "In heat. Don't go in unless you want your arm chewed off. You know how Hollywood bitches can be."

It was not until the front door was shut and locked, and Eunice was in her own room, that Victor allowed Marilyn's crying to pull against his heartstrings. He had sensed all evening behind the false smiles of his guests—her guests—that Fox wanted her to fail, wanted some reason never again to offer her a reasonable contract.

To assure her success, he had to help her rest. Had to hold Norma Jeane at bay.

He went to her room and, easing the door open, stood watching her. The room was lit by a small nightlight plugged into the wall. Despite the semidarkness, he could tell that her eyes were closed. She had removed her makeup; Norma Jeane's features were evident, her face a rictus of emotional pain. Tiny cries intermittently issued through her compressed lips. In a matter of minutes, he was certain, her induced semiconsciousness—one could not call it sleep—would end. The pills, at least the way she was taking them, were not working. Her body had become too drug-tolerant. Greater dosages would not help—and might kill her. The only answer was to increase absorption without increasing the amount.

Her eyes blinked open. God but he loved her, he thought, suppressing his own tears with difficulty. She looked around with wide, frightened eyes, as if unsure where she was. Then she fixed on the triangle of light slanting across the mirror—and at the image within.

Her face contorted with a look of terror. On the way to her side, Victor saw the enema bag that lay on the vanity, the one the drugstore clerk had recommended for ease of use.

"Norma Jeane made me do it," she whispered, to the ceiling. "Please, somebody, help me. I don't want to go." She sighed deeply, and lay still.

"I'm here," Victor said, not knowing yet that she was dead. "I promise, I will never let you go."

1993

"I didn't let go," Victor says to Marilyn's reflection in the dressing room mirror, the same reflection Norma Jeane saw, all those years ago. "Not until today. Until now."

He looks more closely at the mirror and, for a moment, he no longer sees Marilyn, or Norma Jeane, but just an old and worn gay gigolo who finally has to admit the truth to himself.

That he is not Marilyn.

That he is not Norma Jeane.

If only he had known then what he knew now, that administered anally, chloral hydrate enters the blood directly rather than being metabolized by the liver, and thus interferes with the body's ability to metabolize the Nembutal injested earlier.

"They tried to kill you," he whispers. "All of them tried—Norma Jeane, your public, who wanted you to be perfect, time, which excuses no one. Only *I* wouldn't let you die. Your death was just another violation, another casting couch that you survived because I, Victor, kept you alive."

He looks more closely at the image in the mirror, his exit song sounding in his mind: *"All the people staring like we're both just quite insane,"* the face in the mirror sings. *"Some day my name and hers are going to be the same."*

The face has straight, mousy-brown hair cut in a pageboy, eyes nearly without expression. Almost unconsciously he reaches for the medicines he is never without.

Marilyn's medicines.

The voice in the mirror speaks out again, his own this time, clear as a stage call: *"Please, somebody, help me. I don't want to go."*

Only the silence answers, a silence filled with the ghosts of Janis and Judy, and Marilyn and Norma Jeane.

It is four o'clock in the morning, but on the Strip in Las Vegas time doesn't matter. It certainly doesn't mean anything to Victor. Cleansed of his makeup now except for a touch of pink lipstick and pencil-darkened brows, he stuffs a blonde wig, a pair of showy diamante earrings, and a tight-fitting, low-cut red dress into a carry bag. He selects a modest pair of pearl earrings from a small box, clips them on, and picks up a large, messy makeup kit. He selects a few items which he slips into his blazer pocket, shoves the rest of the makeup in with the other things in the bag. Carrying that and a small leather briefcase, he goes back onstage for a few moments. The house is empty except for the cleaning crew and the resonances of performances past.

As miserable as he has ever been in his life, Victor leaves the stage and winds his way through the room to the public exit. It leads into the main casino, which is empty of all but its graveyard-shift diehards who will doubtless stay until security clears the place. He wanders slowly toward the elevators. Ears echoing with the last applause he will ever hear, he presses the button that will take him to his suite. *Her* suite, really, with its satin and lace, its blow-ups of publicity shots and music and pills. Its four-poster bed and French telephone.

Once there, tears streaming, he performs last rites upon the contents of the bag, depositing the items one by one into the hotel garbage can.

"Bye, Marilyn," he whispers, as he drops the bag itself inside. "I love you."

He undresses slowly and reaches for her enema bag, which he has kept with him all this time. She and Norma Jeane are staring at him from the poster on the wall. Smiling. The skirts of their red dresses are blowing in the breeze that comes up through the subway grille beneath their high heels.

AFTERWORD

My oldest daughter—a blue-eyed blonde—was born in mid-May of 1963. Counting backwards, it's pretty evident what I must have been doing when MM died. It's not unlikely that one of her songs was playing in the background. I really adored her. As for this story, it's rooted in a real Vegas experience. Late one night, I ambled along the Strip and stopped to eavesdrop on a cross-dresser who was conversing with a poster of Marilyn. The rest, as they say, is history.

—Janet Berliner

I was fourteen and living in Vancouver, WA, when Marilyn died. For the last several years I have been working with Steve Levi on a deeply researched farce on the cult of fame, which focuses on the mystery surrounding Marilyn's death. It's very different from the take that Janet and I did on this story which, I have to say, was a lot of fun to do.

—George Guthridge

SKIN DEEP

BY ELIZABETH ANN SCARBOROUGH

 THE BIG MAN had just had one helluva dream. He didn't know what they were serving at this joint—couldn't exactly remember how he got here—but it must have reacted wrong with his medication or something. First off he dreamed he'd got old and after a long miserable time of deteriorating in public, died. Then he woke up in a tux to find himself back with his old buddies, big men (though maybe not quite as big) like himself in entertainment, business, and politics. All still young and full of juice, not dead or dried up like in his dream.

There were some good-looking broads there too. There always were at these bashes. "Hi, baybee," a voice said in his ear. He turned around to see if he knew her. He didn't like it when broads he didn't know called him pet names. He liked it when they called him "Mister." "Sir" was okay too, in a pinch. Or a clinch. He was gonna tell her so but when he saw who she was he all of a sudden wasn't sure she was standing on solid ground. She was in the dream too but he remembered her as being dead, really dead. "Marilyn, sweetie. I thought you were dead!" he said.

"Oh, that!" she said with a giggle and a wiggle and a dismissive little wave of her white gloved hand. "Maybe just a *little*." She stepped closer till she was in his face and he smelled her perfume. She didn't smell dead. She rubbed lightly against him and breathed, "Miss me?"

"Yeah, sure, baby, you were—are—the best. But—" he looked a little closer at some of the other people he had recognized earlier. One of the Vegas boys nodded to him, looking right at him. That was when the big man noticed the guy had a bullet hole right between his eyes.

"Swell party, huh?" Marilyn said. She was definitely in her Marilyn role now—all dimples and pout and a slinky white satin slip shimmying across her curves. She wasn't nude or half nude the way several of the other babes here were, but he'd seen her when she was, and when she was drunk, drugged, depressed, bawling, pleading, dying, dead. Definitely dead. He took a step back. She didn't seem offended. She was looking around for someone, someone she suddenly spotted and wiggled her fingers at.

"You know I always told you I thought I was adopted, honey? Well, I was right." A gorgeous redhead and a tall bodybuilder with long blond hair, both wearing Halloween costumes, were suddenly standing beside her. "This is my real mom and dad, Sugar. Mayzie and Earl. Say hi."

The big man glared at her so she'd get the point not to fuck around with him. The two people were no older than she was, which was plain to anybody. No plastic surgeons or personal trainers here either. He'd seen enough of that to know.

"Mom" had tiptilted green eyes, like she was Eurasian. "Dad" looked like he could jump into a dragon boat and go off plundering any time. "So pleased to meet you, Mr.———," Mayzie said. "That's an Italian last name you have, isn't it?"

Where had she been, the moon?

"Yeah," the big man said. "It's Italian." He was nice and didn't say "what's it to ya?"

"I don't suppose your mother told you any Italian fairy tales when you were a little boy, did she?"

"No. What? You gonna tell me some now?"

"Surely that's not necessary," the redhead said. "The customs, the principles of fairy people the world over are similar."

"Speaking of which," Earl said, cupping his hands to his mouth, "Very well, everyone, it's time for a little horizontal refreshment. Choose your companion!"

"Mom" turned to Marilyn, "May I?" she asked.

"Be my guest," Marilyn said.

Mayzie turned back to the big man. "Well, what are you waiting for?" she asked him. "Off with your garments and on the floor. Quickly, quickly. These interludes don't last forever."

Earl had already found a toothsome young thing and Marilyn had turned her attention to someone with whom she made an oddly familiar couple, but the big man had no time to wonder about it. Mayzie was on top of him and she was very demanding. He had been an old man the last time he looked, but she was definitely getting a rise out of him, whether he liked it—like he had a choice—or not. "Hey, lady," he wanted to tell her, "I'm the one who says when we do it. And if there's any S&M going on, I'm the *S* unless otherwise notified, get it?"

But he didn't have the time or the breath to say it. His mouth was pretty full, what with one thing and another. He thought maybe it wouldn't be so bad after all, but about the time she was climaxing and he thought maybe he could come along for the ride, her face changed into something like out of a horror movie. Old and decrepit and about ready to rot away sort of thing. He decided someone had slipped something medicinal in the drinks, because she slumped against him suddenly, and when she lifted her face again it was as perfect and young as it had been.

And as suddenly as it started, it was over. Mayzie was back on her feet again, as was everybody else. She stuffed herself back into her dress, gave her tits a shake, and without another word stepped over him, presumably to go mingle.

Marilyn bent down, her dress just barely holding her in again as she leaned over to help him up. "Goodness, baybee, you'll get trampled if you stay down there."

"That old lady of yours is something else," he said. "She damn near raped me."

"Don't be silly, Sugar. There's no such thing as rape here. Everybody does it with everybody else all the time. It's our native custom, you might say. Now that I understand more about my roots and all, I understand that lots of the things that some people might think were cheap about a girl were simply natural for her if she was of a certain ethnic persuasion."

"Is that so?" He asked, zipping his pants and feeling a little at a loss because everybody else had put themselves back together and continued dancing as if nothing had happened.

"Yes, it is. Mom and Dad explained it to me. Take this party, for instance. It's a dress occasion. Most of the time we don't bother with clothes at all. But dressing up is fun sometimes."

"So, I'm Italian and you're a Nudist, is that what you're trying to tell me? That's why you were always ready to peel at the drop of a hat?"

He half expected her to get sore. The last few times he'd seen her, she'd been all huffy about the sex stuff until she had enough drinks in her to take on anyone and everyone. She might claim to have been in doubt about who her folks were and where she was from, but he'd always known exactly what she was and he enjoyed making sure that she didn't forget it. As publicly and with as many witnesses as possible. Some people—the ex-husband who was still sweet on her, for instance—didn't like that, but that was just tough. He didn't like to see a broad getting ideas about her own importance. He'd mostly put up with her drunken antics because some people would do him favors if he provided them with hers.

He buttoned his tux and straightened his tie. "Well, your old lady is one seriously kinky girl, toots. Got a real problem with her image. Keep her away from me."

Marilyn looked sad, "I was kinda hoping you'd get along. I was glad when she chose you because, you know, it sort of will help you fit in, to have had her pick you right off . . ."

"Fit in? Why should I want to fit in?"

"Perhaps because you haven't any choice," Earl interrupted.

"That's right, Sugar," Marilyn said with a little moue that wasn't entirely nice. "You're *stuck* with us. For the time being, anyway."

"How long is that?"

"However long it takes," Earl said. "You're our guest for the meantime."

"Where *is* this exactly?"

"You're in the Underworld, actually," Mayzie said, sidling up to him.

"You mean, like, in New York? The Village?"

"Oh, no, sweetie," Marilyn giggled. "Not the Underground. The Underworld. It's where my people live."

"The other Nudists, you mean?" he asked with a sneer that at one time would have intimidated her.

Mayzie goosed him and he jumped. "Would you feel more comfortable if everyone stripped, my poppet?" She turned to face the crowd and trilled, "Horizontal refreshment!" The big man, seeing the suggestive way Earl was wiggling his eyebrows at him, clung to Marilyn and pulled her down on top of him.

She giggled. "Why, Sugar! I didn't know you cared. I thought you didn't like me. You and I never—you know—made love before."

"We're not now, either, you dizzy dame. But don't move. I don't want your dear old dad to get any ideas about me."

"Honey, it's not just ideas. Why, imagine! I never guessed after all those parties you gave that you were so shy."

And she proceeded to try to draw him out—which she did to an extent.

Once more he found himself performing without enjoyment and with disgust, and, as she climaxed, saw that she appeared to sag and melt into herself for one brief moment. Then she was standing over him, adjusting her dress, and wiggling her fingers at someone across the room.

"Yoo-hoo! Harold! I think we can start now!" she shouted.

And suddenly trumpets blared, writhing couples reformed into long stately lines, and Mayzie and Earl took seats on two high thrones which he hadn't previously noticed. Marilyn sat on a slightly lower one between them.

He noticed then that the room was so glitzy it made Vegas seem like the little house on the prairie.

"Hear ye, hear ye, the court of His Majesty the Erl King and Maylin the Immortal, the Queen of Faerie is now in session. Their Majesties and Crown Princess Maylin the Second Presiding."

"What is this crap," the big man muttered. Someone shushed him and two Godzilla-sized Swedish-types who looked like relatives of Marilyn's dad propelled him down the rows of people and placed him on his knees in front of the throne. "I thought her name was Mayzie."

"Familiarly, yes, but in court it's Maylin the Immortal, mortal, and you'd do well to say it respectfully."

"Okay, okay, let go, you're wrinkling the fabric," the big man said, adjusting his tux lapels. He noticed for the first time the calla lily in his button hole. Must have been at a formal funeral.

"Thank you, thank you," said Earl, waving his hand like a headliner on opening night. "We're gathered here at the request of Princess Maylin to welcome another of her little friends from the world above. As you know, several of Maylin's other friends have been joining us from time to time. Now it's his turn. What did you say his name was, darling?"

Marilyn smiled at the big man and he particularly noticed her teeth. She gave his name and added, "But I just call him Honey."

"You can't do that, dear," Mayzie said. "You called the last one Honey and the one before that."

"Okay then, Sugar."

"I'd call him Rabbit if he were mine," Mayzie said, poking at him with her scepter so he had to jump to avoid it. "He's not very friendly, is he?"

"You can't compare everybody to the politicians, Mama," Marilyn told her. "They're friendly to everybody. It's their job. This guy was a great performer, weren't you, Sugar? Want to sing a little duet with me to entertain the guests?"

"No way in hell," he growled defiantly.

"Okay, no need to get huffy," Marilyn said with a pout and a shrug.

"Besides, Rabbit, this isn't hell," Mayzie said. "It's Faerie. And you will sing a duet with my daughter if she desires it. See what I told you, child? Not friendly at all?"

"And yet," Earl said, frowning, "you were apparently a good friend to our girl during her time on earth, weren't you, Slick? Inviting her to all those parties, introducing her to all those friends of yours?"

"Most hospitable, according to her," Mayzie said.

Marilyn gave him a look that couldn't have been described as friendly.

"Many opportunities for horizontal refreshment, she said," Earl put in. "How good of you to bear her own customs in mind."

"Her own—what is this?" the big man demanded. "I don't know where this place is, or what customs you're—"

"Time again!" Mayzie chimed. "Horizontal refreshment, every-one." This time he was blindsided by two girls who could have been the twins of the Viking types who brought him to the throne. When they finished, the belligerence he'd been building up had collapsed along with other things, and he began to be afraid he was going to be screwed to death. The sad thing was, there was nobody to brag about it to. Even sadder, he couldn't seem to relax and enjoy it, which had always been his advice to others. Only they were always female others.

"Now then, Rabbit, is further illustration necessary?"

He shook his head, then gathered his courage and said, "The thing is, Mayzie, you're losin' me here. Marilyn and me go back a long ways, but as far as I know, she's pretty much on her own. She always said she was an orphan, even though we all knew her mom was in a loony bin . . ."

"Her foster mother," Mayzie corrected.

"And her old man run off."

"I was always right here," Earl chuckled.

"Yeah, well, and as far as native customs, she's from California, and while it's true broads strip at the drop of a hat, she had a real talent for it, y'know? That and—uh—"

"Horizontal refreshment!" Marilyn said excitedly. Everybody grabbed a partner and headed for the floor but she said, "No, no, I mean, I had a talent for it up in Hollywood and nobody understood why. They all thought I was a nympho bimbo or something. Even you, Sugar."

"Me?" the big man put his hand to his heart in mock innocence. A nympho bimbo was putting it mildly, of course.

She nodded and tears welled up in her eyes.

Queen Mayzie patted her daughter's head and said, "I can un-derstand where you might have been under a false impression. Our little Maylin, as Crown Princess, has always known that her career prospects are somewhat limited here, since I *am* Maylin the Immor-tal."

"Yes," Marilyn, or Maylin Jr., said. "And a girl can hardly be ex-pected to stay down here her whole life doing nothing but running naked through the woods playing with the flowers and animals and having horizontal refreshment with her friends, can she?"

"Nor should she," Earl said staunchly. "A Crown Princess is due her own proper amount of adoration, so we arranged for her to be reborn into another kingdom, where she would be destined to become the most beautiful and sought-after woman in that world, just as her dear mama is here.

"We chose a foster mother we had encountered at one time and had invited to one of our parties, where we very much enjoyed her company. She later bore a little girl who was not destined to live long, so we brought her child away with us and left Maylin for her to raise. She didn't even notice the boon we had granted her, poor thing. While she seemed perfectly normal when we entertained her, she had become—unable to adapt, above ground.

"She wasn't able to look after Maylin at all, much less raise her to the prominence she deserved."

"And sometimes people just completely misunderstood it when I followed my native customs," Marilyn added. "At first, even as I grew up, I could hardly stand to wear clothes, and I took them off all the time. I also missed the closeness we all shared with our horizontal refreshment sessions."

"Speaking of which . . ." Earl said. "I think . . ."

The big man moaned.

"Not at the moment, dear. Poor Rabbit seems to have a headache or something." Mayzie descended her throne and started toward him. He shrank back. "He seems to suffer from confusion. Do let's continue elucidating."

The King sighed a deep and frustrated sigh, as if it had been months instead of moments since his last coupling.

"But it was different up there," Marilyn continued. "At first people would be nice to you but then sometimes they were just awful. A couple of the men I chose for my consorts actually struck me. And others would demand sex in exchange for recognizing my gifts. It was so unfair! Up there it wasn't even horizontal refreshment. Some of it was selfish and one-sided, and no one cared if I had a good time or not."

"Of course, eventually blood did tell and she achieved the prominence she deserved," the King said.

"*And* met the princes of a royal family," Mayzie said with some satisfaction, and a nod toward the politicians. "Actually, they had ancestors among us, which is where they got their own looks and charm—"

"And appetites, eh, lads?" the King called out to the politicians, who smiled and raised their wine glasses.

Marilyn said, "I knew right away that we were kindred spirits, but I thought it meant we belonged together—see, I had forgotten all but the most basic parts of our own culture and got real screwed up with the value systems from the upper world. I forgot what I knew as a girl, that horizontal refreshment was purely for fun and making magic as well as babies, and had come to see it as a medium of exchange. All the great books I read and important people I talked to had made a very big impression on a simple princess such as I. When the boys wouldn't leave their wives or mess up their careers to be with me, I was crushed. I mean, I finally had found some people I knew that I had a connection with, and all of a sudden they were trying to break it. It was only natural that they should make me queen in their world, but they wouldn't do it. And my own success in Hollywood didn't really matter—it was just made up. However I tried to make my own world, they kept controlling me."

The big man noticed that several former Hollywood executives were among those serving drinks, waving peacock fans, and peeling grapes for the crowd. A lot of people in the crowd were taking this bullshit all in. Some were even bawling openly.

"She was completely disoriented, poor girl," Earl said, laying a caressing hand on Marilyn's bare shoulder.

"And very little wonder! The manners of some people!" Mayzie spat like grease on a griddle. "You'll recall, Rabbit, that I asked if your people had fairy tales."

The big man, who was not feeling all that big at the moment, nodded.

"Do you happen to recall any?"

"Sure—Cindyrelly, Snow White, Sleeping Beauty, all those broads. Just because I'm Italian don't mean all I know is Pinocchio. I had kids. I took in some Disney premiers."

"Very *good*, Rabbit," Mayzie said, clapping her long slender hands. "That's a good start. Let's see. Do you remember what happened to the King and Queen in Sleeping Beauty when they failed to invite the fairy who had helped them have their child to the christening?"

"Sure. She cursed them. You think you folks invented it? Hey, I know some guys—some of them are here—who do worse than that if you don't show respect, don't act polite."

"I told you he understood, Mama," Marilyn said. "You're very bright, aren't you, Sugar?"

"Sure he understands," Earl said. "I knew he would. We talked to your friends over there." He indicated the businessmen of the big man's acquaintance, men to whom he had always showed at least token deference. Men who had been helpful to him. "It's the same thing, except with us, we don't like violence too much. It's messy."

"We prefer to use what our girl tells us they're calling behavior modification in the upper world."

"You please us, you get rewarded. You piss us off, and we become creative," Earl said, his smile splitting his face in a way that didn't make the big man particularly comfortable.

"And," Mayzie said, "we naturally wanted to reward our daughter after her long time away and realized she would miss some of her friends on earth. So as they are ready to change worlds, we intercept them and bring them here."

"And here is what? Fairyland?" the big man asked.

She nodded, "Or the Middle Kingdom. Do you know why it's called that, Rabbit?"

He shook his head, warily.

"The road to paradise is on the right, the road to hades on the left. And our own little thoroughfare lies between the two."

"Because we have aspects of both, depending," Marilyn said in that way she always had of overstating the obvious.

"Some of the princess's acquaintances were cruel to her, some just didn't show her respect," Earl told her. "I won't have my daughter abused that way, even in ignorance. Those who did so were brought here to be our slaves for seven years, after which their contracts are negotiable—"

"Servants, Daddy," Marilyn told him. "Slave is such an ugly

word, don't you think, Sugar? Like white slave—that term just sends shivers up and down me. And sometimes people do it and they aren't even called criminals. They're just being big men among the other men and don't even care what the poor girl might be feeling. I got so low, all I wanted to do was come back here. When I couldn't sleep, I took drugs, because I could only come home in my dreams. But it took more and more drugs. Sometimes when I drank, it made me feel more at home too."

Mayzie nodded. "You see, Rabbit, when one of us is above ground and drinks, the wine has the effect of our own *glamorie*—it casts everything in a better light, makes beautiful the ugly and wise the stupid. Most of what you see here before you now is the *glamorie*. We're simple folk, actually, and sometimes, at passion's climax, for instance, the magic relaxes. Mortals among us have a difficult time with that, I fear. And down here, if a mortal becomes intoxicated, he ceases to see the *glamorie* at all. Some find it very distressing."

"Those guys, like those Hollywood bosses, they never see us all pretty the way we look now," Marilyn said. "They had plenty of pretty above ground. Now they deserve a little distress and a little humility so they get to do all the dirty work for awhile instead of making others do so." She gave a defiant sniff.

"The princes, being at least ancestrally of equal status, have simply been assimilated into our ranks after a small object lesson," Mayzie said. "Charming boys, really. And very popular during our sessions . . ."

"Speaking of which . . ." Earl said, and once more, people made feints toward each other and looked hopefully at the floor. One or two twiddled expectantly with the fastenings of their clothing.

"We come to the subject of your reward, Rabbit," Mayzie said. "Your influence upon our daughter was profound. For all of your gifts you are not, I think, a man who is equipped to understand a child such as ours."

"Still, you gave her a social life, a court of sorts," Earl said, "So for you, as we've done for some of the others, there's a special reward. It takes powerful magic though, so—Mayzie, would you like to give the signal, dear?"

"I think that privilege belongs to our daughter, my darling," she said, with a nod to Marilyn.

Marilyn jumped up like a little girl and clapped her hands together, "Okay, everybody, daisy chain!"

The big man cringed and Marilyn said, "Oh, not you, Sugar. You stand in the middle here. Now 'scuse me!" and she slid out of her clothes and under the nearest Viking before he quite knew she was gone. The dame was definitely in her element, which was the only sure thing about this whole crazy scene.

His gratitude was mingled with a brief feeling of being a wallflower while everybody refreshed themselves like crazy with each other, but pretty soon he noticed their bodies were sending out heat waves, which turned into a sort of rainbow-colored mist. The New Age people would have a blast with that stuff, if they knew about it, he thought fleetingly. His little flash of amusement turned rapidly to alarm as tendrils of pink, lilac, primrose, violet, crimson, periwinkle, and peridot slithered closer to him with every thrust and lunge from the bodies around him. He actually screamed when the first ribbon of violet wound itself around his hand and he tried to move, but by then he was being attacked by pretty colors from all sides, like gels on spotlights for Barney the Dinosaur. He really hoped the businessmen he had seen here earlier weren't watching, and if they did, that they had no way of telling anyone he knew at home.

Then all at once he felt dizzy and saw little twinkling stars, all silver and gold and turquoise, and heard birds singing and felt as warm as if he was laying on the beach in Hawaii. He didn't see the bodies anymore, didn't know where he was.

He struggled to open his eyes. He knew when he did, that he would be back in his home in Beverly Hills, maybe asleep by the pool, having a goofy dream.

And then he knew he had to be outside because it was oppressively hot and damp, sticky, wet even. He must have been swimming and then got bad sunburn, but no, the pressure was worse than that, like a straitjacket. He felt himself thrust forward, as if by thousands of hands, pushing, pushing, forcing him out.

He screamed as he fell finally, through the opening. Somewhere nearby a loud voice said, "Congratulations, Mrs. Baker, it's a little girl."

"Oh, she's beautiful," said a masked face—a nurse, probably.

And somewhere deep inside the new wet bald head that now belonged to him someone giggled and said, "and she'll grow up to be the most beautiful girl in the whole wide world. Have a nice life, Sugar."

AFTERWORD

I was only a kid when Marilyn's movies were popular, so my impression of her is colored by that. I liked her in the movies because she was funny and, in spite of being so pretty, wasn't stuck up and always seemed a little baffled. Later, when I heard about her lateness and dependency on drugs and booze, I felt badly for her, and wondered why she didn't have any real friends to help her and take care of her, since she obviously needed taking care of. That's how I saw it as a kid. I don't remember where I was when she died. I don't think I knew until later. Reading about her life now, I still get the feeling that her being here was some sort of big mistake, that she never quite understood what she was supposed to be doing here. The Irish say those touched by madness are "away" with the fairies—and I think even in her lucid moments, maybe that was where Marilyn really belonged. That's what prompted the changeling story.

—Elizabeth Ann Scarborough

COMEBACK

PAMELA J. FESLER

MARILYN STUDIED HERSELF in the makeup table mirror. Was that a line at the corner of her mouth? Nope. Not yet. She breathed a sigh of relief. A line wouldn't do, not before her big comeback.

She'd thought about her return for years, but it was Elvis who prompted her to act. Every Monday morning it was the same thing. People gathered at the Big Blue Sky Clubhouse, chattering about Elvis appearing at some supermarket opening. Elvis on the front page of the tabloids, standing behind that singer who changed his name, stealing the poor kid's fifteen minutes of fame.

If people got excited over catching a glimpse of a long-gone rock 'n' roller the size of a Buick, think what they'd do for a peek at *the* blonde movie star who took a leave of absence in her prime.

Marilyn opened the double doors of her walk-in closet and took inventory of her wardrobe. Everything was back in style, unlike all that tacky Vegas show stuff Elvis insisted on sporting. The slinky, beaded gown she wore when she sang at the president's birthday party showed up annually in some form or other at the Academy Awards. She shook out the white number that brought her fame and fans as she stood over the exhaust grate. Two months ago, it was featured in a major fashion magazine on a flat-chested model who earned a yearly seven-figure income. Marilyn threw the magazine in the trash.

While the styles were retro, prices weren't. Dom Perignon at a hundred dollars a bottle—if you knew where to shop. Chanel No. 5, hair coloring, satin sheets, all cost more every day. She brainstormed late one night with Mary Pickford on how to manage her return.

"You're not stupid, Marilyn. People wanted to think you were a dumb blonde and you let them. You're only thirty-six years old. You can still play Mel or Denzel's love interest or be MacCauley's mother. Let people know you're back. Then start acting and directing. Set up your own production company. That's what I did. That's where the real power and money are."

Could she be that tough? Marilyn thought she could. She'd talked for hours with Freud and Jung and Karen Horney and read a lot of self-help books. As for the drugs that had caused problems earlier, she could absolutely guarantee anyone who asked that she hadn't touched drugs in years. Make that decades.

Marilyn glided across the deep champagne-colored carpet, installed especially for her by a fan. It matched her hair. She admired the sunlit white room and thought about leaving all her friends. She looked at the makeup mirror again. The face she saw gave her a scared, hopeful smile.

"This time, honey. This time, it'll work out right." She hugged herself hard and pulled a map of the United States off her bedside table. Slipping on a pair of black harlequin reading glasses, she scanned it coast-to-coast.

"Let's see. Where hasn't Elvis been sighted lately?"

AFTERWORD

Late one night I watched *Some Like It Hot* and I wondered what Marilyn would do differently the second time around. I decided she'd keep the hope and vulnerability that made her special and let the brains that everyone ignored flourish. Rumor has it that she, Mae West, and Carole Lombard are forming a production company called "No Dumb Blondes."

—Pamela J. Fesler

SUNSET:
A MONOLOGUE
IN ONE ACT

BY CAROLE NELSON DOUGLAS

[THE ACTRESS SITS *at a dressing table. Any wooden chair, any wooden surface, even a plain desk, will do. An empty frame indicates the mirror, and round theatrical lights flank the vacancy. The Actress sits in profile to the audience, like the driver of a car.*

A slender woman with silver-white hair smoothed back by a headband, her erect posture and taut profile indicate a well-preserved fifty, or sixty, or more. She is very much the theatrical grand dame, yet wears only an oversized white terrycloth robe . . . a once-white robe. Smudged at the rolled collar and sleeves with greasepaint, the robe's streaks of undiluted lipstick red and eyeshadow blue suggest a dingy American flag.

During the monologue, the Actress addresses an unseen someone over her audience-side shoulder as she applies makeup. Note: For theater-in-the-round or more intimate proscenium performances, dressing table and actress can face the audience. In this case, the small, concealed TV screen that news anchors use should be set into the makeup tabletop, so that the Actress can watch herself to apply the makeup correctly, but in no case should the audience see the final made-up effect full-face forward until the very end. The Actress addresses the unseen interviewer, her voice an aging contralto. Occasionally a breathless, girlish quality emerges.]

THE ACTRESS: Thank God I didn't die! I was this close. No kidding. Of course, I might as well have died, for all anyone ever saw of me for almost thirty years. Hollywood. After all those years, all that effort, all I took out of there was Maf. Anyway, that's the only thing I wanted when the men dragged me out, my poor little poodle. I couldn't ever stand to see anything left to die, even flowers. That always made my skin crawl, the way some people would just mow them down, all those soft petals, that pretty color. Sometimes I think flowers are souls. You can see them drooping when they don't get enough water. Or too much. Sometimes they get too much water and drown.

I got too much champagne. And pills. I didn't drown that night, though. I floated. Like Ophelia. With flowers. [*Giggles.*] And I didn't "get thee to a nunnery," though where I went was damn close. [*She leans almost into the plane of the invisible mirror, as if checking for facial wrinkles.*] God, I look like Carol Channing's *grand*mother in this light! [*Giggles again.*] Speak of another Marilyn-come-lately. That was the hardest part, watching the imitators go on and on, and get my parts, just like the gossip and lies and speculation went on and on. That . . . and the deaths. Not Joe, though. Not Mr. Arthur Miller. No, I won't talk about him, them. Only about my work. That's always been the most important thing, my work, and I finally saw that I didn't need someone else to believe in it, if I really did.

You still can't buy it: that I could just vanish like that—not with all my fame and the press attention—can you? Let's see you in better light, Junior. Lean forward, kid. What are you—thirty-something? Just a baby. Like my boy. You of all people—a grown-up, East Coast nineties sophisticate like you—should know how easily the unthinkable can be arranged, how fame can make being forgotten the only thing worth living for. I call this decade my Gray Nineties. That's how old I feel sometimes. How can someone wet behind the years like you know about the things people felt they had to do back then? Jimmy Hoffa vanished forever, didn't he? [*Pauses.*] I almost did. I almost went away and didn't come back. Ever.

Now—[*Her arms sweep wide to encompass the bare dressing room.*] I'm finally legit. [*Laughs.*] Me, little Norma Jeane, a stage actress at last, playing the role of a lifetime, of a long lifetime. Ironic, huh? It's never too late. Write that down. It's not the best damn quote you'll ever get, but it's the truest.

Oh, the White House was wonderful, and the First Lady was a doll. The president, though, I think he has a Kennedy complex. He was ogling me pretty good. Poor Peter. Drank himself to death. The Kennedys were a toxic family, you know? Maybe you do. Oh, God. I wish . . . Lee Strasberg could be here to see this, my big comeback, my Broadway debut in the role of the decade. He always said I could be the best on the live stage. Me and Marlon. Marilyn and Marlon. Both of us as dysfunctional as . . . Dostoevski characters. Yeah, I still love the Russian writers. [*Coyly.*] You must have read a lot about me. How could you not? The Russians had soul. They saw the dinge underneath the daisies, right? Oh, and I wish Michael were here. No, that's not my son's name. You're not going to trick that out of me. He, at least, will have privacy, that's one thing Jackie O and I agreed on.

I was talking about Michael Chekhov . . . you know, Anton's boy. Imagine, I knew him! I studied acting with him when I was a starlet. That's a funny word, isn't it? Starlet. Star-let. Like Scarlett. Made up to make a person sound like less than the real thing. Like an av-i-a-tricks. Don't ask me to spell that. I still don't spell. That's when I hit the key for Spellcheck. Computers make me feel like Walt Disney or something. I still write poetry by hand, though. Nowadays everybody calls themselves "actors," even women. I don't know, I can understand why, but it still sounds funny to me. That's all I ever wanted to be, an actress. I like that word. Ac-tress. But you can call me an actor in your story. I know that's politically correct, and I always had a deep interest in politics. . . . [*She laughs at the touch of the old tease in her voice, then sobers.*]

Those were terrible times. For me, sure, but for everyone. Think about it. I sure did that a lot during my Black Hole years. No, I won't say exactly where. I'll just say . . . where the wild horses and misfits hide. Someplace lost and lone, where the town drugstore isn't big enough to have movie magazines. That's another dinosaur, like me—movie mags. Those were the rags. Nowadays, they're toney. *Vanity Fair!* I guess you can't keep an old girl like Gossip down, especially in the print business. It's still the same old shell game, though, with Demi and Michelle and Madonna—don't get me going on Madonna, talk about cheap imitations!—doing cheesecake for the cover, but in their underwear yet! [*She shakes her head, beginning to apply the deep-toned, oil-based face makeup that stage lights require, rather like what burn victims wear to hide scars.*]

Nobody's ever beat my calendar, though! And, back then, they thought it would ruin my career. Instead, it launched *Playboy*. They used to have that magazine even in my drugstore, but behind the counter under plastic, like Hostess Twinkies that are too rich for you. I really had a great body. [*Nostalgically.*] Still do, for my age. If I had only known that plastic surgery would do all this science-fiction stuff with lasers and all, I wouldn't have been so worried. Hey, I'm an actress! I don't apologize for keeping the instrument state-of-the-art. [*Sobers.*]

That's all it was in my day: a body to die for, and when it was gone . . . die. It's still the same, except actresses aren't considered over the hill until forty, instead of thirty. I'm glad I had my awkward years—decades—away from Hollywood. They were right; having a baby does nothing for your figure, but I ran it off later chasing the kid. Nope. It's up to him to come forward. He's not too fond of the press—oops, we say "media" now, don't we? I kept up, you know. I can *read*. I even can act, and that's the one thing I liked reading about when I was missing: how everybody said they underestimated my acting. They never know what they got until it's gone.

[*She slaps rouge under and over her cheekbones, then stops to stare at her feverish reflection.*] You know, that's one thing I found out in Korea when I entertained the troops on our honeymoon. Wow, that sounds . . . *Joe's* and my honeymoon. Joe hated my jaunt to the front lines, but it showed me I could do more than I thought, though I didn't really know it until much, much later. Those boys were so sweet. They were with me all the way, and I was something special to them. Something more than a pinup or a sex symbol. Oh, I was that all right, and I played it to the hilt. Gosh, it was cold! Took real acting talent to wear that slinky spaghetti-strapped dress and not turn into one big goose bump. And those kind of bumps they weren't interested in! But the craziest thing, I wasn't scared! All those men, that sea of faces I couldn't even focus on I was shivering so much, but I didn't freeze or forget. Or stutter. Women seldom stutter, you know. It's a male chromosome thing usually. Unless some youthful trauma kicks in, and my youth was all trauma. That's why I went in for Drama. [*Laughs self-mockingly.*]

I don't stutter now. When I finally got off the shrinks—and I had to in the outback where I lived all those years—and got into self-help, that's when I finally understood it, me, after all those years. Attention, of course. I was seeking male attention in an industry where the father figures were studio heads who kept harems of starlets in "stables" like race horses. Ran us until we dropped, or turned thirty. Like Ruffian. [*Chokes up.*] Only filly to give the boys at the derby a run for their roses, and they overwork her until she hurts herself, and then they kill her. And they don't even pay horses, do they? I was really screwed that way; paid way less than I should have been. Poor Ruffian, one trip-up and . . . kaput. I hated that! I almost came out and bought her then. I could have retired her someplace where she didn't have to run for a place in the sun; my loyal pals saw I got money from all the boom projects after my "death." Ruffian didn't have any loyal pals. How do you suppose they killed her? Didn't shoot her, like in my day. Maybe injection. They did that in my day, too, the studio doctors, those bozos I paid to keep me awake or asleep or just this side of happy. I wasn't the only "actor" to go nova on shots and inferiority complexes. Judy Garland. A whole bunch of us, especially the "looove goddesses." Yeah, I saw *Looove Boat* during my sabbatical.

[*Briskly, drawing businesslike lines between her eyebrows, down from her nose with dark pencil.*] Well, you can't save everything. Your own self is enough is most cases. Who saved me? Who saved me. The Three Stooges, silly! Me. Myself. And I. Just like I made my own career until the people made me a star. And the people kept me alive all this time. Oh, you mean who whisked me out of Brentwood That Night? Who made sure that everyone swore the body was mine, and left it sit for two goddamn days until Joe stepped in like he always did . . . Joe. We shouldn't have married, but people did that sort of thing in those days. Bad publicity otherwise; he was a jerk and she was a slut and her career was over. Now . . . holy Hays

Office! All History. All sorts of actresses have babies by themselves (okay, not totally by themselves). They even own their own production companies, like I did then. Actors, I should say. We're all actors now, but the girls still get stripped and knocked around in movies. They say we're like strippers, all of us actor-actresses who need to peel off our clothes to be famous and feel wanted. They say we all were victimized during our childhoods. Can you imagine that? Your own father doing that to you? Now I'm glad I didn't have one and didn't find the one I didn't have. But I think my tattered gold-diggers—in movies, you know, even though I got some bum blonde parts—I think they had more self-respect than what masquerades as women's roles now. I tried to give them that. And it isn't sex, no matter how much skin and how much bedroom action they show now. Smut! they used to call it. Nobody's *nice* in movies anymore. I used to be naughty, but I was nice.

Oh, you're a media shark, aren't you, Junior! Back to The Question. My son's almost your age, so I'll give you a motherly hint, just as if you were my very own little boy. Who whisked me out of Hollywood and scandal and self-destruction? Do the initials H.H. mean anything to you? And I don't mean *Hubert Humphrey*!

[*Laughs uproariously while dabbing clown-white makeup above her age lines.*] That your best guess? That's rich, and kinda predictable for a high-class rag like *Vanity Fair*. But *he* was married to Jean Peters then, and already pretty reclusive. Had the money and motive, though. Never could resist a sex symbol, though you have to wonder how he was at the real thing.... No, not Howard Hughes. The other H.H. who was big on sex and stars and calendar girls in those days. Still is. Some boys never grow up. I still could pose for him, and don't think I haven't been tempted to show what born talent and cutting-edge plastic surgery can do. Maybe I should be stuffed when I die, like Trigger. Nobody ever can see enough of natural blondes! [*Laughs.*] I guess you *are* pretty young. *Hugh Hefner,* honey! H.H. He owed me a lot. I was the body that launched a billion issues of *Playboy*. The first drawing card, even though he had to print that old calendar shot, *Golden Dreams*. I didn't even need to be air-brushed then. And isn't *that* a nice development?

Saw a photo of Liz the other day and she looked sixteen again.

Skin like *National Velvet.* I'm doing the cover of *Vanity Fair,* did you know? Hey, what I can't fix they can take out. They erase the pixies nowadays. You know, those nasty little dots you could see when you looked at news photos real, real close? Yeah, I know they're called pixels, but I like to think the pixies are helping out all the old broads in the world. Say, listen, Liz and Lauren do it, why not me? [*Shrugs and begins outlining her eyes in vampish lampblack.*] I'll give Hugh credit for never breaking the story, though he kept bugging me to pose. In a wig! Like I used to wear when I wanted to be just me and not Her, not the emmmminent MmmMmm. [*Flutters her long, black false lashes.*] I always knew makeup was a mask. And, no, it doesn't bother me now slathering it on to look older or uglier.

I really became an actress, you know. Actor. I started on the stage, back at the Bliss-Hayden Miniature Theater in Beverly Hills in nineteen-forty-seven and -eight. It was after Fox dropped me; I had to do something. So I got the second female lead in *Glamour Preferred.* Guess what I played? Guess! A silver screen siren! Isn't that a scream? For my first play. Later, they all said that I'd never make it on the stage, not with my neuroses, but they didn't know I did just fine in those early plays. And don't tell anybody, but this isn't really my Broadway debut. Back in 'fifty-five, I slipped into the Martin Beck Theater for a one-night . . . cameo. Did you think I was going to say one-night something-else? It was *Teahouse of the August Moon,* so no one would recognize me made up for a bit part. [*The Actress pulls her eyes into an Asian slant.*] Brando did it, so I sure could! We were both Stanislavski babies. I did my Method work in Manhattan, but after I "died," I practiced in secret for years. Did Little Theater in my little town. Was quite a local celebrity as a brunette. Even did those parts that they gave to my "the nexts" after I was gone, and before I even left. You know, the "next" Marilyn, like the Kim Novak part in *Picnic.* Now I've come full circle, fronting a Broadway musical, stepping in for a Tony-winning stage star. Adding a bit of zing to a long-running show. Me, Marilyn Monroe.

Do you want to see me do Her? I still can. [*Assumes an uncanny pose.*] There. What do you think? Good enough to fool a near-sighted man on a donkey, right? I could still be doing her, like Mae West, forever. Except that Mae was always a worldly broad. Heck, she didn't hit the movies until she was forty. Age never seemed to matter with her and her look never changed. It just got . . . thicker.

Marilyn, though, you couldn't age. She wasn't allowed to age. Marilyn was a child molester's dream. I can face it now. That breathy voice, those innocent, inciting wiggles. The giggle. Marilyn appealed to all the men who want some girl who's so easy they don't have to be afraid anymore that women might get something from them. Some girl they can use and who'll come back for more. Who'll beg and whine for what she's earned. Thank God they liberated the slaves! I feel sorry for Her. In a way she died when I took that bad overdose. At least that's when I began to be born again. And what did I have to lose? It already was all gone. They'd written me off as old and uppity. Everybody seemed to want me dead and gone. And I was scared, too scared to act, all broken up, in pieces like that, before the camera. I was getting better, but it got harder. I needed time to be sure my character was coming through. That's why I demanded all those takes, why it took me hours to face the camera. Cameras capture you forever; it has to be just right. You have to look just right, act just right, all at once at the same moment. A film hangs on a bunch of split seconds spliced together. Like a car accident. Imagine if everyday life were like that! It's terrifying.

I'm not scared anymore, not onstage anyway. I'm finally prompt and I don't need prompting. They all acted as if my good film work was magic, like I got it somehow, instead of made it. What did they call me? A "fey, uncanny talent that made love to the camera"—that was one quote. Always a freak. They always treated me like a freak. I wasn't supposed to be a star. I wasn't supposed to be ambitious, or read good books, or try to be more than my looks. Sure, I used them. We all did then, still do. Looks are what women have to make up for muscles and male ego: looks and a dumb hope that somebody will see them for what they are beneath the pancake and the push-up bra. Of course, nobody can see past *this* crap. [*Indicates makeup tins.*] Sorry, that's not a nice word for *Vanity Fair,* is it? Got it from my kid.

[*Smiles.*] Got a lot from my kid. Confidence. Yeah. I could do it, do what any woman does. No kidding, that meant a lot. And I got a whole new vocabulary. And started worrying about somebody besides myself, my looks, and my career. Later, when he was in that pre-teen stage, he thought his old lady was really not with it. [*Giggles.*] I loved it all, even the PTA. How could I be vain with a teenage son? How could I stay all messed up with *Hollywood*! He'll be out there tonight, for my Broadway debut, but no one will know who, except him. That's one secret I'll never give the press. He can, after I'm gone, if he wants to. But, you know, I kinda think he won't want to. He's that kind of kid. Man, my son's a man now. I never had a real father, and he didn't either.

It doesn't matter who his father is. It matters who his mother is. And that's me. A mother, jeez. First I had to learn to be my own mother, though, and that took years. He went to Harvard. Yeah. M.B.A. Nobody messes with my money now, right, honey? I wouldn't remarry. I didn't need any men once I had my baby.

He isn't obsessed to find out who his father was, like I was. Not after I told him everything. He said, "Mom, you need a new generation man in your life." And he is my new generation man. He doesn't need to own me, he doesn't need me to be what I was, not what I can become.

Oh, ho! That's what you're really here for. The father. Who's the father? Sorry, wrong number. It's nobody famous, it's nobody who hung around. It's nobody significant except to me and he, and maybe thee. I was one of those nameless sixties statistics, a working single-parent. When I had my son, I finally didn't need a father, didn't need Mr. Mayer to like me or Mr. Cukor to have a heart or Mr. Olivier to give me le-gi-ti-ma-cy. As for men, when women get older, a lot of them lose interest and find girls. Men lose a lot more that way, like knowing real people. I don't need romance now to remind me I'm alive. I have my family. My son, my friends in that little place—and not the ones who gave the interviews to *Current Affair* when I "came out" a few years ago—and my family, my theatrical family, just like I had my film family, Whitey and the other tech people who sympathized and stood by me, even when I had been made into a mess.

[*Outlines her lips into an exaggerated bee-sting.*] I used to use five shades of lipstick to make up my mouth. I could still do the glamour thing, like my character, poor woman, but I always enjoyed being a slob. Casual. If you look at my old cheesecake pics, you can see that being outdoorsy was my thing. Waves and wind . . . yes, and the wind from a sidewalk grate, you naughty boy for mentioning that! The legs held up, though, without artificial interference. I could still do the legs part, but you'll never see them, not in this show.

I can't regret anything. I even wear underwear now. Have to. I mean, time does have its way with a girl's bottom. I work out and all that, but I need a little help. Besides, that underwear thing was just adolescent rebellion. Gave the movie mags something naughty that they *could* talk about. Whatever happened to them, they used to be so big? What's *People* and *Us*? Processed celebrity cheesecake. [*By now heavy makeup has transformed her into a glamorous ghoul.*] I'm healthy. Only pills I take now are mega-vitamins and anti-oxidents. Say, you're never too young to start. I've got some plastic baggies here . . . try these. I only drink distilled water and maybe a teensy bit of champagne after the opening tonight. Hey, a girl needs a bit of bubble bath and bubbly now and again, at any age! And as I say— [*standing, she pulls on a brunette wig, then strips off robe to reveal a darkly glittering, loose and garish getup that matches her grotesquely exaggerated vamp makeup.*] They don't make movies like they used to, so I don't miss 'em.

How do I look? Gee, thanks. I'm supposed to look demented. Wait! I'll do my big curtain line for you. Private preview. Sure, I'm scared, but that's natural. It takes adrenaline to carry a show for two hours. And wait'll you hear my singing! No more baby-doll voice. Time and lessons liberated a real range and some guts. Maybe not Ethel Merman, but A-okay. [*Her voice deepens, her mask of makeup twists into a Medusa face, her hand convulsively clutches her bony chest. She resembles a figure from an Oriental opera, a caricature of an ancient, almost alien femininity.*]

After all . . .

"They had voices. They had faces then.

"I'm ready for my close-up, Mr. DeMille." Here comes little ole Norma . . . Norma Desmond in *Sunset Boulevard*.

[*Smiling, Marilyn Monroe slinks toward the footlights and the au-*

dience, an expression of demonic self-absorption on her face, until she drops character to wink at the man from Vanity Fair.]

Sorry, gotta go. I'm never late anymore! Poor Sir Larry nearly went crazy over that, but I almost managed to seduce him anyway. Sleeping with someone was a way of saying I was sorry in those days. I don't do that anymore. Say I'm sorry, I mean. [*She winks.*]

So thanks for coming. Sorry about your mom. It's nice you miss her so much. And don't forget! [*Her tone is mock-maternal, mock-seductive.*] Come back after the show for some champagne, John, and we'll talk about your father. Off the record. 'Bye.

[*The lights dim, except for a pinpoint spot on the film-still frozen, ultrafeminine mask of the Actress.*]

AFTERWORD

Girls who grew up in the Repressed Fifties and grew smart in the Liberated Sixties found Marilyn Monroe twice cursed, whether alive or dead. In the fifties she was a Legion of Decency–labeled "not-nice" girl—a sexy, squirmy film female appealing only (and only too obviously) to men. By the seventies, conscienceness-raised, right-thinking young women deplored sexism and sexpots. MM was politically incorrect before politically incorrect became cool.

Any of Marilyn's on-screen gyrations I glimpsed as a child struck me as embarrassingly phony, but I liked her singing on the radio: ". . . diamonds are a girl's best friend." I'd later reject the cynical lyric, but I never forgot that soft, siren voice.

Working on this anthology, I came to see that she was more than most people knew, and less than she could have been. I don't recall noting her death, but after realizing where I was when she died, I no longer consider myself immune to Marilyn.

On the cusp of high school and college that summer, I had landed roles in two community theater productions: one tragic and Greek about a defiant heroine, Antigone, the other comic and American, Neil Simon's *Come Blow Your Horn*. In the farce I snagged a challenging, totally-against-type part I adored: a dumb blonde. I spent hours on my back porch in St. Paul styling a platinum-blonde wig, teasing the cotton candy cloud into the then-fashionable flips. Only now, after poring over MM photo essays, do I see that I instinctively shaped my wig into a replica of The Way Marilyn Wore Her Hair that last summer of *Something's Got to Give.*

We fifties girls were more than we knew, and lived to become women who, in time, learned that we too weren't expected to become all that we could be. That's why I wanted to imagine Marilyn Monroe as she so easily could have become, growing older and bolder and better, jauntily slouching toward the Millennium with the rest of us.

—Carole Nelson Douglas

IT HAD TO BE YOU

BY NANCY PICKARD

 I'VE KEPT THIS secret for years, but I'm telling it now: My sister, Crystal, was possibly the first person to see Marilyn Monroe's image appear on Mount Rushmore.

Remember that incredible week?

You *don't* remember, do you?

It's the strangest thing, how I seem to be the only person in America who remembers. It's as if we suffer national amnesia. Ask any American, "Do you remember when Marilyn Monroe appeared on Mount Rushmore?" and they'll laugh at you, and say, "Are you crazy? That's a tabloid story, like Bigfoot and Nessie. I suppose you believe in *them,* too?"

Americans don't seem to comprehend that the story of Marilyn Monroe on Rushmore is only treated like a tabloid fabrication *here;* in other parts of the world, people remember it as the actual, astonishing event it really was. Their media run "Marilyn Retrospectives" every year on the anniversary of her appearance. In Japan, she's nearly a religious icon. Believe me, *she's* the reason—not the Presidents—why thousands of foreign tourists stream into South Dakota, like pilgrims to Lourdes.

Americans think they're fools, those Marilyn-worshiping foreigners, but they're fools with money. We're delighted to sell them little Indian tom-toms (made in Korea) to take back home to their kiddies, but they search in vain for souvenirs of MM on Rushmore. They come, in their rented cars and tour buses, hoping to find photographs and commemorative books and souvenir paperweights so they can hold her in their hands, along with with George, Tom, Abe, and Teddy, but all they ever find are the presidents. They don't find any record of her appearance at Rushmore. You know that's true, if you've ever been there. Think about it: Have you ever seen any Marilyn souvenirs sold in the "trading posts" beneath the monument?

No, the event has vanished from *our* national memory, just as she eventually vanished from the face of the mountain.

But I'm telling you—I'm *reminding* you—she was there! For that all-too-brief but magical week, *she* was there. I really do think my sister saw her first, so it's possible I saw her second. But I'm getting ahead of myself.

I remember it all, even if nobody else in this country does.

It took us a couple of endless days to drive from Kansas City, Missouri, to the campground on a pine-forested ridge east of Mount Rushmore: two sweltering, interminable days of driving through Missouri, Nebraska, and South Dakota in ninety-degree heat without air conditioning, and one night in a tacky motel, with Mom and Dad either arguing or not speaking to each other most of the time.

In the car, Crystal and I ate the peanut butter and cracker "sandwiches" that Mom had packed, and drank lukewarm water from the Thermos—because Mom thought Cokes gave me pimples—and sang as many popular songs as we could remember the words to, and stared out the windows of the back seat of the Chevy the rest of the time.

Crystal looked miserable, and I was bored out of my skull and wondering how we were all going to be able to stand being cooped up together for two whole weeks on the road.

I had recently earned my driver's license, and my parents had promised to turn the wheel over to me now and then, once we got out of the heaviest of the summer tourist traffic. But that hadn't happened yet; it seemed as if the entire southern half of America was driving toward the northern half of it. So I was stuck in the back seat with my ten-year-old sister. Our ultimate destination on that year's vacation trip was supposed to be Dad's sister's family in Seattle.

We never made it past Mount Rushmore.

The morning when Marilyn Monroe began to appear on the

monument, Mom and Dad woke up fighting, before dawn's early light, even. Maybe they'd never slept, it's entirely possible that they only held it down—the noise and the nasty words—during the night to enable Crys and me to sleep, and then as soon as they heard me slip out to the campground bathroom, they started in again, lying there in their separate bedrolls on the canvas floor of our tent. They probably figured Crystal would sleep through their furious whispering, where I wouldn't. They knew that if they woke me up, I'd fly out of the tent and run off into the night, and they were scared of that possibility, especially now that I could drive by myself.

I had run off once before, on a family camping trip to the Lake of the Ozarks just three weeks earlier. It had scared them both half to death when they couldn't locate me for several hours—they thought I'd drowned, or some hillbilly had captured me—and it made them start to look with wary eyes at me if I was in the room when they would start to argue, after that. (I'd been perfectly safe the whole time I was gone, having stumbled down a country road to the highway, where I sat on the stoop of a Dairy Queen in the sun for hours, getting a tan and flirting with the boys who drove in for burgers or Cokes. I got burned from the sun and also got poison ivy from my furious plunge through the thick Ozark foliage surrounding our tent, but it was worth it.)

So it wasn't as if they didn't love us, or ever think about us.

They did, but they got distracted by their own heat and noise. What did they fight about? What time to get up in the morning, where to eat breakfast, what to eat for breakfast, when to stop for bathrooms, which road to follow on the map . . . and private things, in angry whispers in their bed and bedrolls, things I absolutely did not want to overhear.

This time, however, it was Crystal who ran away, only she was a quiet little thing who just slipped out without them even noticing at first. None of us knew she was gone.

As I said, I was off in the campground ladies room, getting a shower before the hordes of other women and girls trooped in, holding their toothbrushes aloft like flags to stake their claim to their places in line for the showers. It was worth forcing myself to roust before sunup, just to have the bathroom to myself.

Basically, I hated camping, I hated being on vacation with my parents, and I hated them. Well, what can I say, I was sixteen. I loved my little sister, though, and had long considered it my job to shelter her from the acrimony between our parents. I didn't want her to feel as bad about it as I had during those five years before she came along to keep me company in the misery.

After Crystal was born, it was easier for me to tell Mom and Dad to shut up—or run away from them—because then I had some-body besides myself to do it for, to protect. I felt guilty about leaving Crystal behind that time in the Ozarks when I ran away, but it had seemed at the time as if everything was closing in on me, even my responsibility toward her, when all I really wanted was to be left back home, on my own with my friends, in Kansas City.

As of that summer, I was even beginning to resent Crystal— how much I thought she needed me—and to feel guilty about feel-ing that way, and naturally I hated *those* feelings, too. I was a mess of self-pity and self-righteousness, and Marilyn healed me, and not only me.

What I'm telling you, this story, I've adapted from the diary (we'd call it a journal now, I suppose) which I kept on that trip. If at times I sound a bit young in the telling, it's because I was, then. We were all younger then, we Americans. Perhaps that's why it's hard for people to recall, because children change and grow, but they don't always remember the moment, the place, or the reason.

I kicked rocks coming back from the bathroom, feeling fresh as the piney air around me. Ten steps from the flap of the tent, I heard *them* arguing, and I seriously considered not going back in. But I stuck my head in anyway, kind of to see what they'd do, and sure enough, Mom and Dad looked at my face, then looked at each other, and then silently turned their backs and pretended to return to sleep. I felt suddenly, pleasantly, powerful, because my mere pres-ence was enough to silence them.

Crystal's bedroll was empty.

"Where's Crys?"

"Bathroom," Mom said, sounding muffled by bedding.

I knew that wasn't true, or I'd have seen her myself. It was just barely light out, and I didn't like the idea of a ten-year-old girl wandering around the campground alone in the almost-dark. I also felt suddenly afraid that she'd picked up from me the idea of running away.

When I found Crys, she was sitting on a huge rock on the ridge overlooking the Black Hills and the monument and the valley below. We'd arrived late the night before, so we hadn't seen anything but the campground yet. I was really relieved to find her. She was staring—her knees drawn up to her chin, her arms hooked around them—spellbound into the distance.

I came up behind her and crawled onto the rock to sit beside her.

It was pretty impressive, the sight of those four huge faces.

The first thing I said to Crystal was, "Do you think Thomas Jefferson can hear Mom and Dad yelling at each other?" I wanted to let her know she wasn't alone in her distress, and I wanted to make her laugh.

"They woke me up," she said. "I wanted to scream at them."

"I know."

"Who's the other one?"

"The other one?" On the mountain, she meant. "Well, to our far left, that's George Washington, and of course you know he was our first President . . ."

"We already studied him," she agreed, impatiently.

"And next to him is Thomas Jefferson, and then there's Theodore Roosevelt, and the one on our right is Abraham Lincoln." I wanted to be either a writer or a history teacher when I grew up, which is why I was keeping a diary, and why I frequently took it upon myself to read travel books about the places we visited, and then to educate my little sister. "The sculptor was a man named Gutzon Borglum. He worked on them from 1927 until he died in 1941. Originally, he was going to carve them down to their waists, but he died before he could do all that. The heads, alone, though, are sixty feet high! And the reason they look so real, like they're looking right at you, is that the pupils of their eyes are actually these three-foot long posts carved out of the granite, and—"

"Who's the *other* one?"

"The other one?"

"Her! I never knew we had a woman president. Who is she?"

"What are you talking about, Crystal?"

And then I saw it: a faint outline on the mountain just to the left of George Washington, in the blank space where the sculptor had originally planned for Roosevelt to be. Only it wasn't blank. I could just barely see it at first, but even so, it was most definitely an outline of a female form. Most definitely. Not just a head, either, but a whole body, down through the spaghetti straps, the tight bodice and skirt of her dress, to the high-heel shoes. High-heel shoes? The outline was getting darker, too, as the rising sun shone fuller and fuller about it. Upon her. Now it looked like an etching. Now it was filling in, like an Etch-A-Sketch, so we could begin to see how bouffant her hair was, how wide her eyes, how full her lips, how round her curves. It wasn't a sculpture, like the presidents, but more like a painting in stone.

"Oh, my God," I whispered, and then I jumped up on the boulder, nearly losing my balance in my excitement. "Oh, my God! Crystal, this is impossible, but that's Marilyn Monroe!"

"Be careful!" Crys yelled at me, and pulled at the bottom edge of my shorts, trying to get me to sit down with her again. "What's going on? I'm getting scared! You're scaring me! What's happening? Who's Marilyn Monroe?!"

"It's a miracle!" I shouted to the valley.

Mom and Dad didn't think it was a miracle, when we dragged them out of the tent—away from an argument over whether or not the milk in the cooler was still fresh enough to pour over cereal—and out to the ledge. We wouldn't tell them why we were pleading and begging and insisting, because we knew they wouldn't believe us, not until they saw her themselves.

Once Mom recovered from her first astonishment, she said, "It's a trick of light."

But Dad's opinion was, "No, somebody's projecting it from somewhere in back of us, from an airplane, maybe. It's an advertising gimmick."

Crys and I turned to look up at the pale blue sky, but it was empty of everything including clouds.

"Oh, please," Mom was scathing, and didn't even bother to look. "An airplane? How about a flying saucer, while you're at it? What airplane could hold an image still for so long?"

"A helicopter," he retorted. "A Harrier jet."

"Oh, stop. It's a trick of light, that's all."

Before they could really get into arguing about *that,* I said in a hurry, "Let's get in the car and get closer! Let's see if we can still see her from any direction! Please?" I was, myself, determined to go chasing that image if I had to steal the keys from my mother's purse, and take off with Crystal and the car.

"It's only an advertising gimmick," Dad grumbled.

But he was curious enough to indulge us, and so we all ran back and piled into the car and started driving around the area. We found out that she was, indeed, visible from any angle, and from anywhere you could see the monument. Uphill, downhill, there she was; daybreak, noontime, and twilight, there she still was!

As each amazing hour passed, and more and more people noticed her, her image became clearer and clearer upon the mountain, until there was no longer any chance of anybody denying that she was there. There was one time of day when George Washington's face cast a shadow that covered her face, but you still couldn't miss the hair, or the rest of her body. She was more than five hundred feet tall, for heaven's sake! Her voluptuous figure was turned slightly toward the presidents, but the full and radiant incandescence of her smile was directed toward the land below the monument, where all of us were staring back up at her.

She was there all that first night, too, in the lights which came on every evening to illuminate the presidents. In the spotlights, her tight, spaghetti-strap dress sparkled like sequins.

Crystal and I squatted on our rock, like Indians, for hours in the darkness, until Mom came out and put her foot down, insisting we come into the tent and go to bed. We could hardly bear to wait until morning, to see if *she* was still there.

And that was the first day.

The second day of Marilyn Monroe's presence on Mount Rushmore was the beginning of pandemonium. When people woke up and looked outside their travel trailers and their motel rooms and their tents, like us, and realized her image was still smiling down at them from beside George Washington, they went nuts.

We drove right into town, or what I called "town," although it was really just the big area of parking lots and "trading posts" and information centers for the monument, and hung around there all day, where the action was. Before you could say "Good Morning, America," the television network news shows had crews landing at the airports at Rapid City and Sioux Falls, and then helicoptering out to the monument. Soon, it seemed as if every single one of us tourists from out of state got interviewed at least once by some reporter from some rinky-dink station or newspaper from somewhere in the country. By late afternoon, the international media was on the scene, too, until you could hardly hear yourself think for the whup-whup of helicopters dipping and twirling all around the monument and the parking lots, trying for the best photographic angle.

And you wouldn't have believed how fast some folks could set up a booth to sell "Marilyn Monroe on Mt. Rushmore" T-shirts! That was just the beginning, too. Dad joked that there must have been five factories in Taiwan, just waiting to get the word to put a rush on Monroe salt-and-pepper shakers and little ceramic statues of her with the wind blowing her skirt up, and copies of that nude calendar photograph of her, you know the one. But all of that came later in the week, most of it arriving at the worst possible time, as things turned out.

In the meantime, on that second day—when we were supposed to be well on the road to Seattle—Crystal and I wandered around on our own. We kept walking on the heels and stumbling into the backs of people who would be walking normally in front of us one minute, and then stopped dead on the sidewalk the next minute, staring up at *her,* as if they'd all at once been turned to stone, themselves.

Crys and I got to giggling about all the open mouths and wide eyes, until we had to lean against a stranger's Toyota and laugh until we were crying. We pleaded with each other, as we each kept making jokes about it, to "Stop, oh, please, stop!"

Too late, I realized the Toyota was occupied, only the owner wasn't inside the car, she was seated, cross-legged on its hood. I quickly pulled Crystal to her feet, and both of us moved away from the vehicle.

The woman on the hood, who was pretty obviously a Native American, was staring back at us.

"Some kind of religious hysteria?" she asked me.

"What?" I didn't know what she meant. She looked quite a bit older than I was, but younger than Mom. She had been wordlessly sitting up there—her black hair hanging way down her back and her bold nose pointed toward the monument—like a hood ornament. Now the dark Indian eyes that had been looking at *her* were observing the antics of my sister and me.

"It's a sacred mountain," she said, and pointed with her right arm to the monument. "We've been trying to tell white people that for centuries. So I guess it figures that a goddess would appear on it. I just never guessed it would be one of *yours.*" She laughed in a way that managed to sound indignant, sad, and amused all at once. She didn't seem to be upset that we'd leaned on her car, however, so I tugged Crystal a little closer to the front of it, so we could hear her better. I didn't know how she could stand sitting on the hot metal, until I saw she had a plaid blanket under her.

"We Lakota believe the entire range of hills is our sacred mother from whom comes our food and our shelter," she said then, speaking directly to Crystal, who was clinging to me and looking shy. "Or, at least, it used to provide all that, until you guys took it away from us." She said it with more resignation in her voice than rancor, but I looked down at the ground, feeling vaguely guilty, anyway. But then she commanded my attention again by saying, "Look, you can see the shape of her in the line of the hills. She's lying down. There is her head—"

"I see her shoulders!" Crys let go of me and jumped up and down, thrilled. I understood that we weren't talking about Marilyn now, but rather about a much, much older—even ancient—female spirit that Native Americans attributed to the Black Hills.

"There's the curve of her bosom." The Indian woman pointed, and I thought that I saw it. "The mounds of her belly and her hips."

"I see her legs!" Crys looked up at me. "Do you see?"

I saw the dark, reclining form, all right, of a woman lying on her side, gazing our way. She was a lot bigger than Marilyn's image, because she was the profile of all the hills put together, and she was horizontal, where Marilyn was—for once, as my own father had joked—vertical.

"These hills are womanly," the woman on the car told us.

I thought I could actually feel the Black Hills at that moment, and they felt like a cool embrace on that hot day. I imagined I could feel the pull and attraction of them, and I remembered the way my eyes couldn't stop looking at them when we were driving toward them, the way I couldn't turn away for very long and look at anything else, and the desire that was getting stronger and stronger in me to get as close to them as I could, to walk into that mysterious darkness and let it enfold me. I thought I smelled something in the hot summer air—part baby powder, part some yeasty doughy aroma like bread cooking, part Shalimar perfume, part evergreen, and also something that smelled like my own body, and made me feel embarrassed and excited all at the same time.

Whether it was Marilyn I was smelling, or the sacred mountain mother, or the real live Indian woman beside us, or my own hot, sweaty self, I couldn't tell. Everything was getting confused in my mind as the woman talked to us, and I was beginning to have a hard time telling what was real.

It was real, all of it. And it was unreal, too.

Beside me, Crystal whispered, "Can we go up there?"

The Native American woman and I looked at each other.

"It is a miracle, isn't it?" I said.

She shrugged. "It's a sacred mountain. I'll say this for her: At least she just appeared on it without hurting it; she didn't carve herself into the very flesh of our mother."

"But what about Crazy Horse, down the road?" Crys asked her.

I thought it took some guts for Crystal to ask the Indian woman about that sculpture-in-progress, seventeen miles to the southwest. What Crys meant was: If it's not okay to carve a president into the mountain, why is it okay to carve an Indian chief?

"He never wanted an image to be made of him," the woman told us. "He wouldn't allow paintings or photographs while he was alive."

So it was *not* all right, she was telling us.

But I got the distinct impression that having Marilyn on the mountain was okay, even with her.

That night, the evening of the second day, the story was broadcast all over the world, and front-page photographs displayed the image to millions of people, some of whom believed it was true, and some of whom didn't.

Some of the ones who didn't began to arrive on the third day.

But so did hundreds, thousands, of the ones who did—and that's when the healings began.

The morning of the third day dawned quiet in our tent.

At the time, I didn't recognize that as an early sign that something fantastic was about to happen—a phenomenon that would be even more amazing than an image of a dead movie star appearing on a national monument.

After Crys and I had returned from checking out the view from the ridge (*she* was still there, and her smile competed with the sun, for wattage), for our breakfast of cereal in plastic bowls, we found Mom and Dad not speaking to each other while they were drinking their plastic cups of coffee. But it was a different kind of not-speaking, a kind that seemed peaceful and relaxed, for a change. I held my breath, waiting for the first word of dispute between them.

"More coffee, hon?" my father asked her.

"No, thanks, sweetie," Mom replied, smiling at him.

Crys and I exchanged glances. *Hon? Sweetie?*

"Don't you want some cereal?" Mom asked him.

"No, I think I'll wait for lunch."

I saw Crystal clench her jaw. Here's where it would start, the sarcastic retort from Mom that would poke a withering response out of Dad. Here's where she would say something like, "Great, so we get to look forward to being in the company of a hungry grouch all morning." And then he would say something like, "So? I get to enjoy the company of a grouch *all* the time!"

"Okay," my mother said.

Crystal's eyes widened, as she looked over at me.

Neither of us said a word; we were afraid to break the mood.

What finally moved us out of that idyllic space was an eerie, electric, yet strangely comforting sound, emanating from inside the tent next to us. Crystal heard it first, and she looked up from her Cap'n Crunch and said, "What's that?" With her leading the way, we all four trooped next door to "knock" and to be admitted by our "neighbors," a young couple from New Jersey. There, on their TV, we watched the news of the "Marilyn Miracle," as the reporters were now calling it.

At the moment, the cameras were panning the crowds below the monument, and picking up the noise from down there.

The eerie sound was coming from the crowds.

"Are they chanting?" Mom asked.

"No, listen," the young woman urged us.

And then we could hear that it wasn't *om* the crowds were humming.

It was *MMMMMMM.*

"They say there've been healings," the young woman told us, her eyes as wide as Crystal's had been earlier, when Mom and Dad were courteous to one another. "Sexual healings."

Mom cast a quick glance at Crys and me, and I tried to look bland.

"What's a sexual healing?" my sister blurted out.

Nobody answered her, though I wished somebody would, so I'd

know, too! We stayed in their tent long enough (before Mom shooed us out) to get a hint not only of what that meant, but also of what the rest of the world was saying about "us."

"The vision, itself, appears to be a bonafide miracle, accompanied by actual physical miracles," attested one of the people being interviewed. "It is clearly on the order of Fatima or Lourdes, but is even more astonishing and believable, because it has been witnessed, and continues to be seen, by millions of people, if you include those watching it on television." The expert smiled, ever so slightly. "It is certainly not, however, a sighting of the Virgin."

"What's a virgin?" Crys whispered to me.

You, I thought, *and me.* But I put my finger to my lips.

"It's an illusion," claimed a man who was reputed to be an expert in unmasking fraudulent "miracles." "It's a spectacular magic trick to dupe the gullible."

"It is not!" Crystal shouted at his face on the screen. She may not have known what "gullible" meant, but she knew what the man meant. Dad said, "Shh, honey," and pulled her into a hug, and kept her there.

"Heresy," pronounced a high church official. "Blasphemy, for anyone to call this a religious experience!"

From the political right came similar, heated opinions: "It's a national disgrace, having that woman up there with our most beloved and respected presidents!"

But from down below the monument, the interviews were of a different tone, entirely: "She's so beautiful up there," said a man from North Dakota. And a woman from Minnesota was crying, as she said, "I can't stop crying. When I look at her, I can't stop crying, and yet I feel so happy. I can't explain it." And a man from Arizona said, "I loved Monroe in *Some Like It Hot,* and I love Monroe up there, but . . ." He bent down and kissed the forehead of the woman standing beside him, and smiled, as he said, ". . . I love *her* most of all."

"Oh," sighed the young woman from New Jersey. "Isn't that sweet?"

Mom made us leave their tent when medical experts started talking about the normal incidence of cures of impotence in an av-

erage population of men, and the statistical likelihood of instanta-
neous changes in the sexual responses of previously nonorgasmic
women.

Down among the "trading posts" and parking lots that day, we
drove into the atmosphere that could only be described as part religious revival, part movie star festival.

Clones of Marilyn (not all of them female, by any means) were
arriving by the plane and bus load, accompanied by men dressed up
like Tony Curtis, or Jack Lemmon, or Clark Gable, or any one of the
male movie stars with whom Marilyn Monroe had appeared in pictures.

People were carrying around little statues of Marilyn, and holding them to their lips, and kissing them. Lots of people were kissing
each other, too, which should have been excruciatingly embarrassing, especially for Crystal, but for some reason, it wasn't. As the lady
from New Jersey had said, it was sweet. There was a sweetness to
that crowd, and a tender courtesy in the way that many men and
women were treating one another, a tenderness that only grew as
the day progressed from warm to hot by late afternoon.

We heard men saying "please."

And women saying "thank you."

We saw people move back from doorways and murmur, "after
you," and we saw shoppers wait patiently in the long lines, and we
heard them speak respectfully to waiters and waitresses and sales
clerks. We saw people with their arms around each other, and people laughing, and a lot of people crying, for no apparent reason.

As we strolled—carrying our own Marilyn souvenirs—my father held my mother's hand. By afternoon, they each had an arm
around the other's waist. Crys and I tagged along all day, unwilling
to break away from the feeling of affection that seemed to surround
our parents. My sister and I had stopped staring at Marilyn on the
mountain by that time; instead we stared at those linked arms, as if
they were miracles, too.

And that was the third day, when you would have sworn world

peace was at hand, not to mention peace in the war between the sexes.

On the fourth day, all hell broke loose.

For us, it started nearby, right after cereal.

Both the young couple in the tent to the left of us and the family of five in the tent to the right of us had portable televisions, which they seemed to have turned on, watching the news, more than they actually spent down in "town," or even watching the monument. Maybe that's why a fracas broke out between them—because their experience of *her* was so indirect—and wouldn't you know it began as a religious war?

From the tent to the right, we heard a TV preacher inveighing against Marilyn and her image. They had it turned up loud as it would go, clearly hoping all of us heathens would listen, and heed!

"Heed not the Queen of the Realm of Illusion!" shouted the hoarse-voiced preacher. His voice ripped into the tranquility of the morning. "Turn your eyes from the Whore of Babylon! Turn back your eyes to the Queen of Heaven, to God and Our Lord Jesus and His holy Mother! Drop to your knees this instant, and beg God's merciful forgiveness for so much as glancing at this evil image that has arisen steaming from the foul bowels of Hell! God, forgive us who repent, and punish those who persist in their iniquity! Hear us, believe us, that we who are gathered in Thy Name this day, do not love the Harlot! We do not accept the works of the Whore! We plead for the scourge of Thy Fury across the world, to whip the sin from the backs of the lovers of the Harlot! Blind them! So they cannot see her! Deafen them! So they do not hear her! Cripple them! So they bend their knees at last to Thee! Cast the Whore off Thy mountain! Kill, kill, kill the Harlot, and strike down the wicked who follow her!"

Crystal started looking confused and scared.

"Mom?" she said. "What does that mean?"

Dad was furious, at the noise level, if nothing else.

"I'm going over there and give them a piece of my mind," he fumed, which would once have been Mom's perfect cue to say something like, "That's why you're such a moron! You give so many pieces of your mind away!" But now she only placed both of her hands gently against his chest, and said, "Let's get in the car, and go back to town. Don't you think it might be best to get the girls away from those crazies?"

We were hurrying to do just that, when the couple from New Jersey burst out of their tent and started yelling at the people in the other tent to turn their "damned idiot preacher off!" Which brought out the man from that tent to shake his fist and yell back at them that they were "going straight to hell for worshiping that bitch of Satan!"

It was worse, if possible, in "town."

The forces against the miracle were gathering, even as more "healings" were being reported. Grim-faced people with pamphlets appeared in front of the "trading post." Men carrying large crosses started marching up and down between the cars in the parking lots. Women stood on street corners with their children and yelled Scripture at passersby.

Around lunchtime, there was a rumor that somebody had gone into one of the "trading posts" and had attacked the Marilyn souvenirs with an axe.

Unfortunately, truck after truck of mementos were pouring into the area that day (possibly from those factories in Taiwan Dad had joked about), just as the anti-Marilyn people began arriving in big groups, too. Of course, the sight of all of those bosomy little dolls just fueled the religious and political outrage and determination of some people to "do something about her." We heard several people say, in fact, that they were "going to do something about her."

"What can they do?" Mom wondered, out loud, to us.

"I don't think *they* know," was Dad's opinion.

We, ourselves, actually saw two men shove a man dressed up as Marilyn. The guy in the sequined dress stumbled in his high heels, which caused him to fall against a wall and scrape his bare shoulder. And we heard somebody hiss, "Whore," at a woman who was dressed up to look like Marilyn in the number "Diamonds Are a Girl's Best Friend" from *Gentlemen Prefer Blondes*.

When Mom heard that, she insisted on gathering us up and returning to the campground that minute. When we got there, our neighbors on both sides were quiet, but Dad said to start dismantling our tent, which Crys and Mom and I did, while he went off to try to locate another site for us. I was scared: I didn't want to get hurt, but I didn't want to leave Marilyn, either. I was afraid that if we left Mount Rushmore, our parents might revert to their old ways. The preachers might be screaming about Hell, but the last day and a half had seemed like heaven, to me.

"There's no other space for us here," Dad reported when he returned, and then he looked at all of us, in turn. "Should we go home?"

"No!" Crystal said, and tugged at him. "No! No!"

Dad glanced at me, and I shook my head.

Finally, he took Mom's vote. She didn't say yes or no. Instead, she said, "Let's find a place off by ourselves, in the woods." And that's how we came to move so much closer to *her*, so that we were right where we needed to be in order to become bit players in the final dramatic scene of her last appearance on earth.

By that night, it was—if you'll pardon the pun—crystal clear that somebody was going to have to explain some things to the ten-year-old. Our parents apparently assumed that I'd do the dirty work, as I usually did, but the problem with that convenient theory was that I didn't understand a lot of what was happening any better than Crys did!

It seemed that the healings that hundreds of people were attributing to the apparition were complete cures of an extremely specific sort: All of them were related somehow to sexuality. Some were physical healings of medically confirmed ailments such as ovarian or testicular cancer, while other cures seemed to be more of an emotional or psychological nature. Supposedly, there were men who confessed to having been child molesters, and who now claimed to have no further longings in that direction. In New York City, a convicted rapist was reported to have fallen to his knees in the middle of a prison exercise yard, and to have wept for his victims.

In addition, women who thought they were infertile were finding themselves suddenly pregnant. And women who desperately *didn't* want a baby were discovering their wombs to be mysteriously, blissfully empty! Women who'd always suffered from menstrual cramps were experiencing pain-free periods, and people who had been hiding sexual addictions were publicly declaring themselves liberated from compulsion!

As for me, I just wanted to be hanging around when Mom or Dad explained to Crys the meaning of phrases such as "sustained erection" and "multi-orgasmic"!

Our new campsite was miles closer to Mount Rushmore, close enough so that the lights that illuminated Marilyn and the presidents also cast a soft glow over us.

By suppertime, Crystal's questions were thick as ticks on a leaf.

"Mom, I heard people are getting cured of herpes," Crystal said, over baked beans and hot dogs under the fragrant pines. "What's herpes? I know what AIDS is. Is it true people are getting cured of that, like we heard?"

"I hope so," Mom replied, carefully answering the second question.

"What are genital warts?" Crystal, irrepressibly, asked next.

Dad nearly squirted his hot dog out of its bun, when he heard that.

"Oh, gross!" I blurted, and wished I could disappear.

"Crystal," said my mother, who looked as if she desperately wanted to laugh, "your sister will answer all your questions, after we eat."

"Mom!" I objected, loudly.

"Won't you?" she asked me.

"No! That's your job!"

I didn't want to tell her I didn't have all the answers.

She glanced for help toward Dad, but he only grinned, and said, "Right. That's definitely your job, sweetheart."

"Okay, Crystal," Mom said later, as the two of them sat cuddled together by our campfire. I was right inside the door of our tent, with one ear practically glued to the canvas. Dad had disappeared, on the pretext of gathering firewood. Poor Mom got stuck with the job. I listened for all I was worth, as she stumbled on with her explanations about the facts of life and miracles. "To understand what's going on, you need to understand about Marilyn Monroe."

"She was a movie star," Crys interrupted, in a knowing voice.

"Yes, but a very special one, and there has never been anybody quite like her, either before or since. She was what people call 'sexy.' That meant she was really attractive to the opposite sex—men, I mean—because she was so . . . so . . . uh, well, you know how last year you thought Danny Francis was so cute in your class?"

"Yeah, but Mom, that was last year!"

"I know, honey, but how you felt . . . that, in a great big way, is how millions of men felt about Marilyn Monroe. And not just men. A lot of women thought she was attractive, too. I loved her, for instance. I thought she was kind of embarrassing, because she wore these revealing clothes that made her look practically naked, and she was always flouncing around and wiggling her butt—"

Crystal and Mom giggled, together.

"But even so, I thought she was cute and pretty and funny and adorable." Mom paused, and the campfire filled that quiet moment with the hissing and crackling sounds of its burning. "And now I realize she was also powerful. And intelligent. I can see that in her now, when I look at her old movies. And that power and intelligence, that's all part of being sexy, too. Anyway . . ."

Mom's voice rushed on, before Crys could ask more questions.

"Sex is a powerful feeling of attraction between two people. It's part of what makes people fall in love. It brings people together to have babies. It's perfectly normal. But it can be used in healthy or unhealthy ways. Just like money can, or food, or anything else you can think of. Sex can cause good things to happen to people, or bad things."

Mom's words were coming slower now, as if she was choosing them ever more carefully, or maybe just thinking about what they meant as she said them.

"For some reason that none of us understands, this vision of Marilyn on the mountain is causing good things to happen to people, in regard to sex, and it's also undoing some bad things that have happened to them in regard to sex."

"Why?" Crystal asked.

The fire sang while I, too, waited for Mom's answer.

"Because we needed it, I guess," she said, so softly I barely heard her. "And maybe it had to be her, because she knew what it was like to need—to need so very much—to be healed."

"She?" Crys said.

"Marilyn."

"I love her," Crystal declared.

"I love her, too, honey."

Inside the tent, I thought, *Me, too.*

That was the moment I realized that I didn't hate the vacation or my parents, and that I didn't resent my little sister, not anymore. I felt good, better than I'd ever felt before in my life. I knew what it was like then to feel whole. Complete. Young. Hopeful and happy. *Thank you, Marilyn,* I whispered. I closed my eyes, and pictured her on Mount Rushmore. *Thanks very much.*

By the dawn of the fifth day, many of the people who believed the apparition was an abomination had, with seemingly incredible swiftness, formed themselves into a loud, aggressive coalition.

Dad went into "town" by himself early that morning, and came back talking of rumors of dynamite, of "blowing her off the mountain," of the National Guard being sent in to disperse the crowds and maintain order, of incidents of violence in the crowds, overnight, and of beatings and arrests, and of people being shipped off to jails wherever there was room to hold them in the little towns of South Dakota. He said he didn't know how much of what he'd heard was true. But Dad said he did know this was no longer a happy place to be, and that if there wasn't trouble now, there soon would be.

"I want to get you and the girls out of here," he told Mom.

But she looked thoughtfully at Crystal and me and then astonished me, at least, by saying, "The girls and I aren't ready to leave." She ordered me to take Crys for a walk in the woods "while your father and I sort this out." But before I could turn away, she said to me, "What's that on your face?"

My left hand flew to an itchy spot on my lower left cheek, where I felt something bumpy and kind of rough, and I immediately thought, *Damnation,* how come other people get cured of cancer, but I still get pimples?

Mom drew me close to her and squinted at the thing.

"It's a mole," she pronounced, and then she drew back from me . . . looked up at Marilyn on the mountain . . . looked back at me . . . looked over at Dad . . . and breathed, "Oh, my God, do you know what this is?"

It was a beauty mark, exactly like *hers.*

Mom called it a stigmata—which she explained was like Christ's wounds appearing in the hands of saints and martyrs. But Dad said she'd better not use that word loosely, especially not in "town," what with all the religious fanatics gathered there, and every one of them just looking for any excuse to be offended, and to strike out against the offender, which in this case would be me.

My sister looked at me doubtfully. "A saint?"

I kept touching the beauty mark, until Mom pulled my hand away from it.

"We have to talk," she said to Dad.

As we plodded off together onto our assigned walk in the woods, Crystal muttered, "It's not fair. I want one."

"Maybe when you're older," I told her, smugly.

She thwapped me with the back of her hand, and I laughed, feeling extraordinarily special and pleased with myself.

We stayed, and we even made a brief foray into town that fifth day, though I received stern instructions to keep my head down. Dad wanted to make me wear a head scarf, but Mom said that made me look even more like Marilyn during the period when she was married to the playwright. They compromised by sticking a bandage on my face, which made me feel embarrassed to be seen in public. Protesting did me no good; they said it was for my own safety.

Once in "town," however, we discovered I was not the only one to have received what the agitators were already calling "the mark of Marilyn." Girls and women all up and down the streets, and in the parking lots and "trading posts," were sprouting similar beauty marks, and some of the females wearing them were furious about it, because they were among the agitators. Dad said we were lucky that was the case, because the fact that it was also happening to them was probably the only thing that kept them from actually calling it the "mark of the Beast."

I felt let down, that I wasn't the only one.

People who felt as we did had almost disappeared from the congested area below the monument, because it was getting too dangerous to be there. If you were seen carrying a Marilyn souvenir, or wearing a Marilyn costume, you were accosted by people accusing you of being a traitor to America, or a blasphemer against God, or both, and you stood a risk of having your souvenir jerked out of your hands, or your costume torn off of you, and of being shoved, or worse. People who'd come like pilgrims hoping to be healed were shown on television as they stood weeping in disappointment, some of them, still at the airports in Rapid City and Sioux Falls, afraid to venture any further down the road to Mount Rushmore. At the "trading posts," the merchants swept the Monroe sales items off their shelves and put the presidents back in their front windows.

Mom and Dad hurried us away almost as soon as we arrived, but not before we saw the huge demolition machinery moving into "town," and not before we heard more of the rumors about "pinpoint explosives."

"Why do they hate her?" Crys asked, and asked, and asked. She was hyper with too much energy, bouncing up and down on the back seat of our car and chattering, chattering, chattering, until she drove us all crazy, and we all snapped at her. "Mom? Dad? Why do they hate her? Why do they want to kill her? Why do they call her those names? What's *wrong* with her?"

"Crystal, sit *down*," Dad finally told her.

"And be *quiet* for five minutes!" Mom said, sounding frantic herself.

"Please!" I chimed in.

Of course, Crys burst into tears. Feeling awful and guilty about taking it all out on her, I turned my face to the car window. Out of their sight, I gently rubbed my beauty spot, over and over, with the first two fingers of my right hand.

According to the news bulletins we heard on our car radio, the U.S. government truly was sending in the National Guard to keep order, but nobody seemed to think they could mobilize in time to save Marilyn, not that that was their objective, anyway. Their mission was to maintain law and order, and to protect the presidents.

"How," asked a talk-show deejay sympathetic to the apparition, "can they stop a dedicated cadre of explosives experts, anyway? In that wilderness around the monument? No way! Listen, folks, the bad guys are probably already on their way, armed to the teeth with dynamite, or nitroglycerin, or plastic explosives, or whatever it takes to slice our girl off the mountain. Talk to me, Callers! What's your opinion?"

At our tent, with the Ponderosa pines guarding our privacy like sentinels, we got more and more quiet as the day progressed, even Crystal, who kept breaking into convulsive little bursts of tears, and needing Mom or Dad to give her a hug and stroke her hair and lie to her and tell her it was all going to be all right.

"How can you tell her that?" I whispered, furiously, to Mom.

"Honey," she said, so gently it made me feel even more angry, "it *is* going to be all right. We'll go back home. You'll go back to school. Life will go on as usual. We'll forget all about Marilyn."

I touched my beauty mark. "I'll *never* forget her!"

Mom tried to hug me, but I wouldn't let her. I stalked off a little way into the woods, and my head filled up with the words, *I won't . . . ever . . . forget . . . you!*

At least, we got over making Crys the family scapegoat.

Nobody snapped angrily at her anymore. I came back into camp, my anger spent on hurling pine cones into space, and we just all walked around, or lounged around, like zombies, turning on the car radio every so often, and getting more discouraged and feeling more hopeless as the sun crossed over the monument and slid down the other side of it.

The spotlights came on, illuminating Washington, Jefferson, Lincoln, Roosevelt, and Monroe, for the last time.

The chanting started around 11 P.M.

It floated through the woods to us, winding around the pines, scooting along the ground and carried with the cold breeze of that summer evening. It woke us up, one by one, in our tent, and pulled us by our curiosity out into our little clearing.

"What in the world?" Dad murmured.

Crys and I had slept in our jeans and T-shirts, Mom and Dad had pajamas on, and we were all barefoot and rumple-haired and sleepy. For some reason, Mom ran back into the tent and put her own jeans and T-shirt and a jacket, and even her socks and hiking boots. She threw jackets out at Crys and me, and then she insisted we both put shoes on.

She didn't say anything to Dad, so he just stood there, listening.

By the time Crys and I got back outside, the chanting was louder, and coming near us.

MMMMMMMMMM

That's all it was, a humming of that letter of the alphabet, and it sounded like a melodious, resonant, high-pitched wave rolling toward us, some of it sung in soprano, some in alto, for it was all women and girls who were chanting, and marching across the plain toward the monument. Within minutes, they reached us, and Mom took one of Crystal's hands and one of mine, and the three of us melted into the pines to become notes in the moving melody.

Dad started to hurry back into the tent to change clothes, but Mom stopped him with a softly voiced, "No, sweetheart." And when he then moved as if he'd join us, pajamas and all, she tugged her hand free from mine, blew him a kiss, and called back to him, "Somebody needs to stay here and guard the fort!"

I caught a glimpse of my father, standing there with the breeze whipping the ankles of his pajamas, and he staring at us, looking so worried, as if he were afraid he'd never see us again.

But he didn't follow us.

We left him behind, and joined the other women, dozens, hundreds of women, and more, all of us merging easily into a cadence with one another with every bold and quiet stride we took, softly humming as we marched along together to the base of the monument.

"Others are coming from above," one of the marchers told us.

From the Black Hills, from the west, she meant.

I looked for the Lakota woman, and thought I glimpsed her once, among the trees.

By morning's light, we were fully assembled: hundreds of women and girls, stationed at the base of Mount Rushmore; hundreds more of us lining the top of the monument, standing at the very edge that overlooked the plains and the "town" below.

Through a telescope or binoculars, or from an airplane or helicopter, anyone who saw us could read the words on the banner that some of the women draped over the apparition of Marilyn's hair.

It said, in big, black letters:

IF YOU DESTROY HER, YOU'LL KILL US!

And that's the sight that greeted not only the valley, but everybody who switched on a morning television news show. And there we remained, successfully defending *her,* all that sixth day and all of the sixth night, while the monument lights illuminated all of us: Presidents, Marilyn, living women and girls. Food materialized from somewhere, and water as we needed it, and somehow there were bedrolls for the children, who organized their own games to play.

No one dared to touch her as long as we remained.

I think we could have stayed, if not indefinitely, then certainly a long, long time, because reinforcements, other women and girls, began arriving by the morning of the seventh day. But as it turned out, we didn't have to stay, because *she* took matters into her own hands.

$\star$ $\star$ $\star$

The word came first to us from observers below.

"They say she's fading!" someone yelled.

We couldn't tell from where we stood and guarded her. We were too close to the image to be able to judge whether it appeared as dark and clear upon the mountain as it had all week.

"She's leaving the mountain!" the word came down.

And she was. Slowly, over the course of the seventh day, she took her leave of us, having drawn out of us our courage and our independence, having been protected by us when we believed she most needed it. Now she freed us by vanishing as mysteriously as she had come.

By the time the lights came on that night, she was gone.

As you know, the Crazy Horse monument was never finished.

Some people thought he'd gone chasing after her. If that's true, I'd call that a *really* Happy Hunting Ground! But I think he had too much dignity for that. Personally, I think she pulled his image away with her as a favor to a great man, knowing he would never have wanted to be there in the first place. How could she do that? Well, you know her magnetic appeal! She didn't take the presidents with her—obviously—and, to me, they look incomplete now, without her voluptuous, vibrant, incandescent femininity to balance them.

However, if you compare photos of them now with pictures of them before *she* appeared, you'll swear there has been a softening of the presidential brows, a loosening of tension in Tom's lips, a twinkle in George's stern glance. Abraham looks as if his load's been lightened, he looks encouraged and comforted, I think, and a little ashamed of himself for hanging up there on the Lakota's sacred mountain. None of those four had very enlightened attitudes toward the native peoples, after all, and Abe was no better than he had to be, in that regard. I know I'm reading a lot into stone, but over time even stone changes, doesn't it? The most dramatic transformation I detect is in Teddy, who used to look as if he were only peering over the plains for the biggest stag to shoot. Now I believe there's a hint of awe and tenderness in his gaze, as if he's deeply moved and even humbled by all he surveys. Any woman who could humble Teddy Roosevelt was a saint, in my book!

Everybody has forgotten, except the rest of the world and me.

Maybe, when she left, she took America's memory with her, because the important thing was not the conscious memory of her apparition, but the unconscious changes she wrought in us. We women are different now—stronger, more straightforward and honest—and so are our men, many of them just plain nicer people than they were before.

So maybe it doesn't really matter if everybody's beauty mark faded, except mine, evidently, or that even Crystal thinks I'm crazy when I try to remind her of our astonishing vacation to the Black Hills when she was ten years old.

It's not that I'm lonely with this memory. After all, I've got the rest of the world to remember it with me. It's just that I'd like her to get the credit, that's all.

So, now, can you see *her* there, on Mount Rushmore?

Are you beginning to remember?

AFTERWORD

After reading "biographies" that wildly contradict each other, I've decided I'll never know many indisputable facts about the life and death of Marilyn Monroe. In fact, the more I learn about her, the more elusive and mysterious she becomes, until I am left holding onto a single truth: She's unforgettable. At least, I can't imagine ever forgetting her. She's part of my memories, even though I never knew her. Unforgettable. That's all I know about Marilyn Monroe, even after all of my research, and it's probably all that I will ever know.

That's why my story is about remembering her.

—Nancy Pickard

ABOUT THE AUTHORS

HUSH MONEY

Lynne Barrett, an associate professor at Florida International University in Miami, teaches in the graduate creative writing program. She has a collection of short stories, *The Land of Go* from Carnegie Mellon University Press, and stories in *Mondo Barbie, The King Is Dead, The Lexington Introduction to Literature,* and other anthologies, as well as in *Redbook, Ellery Queen's Mystery Magazine, Quarterly West, The Tampa Review,* and many literary magazines. "Elvis Lives" won the Edgar Award for Best Mystery Short Story and appeared in Best Mystery/Suspense anthologies. Lynne has been cited by the Pushcart Prize and received a National Endowment for the Arts fellowship.

SOMETHING'S GOT TO GIVE

Janet Berliner and **George Guthridge** write the "Madagascar Manifesto" series of novels, including *Child of the Dusk.* Janet (previously published as Janet Gluckman) lives and works in Las Vegas, and has been writing and editing forever. Her recent work includes dozens of short stories, as well as creating and editing the anthologies *David Copperfield's Beyond Imagination,* Peter S. Beagle's *Immortal Unicorn,* and *Desire Burn: Women Writing from the Dark Side of Passion.* George is a multi-award-winning educator who teaches in rural Alaska. Using his revolutionary techniques, his Eskimo students have won the most challenging academic competition in the U.S. As a writer, he has been a Nebula and Hugo award finalist, and has published over sixty short stories in such magazines as *Asimov's, Fantasy & Science Fiction,* and *Analog,* and has written several novels, including *The Bloodletter,* an offbeat Western.

THE COST OF FREEDOM

After a hiatus tending a family and a career change, **Peter Crowther** returned to fiction with true Brit gusto in 1990. *Interzone* called his third postreemergence story (in the award-winning *Darklands 11* anthology) "an object lesson in how to write a ghost story," and 1994's "Cankerman" (from *Phobias*) was nominated for the Bram Stoker Award. Now he has produced forty-some more stories and a TV script, plus seven of his own anthologies (including the World Fantasy Award–nominated *Narrow Houses*). *Escardy Gap,* his collaborative novel with James Lovegrove, came out this year. Peter, his wife Nicky, and their two sons live in Harrogate, England.

DA SVIDANIYA, KHRUSHCHEV

Barbara Collins has written many short stories that appeared in such anthologies as *Murder Most Delicious, Women on the Edge, Murder for Mother,* and the best-selling "Cat Crimes" series. Her "Sweet Dreams, Norma Jeane" in 1995's *Celebrity Vampires* reflects a long-time interest in Marilyn Monroe. Barbara's stories are included in the first three volumes of *The Year's 25 Finest Crime and Mystery Stories.* She lives in Muscatine, Iowa, with her writer-husband Max and their twelve-year-old son.

THE FOUNTAIN STREET GHOST

The Private Eye Writers of America made **Catherine Dain** a two-time Shamus nominee for her Freddie O'Neal series, the sixth being 1996's *The Luck of the Draw.* Catherine reports that she actually made a living as a television newscaster, and that she no longer sees herself as an actress. Sometimes on Saturday nights she still thinks it would be nice to have a significant other. This is her third short story featuring Michael and Faith.

HER BIGGEST FAN

John A. Day is a Texas native. He works as a scientist at a pharmaceutical laboratory and, he says, lives with his beautiful fiancée and two goofy cats. John writes horror, science fiction, fantasy, and role-playing adventures. This is his first professional sale.

SUNSET: A MONOLOGUE IN ONE ACT

Ex-journalist **Carole Nelson Douglas** has written thirty-some novels in various genres and writes two mystery series. *Good Night, Mr. Holmes* introduced Sherlockian adversary Irene Adler as a diva/detective in her own adventures and was a *New York Times* Notable Book. The contemporary Las Vegas–set Midnight Louie mysteries (*Cat in a Diamond Dazzle,* etc.) feature a tomcat sleuth as an intermittent first-purrson narrator. Carole lives in Fort Worth with her husband Sam and seven cats, none of whom write or detect.

FANTASY

Eileen Dreyer lives with her husband and two children in St. Louis. Her four suspense novels with medical backgrounds have been climbing national best-seller lists, with *Bad Medicine* the latest. As Kathleen Korbel she has written twenty-one contemporary romances, winning a 1995 Romance Writers of America Rita Award. She has also done the big time as a trauma nurse, she says, where she developed the "sparkling wit and twisted sense of justice" that serve her suspense fiction so well.

COMEBACK

Pamela J. Fesler is a former advertising copywriter and magazine editor who writes and edits promotional material and speeches for a clientele that includes a psychic, a politican, a computer programmer, and a tepee manufacturer. Her work has appeared in *Mystery Forum* magazine, *Over My Dead Body!*, and *Rosebud*.

O, VIRGINIA

Stephen Gallagher was born in Salford, Lancashire, in 1954. He worked for Yorkshire TV's documentaries department after graduating from Hull University with a degree in drama and English, living in London before returning to the North to join Granada TV in 1975. He became a full-time freelancer after the sale of *Chimera* in 1980. Primarily a novelist and short story writer, Gallagher also has numerous TV and radio credits. His latest novel is *Red, Red Robin* (Bantam U.K.; Ballantine U.S.).

THE CHILD STAR

Ted Klein once called **Melissa Mia Hall** "Fort Worth's answer to Shirley Jackson." *Publishers Weekly* once compared her short fiction to that of Truman Capote. Hall, though, prefers to have her work considered uniquely her own. Her numerous short stories have been published in the U.S., in several foreign languages, and in assorted anthologies. A novel and screenplay, *Stampede,* seek a publisher while she works on other long and short fiction projects.

THE HOUSE THAT NORMA BOUGHT
Floridian **T. J. MacGregor** has explored that sultry terrain in a slew of well-received mystery and suspense novels. The most recent is her eighteenth novel and the tenth book in her Quin St. James suspense/mystery series, *Mistress of the Bones.* Her husband Rob is also a novelist, although daughter Megan, seven, remains unpublished, so far.

MARILYN MONROE ON 165TH STREET
Linda Mannheim has co-authored two folklore collections forthcoming from Scholastic Press. Her fiction, nonfiction, and poetry has been published in *Xanadu III, Bridges, Caliban,* and *Sojourner.*

BLONDE NOIRE
Martin Meyers and **Annette Meyers,** a husband and wife who write together and separately, have had diverse professional lives, also together and apart. Martin Meyers is a born performer: first as a disk jockey in Illinois and New York, then as an actor on Broadway, TV, and in movies. His five novels feature private eye Patrick Hardy. Annette Meyers is the author of six mysteries about Wall Street headhunters Xenia Smith and ex-Broadway dancer Leslie Wetzon. Her most recent is *The Groaning Board.* Under the pseudonym Maan Meyers, Marty and Annette write *The Dutchman* history-mysteries set in seventeenth-, eighteenth-, and nineteenth-century New York. The latest is *The House on Mulberry Street.*

DEAR MOM
Jill M. Morgan is the author of over sixteen novels, including the suspense title *Cage of Shadows,* written as Meg Griffin, and the children's series *The Spider's Child,* written as Jessica Pierce. She is the creator and co-editor of the children's anthology series *Great Writers & Kids,* published by Random House. She lives in southern California with her husband and three children.

MISTRESS FAME
With more than a hundred short stories published in various magazines and anthologies, Edgar-nominated **Billie Sue Mosiman** has also managed to pen seven novels of suspense. Her latest titles are *Widow* and *Stiletto* from Berkley. She is co-editing an anthology, *Armageddon,* for Baen Books with David Drake and Martin H. Greenberg.

IT HAD TO BE YOU

Nancy Pickard is best known for her murder mysteries, even though "It Had to Be You" is not that type of tale. Her mystery novels and short stories have won Agatha, Anthony, Shamus, American Mystery and Macavity awards and have lately become familiar listings in various "year's best" compilations. Most readers know her as the author of the eleven books in the popular and acclaimed Jenny Cain series, the latest of which is *Twilight*.

SKIN DEEP

Elizabeth Ann Scarborough is the author of twenty fantasy novels and "a bunch" of short stories. She lives in a forties-era log cabin in Washington state with four cats and one Nebula Award from the Science Fiction and Fantasy Writers of America for *The Healer's War*. Formerly a nurse, Annie served in Vietnam and lived in Alaska for fifteen years. *The Godmother, The Godmother's Apprentice,* and *Carol for Another Christmas* are her latest novels.

DESTINY

Of Patricia Wallace's seventeen novels, five are mysteries. *Deadly Devotion* is the fourth featuring P.I. Sydney Bryant *(Small Favors, Deadly Grounds,* and *Blood Lies.)* Forthcoming is the fifth Bryant, *August Nights*. A suspense novel, *Dark Intent,* was a 1995 title. Pat has also written eleven horror novels. A former freelance story analyst for NBC, she has communications/film and police science degrees, but notes that she still can't get arrested in Hollywood.

LOVE ME FOR MY YELLOW HAIR ALONE

This year's Edgar-nominated *Mean Streak* is the fourth entry in Carolyn Wheat's detective series featuring Brooklyn lawyer Cass Jameson, who debuted in the Edgar-nominated novel *Dead Man's Thoughts*. Wheat has taught mystery writing at The New School for Social Research, New York City, and was Artist-in-Residence at the University of Central Oklahoma in Edmond for the 1995–96 academic year.

DROWNING IN THE RIVER OF NO RETURN

J. N. Williamson is another prodigious short story writer—155. He edited the four *Masques* anthologies of horror and the supernatural and *How to*

Write Tales of Horror, Fantasy & Science Fiction, featuring such writers as Ray Bradbury, Marion Zimmer Bradley, Dean R. Koontz, Ardath Mayhar, and F. Paul Wilson. His 38 novels include *Bloodlines* and *Don't Take Away the Light.* Both made the 1994 Horror Writers of America awards preliminary ballot.